Adrian McKinty was born and grew up in Carrickfergus, Northern Ireland, at the height of the Troubles. He studied politics at Oxford University and after a failed law career he moved to New York City in the early 1990s. He found work as a security guard, postman, door-to-door salesman, construction worker, barman, rugby coach, book-store clerk and librarian. Having lived in Colorado for many years with his wife and daughters, he and his family have moved to Melbourne, Australia.

In addition to *Fifty Grand*, Serpent's Tail also publishes Adrian McKinty's The Dead Trilogy – *Dead I Well May Be*, *The Dead Yard*, *The Bloomsday Dead*, as well as *Hidden River*.

Dead I Well May Be

'A darkly thrilling tale of the New York streets with all the hard-boiled charm of Chandler and the down and dirty authenticity of closing time…Evocative dialogue, an acute sense of place and a sardonic sense of humour make McKinty one to watch' *Guardian*

'The story is soaked in the holy trinity of the noir thriller – betrayal, money and murder – but seen through here with a panache and political awareness that gives *Dead I Well May Be* a keen edge over its rivals' *Big Issue*

'Adrian McKinty's main skill is in cleverly managing to evoke someone rising through the ranks and wreaking bloody revenge while making it all seem like an event that could happen to any decent, hardworking Irish chap. A dark, lyrical and gripping voice that will go far' *The List*

'Adrian McKinty is a big new talent – for storytelling, for dialogue and for creating believable characters…*Dead I Well May Be* is a riveting story of revenge and marks the arrival of a distinctive fresh voice' *Sunday Telegraph*

'A pacy, assured and thoroughly engaging debut…this is a hard-boiled crime story written by a gifted man with poetry coursing through his veins and thrilling writing dripping from his fingertips' *Sunday Independent*

'Careens boisterously from Belfast to the Bronx...McKinty is a storyteller with the kind of style and panache that blurs the line between genre and mainstream. Top-drawer' *Kirkus Reviews*

'McKinty's Michael Forsythe is a crook, a deviant, a lover, a fighter, and a thinker. His Irish-tough language of isolation and longing makes us love and trust him despite his oh-so-great and violent flaws. When you finish this book you just might wish you'd lived the life in its pages, and thought its thoughts, both horrible and sublime' Anthony Swofford, author of *Jarhead*

'If Frank McCourt had gone into the leg-breaking business instead of school teaching, he might've written a book like *Dead I Well May Be*. Adrian McKinty's novel is a rollicking, raw, and unsavoury delight – down and dirty but full of love for words. This is hard-boiled crime fiction with a poet's touch' Peter Blauner, author of *The Last Good Day* and *The Intruder*

'McKinty has deftly created a literate, funny and cynical antihero who takes his revenge in bloody and violent twists but at the same time, methodically listens to Tolstoy on tape while on stakeouts. He rounds out the book with a number of incredible fever-dream sequences and then springs an ending that leaves readers shaking their head in satisfied amazement' *San Francisco Chronicle*

The Dead Yard

'Adrian McKinty has once again harnessed the power of poetry, violence, lust and revenge to forge a sequel to his acclaimed *Dead I Well May Be*' *The Irish Post*

'McKinty's literate, expertly crafted third crime novel confirms his place as one of his generation's leading talents...McKinty possesses a talent for pace and plot structure that belies his years. Dennis Lehane fans will definitely be pleased' *Publishers Weekly*

'*The Dead Yard* is a much-anticipated sequel to *Dead I Well May Be* and every bit as good. McKinty crackles with raw talent. His dialogue is superb, his characters rich and his plotting tight and seamless. He also writes with a wonderful (and wonderfully humorous) flair for language, raising his work above most crime-genre offerings and bumping right up against literature' *San Francisco Chronicle*

'Expat Irishman Adrian McKinty has just put out his fourth terrific book...and he keeps getting better. He melds the snap and crackle of the old Mickey Spillane tales with the literary skills of Raymond Chandler and sets it all down in his own artful way. This is a writer going places. Hop aboard' *Rocky Mountain News*

The Bloomsday Dead

'Those who know McKinty will automatically tighten their seatbelts. To newcomers I say: buckle up and get set for a bumpy ride through a very harsh landscape indeed. His antihero Michael Forsythe is as wary, cunning and ruthless as a sewer rat... His journey in some ways parallels that of James Joyce's Leopold Bloom on one day in Dublin, but – trust me – it's a lot more violent and a great deal more exciting' Matthew Lewin, *Guardian*

'A pacey, violent caper... As Forsythe hurtles around the city, McKinty vividly portrays its sleazy, still-menacing underbelly' John Dugdale, *Sunday Times*

'Thoroughly enjoyable... [McKinty] maintains the bloody action all the way from Lima to Larne with panache and economy. His hero, the "unf***ing-killable" Michael Forsythe, is a wonderful creation' Hugh Bonar, *Irish Mail on Sunday*

'Packed with sharp dialogue and unremitting action' Marcel Berlins, *The Times*

'Compelling thrillers written in a hard-bitten, muscular style, the novels are given an unconventional twist by virtue of Forsythe's unusually perceptive insights... a fascinating blend of Robert Ludlum's Jason Bourne and Patricia Highsmith's Tom Ripley... McKinty is a rare writer' *Sunday Business Post*

'A tangled and bloody odyssey through Dublin and Belfast... [a] well-paced, edgy thriller' Terence Killeen, *Irish Times*

'A gut-punching gangster story... this illegitimate spawn of a book, with Tony Soprano morality and James Joyce literary weight, ends the Michael Forsythe trilogy' Gerard Brennan, *Belfast Newsletter*

Hidden River

'McKinty is a cross between Mickey Spillane and Damon Runyon – the toughest, the best. Beware of McKinty' Frank McCourt

'A roller coaster of highs and lows, light humour and dark deeds...Once you step into *Hidden River*, the powerful under-current of McKinty's talent will swiftly drag you away. Let's hope this author does not slow down anytime soon' *Irish Examiner*

'[A] terrific read...this is a strong, non-stop story, with attractive characters and fine writing' *Morning Star*

'This is genuinely hard to put down until its conclusion is reached' *Buzz*

'Fast-paced thriller...McKinty's short, sharp delivery manages to make *Hidden River* an engaging read' *Big Issue*

'From an impressive debut to a rock-solid second, neither will disappoint and I am seriously looking forward to number three' *The Barcelona Review*

'A dark, lyrical and gripping voice that will go far' *The List*

'An outstanding and complex crime novel that should appeal to fans of hard-boiled Celtic scribes such as Ken Bruen and Ian Rankin...This is not only an expertly crafted suspense novel but also a revealing study of addiction' *Publishers Weekly*

FIFTY GRAND

GRAND

A NOVEL OF SUSPENSE

ADRIAN MCKINTY

A complete catalogue record for this book can
be obtained from the British Library on request

The right of Adrian McKinty to be identified as the author of this work has been
asserted by him in accordance with the Copyright, Designs and Patents Act 1988

First published in USA 2009 by Henry Holt, New York

First published in UK 2009 by Serpent's Tail,
an imprint of Profile Books Ltd
3A Exmouth House
Pine Street
London EC1R 0JH
website: www.serpentstail.com

ISBN 978 1 84668 723 5

Printed and bound in Great Britain by Clays, Bungay, Suffolk

10 9 8 7 6 5 4 3 2 1

The paper this book is printed on is certified by the © 1996 Forest Stewardship
Council A.C. (FSC). It is ancient-forest friendly.
The printer holds FSC chain of custody SGS-COC-2061

FSC
Mixed Sources
Product group from well-managed
forests and other controlled sources
Cert no. SGS-COC-2061
www.fsc.org
© 1996 Forest Stewardship Council

"Fifty grand is a lot of money," I said.
"No," Jack said. "It's just business."

—ERNEST HEMINGWAY,
"Fifty Grand," 1927

FIFTY GRAND

CHAPTER 1

NOWHERE, WYOMING

The frozen lake and the black vacuum sky and the dead man pleading for the return of his remaining days.

"There must be some kind of mistake."

No.

"You've got the wrong guy."

No.

"You're gonna pay for this."

Viejo compañero, I've paid in advance.

And before he can come up with any more material I unroll a line of duct tape, cut it, and place it over his mouth.

I step away from the car, check back up the trail.

Moonlight on the green Park Service hut. Snow on the dogwoods. No new tire tracks.

Apart from me and my confederates, no one's been here in days, probably weeks. I close the BMW's trunk and take off my ski mask. He kicks at the side panels with his soles but the muffled protests cease after a couple of minutes.

I plunge my left hand into the coat pocket and bring out an orange.

I stare at it obsessively for a moment, but the color and the smell are making my head spin. I return it to the coat.

"An orange," I say to myself with a smile.

I breathe the crisp December air, shiver.

I open the driver's-side door.

The seat. The key. The heat.

I rummage in the bag and find Paco's Mexican cigarettes.

I partially close the door and look at the BMW's rocket ship display. Which of these is the clock? Ah, there it is next to the GPS: 6:02 a.m. At least a one-hour wait. We won't go onto the ice until sunup—no point in taking unnecessary risks in the dark.

I light the cigarette, inhale the loose, sweet tobacco, and let it coat my lungs.

The smoke warms my insides to such an extent that when I exhale I feel empty, scared.

I take an almost panicky second breath of air and smoke.

Keep it there.

Another sad exhalation. Two more iterations but the cumulative effect is the opposite of what I'm expecting, making me jittery, on edge.

I turn on the interior light and examine the pack. A comical English explorer in shorts and pith helmet. Faros. Had them before—when I was a teenager Mexican cigarettes were the only affordable luxury you could get. Uncle Arturo managed to find Marlboros, but my father said that Faros and Rivas were just as good. I must be so nervous that I'm way beyond their power to relax me.

At the bottom of the Faros packet, there is, however, something that looks like a fat joint. I take it out and sniff it. Grade-A narc from Canada—Paco must have stolen it somehow. Maybe the night of the party.

It would be very tempting to light it up, but I should probably save that for *after*. One of those and I'd be on my ass for hours.

I put it away. Check the clock: 6:06 and still as dark as ever.

A breeze cuts through the door and I pull it fully closed. In brittle Euro-trash an annoyed disembodied voice tells me to fasten my seatbelt. I try to ignore it but it grows increasingly demented. "Fasten seatbelt, fasten seatbelt, fasten seatbelt."

I fool the computer by clicking and quickly unclicking the belt.

"Seatbelt secured," the computer sighs with relief.

Clock says 6:08.

I put the cigarettes in the backpack and kill the headlights.

Quick scan through the radio stations. Country. Religious. Country. News. Country. Religious. I nix the radio and max the heat.

Nothing to do now but wait.

I wait.

A gust rustling the tree branches along the ridge.

A starlit vapor trail.

Kicking from inside the trunk.

The radio again, a Nebraska station playing polka. A ten-thousand-watt Jesus station out of Laramie.

The kicking stops.

I relight the Faros, finish it, wipe my fingerprints from the butt, and throw it out the window.

6:15.

I leave the window open and turn everything off.

And sit there.

Sit.

As the day meditates.

Time passes and finally a hint of morning in the black distance and above me a blue, distilled silence as night switches off its stars.

Here goes.

From the passenger's seat I unwrap the ROAD CLOSED—SUBSIDENCE DANGER sign I stole yesterday in Fairview.

Won't be enough to fool a ranger from the Park Service but it should keep away any early-morning hunters or ice fishermen.

I grab the Smith & Wesson 9mm, get out of the car, and walk back up the trail until I find the aluminum swing gate. In the distance I can see the lights of vehicles on the highway. Big rigs, Greyhound buses, nothing that's coming down here. I duct tape the sign to the top bar of the gate. Hmmm. In the light of day it doesn't look so fantastic but it'll have to do.

I drag the gate through the snow, close it, and lock it with the padlock I've specifically brought for this purpose. You're going to need to be pretty determined to come down this road now.

I take a few steps to the side and admire my handiwork.

Maybe a good idea to get rid of all the footprints.

I grab a tree branch and brush over the area on my side of the gate.

That's better.

Not likely that man or beast is going to come by at this time of the morning, but my business is going to take a while and this should help deter the curious.

I wipe away all the tire tracks and footprints until I reach the bend in the road, then I toss the branch and return to the BMW.

I get back inside and warm my hands over the vents. 6:36. Better get a move on. I grab the green backpack and put the sledgehammer, the gun, the handcuffs key, the gloves, and the ski mask inside.

I get out of the car and close the door.

Dawn is a smear on the eastern horizon and light is beginning to illuminate the low clouds in alternating bands of orange and gold.

Ok.

I shoulder the backpack and walk out onto the lake, bend down and examine the ice.

About twenty, thirty millimeters thick. Good enough, I imagine.

I trudge back to the car, open the backpack, and put on the gloves and ski mask.

A click of the button and the trunk pops open.

His eyes are wild, his naked body Pollocked with mud, oil, and paint flecks. His legs covered in yellow bruises. He's been trying to kick open the emergency release lever with his knees.

He's having trouble breathing. I see that the duct tape is partially covering his nostrils. The sort of clumsy mistake that could have suffocated him.

I rip the tape off his mouth.

"Bastard," he says, and spits at me.

Save your strength, if I were you, *compañero*.

I lift his legs out and then grab him by the arm and heft him from the trunk onto the embankment. I shove him facedown into the snow, take the knife, and cut through the duct tape at his ankles. I step away from him and remove the Smith & Wesson M&P from my jacket pocket.

He gets to his feet, but he can't do anything with his hands still cuffed behind his back.

I waggle the gun at him to make sure that he sees it.

"Now what?" he says.

I point at the lake.

"I'm freezing. I want my clothes. I'm freezing to death."

I bring the 9mm up to his navel and press it against his bruised stomach.

The gun and the ski mask are iconic images of terror. It would take someone of sterner stuff than him to resist this kind of pressure.

"All right," he says.

I turn him and push him gently in the direction of the lake.

He mutters something, shakes his head, and walks through the frozen snow to the lakeshore.

His body is pale, almost blue white. And he's a big man. Six foot four, two hundred and fifty pounds, none of it fat. He was a college football player back in the day and he's kept himself in shape. Five miles on the treadmill each morning and rugby training every Wednesday with the Gentlemen of Aspen.

More grumbling, and he stops when his soles touch the ice. He hesitates. The snow was full of air and not too frigid but the ice is dry, flat, and sticky. It's cold enough to burn.

"What do you want me to do?"

I'm about to speak for the first time but the words die on my lips. Not yet. *Not yet.*

I wave him forward.

"On this?"

I nod and extend the gun.

"Ah shit," he says but begins walking.

It's full light now.

The sun advancing over the plains. The moon a fading scar.

Beautiful.

The lake. The trees.

Frost crystals.

Voleries of geese.

Fish in trance.

"Aow!" he says.

Vapor lock. His soles are stuck and he shudders to a halt. Momentum is the key. I give him a shove. His back tenses at my touch and he doesn't move.

I tap him with the gun.

We begin again.

But the sensation of his powerful shoulder muscle through the glove has made me nervous.

I'm going to have to be very careful when I give him the hammer.

In his freshman year at college he had a charge of assault and battery dismissed (so Ricky thinks) through the influence of his father; and in his senior year he broke another man's jaw, but that never came to anything because it was on the football field.

He's strong. He could snap me in half. Would too, given half a chance.

"How much farther? What is this?" he asks and stops again.

I push him.

Although he moves, there's a little jaunt in his step that makes me think he's up to something.

Got to be careful in spades.

"What's with the silent treatment, buddy? Do you even understand English? Are you mute?"

He turns to look at me.

"Huh? Get me? What are they paying you? I'll give you ten times what they're paying you. What's your price? Name it. Just name it. I've got the money. A lot of money. Everyone has their price. Tell me what it is."

Can you run back time? Can you do that? Are you a mage, a necromancer?

"What have you done with my clothes? I want my clothes. I want my goddamn clothes!" he shouts, furious, stubborn.

Naked in, *amigo,* and perhaps if things don't go well, naked out.

Even so, when the gun waggles he keeps walking.

"What is this? I want my clothes!"

The echo back over the lake opens the floodgates.

"This is insane! This is crazy!" he yells. "You can't shoot me, you can't. You can't shoot me. You can't. I haven't done anything. You got the wrong man. This is a goddamn misunderstanding."

I'm not going to shoot you. That would be far too easy. That would not give us sufficient comfort in the long years ahead.

"Listen to me, listen to me. I know you're not mute and I know you can hear me. Say something. Speak. You think you're being so smart. You're not. I want you to speak. I'm ordering you to speak. Speak to me!"

You want part of it? How about this: enshrined within the Colonial Spanish penal code is the Latin maxim *talem qualem,* which means you take your victim as you find him. American cops call it the eggshell skull rule. Slap someone with a delicate cranium, break it, and they'll still charge you with murder. *Talem qualem.* Take your victim as you find him. In other words, be careful who you kill. Be careful who you kill, friend.

"Madness. This is madness. You've obviously made some kind of mistake. I'm not loaded. You want to go to Watson, he's worth a billion. I'll show you. I'll show you. He's got a van Gogh, a Matisse. Him, not me.

Dammit, talk to me! Who do you think I am? What is this? Who do you think I am?"

I know exactly who you are.

It's who I am that's the mystery. What am I doing here? That one I still haven't figured out.

He stamps his heel into the ice, flexes his shoulder, turns again.

"This is crazy. You don't . . . Have you any idea what you've got yourself into? Do you know who you're dealing with? Ok, I'm no goddamn Cruise but let me tell you something, I'll be missed. They'll come looking for me. Are you listening? Take that thing off your head. I don't know what they told you. I don't know what you think you're doing but you're making a big mistake, pal. Big mistake. Biggest mistake of your whole life. That's it, isn't it? You don't know who I am, this is just a job to you, isn't it? Isn't it? Well, let me hit you with the truth, bud, you're making a life-changing error."

His confidence is starting to return. It didn't take long. His default position is the black rider, the boss, the center of the Ptolemaic universe. I prefer that.

"This has gone on too far. Way too far for a practical joke. Right now you're doing permanent damage to the soles of my feet. I'll see you in court for this."

He still doesn't get it. He still doesn't see why we're here.

"Listen to me, pal, you have no idea what you're mixed up in. You don't. Name a sum of money. Go on, just name it. A hundred thousand dollars? Two hundred thousand dollars? How about a cool half mil? Half a mil. Easy money. Easy money. Come on, buddy. You and me. We'll pull one over on 'em. We'll show them. Come on, whaddya say? I'm a grifter, you're a grifter. Come on, man, you can see the angles, we'll play 'em together."

Oh, *compañero*, is everything about you fake? A performance? Where did you learn to talk like that? The movies? TV? Isn't there anything real under that sheath of skin?

I slide the breech back on the M&P and it makes a satisfying clunk.

He continues shuffling, but only for a few paces.

"Come on, man," he says, and turns, and he's so fast I don't even see the drop kick coming.

He jumps with both feet and crashes into my stomach.

The wind is knocked out of me and the gun goes flying. Both of us go down onto the ice with a crash. He falls on me, his thighs crunching against my ribs.

Water and a big fissure forming under my back.

He pivots on top of me, and although his hands are still cuffed he's trying to bite my face.

His teeth snag on the ski mask at my chin, his breath reeking of booze and fear.

I make a fist and thump him so hard the first blow probably breaks his nose. The next gets him in his left eye, and the sideways kick to the crotch is the clincher. He doubles up in agony and I push the writhing mass of naked flesh away from me.

I get to my feet, retrieve the gun, suck O_2.

I look nervously at the crack under my feet. I stand there for a few beats but it doesn't widen.

"Jesus," he says.

Jesus is right. That was really something.

We both could easily have gone right through the surface. The hammer in my backpack would have taken me down to the lake bottom and if the shock hadn't sent me into cardiac arrest, the current would probably have taken me away from the crack and up under unbroken ice. And if I hadn't been able to break through I would have drowned. Shit, even if I'd gotten through somehow, I'd have been too exhausted to get out of the water. I'd have frozen to death in about half an hour. Mary, Mother of God, that would have been too perfect. It almost would have been worth it, just for that. What a wonderful, circular, karmic joke on me.

Yes.

I underestimated you, friend. And if I was a better person I'd let you go.

More deep breaths, hard, until I feel that I'm balanced again, poised between fight and flight.

Behind me the startled ravens stop squawking and resume their perches.

He is gasping for air, blood bubbling in his mouth.

After all the excitement we'll both need another minute. He returns my gaze and, observing the gun, backs away crabwise, trying to make it to the shore. Painful to watch: hands resisting the desiccated ice, heels dragging.

Squeak, squeak, squeak. Clouds. Snowflakes. Squeak, squeak, squeak.

I walk to him.

"No," he says.

His ass sticks to the ice. He rips it free and the crab walk recommences. It's so pathetic I'm starting to feel bad. I point the gun at his stomach.

"No," he repeats in a whisper.

Nooo. His breath a ghost that vanishes like all ghosts. Desperation in those red, coke crash eyes. I go behind him and lug him to his feet. Ice-burned skin. Human skin.

Sickening, but not much farther now.

"Listen to me, buddy, I can make you rich. I can get you money. A lot of money. Millions. Do you understand? Millions of dollars. Goddammit! Why don't you understand, what's the matter with you? Millions of dollars? Do you speak English? Do you understand the goddamn English language?"

I do. It was my major.

"I hope you understand me, because you're making a mistake. A life-altering— I have men, they'll find me, and when they do I wouldn't like to be in your shoes."

Better my shoes than no shoes.

"You just don't know who you're dealing with. You have no idea."

What next? You're connected? You're high up in the mob? Your movements are tracked by drones piloted by the CIA?

Just a few more steps: one, two, three, four.

There, we're about thirty meters out now, which is far enough.

I give him the universal "stop" sign and signal him to lie down.

He shakes his head. I place the barrel of the gun against his heart.

Still he doesn't obey.

I walk behind him and kick him in the left calf. His knees buckle and I push his head down, shoving his face against the ice. His body goes limp. Bracing himself.

I put the 9mm in my pocket, remove the handcuff key, unlock one wrist, and quickly get out of his way. I grab the gun again and wait. For a moment he doesn't believe that I've unlocked him, but then when he sees that he's completely free he gets to his feet and begins rubbing the circulation back into his wrists.

Keeping the gun on him I place the backpack in front of me and unzip the central pocket. I take out the sledgehammer and slide it to him over the ice.

He looks with astonishment at the vicious maple-handled, steel-headed five-kilo sledgehammer.

"What's this for?" he asks.

I point at the ice.

His face shows incomprehension, but then he gets it. "You want me to make a hole in the ice?"

I nod.

He picks up the hammer.

As I knew it would, my heart starts to race. This is by far the riskiest part of the whole plan. Now, if he tries his trick, I'm dead.

Maybe we'll get that sweet karmic ending after all.

He's got a fantastic weapon, he's strong, he's angry, he's free.

He holds all the cards but one.

Information.

He doesn't know that the gun is empty.

He stares at my masked face for a moment, smiles unnervingly, and tightens his grip on the maple.

He looks like Pitt at the party, like Thor at Ragnarok—the hammer, the ice, the bloody face, the blond locks.

I raise the Smith & Wesson and hold it in both hands. I sight him with the utterly useless gun.

"And what if I don't?" he says.

I nod as if to say, Try it.

"This is totally insane," he mutters. He shakes his head in disgust. "What kind of a man are you?"

No kind of a man.

Smith & Wesson. Hammer. Blue eyes. Brown eyes.

"Hell with it then," he says and violently smashes the hammer into the ice. The first hit cracks the surface. The second makes a hole the size of a football. The third makes a large pancake-size fissure that I can easily lift out.

I put my hand up to stop him. Then with the flat of my palm I signal him to drop the sledge.

It would be easier to start speaking now, to actually tell him stuff, but I'm reluctant to reveal that much of myself until he's completely where I want him to be.

"You want me to lose the hammer?"

I nod.

"How about I lose it in your head?"

He looks at me and then the gun and he lets the sledgehammer fall out of his hands. Keeping the 9mm on point I walk behind him and push him back to the ground. The car ride and the cold and this last piece of work have so wasted him that he embraces the ice like an old friend.

I put the snout of the gun on his neck and let him feel it there for a moment; then I take his hands and place them on his lower back; before he can try anything I quickly recuff him.

And that's that. It's over. No escape. If he gives me the wrong answers he's dead.

I lay the gun on the ground, walk to the hole, pick up the ice debris, and throw it out. I widen the hole a little with the sledgehammer and then toss it away as far as I can.

Before he has the time to think I drag him backward by the cuffs into the ice hole. Takes all my strength, which isn't much. When his legs touch the water, he begins to buck wildly but I've got enough momentum now to finish the job.

I shove the rest of him into the freezing lake.

Almost immediately his body begins to convulse in pain. I wouldn't know but I imagine it's like being electrocuted.

For a moment his legs stop kicking and he sinks beneath the water, but then—thankfully—he fights his way back to the surface.

Treading water, looking at me. His legs are powerful and he's so strong I suppose he could keep this up for half an hour or even forty-five minutes if I assisted him a little from time to time.

I sit next to him on the ice and open the backpack.

I take out the Ziploc bag I found in his nightstand. Inside there's six rolls of hundreds, a key of scag, and enough crank to animate half the corpses in Colorado. I suppose it's some kind of emergency treasure. About a hundred thousand in currency and convertibles.

I catch his eye and make sure that he sees what I'm doing. I place the heavy bag in the water in front of him and we watch it sink to the bottom of the lake.

Does that help you understand? This isn't about money.

In fact I can illuminate this even better for you now that you're cuffed and in the goddamn hole. I take off the ski mask.

Recognition dawns immediately, recognition and amazement.

Good. And now for the most important part of all. This is the bit I've been dreaming about. For this I want your full attention.

I lean forward, crawl toward him, and turn his face so that he's looking at me. When his eyes meet mine, I raise the gun, tip it vertical to show him the empty chamber, and then I click the magazine release and show him the empty clip.

Do you get it now, *compañero?*

Who did this to you? A girl. A wetback armed only with an unloaded pistol. At any time you could have run away and, my friend, when you had that hammer you could have ended this whole thing. But you didn't. She bluffed you out. This girl, this *perra latina.*

He looks at the gun, says nothing.

I'm a little let down.

Where's the fireworks? The fury?

Nothing. Well, you can't have everything.

He saw and he knows.

His legs continue to kick furiously but his feet, in the cold currents of the hypolimnion, are beginning to tire already.

I nod, slide back from the hole, stand, retrieve the hammer, and put it, the gun, and the ski mask into the backpack.

"Help me! Help me! Help me!" he begins to yell.

I scan the shore. Nobody.

"Help me!" he screams, his eyes darting madly. Expecting what? Duck hunter? Ice fisherman?

No. No one comes here in the winter, and just to be on the safe side I've put up a sign, I've locked the gate, I've wiped the footprints.

"Help me! Heelp meee!" he screams.

The words hang for a moment and then freeze onto the ice.

His lips are turning blue. His skin, red.

He's whispering. I can barely hear. I lean in. "Bitch, bitch, bitch, bitch, bitch, bitch, bitch," he says.

Words are finite. The set of all the words that will ever be spoken is small and the subset of each human's allotment is tiny. These could be your last. Is this really what you want to leave the Earth proclaiming?

"Bitch. Bitch. Bitch. Bitch."

Apparently so. Well, you're going to have to give me more than that if you want to get out of this alive.

After a minute the mantra changes but not by much: "Bitch, bitch, bitch, get you, bitch, you'll see, won't be fun for you, get you, teach you, yeah, bitch."

But then he whispers something else. Something surprising. "Bitch, you've got no goddamn shame."

That's more like it. Where did that line come from? Shame—how old-fashioned. Hector says that shame was one of the casualties of the twentieth century. Hector comes out with a lot of stuff like that. Hector says that Cuba is a woman's mouth, her lips squeezed together in a grimace, bruised and twisted at one end from all the beatings she's taken over the years. You'd dig Hec, maybe we could get him a job in Hollywood. A character actor. A cigar-chomping Miami cop. Do they still make cop movies?

"No shame, get you, bitch . . ."

But you're wrong. I have no morals, no husband, no children, but shame I have by the bucketload.

He starts to scream again.

"Help me! Help me! Help me!"

The duct tape is still in the backpack. I could cover his mouth, but what's the point? Let him scream.

"Help me! Help me! Help me!"

In a minute he wears himself out.

His teeth chattering. His eyes closing.

I pull out the pack of Faros and put two in my mouth. I flip the Zippo and light both. I offer him one of the cigarettes. He nods and I put it between his lips. It'll help him. In a couple of seconds the dissolved nicotine molecules will be firing neurotransmitters that'll release small quantities of dopamine into his brain. As the cold starts to get to him, blood will retreat from his extremities and his brain will become overoxygenated, perhaps releasing more dopamine and endorphins. The feeling will not be unpleasant.

I put my hand beneath his armpit and lift him a little.

He draws on the cigarette and nods a thank-you.

"I just g-gave up. M-man, this is ironic, it r-really is," he says.

Oh, *compañero*, don't you read the poets? Irony is the revenge of slaves. Americans are not permitted to speak of irony, certainly not Americans like you.

He grins.

He probably thinks I'm starting to crack, that I'll change my mind about this business.

I won't but I am so caught up in that grisly smile and the fading blue of his eyes that I don't see the black Cadillac Escalade idle its way to the locked gate behind us. I don't see the doors open, I don't see the men with guns get out.

I don't see anything.

I'm in this moment with this man.

Are you ready?

Are you ready to speak the truth?

Or do you want to wait until the black angel joins us on the ice?

"D-d-don't d-do this. D-don't d-d-do this." His voice drops half an octave, keeps the imperative, but loses the *tone*. "Don't, p-please."

Much more effective.

A call to prayer in the wilderness.

We Cubans are the vagabond descendants of the Muslim kingdom of Granada. We appreciate that kind of thing.

A call to prayer. Yes.

The dogwood minarets.

The ice lake sajadah.

The raven muezzins.

"How d-did it c-come to this?" he asks, crying now.

How did it come to this?

Mi amigo, we've got time. I'll tell you.

CHAPTER 2

BLOODY FORK, NEW MEXICO

The future paid a shivery visit to the back of the car. I woke, half opened my left eye. A yellow desert. Morning. I let the eyelid fall. Blackness. But not the blackness of negation. Nothing so fortunate. Merely the absence of light. Too hot to sleep. Too uncomfortable, too much background noise: radio in the front cab, annoying chitchat, stones churning against the bottom of the vehicle like lotto balls.

I felt weak, my bones ached, my jeans and sneakers were drenched with sweat.

The Land Rover rattled over a bump on the coyote road, the engine grumbling like an old horse.

No, no point trying to sleep now. I removed the cheap plastic sunglasses, wiped the perspiration from my forehead, rubbed at the dirt on the rear window.

Vapor trails. Red sun. Hot air seething over the vast expanse of the Sonora. No cacti, no shrubs. Not even a big rock.

Where were we? Was this a double cross? Easiest thing in the world, drive half a dozen desperate wetbacks to the middle of nowhere, kill 'em, rob 'em. Happens all the time.

I turned to look at Pedro, our driver. He caught my eye in the rearview, nodded, and gave me a tombstone grin. I nodded back.

"Yes, we're across," he said.

We crunched into a pothole. Pedro grabbed the wheel and cursed under his breath.

"Keep your eyes on the road," someone said.

"What road?" Pedro replied.

I wasn't sure I'd heard him correctly.

"We're across the border? We're in the United States?" I asked.

"For the last kilometer," Pedro confirmed. Both of us waited for any kind of emotion from the others. Nothing. No one applauded, cheered, reacted in any way.

Most of them had probably done this journey dozens of times. Pedro, however, was disappointed. "We made it," he said again.

I peered through the window and wondered how he could be so sure. It looked like fucking Mars out there. A thin brown sand worrying itself over a bleached yellow ground. Nothing alive, all the rocks weathered into dust.

"The land of Frank Sinatra, Jennifer Lopez, Jorge Bush," Pedro was saying to himself.

"Thanks for getting us over," I said.

Pedro tilted the mirror down to look at me. He gave me an ironic half smile. My friend, I don't do this dangerous job for praise, but I certainly appreciate it.

I'd made my first mistake. Now Pedro had singled me out in his mind as a classy sort of person, different somehow from the others. Someone with enough old-fashioned manners to say thank you. That, my demeanor, and my odd accent—all of it more than enough to burn my way into his consciousness.

Keep your mouth shut in future. Don't do anything different. Don't say a goddamn word.

I stole a look at him, and of course all this was in my head, not his—he was far too busy. The windshield wipers were on, he was smoking, he was steering with one hand, shifting gears with the other, while repeatedly scanning the radio, tapping the ash from his cigarette, and touching a Virgin of Guadalupe on the dashboard every time we survived a pothole.

He was about fifty, dyed black hair, white shirt with frills on the collar. The M19 spiderweb tattoo on his left hand meant that he'd probably feel bad about leaving us for the vultures but he'd do it if it came to that.

The kid looked at me. "United States?" he asked, pointing out the window.

"What's the matter with you, don't you speak Spanish?" I was going to say but didn't. He was an Indian kid from some jungle town in Guatemala. His Spanish probably wasn't so great.

"Yeah, we're across the border."

"So easy?" he asked, his eyes widening. He, at least, was impressed.

"Yeah."

He craned his neck through the glass I'd cleaned.

"United States?" he asked again.

"Yes," I insisted.

"How?"

From what I'd been led to believe we were somewhere on a sovereign Indian nation that didn't allow fences, or the border patrol, or even the local cops. Law enforcement was done by the FBI and they had to come in specially from Austin or Washington, D.C. It had been a coyote road for years.

"We just drove over," I said with a smile.

The kid nodded happily. He was the youngest of us. Sixteen, fifteen, something like that. Sweet little nonentity.

He and I and three others jammed into the back of the ancient Land Rover. Seats opposite one another. No way to stretch your legs out. Empty chair next to Pedro but he wouldn't let anyone sit up.

I drifted for a bit and felt drool on my arm. The old man from Nogales was napping against my shoulder. I wiped the spittle with my T-shirt sleeve.

Yeah. Five of us. The Indian boy, me, the old man, a deaf woman from Veracruz, and a punk kid from Managua who was sitting directly across from me, pretending to sleep.

Didn't know any of their names. Didn't want to know.

I stared through the window at the sameness.

So hot now the air itself was a gigantic lens distorting the landscape, bringing distant mountains dizzyingly close, warping the flatland into curves.

I pressed my face against the glass. Time marched. The heat haze conjuring ever more intense illusions from the view. The yellow desert: a lake of egest. The cacti: dead men crucified. The birds: monstrous reptiles from another age.

I watched until nausea and vertigo began to zap my head.

I took a deep breath and closed my eyes and for the hundredth time since that last interview with Ricky I wondered what exactly I was doing here. Revenge is a game for *pendejos*. Hector says that tit for tat is a base emotion, from the lizard brain, from way, way down. He says we've evolved beyond revenge. Witnesses at executions always leave dissatisfied, and he would know, he's seen dozens. But it's not about feeling good, Hector. It's about something else. It's about tribal law, it's about the restoration of order. Entropy increases, the universe winds down, and one day all the suns go out and the last living entity ceases to be. It's about accepting that, accepting that there's no happy place, no afterlife, no justice, just a brief flowering of consciousness in an infinity of nothing—it's about seeing all that and then defying the inevitable and imposing a discipline on the chaos, even as the boilers burst and the ship goes down.

Do you see? No, I'm not sure I do either.

I wasn't the only one suffering. "It's like being born under glass," the woman from Veracruz was saying. Whatever that was supposed to mean.

The Land Rover rattled through a huge sand-filled pothole on the coyote road.

"As long as we don't break an axle we'll be ok," Pedro muttered, and as if in response, the engine grumbled, stuttered, stalled, caught again. Jesus, that's all we need. Outside of Delicias, Pedro had to start it with a hand crank. He boasted that the old Land Rovers were better than the new ones, but none of us was reassured.

I affected an unconcerned yawn and reached in the bag for my bottle, but when I took it out I saw that it was empty. The tortillas were gone, the tequila was gone, the water was gone.

The kid from Managua nodded at me. He'd been twitching in his seat for twenty minutes. Jumpy little torta. Could be a sign of anything from schoolboy nerves to an ice habit.

"*Güey*, what's the matter?" he asked in slangy chingla Spanish. He had a sly, pinched face with big green handsome eyes and a throwback Elvis haircut.

My type. A dozen years ago.

"I'm out of water," I said.

The kid nodded, reached into his own grubby backpack, and produced a bottle of tap water.

"Thanks," I said, reaching for it.

"Five dollars," the kid said.

I smiled and shook my head.

"Four," the kid persisted.

"You're kidding."

"Three."

But I was done talking to this Nicaraguan street punk, this half-chingla trash. Clearly he was a mother of the first order. Give him a taste of this and a year from now he'd be coyoteing grandmas in meat lockers, leaving them to fry on a salt pan at the first sign of the INS.

I leaned back against the side of the vehicle and continued staring out the window.

A cerulean sky.

Cloud wisps.

Tardy moon.

I wondered where we were. The brief hint of mountains was over. The desert was becoming white.

"One dollar," the kid said, tapping me on the leg. I looked at the long-fingered, grubby-nailed paw resting on my knee. I removed it with my left hand and replaced it on the kid's lap. I stared at him for another sec. High cheekbones, coffin-shaped face, and a kind of faux menace in his sarcastic grin. I could tell that he thought of himself as a heartbreaker. Shit, he probably was back in Managua. Girls under sixteen or widows over fifty would be susceptible but everyone else would see right through him.

He was wearing an oversize black T-shirt and blue Wrangler jeans that had been hemmed by a tailor. His shoes were interesting. White Nike Air Jordans that seemed to have two different soles. He was dressing up, but he was dirt poor—in his brother's pants and someone else's used sneakers.

Still, that was no excuse.

"One dollar for a refreshing drink," he insisted.

I decided to work him a little.

"Where I'm from, *güey*, we have a saying: 'Refuse a man a drink and he'll refuse to speak for you at the Gates of Heaven.' But maybe you don't believe in Heaven. That's ok. Most people don't, these days," I said icily.

The deaf old woman genuflected.

The Indian kid looked uneasy. "And what do you know about it, *señora*?" he asked.

Señora, not *señorita*. That was ok. It was better than *güey*.

"It's just a saying, forget it," I assured him.

His eyes frosted over and he looked at me with disdain, and I knew the hook was in. Too damn easy. Poor kid, I thought, and returned to the view of the flatland. A few scrabble trees, a dried-up creek.

"Ok, fifty cents, you can have it. . . . Hell, you can have it for nothing."
I yawned.

"Go on, take it," the kid said finally, resting the bottle on my knee.

No point torturing him anymore. "For your sake," I said.

He smiled with relief. A big easy grin. A kid's grin. Life hadn't ground that out of him. Hadn't seen too much of the world.

Twenty-one, twenty-two. Half a decade separated us. Half a dec and a lot of experience.

I unscrewed the bottle top, took a drink of the tepid water, and passed it back.

"*Muy amable,*" I said.

He put his hand over his heart. "Please think nothing of it," he replied formally.

Somewhere, at least for a while, he'd been raised right with a lot of sisters and aunts. It made me curious.

"What's your name?" I asked.

"Francisco."

"I heard Pedro say you were from Nicaragua."

"Originally, but I lived in the DF for a few years."

"The DF?"

"That's the Distrito Federal, you know, Mexico City, and then after that I moved to Juárez."

Shit, I'd been planning on saying that I was from Mexico City too. Have to change that idea. "I see," I said hastily. "So what are your plans in America?"

"I want to make money," he said flatly. The old man murmured, the little kid grinned. Of course. I was the odd fish here. That's why everybody went to America.

"Why didn't you cross in Juárez?"

He leaned forward. "Vientos Huracánados," he said in a whisper.

I nodded. One of the newer, nastier drug gangs. They don't kill you. They go to your house and kneecap your children. Then they go to your mother's house and torch the place with her in it. And then they go to the cemetery and dig up your father's corpse and behead it. Not to be fucked with.

"What did you do to them?" I asked.

Francisco shook his head. He didn't want to talk about it.

"I was a mechanic in Belize, I can speak English," the Guatemalan kid chimed in. I nodded and put my sunglasses on—see, that's why you don't make conversation; now here I was caring about two people.

I pretended to doze.

The two boys started to chat about soccer and the old man next to me began chanting some ancient Gypsy ballad.

After a while I really did sleep.

Hector says the mammalian brain is the most amazing thing in the world. Even when you're asleep your brain is taking stock of things, measuring the temperature, processing auditory input, sniffing the air.

When I woke I knew immediately that something was wrong.

The bitter taste in my mouth was adrenaline.

The Land Rover had stopped.

"What is it?" I asked.

"There's a car in front of us," Francisco said.

I looked through the filthy windshield. Sure enough, about a quarter click ahead, a red Chevy pickup. New one. Big one.

"*Pitufos,*" Francisco speculated, but they didn't look like cops to me.

"Where are we?" I asked.

"We're northwest of Palomas at a junction called Bloody Fork. Just south of the road. This is our way up," Pedro said.

"Can we go round 'em?" Francisco asked.

Pedro shook his head. "Only way is back the way we came, and they'd catch us."

"They won't chase us over the border," I said.

"Won't they?" Pedro muttered.

"So what are you going to do? Just wait?" I wondered with impatience.

"I don't know. I don't think it's the border patrol."

"What's happening?" the old man asked, suddenly becoming aware of the situation.

"Cops, or something," I told him.

"We should get out and make a run for it," Francisco said.

Ni madres. "Are you crazy? On foot? Across the desert?" I exclaimed.

"They can't chase all six of us," Francisco replied, attempting to open the rear door of the Land Rover.

Pedro turned around in his seat. "Everyone stay put!" he snapped.

"I can't afford to get deported back to Mexico," Francisco said, pushing at the door. He looked at me. "Come on, let's get out of here."

"If we run for it, they get us all sooner or later. Get the old-timers first and then us," the kid from Guatemala said.

"They're going to murder us," the old man said, insanely grinning at this prospect.

"Look, they're coming up," Pedro muttered. "Everyone relax and stay put and let me do the talking."

The big truck gunned the tires and came toward us in a cloud of dust. When the two vehicles were about six meters apart the cabin door opened and a man in a baseball hat produced a rifle and a bullhorn. He wasn't pointing the weapon at us but he made sure everyone got a good look at it.

"Everyone out of the vehicle," he said through the speaker.

"Everyone has to get out," Pedro said in Spanish.

No one moved.

"Everyone out," Pedro repeated.

I didn't like the look of it. "He's not wearing a uniform," I said.

Pedro took the keys from the ignition and opened the driver's-side door. He exited and walked toward the truck with his hands up.

"Lie down, with your arms and legs spreadeagled," the American said.

Pedro lay down.

"The rest of you. Come out slowly with your hands in the air," the man said, still hiding behind the door.

Nothing else we could do. "Pedro took the keys," I said.

Logic worked us; we got out of the Land Rover and lay down next to Pedro on the desert floor. When they were sure that everyone had exited, the two American men cut the Chevy's engine and walked over, one carrying a hunting rifle, the other a double-barreled shotgun. They were both tall, wearing boots, jeans, plaid shirts. The one with the rifle had a John Deere hat pulled low over his face. The other was sporting a baseball cap of some description. Both seemed to be in their early thirties.

"Well, looks like we got ourselves something better than javelinas here, Bob," the John Deere man said.

"Fuck it, Ray, they's sorry-lookin' wetbacks, maybe we should just leave 'em," Bob said.

Ray shook his head and dropped the bullhorn.

"Please, sir, we got lost, we were driving—" Pedro began, but Ray kicked him in the ribs before he could finish.

"Listen up, dinks, nobody speaks till they gets asked a question. Is that understood?"

I didn't know if all of us could follow English but the message was clear enough.

"Everyone's gonna have a stash, Bob, keep 'em covered and I'll shake down their gear," Ray said.

"Why do I have to keep 'em covered?" Bob asked a little nervously.

I stole a look at him. He was the younger of the two—might be persuadable if things got hairy.

"Cuz you have the shotgun. Anyone gives you any trouble, plug 'em. Hear that, dinks? Anyone moves and Bob here will blow your fucking head off, *comprende*?"

We nodded dutifully, mushing our faces up and down in the dust.

Ray went to the Land Rover and began violently opening our stuff.

"Hurry up, man," Bob said.

"Shut the fuck up, Bob," Ray told him.

Ray rummaged in our backpacks for a couple of minutes. What he didn't find there made him angry.

"Well?" Bob asked.

"Search the dink driver."

"What you get so far?"

"Squat, a couple of hundred, few bags of c, some grass. Nothing."

"Let's go, man, let's get out of here."

"Somebody's holding. Search the driver . . . hell, we'll search all of them. Two hundred bucks won't cover our expenses."

One by one he turned us over and began patting us down.

Pedro had about a hundred dollars in a billfold but apparently none of the rest had much of anything. If they looked in my ratty sneakers they'd have themselves a handy little score but I knew they wouldn't think to do that.

When they flipped the Guatemalan kid they found that he had wet himself.

Both men laughed. Bob's mood lightened.

"Probably shitted himself," Bob said.

"Yeah, well, I ain't checking. He can keep that coke he jammed up there too," Ray replied and they both laughed some more.

Ray flipped me with his boot.

"Look at this little piece of fucking ass," Ray said. I could see him now. ID him pretty easily. Flinty brown eyes, light tan, hard gray stubbled chin, hog nose.

"Little spitfire, you can tell," Bob agreed.

"Not your type."

"How do you know?"

"Seen your ex-wife. This one, nothing to hold on to. One-twenty, one-twenty-five. Can't be five-five. Pretty little thing, though. Let's see what she's holding. Turn out your pockets."

I came up with about fifty bucks in assorted bills. Ray patted me down and didn't find anything else.

He stood up, looked into the sun.

"This is one sorry bunch of dinks," he said.

"What about the Land Rover?" Bob asked.

"Land Rover's a piece of shit."

"So what now?" Bob asked.

Ray signaled his friend to come over. They leaned against the hood of the Chevy and looked at their plunder. Ray opened Pedro's bag of junk cocaine, cut with God knows what—meth, rat poison, whatever. Kind of shit that made you want to shoot at people from freeway bridges. He took a pinch on the back of his hand, snorted it, and shook his head. It was practically worthless.

Bob obviously wanted to go now but Ray was working himself up. Had they been tipped off about us, or did they just sit here and watch the coyote road? Either way, this wasn't the big one they'd been hoping for.

Ray came back over and looked at us all lying on the ground.

He kicked Pedro in the gut.

Pedro curled into the fetal position, expecting more blows, but Ray couldn't be bothered.

"If anybody's holding out I'll fucking kill yaz, every one," Ray said. "Come on, what else you got?"

But nobody had anything.

Heat on our necks.

Still morning but the ground was burning.

The old man from Nogales took off his watch and held it out.

Ray looked at it. "The fuck is this?"

He took the watch and threw it into the desert.

"Fuck," he muttered.

He unslung the rifle and fired it twice into the side of the Land Rover. The bullets whizzed through the metal plates and continued in a dying parabola for a thousand meters.

"What are you looking at?" Ray said, staring at me.

I shook my head.

"I said what are you looking at, bitch?" Ray demanded.

"Nothing," I told him.

"Yeah? I think you're looking at me. I think you can't keep your eyes off me. Is that right?"

Ahh, so this was how it was going to be in America.

Hoping for a little time to get my bearings but that wasn't going to happen. Gonna be ugly from the very start. Straight from the get-go. Mother of God, how does it feel, Hector, to be right about everything?

"Cover me," Ray said to Bob, and he took a hunting knife from his belt. He safetied the rifle, slung it over his shoulder, tightened the strap.

"What are you doing, man?" Bob asked, his voice quivering. He knew what was going to happen.

Ray didn't reply. Ray was gone. Ray was a character from an old story of his uncle or his paw, propelled by forces he didn't understand.

He kneeled down on top of me. His groin over my groin. I tried to push him off but he put my hands under his knees. He was about a hundred kilos, mostly muscle. I was pinned.

He leaned forward and placed the knife against my throat. It was cold. Very sharp.

My head hurt from the fear. I couldn't breathe.

The desert burned off the sweat pouring from my back.

"Get off her!" Francisco said, sitting up.

"Shut the fuck up, dink, or I'll fucking kill all a yaz," Ray said.

"Get off her!" Francisco repeated.

"Bob, if this one doesn't lie down in five seconds, blow his fucking dink head off. One . . . two . . . three . . . four . . ."

Francisco hesitated for only a moment before lying down.

You did the right thing, kid. You can't argue with a shotgun. Proud of you, *güey.*

"What are you doing, man? We better go. We have to go. The BP has drones and choppers. This is taking way too long," Bob said, trying to talk some sense into his partner. But that moment had passed. Ray couldn't back down now.

His eyes narrowed and he mumbled something I couldn't catch.

He let the edge of the knife rest against my chin and then he dragged it slowly down my neck, bumping it over the carotid artery before bringing it to a halt above my clavicle.

"You understand English?" he said in a whisper.

I nodded.

"You wanna live?"

I nodded again.

"Don't do nothing stupid."

Holding the knife against my throat with his right hand, he began ripping open my shirt buttons with his left.

"Rest of you turn over, face into the dirt, I don't need no audience, goes for you too, Bob, think I can handle this little lady. Seems eager to please."

One by one they rolled over. All except for Francisco. His eyes were blazing. Boy was going to get himself killed. He'd clenched his fists and was thinking about a rush.

I couldn't help. I was deep in the pit. I could barely see. Paralyzed by fear. Fear a blanket smothering me. Fear in my throat.

Ray's mouth. Desert. The pit.

But now I had to climb out.

I caught Francisco's eye and gave him a minute shake of the head.

It's all right. It's all going to be all right.

But he was still going to come.

Jesus.

It's all right, little Francisco. Don't do anything. It's all right.

Eyes narrowed, fixed, he was gonna rush Ray. No. No. Bob will kill you.

I stared him down and, seething, he finally turned over and forced his face into the dust.

"You want it, baby, don't ya?" Ray said in a whisper.

The knife was on my thorax.

I owned it. I felt it there. I let it be there.

I would let it be there for a while and then I would move it away.

"What's your name?" Ray asked.

I tried to think whether I'd used a name with any of the passengers on the bus. But I hadn't. I'd been careful.

"María," I said.

Half the girls in my elementary school had been called María. That would do just as well as any other name.

"Ok, María, you look like you got a nice pair, let me see them tits," Ray said.

"We don't have fucking time for this, man," Bob grumbled, scanning the horizon, nervously. The gun not pointing at anyone now.

"Ain't gonna take but a moment. Ok, María, let me see 'em," Ray repeated.

He had ripped two of the buttons off my shirt.

"Let me do it," I said in English.

Carefully, I wriggled my hands free from under his knees. He didn't stop me. I undid a third button and a fourth. I smiled at him and gently pushed him upright. He resisted at first but then moved back. He was still straddling my pelvis and he still had the knife.

The knife.

A four-inch serrated hunting weapon. Lovingly honed. You could skin a bear with that thing.

He was holding it lightly in his palm, face open. It might be susceptible to a blow to the wrist. He might drop it. But then again, he was big and strong and wary.

Knife fights are bad news. In self-defense class they tell you that you have to be prepared to lose a hand. You have to commit.

To save your life, grab the blade and twist and know that it's going to hurt and it's going to cost you fingers.

I undid another button. The shirt was open to my navel.

"That's it, that's my girl," he said. Slobber at the corner of his mouth. His eyes filming over.

And me light, floating.

The knife.

The grinning face.

The partner turning away.

Commit. Lose fingers. The hand. And more. Never killed anyone. Nothing bigger than a wasp.

Commit. Lose fingers.

"Yeah, that's it, let me see," he said.

And then, just when I was ready to grab the knife with my left and punch him with my right, he rolled back onto his heels and stood.

I was puzzled for a second, but then I saw. He was undoing his belt and pulling down his jeans.

"You, too," he said excitedly.

"Ok," I said.

I pulled my jeans and underwear to my ankles. I slid them off.

Half naked.

The fear a river.

My arms shaking.

"Come on then," I told him and offered another smile.

He leered back.

Yeah. He liked this better. He wasn't getting off on the terror. He wanted a fantasy in his head. The willing victim. The fiery Latina. The sex-starved maid. Just like in his DVDs.

His jeans came off.

"Come on, honey," I said in a voice that was half willing accomplice, half frightened victim. Evidently the right mix.

"Yes, ma'am," he muttered. He spread my legs with his feet.

"Hurry up, Ray," Bob said.

"Don't worry, man, you'll get your turn," Ray said.

"Just fuck the bitch," Bob grunted.

I opened my shirt.

"You're gagging for it," he said. "It's going to be like making guac, María, we're gonna scoop all the love right out of ya. Show you a trick or two. I've had compliments from pros."

I nodded.

He kneeled between my legs and put down the knife to take off his boxers.

There would be one play.

I knew that he had the capacity to kill me. I knew that as a wetback my life wasn't worth anything and more than likely if he did kill me, he'd have to kill all of us. Six deaths for what?

No two ways about it. A commitment. A trade. Your lives for ours. In advance I ask forgiveness.

His tossed his cartoon-covered boxers and when they were gone he grinned and reached for the knife.

The knife that wasn't there.

"Huh?" he said.

Watching his brain tick over was like watching a dinosaur step on volcanic glass. Confusion showed between his eyes and before he could say or do anything his own treasonous hunting knife slashed him across the belly.

Maroon venous blood, stomach fluids, coffee.

A deep laceration, nothing punctured, but enough to sear his nerve endings and get his attention. He reacted faster than I was expecting. His fist hammered into the ground a few centimeters from my swerving head. I slashed at his face and the serrated blade opened his cheek like a sushi knife into yellowtail.

"Christ," he screamed, lurched back, and fell.

With his weight off me, I got to my feet, and before his head had hit the ground I slashed him again. Gut shot. The blade cutting vertically from his belly down through his urethra and into his scrotum—gravity helped and this one was deeper, piercing his bladder, cutting a chunk from the head of his penis and opening his epididymis. Blood, piss, one of his testicles rolling onto the ground.

I scooted away from him, kicking up a tornado of dust with my hands and feet.

"Fuck! Fuck! She cut my balls off," he managed between screams.

Bob was horrified. It had happened in about four seconds. He couldn't compute it. I kicked up more dust and he didn't even see me running at him until I was three meters away. He tried to raise the shotgun but in his panic discharged both barrels into the ground in front of me. Pellets struck me in the legs, burning like fat flying from the pan. Didn't stop me at all.

He looked at the gun. Had he really shot *both* barrels?

Yes, Robert, and on such things turn the world. We'll live and you'll die.

I jumped at him like a fucking puma. He didn't even think to hit me with the seven-kilogram wood-and-metal shotgun. He just sort of crumpled, absorbing the blow and falling.

The dagger entered his throat, my momentum so great that the serrated edge tore through his larynx and embedded itself in the cerebellum at the bottom of his brain stem.

He was probably killed instantly, but when we crashed into the ground I removed the knife and stabbed him hard in the forehead just to be on the safe side.

A crunching sound as the blade wedged itself into his skull.

I left the knife between his eyes, broke open the shotgun, and took fresh shells from his gun belt. Everyone was up now and the deaf woman had started to scream.

I pointed at Francisco.

"Calm her down," I said.

He nodded, put his arms around her.

I found my underwear and jeans and pulled them on. My skin was crawling. It was ninety degrees but I was shivering. I gagged back vomit. No one had ever touched me like that. I wanted to lie down and cry. I wanted to shower for ten hours. I wanted Hector, Ricky. I wanted to swim in the current. I wanted moonshine or a fix. No time for any of that.

I pulled myself together, loaded the shotgun, and walked over to Ray, scrabbling like a redneck Uranus among the blood and sand for his missing testicle. His voice had taken on the high-pitched whining so familiar to those of us who have worked in abattoirs or the torture chambers of the police headquarters on Plaza de la Revolución.

He yelled when he saw me coming and threw an arm over his face.

"No, wait, no," he said.

Despite the pain he scrambled to his knees and brought his hands together in a gesture of supplication.

"Please, I'm a family man," he said.

I gave him both barrels from a foot away.

His head disintegrated.

His body quivered and fresh oxygen-rich blood spouted like a fountain from his neck. It flowed for half a minute before slowing to a trickle when the heart had no more of it left to pump. His torso kept kneeling there, spookily, until finally I kicked it over.

I looked at the crew. They were pretty junked.

I was pretty junked.

I walked to Francisco, who had calmed the deaf woman. I took the pack of cigarettes from his shirt pocket.

"Lighter?"

His eyes glazed.

"Lighter?" I asked again and snapped my fingers in front of his face.

"Oh," he said and reached into his pants.

I lit three cigarettes, put one in my mouth, gave one to the deaf woman, gave him the other.

"We're gonna need to get these bodies in the pickup. I'll bring it over," I said.

He nodded. I passed out smokes to the others, walked to the red Chevy, got in the cab. Keys were in the ignition. I moved the seat closer, turned the key, hit the gas. I drove it next to the Land Rover, wiped my prints from the wheel, and got out.

Pedro was looking at me.

"Why did you move the car? Are we going to call the police? This was self-defense," Pedro asked.

"What police?" I asked dismissively.

I left him to think things over and went to the Guatemalan kid. He was sitting on the ground with his arms wrapped around his knees, crying hysterically. He was freaked. He'd never seen anything like this, not even in those jungle border towns.

"What's your name, partner?" I asked him.

"F-f-f," he tried, but he couldn't get it out.

"Ok, Fredo, we need you to help us."

He looked at me.

I was covered in blood and brains and bits of skull.

He shrank away.

I took him by the wrist. He disengaged my hand immediately.

"Are you ok?" I asked him.

He nodded.

"Speak to me. Are you ok?"

"Yes," he managed. "You?"

"I'm fine. We gotta move fast. We're going to need to get everyone back in the Land Rover. You gotta help us. Help the lady first, you and Francisco. Understand?"

He nodded. I left him, went to the old man and kneeled beside him. "Can you stand, *abuelo*?" I asked.

"Yes."

He didn't look too bad.

"We have to go," I said.

"Yes," he said. Somehow his cheek was bleeding. He was touching it, staring at the blood. Fixated.

"You're ok. We'll get you a Band-Aid in the car. Come on, Poppa," I said and offered him my hand.

"You speak English good," the old man said.

"I studied it in school," I replied.

That fact helped him. Anyone who could speak English that well was practically a Yankee. And Yankees could do this kind of thing to other Yankees. He blinked slowly, rubbed the tears from his cheek. I got him to his feet.

"Pedro, you and Francisco get over here. Everyone else back in the Land Rover," I said.

I rebuttoned my shirt and slid some of Ray's face from my hair.

When the Guatemalan kid and the old-timers were in the Land Rover, I rifled the two corpses and took back our money and possessions. Both bodies were still warm.

"What the hell are you doing?" Pedro said.

I gave him his billfold and that shut him up for a second.

"Is there anywhere we can hide this truck?" I asked him.

"What?"

"Is there anywhere we can hide their vehicle?" I repeated with more urgency.

He thought for a moment. "I don't think so," he said finally. "I don't remember any gullies or canyons around here. Nothing back on the reservation."

"Gotta leave it then. We'll put the bodies inside, buy us some more time," I told him.

"You can't move those bodies," he said.

"Not without help."

"That's not what I mean."

"Pedro, listen to me. They're gonna bring birds and attention. Get the bodies in the truck and it might sit here unnoticed till nightfall. Might buy us a whole day. Maybe two."

Pedro could see the sense in that. "What do you want us to do?" he asked.

"Let's get 'em in the cab. Don't touch them with your hands if you can help it, they can take prints off anything these days. Roll your sleeves down or make fists."

I looked at Francisco. "You gotta help too, ok?"

He nodded.

"Good, let's go."

First we went to Ray. I took one leg, Pedro took another, Francisco an arm. We dragged his headless body to the truck. I opened the door and with some difficulty we heaved him into the cab.

"Good. Let's get the other one."

We dragged Bob to the truck and before we hoisted him up I pulled the knife from his forehead. It made a terrible sucking sound. I'd hit him so hard that I'd punched all the way to the back of his skull, and as we lifted him into the truck, his cranium cracked. Daylight streamed through the hole in his head, sky where his face had been. Sky and brains and blood. Pedro began to throw up but Francisco and I kept at it, heaving Bob into the cab and dumping him in the driver's seat.

"Damn it," Francisco said, wiping goo off his shirt.

Bob's brown eyes were still looking at me. Half accusation, half amazement. I wasn't going to take it. Fuck you. Is this what you wanted, *Bob*? Is this what you thought would happen when you got up today, when you had your coffee and met up with your good buddy Ray? Save your look, friend, save your accusations, you had a dozen chances to let this go.

I closed his eyes with my knuckles.

"Let's give them something to think about. Gimme one of your bags of coke," I said to Pedro.

"I'm not a dealer, it's just to keep me awake," Pedro said defensively.

Mother of God, what was his problem? Was he sniffing cop? Maybe I was being a bit too professional, a bit too cold. If only he knew how sick I felt inside, fighting back the waves, pushing them deep where no one could see.

"That's ok, man, we just need to give the feds something to worry over," I said. He gave me a dime bag of his stash and I opened it and poured a little on Bob's pants.

"Make 'em think it was a double cross," I said.

"Yeah," Francisco said. "I can help with that."

I wiped prints everywhere I thought they'd be and Francisco dipped the knife in the blood and drew a T on the windshield. We both knew what it meant. CSI would pin this on the Tijuana cartel. At the very least it would set them off on a tangent.

"Ok, now we can—" I began but was interrupted by Bob's cell phone. The ring tone was one of those jazzy Vince Guaraldi numbers from *Charlie Brown Navidad*.

We stiffened.

"What do we do?" Francisco asked.

"Well, we don't answer it," I said.

We let it ring and ring and then we walked back to the Land Rover.

"Now what?" Pedro asked, his face ashen, his eyes exhausted.

"We continue on like nothing happened," I said.

"How can we just go on?" Francisco muttered.

He was cold, trembling. I put my arm around him. Poor kid. He'd lost about seven years. Thirteen again. Now I wasn't the next privileged chiquita in line for his attentions, now I was his way-too-young mother comforting him on the dirt floor of some Managuan shanty.

"It's going to be ok," I said.

He nodded and tried to believe it. And then he turned and looked at me. "What about you, are you ok?" he asked.

I hadn't thought about it.

I wanted to fall down, I wanted to scald my body, turn it inside out. He had touched my hair, between my breasts, my legs.

"I don't know. . . . I think so."

"Did, did they?"

"No."

He nodded and stared at the yellow sand spiraling around his shoes. "I'm sorry," he said.

"It's ok. We're alive and in one piece," I said.

It was one of Hector's lines. We're alive and in one piece and we're not in a DGI dungeon.

Francisco frowned, said nothing. He was a bit fucked up, but really it didn't matter if Francisco was fucked or not. Pedro was the one we needed. He knew the way.

I walked to him. He had stopped throwing up. He was trying to light another cigarette. I cupped the match and helped him.

He inhaled, coughed, inhaled again.

"Ok, Pedro, tell me the story, what were you supposed to do? What was the original plan?"

But he was too shaken and couldn't yet manage an answer.

With the patience of Saint Che I gave him two minutes to drain the cigarette and then repeated the question.

"I-I'm supposed to drive you up through New Mexico. We meet the 25 and then we stop at a motel we use in Trinidad, Colorado."

"How long will that take?"

"I don't know, ten hours."

Could I keep my breakdown away for ten hours? I'd have to. I took the keys from his hand, lit him another cigarette, opened the driver's-side door of the Land Rover, reached across the seat, and turned the ignition.

"What are you doing?" he asked.

"Ten hours, *hermano*. We'd better get moving."

CHAPTER 3

HABANA VIEJA

Tears. Tears at the rise of the moon. Tears under a starless sky. Tears down my pale cheeks while Death busses tables in the restaurant.

I sip the mojito, stare at the busboy, and shake my head.

That's a guilty man if ever I saw one. Hector's right. The baby's dead.

I dab my face with a cocktail napkin and shake the glass. The ice melts a little.

It is, as my mother would say, a close night. Every night for her is close. Way back her family is supposed to be from Galicia, which means, she says, that she is a martyr to the heat.

"What are you doing over there?" Hector asks in my earpiece. His voice is mock serious, sonorous, gruff. He talks like someone from the provinces who has tried hard to lose the accent, which, of course, he has. "Come on, Mercado, we don't have all night," he adds. You can hear the twang of Santiago in some of his vowels, but the way he enunciates is more Castilian Spanish than anything else. I know he watches a lot of illegal U.S. and European DVDs; maybe he's picked that up from them.

I raise the Chinese cell phone, which I've switched to walkie-talkie mode.

"Take it easy, Hector, I'm having a drink," I tell him.

"Did you make the arrest?"

"What does it look like?"

"I don't know."

"Father my babies, Hector. They'll be ugly sons of bitches, but with that big brain of yours I'm sure they'll go far," I say into the mouthpiece.

He doesn't respond.

A kid comes to the rail. Normally you don't see beggars in the Vieja because the CDR goons will chase them away with baseball bats. Whores aplenty but not beggars, because pimps have dollars to kick back. The CDR is something between a police auxiliary and a neighborhood watch. Real cops hate them because they're even more corrupt than they are. *Than we are,* I should say.

The panhandler is a skinny little boy with long black hair. Picked a good spot. Stone's throw from the plaza, which is packed with Canadians and Europeans. Behind me the cathedral is lit up by spotlights and the relentless music from the street musicians is entertaining those tourists who don't realize that they're having their pockets picked.

"You're too old to have babies. A woman of your advanced years," Hector says in my earpiece. I'm twenty-seven, Hector, I almost yell with indignation, but that's what he wants.

"In a minute and ten seconds that's the best line you can come up with? You should tell Díaz to write you some fresh material, he's got the filthiest mouth in the station," I say instead.

"Can you see us?" Díaz asks.

Certainly can. A bright green Yugo near the Ambos Mundos with the windows wound up and the two of them looking as suspicious as hell. If they weren't cops they were Interior Ministry secret police or something. All the pimps and dealers had cleared out of here twenty minutes ago.

"Yeah, I see you."

"Watch this."

I see him wave at me from the front seat of the car, a wave that quickly becomes a sexual pantomime I can't really follow. Some kind of insult, I'm sure. Díaz was originally from Pinar del Río, and they're an odd crew over there.

"I feel lucky to have met you, Lieutenant Díaz," I tell him.

"Oh yeah, why's that?" he asks, taking the bait.

"To know that such an idiot can rise so high in the cops gives hope for all of us junior detectives."

"You're not rising anywhere, Mercado, you're lucky you're not handing out parking tickets or sweating with the other girls down in the typing pool," Hector says quickly.

"The typing pool? That dates you, man. I think the department got rid of the typing pool ten years ago," I tell him, but actually I take his point. I'm not likely to go anywhere in the PNR. He knows it, I know it, even the kingpins who pay off the rising stars know it. No envelopes filled with dollars left on my doorstep—not because I'm not susceptible to corruption but simply because no one thinks I'm important enough to corrupt.

"At least the typing pool girls knew their place," Hector mutters.

"Yeah, anywhere but under you," I tell him.

There's an annoyed grunt in my earpiece that is Hector trying to conceal his laughter.

The kid's looking at me with big dark eyes. Not saying anything. It's a fantastic angle, makes you think that he can't speak. Mute, cancer, could be anything. I give him a few pesos and tell him to beat it. He takes the money but he only drifts back a couple of meters toward Palma. He looks at me with infinite sadness. Yeah, he's good. I check that my watch is still on my wrist.

Hector's mood is better when he comes back on a minute later.

"What's keeping you? Come on, we have other things to do," he says.

"Ok. Ok. I was waiting for an opening but if you want I'll just call him over."

"Yes, do that. Do it now."

"You're looking for an admission?"

"Anything. Anything at all. We'll have to try this *new directive* for a while before the even newer directive comes in."

The *new directive,* straight from the president's office, was an end (or more likely a suspension) of coerced confessions. Now we were supposed to gather evidence and arrest people in the modern manner. With an American election coming up in less than a year, the powers that be wanted us to look like we were a country in transition, ready for a new chance. And that's why they had me out here tonight, because that was one of the things I'd been pushing since I'd made detective.

"Ok. See what I can do," I say.

I scan the place and spot him waiting on a *gabacho* table near the fountain. Two Québecois executives who'd probably tip 15 percent. The restaurant is a staple of the Vieja, with spillover from Hemingway groupies at the Ambos. All the trendy people and the youngsters are farther up O'Reilly, but this is an older crowd who appreciate a good cocktail and slightly out-of-date cuisine. Almost all tourists.

"Ok, Hector, I'm going to go for it. I'll leave this on. If it looks like things are going bad I expect you and Sancho Panza to come charging in," I say, and before they can give me further instructions or Díaz asks if that was a crack about his weight I remove the earpiece and push the phone away from me.

It's transmitting and they're recording, so if he says anything incriminating we should have it on tape. Our boy's pretty close to me now anyway, fussing over two foreign ladies and pushing the priciest wine on the menu. When he's done I catch his eye.

He shimmers across and stands next to me.

"Yes, madam?" he says in English.

I'm dressed like a foreigner. A white blouse, a tartan skirt, half pumps, a faux pearl necklace. I've even put on lipstick and eye shadow and my short hair is styled with bangs. I'm supposed to look like a Canadian business-woman, but as soon as he speaks I realize I'm not going to play that game: teasing information out of him, flirting with him, pretending to be drunk . . . Now it all seems so tacky and pointless.

"Yes, madam?" he says again.

Young. Twenty-four, it said on his employment application, but I think he's a few years younger than that. Thin, handsome, probably using this gig to make connections for the bigger and better.

"Can I get you another mojito, *bella señorita*?" he asks and flashes a charming smile.

"You're the head waiter?" I ask him.

"Well, for tonight."

"I'm only asking because I saw you bussing tables earlier."

He smiles. "When it's like this we all have to pitch in."

"Take a seat," I say.

He smiles again. "I'm afraid that's not permitted and even if it were, on a night like this, with the place packed to the rafters, it would simply—"

I take out my PNR police ID and place it discreetly on the table. He looks at it, looks at me, and sits. No "What is this?" or "Are you for real?" or a glib joke about the health inspectors finally coming for the cook. No, he just sits, heavily, like his legs have given way. If my thoughts were miked up I'd be saying to Hector, "Man, take a look at his face." His whole expression had changed as instantaneously as if he'd just been shoulder tapped in improv class. Poker's not his game, that's for sure.

"Please, Detective, uhm, Mercado, uhm, can you tell me what this is about? Will this take long? I'm very busy. I have a job to do," he whispers.

"I've come to ask you about the murder of María Angela Domingo," I tell him.

"Never heard of her."

"No?"

"No."

"That was the name they gave her in the morgue. Domingo, because it was a Sunday when the body was found."

He frowns. His foot begins to tap. There's even sweat beading on his upper lip. Christ, what's the matter with you? You wanna get life in prison, Felipe? Calm down. At least make it look like I'm working you a little.

"I don't know what you're talking about," he says, finally.

"Don't you?"

"No. I don't. And I don't appreciate this. Who put you up to this? I suppose you're looking to get a few drinks or something. Well, have your drink and leave. We have good relations with the police." He gets to his feet. "Now, if you don't mind—"

"Sit where you are."

He doesn't move.

"I said sit!"

He almost jumps and then he doesn't so much sit as collapse. Better be getting this on video, Díaz, we could use some of this stuff with the judge advocate.

"It will only be a matter of time before we match the baby's DNA to the DNA of your girlfriend and, of course, you," I tell him.

His mind is racing. He takes a drink of water.

"Do you know the law?" I ask him.

He shakes his head.

"Whoever makes an admission of guilt first can become state's witness against the other," I say.

He looks dubious.

"I mean, we don't know how she died. Not yet. We don't know the details. Maybe the death was an accident? You're both young. You don't know what you're doing. How could you know how to care for a baby? Come on, Felipe. Come on. We don't want to take two young lives and ruin them. We don't want you to go to jail for twenty or thirty years. That'll cost the country a fortune. We don't want that. All we're interested in is finding out the truth. The truth. That's all we care about."

I take a sip of the weak mojito and keep my eye on him.

He's on the hook, yes, but he's still some way from the fish fryer.

Time for another gamble.

"We arrested Marta earlier today. We had to take her in first. She didn't seem surprised. They took her to a different precinct, so I don't have all the details yet, but I'll get them eventually. I wonder what she's saying about you right now?"

His eyes flash and I see that this is the tipping point. If he's going to blab it's going to be now.

But I'm wrong, he doesn't say a word.

Instead he makes a fist and brings it down on the table. My phone bounces and lands on the sidewalk. The beggar kid runs from the shadows, snatches it, and instead of running off into the night, gives it back to me. Yeah. He's good. That's how you do it, Felipe. That's called the soft sell. I slip the kid a dollar bill and check the phone's still broadcasting. It is.

"What is she saying about you? I mean, who did it? It must have been you. A mother couldn't do that to her own child."

"Don't you believe it," he says in a whisper so low the phone mike won't have picked it up.

"What was that? Tell me. Let me help you. What did she make you do?"

He closes his eyes, brings his fists to his temples.

"You've got the body?" he asks.

"Yes, of course. Little María Angela."

"Will they let me see her?"

"Yes, you've every right to see her, you're her father."

He nods and takes a breath and it all comes tumbling out: "I am. I am her father. Although she pretended it was someone else's. What happened to that guy? Eh? Don't believe anything she says. Don't believe a thing. She's the one. Her. I didn't do anything. She's was the . . . She killed her. I had nothing to do with it. Nothing. When I came over the baby was already dead. All I did was get rid of the body. I didn't ask her to do it. You gotta believe me. I didn't ask her. Why would I? We would have managed. I've got a good job here. We would have been ok."

He opens his eyes and stares at me.

"She killed the baby?" I ask.

"Yes."

"How?"

"She drowned it . . . *her*, in the bath. That's why I thought to put the body in La Ceiba. You gotta believe me, I had nothing to do with this. You believe me, don't you?" he says, his voice breaking. On the verge of crazy.

A couple more pushes. "Was it your idea? She wouldn't have done it. You must have told her to do it."

Eyes like catcher's mitts.

The waterworks.

"No. No. Haven't you been listening. I told her noth— I didn't tell her anything. It was her. It was all her. It's madness."

"But why did you keep the birth a secret?" I ask gently.

"She wanted me to," he says between sobs. "She begged me to keep it quiet. And I did. God forgive me."

"You delivered the baby alive. And then, at some point, you left the apartment. And then what happened? Later on she called you to let you know she had killed the baby?"

"Yes. That's what happened. I wasn't there. I had to go to work. She called me. I came home and the baby was dead."

I nod sympathetically.

"You believe me, don't you?" he asks and grabs my left hand.

"Yes, I believe you. La Ceiba," I say, enunciating the words clearly. If I know Hector, he'll have divers down there with underwater flashlights before I've finished this mojito.

I release my hand from Felipe's strong fingers. I push my chair a little way back from the table. He wilts, puts his head down on the stained mahogany top, and starts crying like a good one. It's pathetic. What does he want me to do? Pat his back? Give him a hug?

"She killed the baby and you hid the body?" I ask to confirm the testimony.

I push the phone close to him.

"Yes, yes, yes!" he mutters.

That's good enough for me. I swivel in my seat and signal the guys on the corner. I hold up two fingers and almost immediately two uniforms come out of a car I hadn't noticed before.

The beggar kid disappears.

Felipe looks up as the cops clamber over the barrier around the patio tables. His eyes are desperate, darting left and right. He grabs the back of a heavy metal chair.

Shit.

Quick flash of a possible future: table overturned, chair on my head, dislocated eye socket, smashed teeth, blood in my mouth, fumbling for the gun in my purse, second swing of the chair, roll to the side, revolver in my hand, trigger, two bullets in his gut.

Sort of thing you never get over.

"Don't even think about it," I tell him severely.

He lets go of the chair.

"Please," he says and tries to grab my hand but I slide away and he clutches air.

Finally one of the uniforms puts a hand on his shoulder. He flinches.

"You know where I was when she called me?" he asks me.

"Where?"

"The cathedral."

I raise an eyebrow.

"Yes. Yes. It's the truth. I was there," he says, pointing up the street.

"Praying for forgiveness?"

"No, no. No. No. You've got it all wrong. The baby was still alive when I left. She did it. She killed it. Drowned it."

The uniforms look at me as if to ask "Is this one a runner?" I shrug my shoulders. Their problem now.

"Come on," one of them says and cuffs himself to Felipe. With surprising efficiency an old Mexican *julia* appears from the plaza—brakes screeching, lights flashing, but, because it's the Vieja, siren off.

"You believe me, don't you?" Felipe asks, his eyes wide, tears dripping off his face like a leaky tap.

"I believe you," I reassure him.

He walks meekly to the *julia* and gets in the back.

The doors close and just like that he's gone, whisked off into the night as if he's part of a magician's trick. I look around the restaurant but the place is so busy no one except the Québecois has noticed any of this. The two widows at the next table are still studying the menu and everyone else is getting quietly hammered on daiquiris.

Only the gamin seems to care. I feel his glare from the semidarkness. His unasked question needs no answer but I give it to him anyway. Gratis. "He killed his girlfriend's baby. A little girl. Ok?"

The boy looks skeptical. My cell phone vibrates. I stick in the earpiece.

"Hell of a job, hell of job," Hector says.

"Thank you."

"Where did you come up with that stuff? 'María Angela.' Fantastic. That's exactly what they would call her, will call her when they find the body. You took a risk, though, no?"

"What risk?"

"You didn't know it was a girl. What if it had been a baby boy?"

"They wouldn't have killed it if it had been a baby boy. They would have sold it."

Hector sighs. "Yes, you're probably right."

"I've given you enough to go on, right?"

"More than enough. Wow. The things that come from nothing. All we had was a tip from the old lady that she was pregnant and wasn't pregnant anymore. We didn't have proof of anything."

"Well, now you got two losers whose lives are ruined."

"Always the downside, Mercado. Don't look at it like that. You did good. You really did good. You broke it open. In about two fucking minutes."

"Like to take the credit, Hector, but it really wasn't me. He wanted to talk. He was itching for it. I believe him about the cathedral, by the way, but he probably went there afterward. To ask forgiveness from Our Lady."

Hector doesn't want to think about that. "No. You really scored for us. Come on. Put down that glass and let me buy you a real drink. We'll go to that place on Higüera. Let's go celebrate."

I shake my head. "I can't."

"Why not?"

"I'm meeting my brother."

"Here?"

"Yeah."

"Why do you want to meet here?"

"I knew I was going to be here."

"What if Felipe had gone crazy and strangled you or something?" Díaz chips in.

"He wasn't strangling anybody. He was glad. Relieved."

"Well. We're all pleased. You should come . . ." Hector says, then his voice drops a register. "You should come, Mercado, we're, uh, we're meeting our friends from the embassy, uhm, I'd like to introduce you."

"You should definitely come," Díaz seconds.

Our friends from the embassy.

Which embassy? The Venezuelan? The Chinese? The Vietnamese? They all have what works in a plutocracy. Money. And Hector wants to introduce me to some of the players. Never done that before. It's what all ambitious cops want. The way in. The party, the drinks, the jokes, the dollars, an end to the sweatbox on O'Reilly, bigger cases, DGI contacts, maybe even a car.

Our friends from the embassy.

"Sorry, Hector, rain check, I can't do it tonight."

"Tell her, Díaz," Hector says.

"She doesn't want to go," Díaz replies.

"Can't do it, I'm meeting my brother, he's flying in from America."

A long pause before Hector decides it's not worth it. "Ok, well, if you change your mind you'll know where we'll be."

"I will, thanks, guys. And Díaz, please don't let him tell any jokes—you two on a bender with embassy people has 'international incident' written all over it."

I hear them chuckle and they flash the lights on the Yugo and wave as they drive past. No obscene gestures this time.

I finish the mojito and look about for a waiter. I suppose I should tell the manager that I've just arrested their—

A pair of hands covers my eyes.

Too clean and presumptuous to be the boy beggar.

"Ricky."

He laughs and kisses me on the cheek. He puts a chic black bicycle messenger bag on the table and sits in Felipe's seat.

"I thought they'd never go. Fucking cops," he says.

"Hey—"

"Present company excepted. Jesus, we're the youngest people here. Why did you want to meet in this cemetery?" he asks.

"I like it here."

He shakes his head, takes off his raincoat, and as an antitheft device wraps the strap of his messenger bag under his chair.

"How was your flight?" I ask.

"It was fine. I came direct."

"Really? Didn't know you could come direct."

"Yeah, you can. Two flights a week from Miami to Havana. Shit, I really could do with a . . . Have you seen a . . . Jesus. Pretty slow service in here, no?"

"I just arrested the head waiter."

"You're joking."

"No."

"Did he grab your ass or something?"

"No."

"What did—oh, wait, here's one finally . . ."

A harassed-looking kid shows up, seemingly dragooned from the kitchen.

Ricky orders half a dozen things off the tapas menu and a martini. He looks good. He's fit and handsome, with a mop of black hair that hangs over his left eyebrow in a fey, Englishy sort of way. He's almost too handsome, with none of Dad's flat, jovial peasant charm or Mother's fleshy good looks. He's angular and trim. His teeth are American white and his smile broad. The only thing we share are the dark green eyes from Mom's side of the family.

The eyes twinkle in the moonlight as he sips the martini.

"*Yech,*" he says. "Local gin."

When we were younger, people used to say we resembled each other, but not anymore. He's grown prettier and I've grown duller. Although perhaps tonight because he's just gotten off a flight and I've put on eye makeup and my best clothes we are like siblings once again.

"The mojitos are ok," I tell him.

"A mojito?" he says as if I've just suggested human flesh.

It makes me laugh and he laughs. Because of his good looks and the fact that he works for the *Cuba Times* and the YCP magazine, everyone assumes that he's gay. For years he wheeled a few girls around and tried to beard them but when he saw that it wasn't going to hurt his career he quietly let the girls go. He's not "out" like some of the famous Havana queens, but I've met his sometime boyfriend, a captain in the MININT—the Ministry of the Interior—and almost everyone knows. One time a low-level *chivato* (a paid informer) tried to blackmail him about his cosmopolitan tendencies, but the *chivato* ended up losing his job and being moved to Manzanillo.

He swallows the last of his martini, orders a Cuba Libre, and eats most of the food before he even thinks about having a conversation. Ricky's one of those men who can eat anything without it ever showing. If he weren't my brother I'd probably hate him. No, if he weren't my brother we would never have met in the first place. His circles are kilometers above mine.

"I'm surprised they can still pull it together," he says, munching on something that yesterday was swimming happily in the Florida Strait. "I would never have eaten here in a million years but it's not bad."

I let him nibble at two more side dishes before I press him.

"So what did you find out?" I ask with a trace of impatience.

"In a minute. Let's do you first. You arrested a waiter?"

Typical Ricky, always looking for a story.

"Yeah. One of the head waiters."

"The head waiter? What did he do?"

"He was a murderer."

"You don't say. Who did he kill?" he asks, affecting casualness.

"Killed a lot of people. Real nutcase. Poisoned them."

Ricky looks at his empty plate of tapas.

"Poisoned them? Are you serious?"

"Yeah, a dozen victims at least."

Ricky pales, but then I wink at him and he laughs.

"You're wasted in the goon squad," he says.

"I like the goon squad."

"That's why you're so weird, big sister."

"So. Tell me. What did you find out?"

He reaches into the messenger bag and hands me a folder full of typed sheets, drawings, and photographs.

"You wrote a report? Where did you get the time?"

"It was easier to write it out on the computer. I can type at a hundred words a minute, you know."

I look through his notes. They're clear and well organized and give me everything I need to get started.

"What's your conclusion?" I ask.

"Hey, do you like my bag? I got this in Manhattan, it's the latest thing," he says, trying to be frivolous.

"You're not going to distract me. What did you find out, Ricky?"

He shakes his head. "My conclusion, dear sister, is that your suspicions are *probably* correct," he says with deliberate caution.

"I'm right?"

"I think so."

We both consider this for a moment.

"You went to the garage?"

"Yes, I went to the garage."

"What did you learn there?" I ask.

"It's all in the notes."

"What did you learn, Ricky?"

"There were two accidents that day. That means two suspects: one of them's an old lady, one's a Hollywood type."

"A Hollywood type? What are you talking about?" I ask.

"Didn't I tell you? Fairview is full of Hollywood types. Tom Cruise moved there, and around his sun lesser planets revolve. It's where the elite go to ski now that Aspen and Vail are full of the hoi polloi. I met some of them. I got invited to a party."

"You didn't!"

"I did. I met a charming young man with whom I had a meeting of minds."

"I hope you were careful."

"I'm always careful, darling."

"How did you get all this stuff through airport security?" I ask.

Cuba was one of the few countries in the world that put you through a metal detector and scanner and searched you after you got *off* the plane. It was so that they could seize any contraband such as banned books, newspapers, magazines. The agents must have read Ricky's typewritten notes and asked him questions about it.

Ricky sighs as if this is a stupid question. "They're not very bright. I did a cover page about the conference, made it really boring. I knew they'd only glance at the first few lines, which were full of praise for the brothers."

"Smart," I say and examine the photographs. A motel, a mountain, a lonely mountain road. A Range Rover with a dent on the left front.

"This is amazing. This is more than I'd hoped for. You did really well, Ricky," I tell him with genuine affection.

"Yeah, I'm good," he says and lights a postmeal cigarette. American one.

"Tell me about the Range Rover in the photograph."

"Oh, that's a man called Esteban, a bear, straight, second-gen Mex, he did not bring his car into the garage for repair but he seems to have damaged it at around the same time. Apparently he hit a deer. It's only a small dent, but I knew you'd be intrigued."

"Why isn't he one of your suspects?"

"I don't know if anyone would have the *cojones* to kill a man and drive around with his blood and DNA on his car for half a year."

"Hmmm, you might be right about that. Who's this Jack Tyrone character?" I ask, skimming his conclusions.

"He's the movie star I was talking about."

"Never heard of him."

"No, he's an up-and-comer. I met him at the party, talked to him, also straight as they come, alas."

"Ricky! You've got him down as a suspect!"

"Secondary suspect. I suppose someone might be covering for him but his alibi seems watertight. He was in L.A. at the time of the accident. He was ok, but, like I say, straight as the fucking gate. At least he didn't try to get me to attend a Scientologist meeting like my charming new friend did the next morning."

"What's a Scientologist meeting?" I ask innocently.

"Oh, my God, sister. Don't you read the Yuma magazines?"

Yuma was street slang for anything Yankee, and of course you could get the magazines but why anyone would pay hard currency for a copy of *People* or *Vogue* was beyond me.

"I need my money for things like food and electricity," I say.

"Oh, boo hoo, the poor, starving public servant."

"Shut up."

He shakes his head as if I'm hopelessly uncool.

"Oh, speaking of Scientologists. One other thing I put in there at the end. The same night as the accident, one of them apparently crashed a golf cart on Pearl Street. I don't think it's anything to do with us but you might want to check it."

I put the notes back in the folder and grin at him. "Well, I'm impressed, you've done really well here, Ricky."

"I risked a lot."

"I know."

"I was proud of the photographs. Thought they might help."

"Did you talk to Karen?"

He conceals his distaste in a comic pretense of distaste. "No. That little chore I will leave to you. If you go."

"When I go."

"Oh, the one thing I couldn't get was the sheriff's report. They told me I could file a Freedom of Information request—if I were a U.S. citizen."

I look at him. "They said it like that?"

"Yeah, they said it like that."

Ricky waves at a friend walking past the Ambos.

"Well, I guess I'm going too, then," I say.

Ricky leans back in his chair. "Not necessarily, sweetie. We have an interests section at the Mexican consulate in Denver. Maybe we could do something through them," he suggests.

"No, Ricky, my mind's made up. I don't want a snow job. I want to do it myself."

"And of course you're the only one who can do it, right?"

I note the sarcasm in his voice but I don't want to make an issue out of it.

"I've decided, Ricky."

He says nothing, blows a smoke ring, and waves hello to yet another friend.

I tap the folder. "Seriously, thank you for this."

"You're very welcome," he replies and flutters his eyelashes.

A long silence.

This is always what it's been like between us. What's not said is just as important as the dialogue.

"So when are you thinking about popping off?" he asks, in English, his brows knitting.

"Soon. Next week. I've put in for a leave of absence."

"Next week? I've got an article coming out in *El País*. Big break for me. I'm having a party."

"And I would have been invited?"

"Of course. But you wouldn't have come."

"How do you know?"

"Because you feel out of place around my coke-snorting, bisexual, decadent contra-revolutionary pals."

"Yeah, I wonder why. What's the piece?"

"Feature article in the magazine on *the new Cuba*. All sorts of rumors coming down from the MININT."

"*El País*. Dad would have been proud."

"You think?" he asks dubiously.

"Of course, Ricky."

He nods but doesn't answer.

His face assumes a dark expression and he reaches his fingers across the table.

"Hands," he says.

I put my hand in his.

He clears his throat.

"Oh no, Ricky, you're not going to give me a lecture, are you?"

He ignores this crack and says what he's going to say: "Listen, sweetie, I know you're two years older than me but in some ways I've always felt that you were my little sister and I should be looking out for you," he intones very seriously.

"Don't do this, Ricky," I say and wriggle my hand free from his grip.

He shrugs, reaches into his jacket pocket for another cigarillo, lights it, takes a puff. "Ok, sis, I'll cut it short, but I'm going to say it and you're going to listen. That way if anything happens to you, my conscience will be clear. I'm doing it for me, not you. What do you think?"

"Ok," I mutter.

"All right, I'll give you a précis of the big speech I was going to hit you with. Basically it's this: There's no point at all risking your life and your career for Dad. Dad didn't give a fuck about us. Not one letter, not one dollar in all those years. Dad was a selfish bastard and although I'm sorry he's dead, that's about all I feel. We don't owe him a thing. And furthermore, he probably *was* drunk that night, and although I'm upset that he went the way he went, it's nothing to do with us."

Ricky smiles grimly and takes a long draw on the cigarillo.

I can see his point of view, but it's not mine.

"Who else is going to do anything about it?" I ask him.

"That's not the issue."

"What is the issue, Ricky?"

"The point is that this isn't how grown-ups do things," he says.

"How do grown-ups do things?" I say with a trace of anger. Sometimes his condescension is hard to take.

"Not like this. This is the way people behave in comic books or TV shows. It's preposterous. It's a throwback. It's theatrical."

"I'm theatrical?"

"Yes. You're pretending. You're acting. Look at you. You're someone with a promising career, a cheap apartment, a new promotion. And you want to throw all that away? For what?"

"I'm not throwing anything away. I'm taking a week's vacation, I've planned it all out in adv—"

"Planned what out? How dumb do you think they are in the DGI? If you don't defect when you get there, if you really do come back, you're going to be spending the next ten years in some plantation prison."

"I told you. I'm not defecting. I'll be back, I've got a plan all worked out."

"Fuck the plan. The DGI, the DGSE, the Interior Ministry are always one step ahead. It took me all day to lose my tail in New York."

"But you lost him."

"Yeah, I did, I've done it before. You never have."

"I'm a cop, I know when I'm being followed."

"*Ojalá,*" Ricky mumbles, looks at the stars, and shakes his head.

Another long silence. *Jiniteros* and *jiniteras* start filtering back into the street. The boy beggar resumes his perch. The piano player at the Ambos breaks into the "Moonlight Sonata."

"What does Hector think about all this?" Ricky asks.

"I wouldn't tell him. I don't trust him. Why do you mention Hector?" I ask.

"You're screwing him, aren't you?" he says.

"Mother of God, what makes you think that?"

"Well, because he promoted you to detective and because you always talk about him."

"I'm not screwing him. I got promoted because I'm good at my job, Ricky."

Ricky orders another rum and Coke. He looks at his watch. Obviously I'm only the first of several appointments in his busy evening. I smile gently. "Look, Ricky, I know you've risked a lot, slipping out of Manhattan, going to Colorado, but I can take care of myself too."

He nods slowly and sinks back into the chair. His shoulders slump as if all the life has been sucked out of him, as if I've just told him I've got terminal cancer. He starts to say something and stops. "You've never been out of Cuba," he says.

"No, but I can speak English as well as you and I'm a damn fine cop."

Before he can respond the beggar boy pulls at his arm. Really pushing his luck, this one.

"It's your turn," I tell Ricky.

Ricky reaches into his pocket and gives the kid a few pesos. The kid takes it to one of the *jiniteras*, who might be his mother.

Ricky looks at me, beams me that get-out-of-jail smile. "Ah, fuck it, it's your decision, if you want to go, you go."

"Thanks for the permission. Now let's end this. You know I've made up my mind. And once it's made, it's made."

"I like your outfit," he says.

"Shut up. I didn't want to look like a cop."

"You don't."

The street has completely filled now. Whores back under the streetlamps, pimps playing craps against alley walls. A CDR man I know shooting dice with the pimps. Ricky finishes the cigarillo. "I suppose it should be me. The only son," he says.

I hide the surprise on my face. "You've done enough," I tell him.

"It should be the son. It's my responsibility. I owe it to Mom, to you."

I shuffle my chair next to him and put my arm around him. I kiss him on the cheek.

"No."

He blinks, turns his head away. "It should be me," he continues. "I thought about it when I was up there, but then—well, then I knew I wasn't going to do anything."

"You did what I asked you to do."

He nods. "It wouldn't be justice. It would be murder."

"Maybe nobody has to die."

A tour group of elderly Canadians comes up from the harbor and files solemnly into the Ambos Mundos. They walk through, buying neither a drink nor anything else. The piano player starts riffing on a song by Céline Dion, either to bring them back or perhaps as ironic commentary.

Ricky politely disengages my arm. "So how are you going to wangle the visa?" he asks.

"I'm telling Hector I'm interviewing for a master's degree at UNAM in Mexico City. I am too."

"Jesus Christ, when did you start planning that?"

"Three days after the funeral."

Ricky laughs and takes my hand. "Oh, you're good, Mercado, like I say, too good for the cops. You need an outlet. When was the last time you wrote a poem?"

"Are you kidding? When I was thirteen."

He smiles. "You had talent. Your place is full of poetry books. You should start up again."

"You need to be in love with somebody to write poems," I tell him.

"That's not true. Dad thought you were good."

He is getting on my nerves again. "You wanna hear a poem?"

"Sure."

" 'The singing bird is dead as dust, he won't revive, alas, / so you can take that golden quill and shove it up your ass'—Heinrich Heine."

Ricky laughs, shakes his head, looks at his watch, yawns. "Well, I suppose I better . . ." he says.

He stands and leaves a twenty-dollar bill on the table. I give it back to him.

"The police are paying for this one," I tell him.

"Hey, you want to come with me? Yeah, you should come," he says.

"Where to?" I ask suspiciously, imagining some sweaty basement Sodom and Gomorrah filled with rail-thin boys and army colonels with fat mustaches.

"To see Mom. I smuggled in American chocolate from Miami. Come on, she'll be thrilled."

"To see Mom?" I say, aghast.

"It won't be that bad," he says.

But of course it is.

Water leaking in her apartment. Buckets over the voodoo gods. The smell of incense and a backed-up toilet.

Ricky tells her all about Manhattan.

An isle of joy, he says. She doesn't really understand. She brews herbal tea and casts the tarot. Makes predictions. Not a surprise when she mentions death. She always predicts death. We always ignore it. Laugh about it.

Death.

Oh God.

My eyes open.

Out into the hard blue night I gaze. Through the mountain and the desert. Through the tears. Tears for me. Tears into the black seat. My denim shirt thick with tears. I picked this shirt because it looked sexless, like a drab uniform for a drab nonentity. For an invisible. The person who cleared your table or cleaned your toilet or mowed your lawn.

I hadn't wanted to be noticed. But two miles into the United States I'm noticed. I'm nearly raped. And now I've killed two men. Unmade them as if they never were.

And there's nothing I can do but wipe my tears.

My face pressed against glass. Yellow lines. Scrub. Incandescent creatures following the van. What do they want?

More blood.

The deaf lady talking to me.

She can see I'm crying.

"We're nearly there," she's saying.

Francisco gives me a handkerchief, asks me something.

"No, I'm fine."

Headlights lick asphalt.

Moths call my name.

Close my eyes. Mom's apartment, Ricky's chocolate, me looking for the container holding Dad's ashes. It isn't there. No doubt Mother sold it to the witches on the floor below.

This is stupid.

This is crazy.

Hector was right. Ricky was right. They were all right.

Lights in the distance. Gas station. Another gas station.

"Ok, friends," Pedro says. "We're just about there."

A strip mall. 7-Eleven. Liquor store. Smoke shop.

Bits of tire. Fenders. License plates.

A gender reassignment clinic.

What is this place?

"America."

America.

"I don't feel good."

The car pulls into a parking lot.

"I don't feel good, Francisco."

"Call me Paco, everyone does."

"Paco, I don't feel . . ."

"Let me help you out. We're here."

"Where's *here*?"

"Come on. I'll help you to the motel room. It's been a long day."

His hand on my arm. The trucks. A chill in the air. Snow clouds to the north.

"It's ok, you're safe now."

Safe. Burn this shirt when I get the chance. Burn all these clothes.

"I need to shower."

"Yes, a shower."

Voices. Paco to Pedro. "She's in shock. Delayed reaction. Give her some brandy."

"I've got some 4H, do you think she would take some of that? Mellow her right out."

"Worse thing you can do. Get some hot chocolate."

Chocolate.

Snow clouds.

An outdoor swimming pool.

"Does anyone have a bathing suit that I can borrow?"

"Well, I don't know, I can check."

"Check."

A bathing suit.

"We got it in the lost and found," Paco says, grinning.

Flip-flops. The edge of the pool. "Gotta warn you. The guy says it's not heated."

"It's ok."

I step in. The cold clears my head. The chlorine scalds my cuts. I stay in till midnight. Quarter moon. Stars between the clouds.

A towel.

Food.

Whispers.

"Get some rest. Long day tomorrow."

"Rest. Yes."

The women in one room. The men in another.

A picture of Jesus. Mosquito corpses on the walls. A calvary for mosquitoes. The fabled mosquito graveyard.

The bed sags. I lay the mattress on the floor.

Sleep comes like a guillotine. And I'm down. No bad dreams. No dreams of any kind.

It's ok, Ricky. It's ok, Mom.

It's ok.

I'm in America and I've begun my task and the night is quiet and the world at peace.

The peace of Carthage.

The peace of baby María Angela.

The peace of a frozen grave.

CHAPTER 4

SLAVE SOUK

The warehouse bakes. Outside, snow. Snow I have never seen. I looked for it in Mexico City on top of Popocatépetl. Saw nothing but ozonic haze.

"The fuck is this?" the man asks, folding his hands behind his back, looking at us skeptically.

He points his finger at Paco.

"What the fuck are you supposed to be?" he asks.

Paco shrugs. The man towers over him, could pulverize him, but somehow Paco's slouch and silence is all insolence, as if he has the power, not the tall American.

The man turns to Pedro. "I mean, seriously. Two boys, two women, and a fucking old man. This is gotta be a joke. Where's the real merchandise?"

Merchandise. That's what we are.

"I just bring them in," Pedro says.

"Yeah, that's right, you just fucking bring 'em in."

"At considerable risk," Pedro adds, and he can't help but give me half a glance.

"How old are you?" the man asks Paco.

Pedro translates the question. "Twenty-eight," Paco says.

"Like hell, and the other one's even younger. Hold out your hands, both of you," he says.

Pedro translates again.

Paco and the Guatemalan kid hold out their hands. He examines them for scar tissue and blisters and shakes his head.

"These are town boys. Juárez trash. Neither's done a hard day's work in their fucking lives. Christ . . . This is really pathetic. I need strong guys for construction. Not fucking children, women, and old-timers."

He takes off his hat, a peaked cap that says DON'T TREAD ON ME, whatever that's supposed to mean.

Without the hat he seems even taller. Six foot six. Two hundred and fifty pounds. About forty-five. I give him a cop's look and memorize the details. Lines on his face, scar below his ear. He dyes his crew-cut hair a chestnut brown, but lets his goatee keep the flecks of gray. His voice is harsh but not strained. He's used to having authority, to being in command. Likes it. His back is straight and his belly fat is contained. Not like the Americans of *The Simpsons* or the Yuma flicks. Athletic. Strong. Jaw like an axe head. He's the type that landed on the moon when Jefe was boasting about a 10 percent increase in sugarcane production.

"You. What's your name?"

"María."

"María. Course it is. You know what the problem with your fucking culture is? No fucking originality. Indian blood. Fucking ten thousand years and no one invents the wheel. Shee-it."

"María, Elizabeth," I improvise.

"Where are you from?" he asks.

"Yucatán."

"The Yucatán. I know it. Ever been to Chicxulub?"

I shake my head.

"Fuck no. Why would you? That's where the comet hit the Earth that wiped out the dinosaurs. Why would you want to go there? Jesus, no fucking curiosity either."

I nod and our eyes meet and I look down at the concrete floor.

"And what do you do María, Elizabeth?" he says, coming close, his sternum an inch from my nose.

He's wearing cowboy boots, boot-cut black jeans, and a long wool overcoat. On another man it would be a costume in lieu of a personality, but not him. This is his attire. And you couldn't see it unless you were looking, but I am looking, and the bulge is a gun in his coat pocket.

He puts his finger under my chin and tilts my head.

His eyes are blue-gray, distant, like ash.

"I was a maid," I say. "I worked in many of the Western hotels in Cancún."

"This ain't Cancún," he says.

Pedro senses trouble. The others think I'm lucky, but Pedro knows I'm good. He's never seen moves like that before. I'm not a cop or a *federale* otherwise I'd have called it in. But I am *something*. And the sooner he's shut of me, the better.

"She has worked also as a nurse and she is strong and she is good with children," Pedro says.

The man sniffs me like a bear. "Whored before?" he asks in Spanish.

I shake my head.

"Well, if you're gonna start, you better start now. Getting too old as it is."

He turns to Pedro. "Is she a breeder or what?"

Pedro shrugs.

"You got kids?" the man asks me.

"No."

"A hundred a week, domestic. Hard fucking labor. But five times that giving working guys a little R-and-R. Think about it. Esteban will give you the lowdown," he says.

He touches my cheek with his forefinger. Paco flinches, but I look at him to show that it's all right. The man smiles and strokes my hair. I decide that—despite the plan—if he touches my breasts I'm going to kick him in the ballsack and when he's down I'll attempt to break his nose with the bottom of my shoe.

He looks at me for a long ten seconds.

What do you see there, friend?

Do you see the future? Or the past? The dead men in the desert, one with his head blown off, bodies black with egg-laying flies.

And what do I see when I look at you?

A hint.

A glimpse.

Before New Mexico I hadn't so much as killed a fish. But now I know there will be more.

I'm shaking.

Maybe it should be you, Ricky. I don't think I can do this either.

The man parts my hair to look for lice.

No, if this gets worse I won't kick him. I'll just go home. I'll quit the game and go.

"She ain't lousy," he says.

"They are all clean," Pedro insists.

He opens my mouth with two fingers. The smell of tobacco, leather. He nods to himself.

"You could make a lot of money . . . Yeah, I like this one. She could pass for white if she weren't so dumb. Ok, you'll do, step over here."

I walk behind him. Away from the others. The gap between me and them no longer merely metaphorical, but now delineated in geography. Paco twitches, looks at me, looks away. He wants to be on my side of the invisible line.

The American lights a cigarette.

Silence.

Smoke.

Snow.

The air in the warehouse perfumed with diesel and Marlboros.

"You are taking one?" Pedro asks, outraged.

The American nods.

"Now you are making the joke," Pedro says.

"I don't see anybody laughing," the man replies.

"This is, uh, madness," Pedro insists. "Do you know the risks that we run?"

"I don't like what you brought me. Whatcha gonna do about it? Tell me, little man, whatcha gonna do?"

Pedro spits on the concrete. "You are right," Pedro says. "I am nothing. You must not have to worry about me. But the people I work for—"

The American cuts him off. "Before you say something you'll regret, let me stop you right there, *friend*. The people you work for would never try to fuck with me in my town. Now that bullshit might play in fucking El Paso or Juárez but it don't work here. This is Fairview, Colorado. This is my city. I'll give you five hundred bucks for the girl. Take it or leave it."

"Five hundred dollars!" Pedro says.

The man nods, throws down the cigarette, clenches and unclenches a fist. His hands are huge. Bigger than my whole head. Meat axes. Hold a basketball upside down with his fingertips. And they say a lot. Tan line where a ring used to be, but no wedding band. Divorced. Knuckle scars. Hint of a tattoo running up his wrist. The bottom of an anchor. Navy. Marines. Something like that. A bruiser whose wife left him when he blew his last chance and beat the shit out of her.

"Take it or leave it. Take 'em all back, for all I care," he says.

"I take them all to Denver. I take them to Kansas City!" Pedro protests.

"Do that," the American snaps.

"This would not happen in L.A.," Pedro seethes.

"We're not in L.A.," the American says.

Pedro plays the angles, dreaming cartels and professional icemen who'll deal with this Yankee fuckface.

"Where is Esteban? I want to talk to Esteban," Pedro says.

Esteban, one of the guys on Ricky's secondary list—the guy with the dent in his Range Rover.

"Esteban's busy, but it doesn't matter, you ain't been listening, this is my town. I say who stays here and who goes." His voice a rasp. Metal grinding on metal—grinding on us. He's the vise and the plane and we're the thing in the jaws to be scraped clean.

"I do not do fieldwork, but I do construction. I lay down bricks. I am skills, my hands are, uh, *mis manos . . . no son asperas*, uh, because, bricks are skilled. I am waiter in restaurant, I am clean sewers. In Managua I work as house painter in morning and in laundry at night. Eighteen-hour day. I work hard," Paco says.

"And you speak English," the man replies.

"I speak English, good," Paco agrees.

"Yeah, ok. You sold me. You come over here too."

Paco crosses to our side of the invisible line.

When he's beside me he touches me on the small of the back. It's comforting, not irritating. I smile at him. *Nicaraguan bullshit artist,* I want to whisper in his ear but I don't.

"For him?" Pedro asks.

The man walks behind us and this I don't like. Him behind me. Hairs on my neck. He stands there for a beat. Comes around the front. He looks at me and Paco. He reaches into his pocket and feels the money in the billfold.

"You know how to work a nail gun?" he asks Paco in Spanish.

"Of course, señor," Paco says.

"Sure you do. What's your name, boy?"

"Francisco."

"Ok, good, I'll take Miss America here," he says, putting his big right hand on my head. He claps his left on Paco. "And if for any reason Miss America is unable to fulfill her duties, you, Francisco, the first runner-up, will step into her shoes."

Paco doesn't seem to catch any of it but smiles uncomfortably.

He turns to Pedro. "Seven-fifty for him. Twelve-fifty for both."

Pedro nods. That figure is a bit more reasonable. "Seventeen hundred and fifty and you will have a deal," he says.

The American yawns. "I'll tell you what, I'm feeling generous. Let's call it fourteen hundred even."

"Fifteen hundred and we will shake on it."

"Fifteen it is," the American says.

"And the others?" Pedro asks.

"You can take the others to Denver."

Pedro shakes his head, but you can tell he's going to take the deal. Fifteen hundred dollars in all those big bills. And there's something about the American. I can't quite put my finger on it but it's something to do with his height and the way he carries himself. His authority is absolute. Once he's decided, the conversation, the negotiation, the interaction are all over.

"I do not know," Pedro says.

"Take a second to think on it."

The American goes to the warehouse door, trundles it open. He sucks in air as if he's getting more than just oxygen from it. As if nature's rejuvenating him like one of my mother's voodoo gods.

Wind blowing around our ankles.

Pedro pretending to mull it over.

Time counting out the moments before the grave.

"Well?" the American asks finally, without turning.

"Take the other boy," Pedro says. "He is from Guatemala. He will work hard. Three hundred dollars."

"Can't do it. Too young. Stick out like a sore thumb. This is Tancredo's district. Motherfucker's running for president. Immigration's his bête fucking noir. INS breathing down our necks. Raided the ski resort preseason. Fucking decimated it. Dumb bastards."

Pedro nods, looks at the pair of us, gives us a look. We're both happy to go.

"Ok, a deal. You will have these and I will take the rest to Denver."

"Made a wise choice, friend," the American says.

In a dizzying two minutes we're bought and paid for and led outside to a new black Cadillac Escalade.

We get in the back.

The old lady and the Guatemalan kid wave.

Blub, blub. Never see them again. Have a good life.

Paco puts his hand up to the window.

"Get your greasy paws from the goddamn glass," the American says from the front seat. "Should have put the fucking sheet down. Forgot. Esteban normally does this."

Paco's hand falls.

We drive away from the warehouse and down a gravel slope to the highway.

The American flips the stations on the radio until he finds seventies rock.

We join the highway and head west into a sinking sun.

More mountains. Light snow. Dry air. Paco's jittery. Not talking. Nervous. Jesus, what about? The worst that can happen to you is the INS and a one-way back to Juárez. I'm the mark who's all in.

The snow comes on wetter and changes to rain.

"Ach," the man says and doubles the wiper speed.

The window shows Rockies. Never seen mountains before. Unreal. Hypercubed. Landscape by Henri Rousseau. Absurdly overblown. Too much. Aspens, firs, pine. Jagged peaks, crazy high.

Paco starts biting his nails. Fidgeting. But not for long. His eyes are drooping and soon he's dozing next to me like a big dead bird. I wonder how old he really is. Certainly a lot younger than I am. Kids need more sleep.

We follow the highway for an hour and then turn off on a two-lane road winding its way deep into the mountains.

The spine of America.

The same mountains that run from the Arctic Ocean all the way to southern Mexico. "Rockies" is a juvenile name. Doesn't do them justice. In Spanish they're called the Montanas Rocosas, which is much more dignified.

Paco starts whimpering. Hair over his eyes. Lips pouting. Bad dreams. I look away. Trouble, that boy. Corrupter of nuns and babysitters.

The rain stops and the sun comes out.

"Are you ok back there?" the American asks.

"Yes, we are fine."

"Not far now, look around, useful to learn a few landmarks."

Power lines. Telegraph poles. The occasional house between trees. And then the outskirts of the town.

"That'll do us," the man says.

The Escalade slows.

I nudge Paco. "We're here," I tell him.

We stare through the tinted glass.

A long street with huge sidewalks on either side. A lot of wealthy-looking people walking, talking on cell phones, window shopping. White, tall, healthy. Blond wives, older guys, but mostly women at this time of day. The stores are names from magazines: Gucci, DKNY, Versace, Dior, Prada. The restaurants are black, minimalist affairs with big windows. There are a few ski apparel shops but no fast-food restaurants, no bars, no lottery vendors, nothing messy. It looks different from Ricky's photographs. Smaller. Much smaller than Havana or even Santiago. It's not much bigger than a village. The main street, a few side streets, parking lots, and then trees. Five thousand people in the town and outlying districts, Ricky says. But he also pointed out that Fairview has doubled its population in just three years and it's supposed to double again in another three. Huge tracts of forest have been zoned for condos and a new ski resort.

We turn at a large bookstore and park outside a police station.

Panic. What is this? Have we been turned in to the feds already? Who is this guy?

"Out," the American says.

"Señor, what—"

"Get the fuck out!"

We unclick the seat belts and open the door. The sunshine is deceptive. It's very cold.

"Follow me, don't say a fucking word, just do as I tell ya," the American mutters, and then, with a sympathetic shake of the head, "It's going to be ok."

He leads us up marble steps into what a sign says is the Pearl Street Sheriff's Station.

Inside. Computers, laptops, fax machines, phones—and it's painted white. No one would paint a police station white in Havana. Wouldn't last five minutes.

"Sally, gather the staff," the man says to a pert woman in a pink dress.

A minute later three uniformed cops are scoping us. Note the badges. A. J. Klein, M. Episco, J. Crawford. All of them around forty. Crawford, a brown-haired skinny cop with a scar on his lip, is probably the oldest, probably the second in command, for I realize now that the man who drove us here must be the sheriff or the chief of police.

"Get a good look, boys. These are the newbies. Couple of Mexes. This one's called María, from the Yucatán, the other one's called . . . What's your name again, son?"

"Francisco."

"Francisco—from Juárez, he says. She won't be whoring, so if she is, I want to know about it. Both of them will be living with Esteban and he's responsible for them. If either of them fuck up, you tell me."

"Yes, Sheriff," the men respond.

The sheriff turns to us. "You two, these are my deputies. You do everything they tell you to do, always. First step out of line and it's the fucking federal detention center in Denver. Get me?"

"*Sí, señor,*" we say in unison.

"My name is Sheriff Briggs. This is my town. It's a peaceful little spot. We got our problems but we ain't had a murder in five years and if it wasn't for teen suicide we wouldn't ever make the papers. That's the way I want it. Either of you step out of line, cause me the slightest fucking headache, you're history. Understand?"

I nod and Paco says, "Yes, sir."

"We got a sweet deal and it's only going to get sweeter if we play our cards right. I ain't telling no secrets if I let you all know that certain parties are eyeing Fairview as the Clearwater of the Rockies. And if the Scientologists do move in en masse we're all going to make a lot of money. That's why we don't want any trouble from anyone."

"No, *señor.*"

The sheriff turns to his deputies. "Burn them into your retinas, boys, I don't want you relying on no crib sheet, I want you to know instantly who belongs and who doesn't in my patch."

The deputies examine the pair of us. Crawford winks at me.

Yes. Look hard. Do you know what you're seeing? Ask your boss, he saw it too.

"Did you get a good gander, boys?" the sheriff asks.

They nod.

"Good, then get the fuck back to work."

They scatter. Briggs smiles and then clouds as he spots an empty Starbucks cup lying there in broad daylight next to, but not in, the trash can. He grabs the unsuspecting cup from off the pristine floor tiles and throttles it into a paper tube.

He tosses it in the trash can and shakes his head.

"Oh, one last thing," he says, and he takes a quick photograph of us with a digital camera.

The sheriff leads us outside to the Escalade. The sun has set behind the mountains and I notice that the streetlamps on Pearl Street are ornate wrought-iron affairs like the ones you used to see in the Vieja. These are fake old, though. Brand-new fake old.

"How do you like my sheriff's station?" Briggs asks us.

"Very beautiful."

"Proud of it. Special bond issue to get it built. I hope that's the last time you'll ever be inside it."

"*Sí, señor.*"

We drive back along Pearl Street. Hermès, Brooks Brothers, Calvin Klein, another Versace. A Scientology drop-in center with a golf cart parked outside. Small dogs, a few more men, but still mainly women. Stick women, pipe-cleaner women, women with great heads on rail-thin frames. If this were Havana they'd be tranny whores. But in Fairview they're überblondes and trophy wives with money. Here and there a dark-skinned man is emptying the trash bins or a very young foreign girl is pushing someone else's child in a stroller. The dark-skinned men step onto the road to let the whites pass; step into the gutter while the tall ladies talking on cell phones keep their straight line. Cuba is no racial paradise—the Communist Party is 1 percent black while the prison population is 80 percent black—but even so, I've never seen anything like that before.

It makes me feel good.

Good because I'm going to need anger to carry out this plan of ours.

"Ok, busy day, next stop Wetback Mountain," Briggs says as we turn left at the traffic light.

Five-minute drive out of town. More trees, narrower road. We stop at a shit-color two-story building not far from what is obviously a major highway. Before the sheriff pulls into the parking lot a large man with wild salt-and-pepper hair and a black beard waves him down.

Sheriff Briggs double-clutches the Escalade and the man gets into the front passenger's seat.

"Drive," the man says.

"What?"

"Drive. Away from here."

"What's going on?" the sheriff asks.

"INS."

"Christ."

"Yeah, but we're lucky they came now. Everyone's still working."

"You get a tip-off?"

"Hell, no. We just got lucky. Did you listen to the radio? Raids in Denver, Vail, Boulder, Aurora, the Springs."

Sheriff Briggs accelerates out of the lot and drives down to the highway.

"Where to?" he asks.

"Just drive. It's finishing. Two INS guys and a couple of FBI to back them up. Bastards. They got three of my girls and that kid from Cabo. I hope to God they didn't make it to the construction site."

Sheriff Briggs nods at us. "Well, I got two replacements for you, Esteban."

So this is Esteban. Ricky's sheet: Mexican parents but born here. University-educated. Big guy but athletic. Plays soccer in a Denver Mexican league and even rugby—a violent game I only have vague notions about.

Esteban turns. "What are you talking about? Where are the others?" he asks in perfect English with no trace of an accent at all.

"I just took these, the others didn't look good," the sheriff says.

"Are you fucking crazy? We're shorthanded as it is, we need every hand we can get. There was supposed to be five coming in. We need them all."

"I said I didn't like the look of them."

"You didn't like the . . . Shit, you fucked up, Briggs, the INS has grabbed God knows how many of my men and now you—"

But before he can finish the sentence, Sheriff Briggs takes a 9mm out of his pocket.

He doesn't point the gun at Esteban. Drawing it is enough, and face red with fury, he can barely speak. "Listen to me, you wetback motherfucker. This is my town. You're here on fucking sufferance. I can fucking disappear you anytime I fucking want. Never talk to me like that again. Do you fucking understand, bitch?"

"I'm an American, Briggs, I'm a citizen just like you, you can't—"

"I can do anything I damn well fucking please," the sheriff says. Veins throbbing. Knuckles white.

Esteban looks at the sheriff and the gun. He doesn't flinch. Makes me think that Briggs has pulled this one before or else Esteban is made of sterner stuff. Hasn't been a murder in five years, he said. I wonder if that includes dead Mexicans?

Finally Esteban smiles. "You want an apology? Of course. I apologize. We're friends. We work together." He even forces a laugh. "Oh, Sheriff, why do you have to be so dramatic?"

Briggs puts the gun back in his coat pocket, satisfied. "Good. Now take a look at what I got ya at the auction block."

Esteban turns and smiles at the pair of us. "Two hard workers, I can tell," he says.

"We'll see. They better work hard. I make this a tough town for slackers. Now let's circle back to your motel and deal with these fucking feds and see what's going on," Briggs mutters.

"Welcome to Fairview," Esteban says, and adds with a grin, "Don't worry, it's not always this exciting. It's normally very dull."

Yeah, I'll bet, but I'll do my best to change that.

CHAPTER 5

WETBACK MOUNTAIN

When we got back it was all over, the feds high-fiving it back to Denver with a couple of little fish for the TV news. As we got out of the Escalade half a dozen people besieged Esteban, waving their arms and venting in fast, barely intelligible Mexican Spanish: "Sudden raid. No warning. They took Susanna, Juanita, Josefina, two others."

"Where did they take them?" Esteban asked.

"Who knows?"

"I've got other things to do. You got this under control?" Briggs asked.

Esteban nodded. "I'll get my lawyer on it."

"Then I'm gone. You two, nice to meet you, remember everything I told you, keep your noses clean," he said to us.

We got out of the vehicle and we were glad to see the Escalade depart.

The remaining population of the motel had surrounded Esteban now. "They took my money. They broke my door. Josefina's daughter is at day care . . ."

Everyone talking at once and pantomiming particular parts of the events in case Esteban didn't quite understand.

Esteban's phone rang in the middle of it. He turned to Paco. "Keep them away from me," he said in Spanish.

Paco took charge like he was born to it and herded the petitioners back to the motel.

Esteban answered the call. His English was as fast as his Spanish. "Yeah,

I know. . . . I'm here right now. . . . Page them, call them, whatever it takes, and if they come to the construction site remind them that it's a violation of safety regulations to allow anyone on-site who does not have a warrant from OSHA. . . . Doesn't matter if it's the fucking pope. . . . Yeah, keep 'em working."

He made two more phone calls and then turned to Paco and me.

"Names?" he asked.

"María."

"Francisco."

"Ok, María, Francisco. I've got a room for you upstairs. You'll have to share for a couple of days but if we really have lost some people then I suppose you'll have your own room."

I nodded and looked at the dreary motel. It wasn't pretty but at least it had a roof and four walls, which was more than you could say for some of the apartment buildings I'd lived in.

Ricky had taken a few photographs of the place but they didn't quite square up in my head. It wasn't that important, anyway. As far as we know Dad had never lived here.

Most of the illegals in Fairview, however, either stayed here or at another motel farther up the mountain.

Esteban was still talking, selling us on the gig. "Yeah, you'll be living high on the hog. Your own room. Money. Maybe even get you a car. Can either of you drive? Juanita had a car, won't be much good to her now."

I looked at the collection of ratty pickups and junk cars in the lot. These *were* as bad as Cuban vehicles, maybe worse.

Esteban flipped open his cell, took another call.

"Yes? . . . Now? . . . Who for? . . . Ooh, yes, he's an important client. . . . No, never say no, no matter what the circumstances. . . . I'll be right up. I got two right here. They just got in. You got uniform requirements? . . . Ok, tell them I'll be there in ten."

Esteban smiled at us salesmanlike, grabbed a gray-haired little man lurking by the door, and gave him a bunch of keys. "Lock the rooms, don't let anybody touch the stuff of the arrested, we might yet be able to get some of them back out. Ok?"

"What if the *federales* come back?" the gray-haired man asked.

"I doubt they'll come back. They never hit the same place twice."

"Not yet," the man said.

"What do you want me to do? Tell everybody to go live in the fucking woods? Just lock up their rooms and make sure nobody takes their stuff, ok?"

"Ok."

Esteban turned back to us. "Ok, folks, look, things *only appear* fucked up. They're not. There's absolutely no reason to panic, everything's fine, we're fine, they didn't hit any of my crews downtown, they sent a small team, and I think that's it. The main raids have been in Denver metro."

"Good," I said, unclear what this meant for us.

"And look, guys, I know you're tired, but I'm shorthanded. You gotta go straight to work, ok?"

"Ok," we said.

"Excellent. Excellent, that's the spirit, now follow me, quick tour, shower, and then out."

He led us inside the motel.

Red concrete walls, tiles, seventies American TV vibe. Nothing broken, though, and cleaner than even Ricky's place in Vedado.

"Shower's to the right, María. In and out in ten minutes tops. When you're done you'll find a uniform on the hook. Put it on. I'll find one for you, too, Francisco. Hey, is it ok to call you Paco?"

"Everybody does."

"Good, we don't have much time. Have a shower and I'll get you something to eat. Think I'll take one myself, it's been one of those days."

The shower felt good. *Hot* water. High pressure.

I soaped and cleaned and got out the smell of Sheriff Briggs.

I put on the clothes Esteban had found for me: a white blouse, a pair of black slacks, black shoes a size too big.

Paco came out of his shower in the same getup. White shirt, black pants. He'd shaved and slicked back his hair. He looked handsome and I told him so.

"I knew you'd succumb to my wiles, they all do," he said with a grin.

After Paco, Esteban came out of the shower fixing his shirt.

The big winter coat had concealed his true bulk. Six foot something, nearly three hundred pounds. He looked small next to the sheriff but he was bigger than all the Mexicans. Powerful arms and chest, a pale yellowy pallor to his skin. Not an unattractive man, and I imagined he could turn on the charm when he wanted.

He buttoned the shirt, smoothed out his beard.

"That's better, eh?" he said. "Now, follow me, my car's around the back."

His car was the newish black Range Rover from Ricky's photograph. Huge. Did everyone drive boats in this land? I saw the dent above the left front light. It was still unrepaired. About the size of a dinner plate. I stared at it. I didn't get a vibe from it. But as Hector and Díaz were always telling me, vibes were unscientific.

Ask him about it in a day or two.

We got in the back and Esteban sped out of the parking lot before we'd even got the doors closed.

"Normally I'd give you guys the speech over some tequila, but we don't have much time tonight, so just listen, ok? You'll stay here in the motel, you'll work for me, and you'll do what I tell you to do. You'll pay me a hundred dollars a week for the room. Most weeks you'll earn a good bit more than that. But when you don't you still owe me the money. Understand?"

His dialect was slangy chingla Spanish but I understood it.

"Yes," I said.

He patted my arm. "María, you were probably pretty cagey with the sheriff. Are you sure you don't want to work as a prostitute?"

"Yes."

"Even blow jobs? You're not bad looking. Ad on Craigslist. Fifty dollars a pop. You get twenty-five, I get twenty-five. Small commission to the SD. Take Sundays off, still make six, seven hundred a week. Good money."

"No."

"All right. It's going to be harder for you, but if that's what you want. Anytime you wanna change your mind, lemme know, ok? Paco, you'll be working construction here until we finish that building on Pearl Street, then I'll probably move you to Boulder or one of the ski resorts. I'll talk to Angel about your skills and we'll work out your pay later, ok?"

"Ok," Paco said.

"Fine, now both of you listen up. I'm a good guy, easygoing, but I don't take any shit. This is the way it's gonna be: you work real hard, you don't complain about anything, you do what you're told. Don't fraternize with the locals and don't try to fucking freelance, because the sheriff and I will find you out. He'll beat you half to death and I'll fucking turn you over to the INS. We don't allow drugs in the motel. In fact, no drugs period except what you move for me. Booze is ok. Understand?"

"Yes," we said.

"Now, where we're going tonight is a party up on what they call Malibu

Mountain or Malibu Mesa. . . . Oh, we live on what the sheriff calls Wetback Mountain—it's kind of a joke—but if you ever get lost, just ask for the Bear Creek Motel. That's what the place is called in the phone book."

It was pitch-black outside but as we climbed up the hill I could see huge houses on either side behind elaborate gates and stone walls. It was familiar.

Another of Ricky's black-and-whites.

Yes.

And this time on cue: *the fucking chills.*

"What's the name of this road?" I asked.

"This is the Old Boulder Road, some of the locals call it Suicide Stre—"

Rushing sound in my head.

The Old Boulder Road.

The very place.

Blood, ice, death.

"Are you ok?" Paco asked.

"Yes."

"What's the matter back there?" Esteban asked.

"We're very hungry. We haven't eaten anything since New Mexico," Paco said.

"Forgot about that," Esteban muttered and rummaged in the glove compartment for a moment. He found a couple of candy bars and passed them back to us.

"Ok, eat fast, we're here," Esteban announced.

Here was one of the houses from the seventies that people back then thought were futuristic. A curved roof, brushed concrete walls, concrete pillars under a wide deck, big glass windows that would make it an oven in summer and an icebox in winter.

"You're going to be working for Susan. She's good. She's CIA."

My face paled again.

Esteban laughed. "Hyde Park, not Langley."

I still didn't get it.

"She's a caterer. A chef. Come on, wake up, María. You're overspill, nothing more. Do what she tells you to do. Don't talk to the guests. When you're finished she'll call me and I'll pick you up. And really, don't talk to the guests, they're big shots, but if anybody asks you for drugs, you tell them you can get them quality stuff. Canadian pot, cocaine from Mexico, and we got a new type of meth from Japan. Are you listening? What did I say?"

"Cocaine from Mexico, local pot, and meth from Japan," I said.

"Good."

"What about heroin?" Paco asked.

"Good question. I like you. Thinker. We don't sell heroin in Fairview. We've had supplier problems. If anybody asks for heroin, of course tell them you can get it. If the price is right I'll send someone to Denver to buy it. Ok, in you go, around the back, Susan's waiting for you, she'll tell you what to do. Do everything she tells you to do, don't give her any fucking grief."

* * *

A bowl of fruit. Oranges. Pears. Bananas. Kiwi. I'd never seen a real kiwifruit before. A day of firsts.

"What's the matter with you? Are you retarded? Stop staring at that and help get the rest of the stuff back into the van. We're contracted until midnight and I'm not paying overtime to anyone."

Susan was a thirty-year-old American with an efficient black bob, a twitchy nose, a pretty face, and an unpleasant demeanor.

"Sorry," I said in English.

"Sorry? Sorry? Fuck sorry. I didn't hire you as a conversationalist. We don't have time for sorry. Get a fucking move on. Come on."

Close to midnight. The food portion of the party was over. Four hours had gone by slowly.

Paco and I had been confined to the kitchen, washing dishes, emptying trash, taking food and drink to and from Susan's van. Her staff, white girls and boys, did the serving, and when they weren't doing that they stood there gossiping and watched us at the mucky muck.

"This is how Spartacus got started," I muttered to Paco as I picked up the fruit bowl.

"Who?"

A girl nudged me and I stumbled in the too big shoes. Gravity worked the fruit bowl, oranges, pears, and kiwis trundling over the floor. I bent down and started putting them back.

"Trash," Susan said.

"Pardon?" I replied.

"*Basura*. Fucking *basura*. They're soiled now. Put them in the trash," Susan said.

"The bananas have a, uhm . . ." the word escaped me. "*La piel de banana*, it, uh, it protects it."

"What's your name?" Susan asked.

"María."

"You I won't hire from Esteban again. Now shut the fuck up and put the soiled fruit in the trash bags."

Susan went into the living room and announced the departure of her catering team. There was a brief discussion before she came back into the kitchen.

"We're done, but there's some tidying to do in the living room, a spill. You, er, wouldn't mind awfully staying until it's done," she said to me with bogus conciliation. "I'll tell Esteban to come for you in twenty minutes."

"Of course," I said and added "*hacete cojer*" under my breath.

She and her minions filed out the back door and Paco and I went into the living room to look for the spill.

Dim lights, smoke, half a dozen men sharing a joint and listening to Pink Floyd on a gigantic silver stereo. The men were all in their thirties or early forties. They didn't notice when we came in but I could see immediately why we were required. Someone had spilled red wine on a Persian rug. We went back into the kitchen and got a sponge and a bowl of water.

When we returned, the movie actor Brad Pitt was at the front door waving to the party guests.

"I can't stay. I just popped in to say hi," Pitt said.

"Oh, come on, man," someone replied.

"No, no, I really can't stay, I was up at Cruise's and now we're going to Vail. I just thought I'd say hi," Pitt went on.

I stood there looking at him, covered in grime, dripping sweat, holding a sponge and a bowl of filthy water—the dissonance between this moment and the encounter of my fantasies was quite marked.

Of course, I had seen Brad Pitt many times on Chinese bootlegs. Troy was the last movie Ricky and I had watched together—that's the one where Pitt plays Achilles, son of Zeus. Tonight he had a beard and was wearing an ugly wool hat, but he still looked like a god.

"What's the matter?" Paco asked beside me.

"Brad Pitt," I hissed.

"Who?"

"*Mierde*, haven't you heard of anybody?" I muttered.

Pitt grumbled something, waved, and was gone. The rest of the men went back to their marijuana.

We started cleaning the stain but it was heavy going. The carpet was thick and it looked like a whole bottle had gotten spilled on it and soaked there for a while before anyone noticed.

When the music ended the men's conversation drifted over.

"Where's Doctor Marvin?"

"He's gone."

"Thank Christ. Shrink with a chip on his shoulder, last thing we need when Cruise comes in."

"Cruise isn't coming."

"He's coming."

"Dude, it's after midnight, Cruise isn't coming now."

"Fuck."

"Hey, did I ever tell you that I was in *Mission Imp*—"

"Only a million fucking times."

"Jesus, no need to jump down my throat."

"Nice of Pitt to drop in."

"Yeah, he's like that. Probably the whole clan with him, out in a fucking minivan or something."

"Spacey was here before you came."

"Shit, was he? He's the fucking bomb."

"Jesus, update your slang, why don't ya?"

"They were good together in that movie."

"Yeah."

The marijuana smoke came our way and I began to feel light-headed. It was strong stuff, much stronger than the black rope they sold on O'Reilly.

"Worse than the Scientologists are the fucking born-agains and the—"

"Oh, I saw this bumper sticker today, 'Come the Rapture, Can I Have Your Car?' "

"Man, that's funny, I got to get one of those."

"No, dude, it's only funny if you got a shitty car. You drive a fucking Porsche, that's not funny."

Paco looked at me. "We need more water," he said. I didn't answer. The pot was tripping me.

"María," he said and snapped his fingers in front of my face, his gesture the reversal of me to him, yesterday.

"Sorry, I was listening to their conversation," I told him.

"Dope bullshit," Paco said with contempt.

Paco took my arm and helped me back to the kitchen. I opened a window and breathed cold air.

"Where's the garbage bag with all those bananas and oranges?" I asked Paco.

"Why?"

"I would love an orange."

Paco fished out the oranges, the kiwis, and the bananas and washed them off.

"Take them with us. We'll have them later," he said.

We went back into the living room with clean water and a new sponge. Two of the men had now gone and there were only four left. I recognized one of them from Ricky's photographs. Jack Tyrone, a minor film star and, more important, someone on Ricky's list. I wondered if this was his house. I looked around me. Was this the home of a movie star? It was hard to tell in the dim ambient light. It was certainly huge but weren't all American houses huge? The apartments on *Friends* were fucking enormous.

Tyrone's picture didn't do him justice. He was more charismatic and certainly more handsome than Ricky's snap, even now when he was stoned and obviously on the verge of passing out.

We got back to the stain. More snippets:

"Yeah, you don't fucking know."

"I do know. I am a connoisseur."

"Just as Christopher Hitchens is no George Orwell, so Beth Gibbons is no Sandy Denny."

"Yeah, the way Cruise is no Gary Cooper."

"Shut up, he might still come."

"Fucker's not coming."

"The way you talk, I should tell your mother."

"My mother's from Brooklyn. Outswear you any day."

"Well, he's no actor."

"Sure he is. You ever see that Oliver Stone one?"

"He can't be a good actor because he holds back. You gotta give everything. You gotta commit to the truth. I don't think he's ever given us a genuine performance?"

"That's bullshit."

"Dude, pass that over . . . thanks . . . Shit, can you get me some of that?"

"Maybe. What'll you do for me?"

"I'll get you a part in the new J. J. Abrams."

"Really? I'd do anything to be in a *Star Trek* movie."

"He's shitting you."

"Are you shitting me?"

"Yeah."

"You fucker. Christ, Jack, you've got more mood swings than Robin Williams backstage at an awards show."

"Leave him alone, he's just a kid."

"Jack's not that young. On his headshots he says he's twenty-nine. And on Wikipedia it says he's thirty, but really he's thirty-one."

"Damn it, Paul, you've got a big mouth."

"I think that's it," Paco said, looking at the stain.

It *was* it. The stain was mostly gone. Baking soda might have done a faster job, but muscle and hot water can do just about anything.

We went back into the kitchen. Paco couldn't stand to listen to any more of their dialogue so he closed the shutters to the living room. I sat on a stool at the marble breakfast bar and got a glass of water.

"What now, do you think?" Paco asked.

"I don't know," I said.

We killed ten and Esteban came in through the back door.

"All set?" he asked.

I could see by his watch that it was nearly one in the morning. No wonder Paco and I were both exhausted.

"We're done," I said.

"You did well, guys. I threw you right into the fire and you did well," Esteban said with a wide, expansive grin.

"Can we go home now?" Paco said.

"Yeah. I'll say our good nights."

Esteban went into the living room and after a moment he came back with Jack Tyrone. Jack's eyes were red and his face puffy.

"I want to thank you for helping out tonight. You guys were probably on the go from early this morning," he said.

You don't know the half of it, I thought.

We nodded and Esteban said, "Well, good night, Señor Tyrone."

But Jack wasn't ready to let us go just yet. "Wait a minute," he muttered, then yelled "Paul!" back into the living room.

Paul was another giant. This was the land of the giants. I wondered if this was Paul Youkilis from Ricky's file?

If so—

"What is it?" he asked Jack.

"Tip?" Jack wondered.

"Oh God, yeah, fantastic job. Where's what's-her-name? Left already? You guys did the hard work, I'll bet," Paul said. Jack opened Paul's wallet and gave us each a fifty-dollar bill.

"Oh, come on, Jack, a hundred bucks?" Paul complained.

Paco took the bills quickly. We nodded a thank-you.

"Job well done, even if fucking Cruise or Travolta didn't show. Pitt came and he can buy and sell those guys," Jack said and leaned against a door. He shook Esteban's hand. "Esteban, is it?" he asked.

Esteban nodded.

"Yeah, I swear to God, I'm on your wavelength, man, Mexicans are just like us Micks, we're Catholics, we have lots of kids, we're religious. Difference is that you guys work harder and, truth be told, you have better food."

Esteban faked a laugh and Jack started laughing. The laugh turned into a hacking cough. Paul got him a glass of water and led him back to the others.

"Let's go," Esteban said with disgust.

We grabbed the fruit and went outside into the cool mountain air.

At the side of the house I noticed a white Bentley. *The* white Bentley. No chills this time. Over that.

"Whose car?" I asked Esteban.

"Señor Tyrone's, I think," he said.

It was too dark to examine the paintwork but I'll bet the garage had done a good job. Invisible mending. All traces gone.

"Home?" Paco said to Esteban.

"Wait a minute," Esteban muttered, then took one of Jack's fifties from Paco and pocketed it. "I take fifty percent of all tips. You two can split the other."

Paco was too tired to complain. I was hypnotized by Jack's car.

Esteban drove back to the motel and showed us to our room. Clean, small double with two beds, a shower, and a heater that you had to feed with quarters.

Beat as we were, we were too pumped and hungry to go to bed just yet and we found ourselves in the second-floor communal kitchen.

"Beer?" Paco asked and passed me a Corona.

I knocked it back in one and he cracked me another.

"What's there to eat around here?" he asked.

"Let me see," I said.

I opened up cupboards. An embarrassment of riches. Cilantro, chives, tomato, onion, garlic, peas, lettuce, peppers, and a fridge full of meat and cheese and beer. Like the house of a Party member.

I found that I wanted to cook for him, this kid, this man. I wanted to provide, the way you couldn't in Havana.

"Put some rice on," I told him. "And look for tortillas."

While he did that I chopped an onion, mashed the garlic, diced a jalapeño, and fried them in olive oil. I threw in some cooked chicken and chicken stock and when they had all gotten to know one another for a while I slid in chopped tomato and minced cilantro and let them cook. When the chicken was brown I added a can of black beans and a can of red beans and let it reduce while the rice finished. Finally, I took a couple of tortillas and placed them in the oven.

"Man, this is good. What do you call this?" Paco asked.

"Havana chicken stew."

"Havana?"

"Oh, I mean, just a regular chicken stew, that's all it is."

"Well, it's good."

It was good. The ingredients were fresh and plentiful and we were famished. It made me *feel* good. This was how life was supposed to be. Not scrimping and saving and fighting over scraps.

We ate by the window and looked out at the street. No cars, no snow, just trees and vague distant lights on the highway. We talked. He told me about Nicaragua. He'd been orphaned early, begged in Managua, ran off to the jungle to be a soldier, drifted to Guatemala and then Mexico.

I made up lies about Yucatán, bringing in things from Santiago and Havana. Paco nodded and was so kid sincere it made me feel terrible.

For dessert we had more beer and I ate the orange, the kiwifruit, the banana, and an apple. I couldn't figure out the kiwi and Paco had to show me how to prepare it. He took the skin off with slender cuts and sliced the inside into five pieces. It was delicious. All the fruit was delicious and it made me hate the Party bureaucrats who deprived us of fruit so that it could be exported for foreign currency or turned into juice or made available only in the off-limits beach hotels.

One more beer and we staggered to our room and before I even hit the pillow I was gone, gone, gone.

CHAPTER 6

ALONG THE MALECÓN

Gone to the dream island.

A city in free fall.

A country in free fall.

Every one of us on deathwatch, waiting out the Beard and his brother's final days.

Tick-fucking-tock.

Hector says (in whispers), *After Fidel and Raúl, le deluge.* The successors will end up like Mussolini—upside down on a meat hook in the Plaza de la Revolución, if there's any justice. Which there isn't.

Calle Gervasio to San Rafael. Walking. Everyone walks in Cuba. You need to be in the Party or have at least a thousand in greenback kiss money to get a car. Early. So early it's late. High on brown-tar heroin, the whores don't care that I'm a woman or that I look like a cop. They raise their skirts to show pussy lovingly injected with antibiotics or mercury sublimate by our world-beating physicians.

"*Qué bola, asere?*" they ask.

"*Nada.*"

"*Qué bola, asere?*"

"*Nada.*"

"We swing with you, white chick. We'll show you tricks to impress your boyfriend."

I'm in no mood. Finger and thumb together, "*No mas*, bitches. *No mas.*"

In this part of town the hookers are all black and mulatto teenagers, the kind patronized by German and Canadian sex tourists whose fat white asses are also here in abundance. Go to bed, Hans, some pimp will knife you for that watch of yours. That watch will get him to Miami.

San Rafael all the way to Espada.

People thinning out. No plump anglos. Kids sleeping in doorways. An old man on a bicycle.

Past the Beard's hospital. Party members, diplomats, and tourists only. "The best hospital in Latin America." Yeah, right. Half the night staff probably outside soliciting blow jobs.

Espada to San Lázaro.

The police station.

A few lights on. Shutters closed. Couple of Mexican Beetles and a midnight blue '57 Chevy parked outside.

Sergeant Menendez urinating into a storm drain.

Sees me. "What are you doing here?" he asks.

Play it cool. Buddy-buddy.

"I heard that in Regla a guy pissing in the bay had his dick bitten off by an alligator," I say.

He laughs. "I heard that too."

He grins and strokes his mustache.

I smile back, flirty with the DGI pig. "I heard you got a lot to lose, Menendez."

Blushes. "Word gets around," he replies.

"It's just what I heard."

Again flirty, not that I ever would in a million years. No one would unless they had a thing for cadaverous bastards with pockmarked skin, greasy hair, and a vibe that would creep out an exorcist.

He leers but it's not really for me. I'm way too old for him. Hector says he goes for schoolgirls. Hector says the PNR had a file on him for child rape, but it was mysteriously pulled. Hector says a lot of stuff, but this I believe.

"No, really, what are you pissing in the street for?" I ask.

"Plumbing's out."

"Again?"

"Again."

"Not in the ladies' room, too?"

Another laugh. There is no ladies' room. The whores piss in a bucket in the communal cell and the secretaries go next door to the Planning Ministry. Since Helena González retired, I've been the only female police officer in the place.

"What are you doing here so early?" he wonders again.

Persistent little fuck.

Careful now. Tightrope walk. Menendez is the DGI *chivato* for the Interior Ministry, an informer, but almost certainly a low-ranking DGI officer himself. Thinks he's smart, but I know and Hector knows and so do half a dozen others—everyone who lets him win at poker.

I smile. "Oh, you know me, anything to get ahead, catching up on some currency fraud cases," I tell him.

He nods and spits out the stub of his cigarette. His eyes check me out. I'm wearing a white blouse with the top button undone. Blouse, black pants, black Czech shoes. No jewelry, short crop. Cop from a mile away. He looks down the shirt and back up at my eyes.

"Trying to get ahead. I heard you put in for a leave of absence. That won't help your career," he says.

Christ. How did he hear that already?

Flirty, young, bubbly: "You'll see, Menendez. I'm studying criminology. I'm hoping to do an M.A. at the Universidad Nacional Autonoma de Mexico," I say with a hint of pretend pride.

"Never heard of it," he says sourly.

"It's the oldest university in the western hemisphere. One of the biggest, too. And when I get the M.A. they'll make me a sergeant for sure. You better watch out when I'm in charge of you."

And for icing I add a little laugh, a little girlish laugh. Oh, Menendez, *cabrón*, am I not so cute to have such big dreams? Oh, Sergeant Menendez, aren't you moved by my naïveté. Doesn't it make you laugh to see how little I know about how things work in the Policía Nacional de la Revolución.

He grunts. "They're going to let you go to Mexico?"

"Well, they haven't given permission yet for the whole year. I haven't even applied formally yet, but I have an interview at the university next week. I think they'll let me go for that at least."

"Maybe," he says coyly. "But on the whole college is a waste of time. Good solid police work you learn on the job. And a year away: big mistake if you ask me, Officer Mercado."

"Well, we'll see what they say."

"If you want to get ahead you should join the Party," he adds.

"I'd like to, but I can't. Because of my father."

His forehead wrinkles, as if he's bringing up the mental files he has on the whole police department: cops, secretaries, cleaners, other *chivatos.*

"Ah, yes, your father. A terrorist. Defected in '93."

"He wasn't a terrorist."

"He hijacked the bay ferry to the Keys."

"No. He was on the ferry at the time but he wasn't one of the hijackers."

"Did he attempt to come back?"

"No."

Triumph and a snort. "Well, I won't keep you, Officer Mercado."

"Good day, Sergeant Menendez."

I walk inside. One of the newer precinct buildings, but already paint peeling off the walls. Uneven black-and-white floor tiling. Frozen ceiling fan. Big painting of Jefe, Mao style. No one around. A snore. Sergeant Ortiz sleeping behind the front desk. I tiptoe past him up the steps and through a set of grungy glass doors that squeak open, almost waking Ortiz.

Through central processing.

Officer Posada asleep under *his* desk. The male hooker cage empty, the female hooker cage with one lonely occupant, a black girl, maybe fourteen, curled under a blanket.

The stairs to the second floor.

Crumbling concrete, cracks in the floor the size of plantains. A corridor-length mural depicting Cuban history from the time of Cortés to the glorious Pan American Games in 1990 when the socialist system triumphed again over the Yankees and their vassals.

Hector's office.

Knock.

"Come in, Mercado."

I open the door.

Books and papers everywhere. Two telephones. Another dead ceiling fan. A window looking down to the sea. Hector nursing a rum and coffee. He looks tired. He hasn't shaved. Wearing the same shirt and jacket as yesterday.

"Sit."

I sit.

"You wanted to see me," he says. This early and this unguarded, his accent has that provincial eastern lilt he's been trying to eradicate his whole life. If he weren't bald, fat, married, and very ugly I'd find it sexy.

"So what's this about?" he asks sipping from the coffee flask.

"It's about my leave of absence," I say.

His eyes flick toward the door.

"You're early; I like that. Who else is in the building right now? Who did you see?" he asks.

"Posada."

"Awake or asleep? The truth."

"Asleep."

"Posada asleep," he sighs. "Before your time, Mercado, a posada was a hotel room you rented by the hour. We'd be lucky if Officer Posada used his brain for one hour a day. One hour in a day, that's all I ask."

I nod.

Hector sips his coffee.

"What about Ortiz?"

"Oh yes, Ortiz."

"You could have brought me something from the bakery. The bakeries are starting to open, yes?"

"I didn't think to. Sorry, sir."

"Hmm, so what's this all about?" he asks.

"Uhm, sir, as you're aware, I've put in for a one-week leave of absence."

He rummages through the papers on his desk. "I saw that. And you've applied to the Foreign Ministry for a travel permit to Mexico."

I nod.

"Speak up," he says.

"Yes, I wish to travel to Mexico City. I have applied to study at the university. I am meeting with a Professor Carranza at UNAM about the possibility of taking an M.A. in criminology."

Hector nods. "Yeah, I read the letter. And if the university takes you, I suppose that means you'll be taking an even longer leave of absence from the PNR? We'll be losing you for how long? A year?"

"A year. Yes."

He shakes his head, starts writing something on the piece of paper. "Hmmm, I don't know about this, Officer Mercado. Has the ministry given you permission for this first trip?"

"Well, I applied weeks ago and it's getting close to the deadline, sir. I was hoping that you could—"

Hector puts his finger to his lips and points at the wall and then at his ear. The implication is that his office is being bugged by the DGSE or the DGI. A second of dead air before he jumps in: "Hoping that I could what, Officer Mercado? Put in a good word for you? Why would I do that? Why would I want to lose one of my best detectives for a week, never mind a whole year? Well?"

He grins at me and passes me the note that he's been writing. It says: "I'll gain expertise that I can use to train fellow PNR officers, saving the department a lot of money."

I clear my throat. "Because, sir, when I come back I'll be a better detective and I will have studied all the latest techniques and I can bring my expertise to bear on our current caseload and of course I can then train fellow officers in the new techniques."

Hector nods, satisfied. "We'll all be like the gringos on *CSI Miami*, no?"

"I haven't seen that show, sir, but I suppose so, yes," I say.

"No, you wouldn't have seen it. It's good. Well, I must say I'm intrigued by your idea. This first trip would only be to meet the professor and visit the university? One week, you say?"

"One week."

"Hmmm. I have very little clout with the ministry but I will see what I can do."

"Thank you, sir."

Another grin. He lights a cigarette and leans back in his chair.

"There are some things I must ask you first, Officer Mercado, some formalities, some important formalities."

"Of course, sir."

"Your father was a defector to the United States."

"He was on a boat that was hijacked to the United States; he did not return."

"He was a defector!" Hector says, his voice assuming an angry tone for the listeners in the wall.

"Yes, sir," I reply meekly.

"That makes things much more difficult, you see that, don't you?" he says, rubbing his bulbous rummy nose.

"Of course, sir."

"Travel permits are given only to those with exemplary records, and you're not even in the Party."

"Because of my father I am not permitted to join the Party, sir."

"Yet your brother, Ricardo, is in the Party," Hector says.

"Yes, he joined the Party two years ago. He was granted a special dispensation."

"How did that happen?" Hector asks, again for the listeners, or more important, for the people reading the transcript.

"Ricardo has proven his loyalty to Cuba. He was president of the National Students Union and is an executive member of the National Union of Journalists."

"And he has been given travel permits?"

"Yes. He has been to Mexico several times, Haiti, Russia, China. When my father died in the United States, Ricky even went there to clear up some of my father's personal effects. He had the body cremated."

"Ricardo went to the United States?" Hector asks, though of course he knows that only too well.

"He has been to the United States twice. Once when my father died and only last week to attend a UN discussion on Cuba in New York City."

"And yet he did not defect?" Hector says.

"No, sir, he is loyal to Cuba and the Revolution, as am I."

Hector nods to himself and lets the silence play out. His hand makes the turning "give me more of this" sign.

"And of course my mother is old and dependent upon state subsidy. I would not do anything to jeopardize her well-being," I add.

Hector smiles, pleased. "Well, Officer Mercado, I am sure that all of this will stand you in good stead, and for what it's worth, I'll try to put in a good word with the ministry. Mind you, there is a lot of bureaucracy involved and these things are quite strict. If you do get a travel permit it will only be for Mexico City. You won't be able to go to Acapulco or anywhere like that."

"No, sir."

"A week seems a little excessive for an interview and a look around the university."

"Uhm, I will also wish to purchase some books and to search out cheap accommodation."

"Yes, of course. Well, I have a lot to attend to today, Officer Mercado. Like I say, I'll see what I can do. Allow me to walk you out."

Walk you out.

Away from the bugs and the performance. The dialogue for the MININT goons.

We walk.

Along the corridor, down the stairs, through the flaking orange paint, past the sleeping Posada, past Ortiz, who has miraculously awoken.

"Good morning, sir," Ortiz says.

"Good morning," Hector replies curtly, and with that we're out into the street.

"You must have seen Sergeant Menendez as well today, did you not?" Hector says.

"Not inside the building," I reply.

"You were wise not to mention his name. Never mention his name in my office. He believes that he keeps a low profile."

"I don't know what you mean, sir," I reply.

"Good. Come with me to the Malecón," Hector says.

The Malecón: the corniche that runs along the seafront of Havana. Now that they've fixed up Alexandria's promenade and Shanghai's Bund this is the paradigm case of faded grandeur. Think Rome in the Dark Ages, Constantinople in the last years before the Turk. In any other city in the world this would be prime real estate: the main drag of the city between the headland and the entrance to Havana Bay. There's no beach, but beyond the seawall bathers and fishermen gather all along the gentle curve of the croisette. On most days there's a spectacular view east to the castle and beyond to the blue waters of the Florida Strait. The Malecón could be beautiful, but in our Havana this particular piece of real estate is just a shabby row of boarded-up three-story buildings and empty lots. In the fifties these were bars, cafés, hotels, private casinos, ice cream parlors, Cadillac dealerships, and so on. In the sixties they all got turned into workers' apartments. And now they aren't anything. When the hurricanes come the seawall doesn't protect them and the buildings flood and the windows break and the wood rots and no one has the money for repairs. The bright paint has long since gone and the buildings that are still standing look like a collection of toothless old men waiting for their own personal apocalypse.

The trick to the Malecón is to look left as you're walking east and right as you're walking west. Keep your eyes fixed on the sea and it doesn't seem so sad.

Gentleman that he is, Hector lets me walk on the seawall side.

"What's the matter with you, can't you keep up?" he asks.

Despite having no sleep and existing purely on rum, pork fat, and cheap cigars, he's setting a blistering pace.

"What's the hurry?" I ask.

"I want to put some distance between us and that son of a bitch."

"He's not even here. I saw him pissing outside and I think he went home after that."

"That's what he wants you to think," Hector says.

"He's a lazy good-for-nothing with bribes up the ass."

"Saints preserve us, Mercado, he's got you right in the palm of his hand. The good ones always want you to underestimate them. Don't make me think I made you a detective too early."

"No, sir, you did not," I reply immediately.

Hector chuckles. "How would you like to be back in that lovely blue uniform?"

I shudder. The blue uniform with the awful peaked cap was almost South American in its hideousness.

"What about my arrest? That impressed you," I point out.

"What arrest?"

"The waiter."

"Oh, him? We would have got him one way or another," Hector sniffs.

"That's not what you said to Díaz," I mention in my defense.

"No, it's not. I wanted Díaz to think that you're invaluable. But anyway, it's irrelevant, that episode ended badly."

"Badly? I hadn't heard. I know you didn't find the body but surely the confession . . . ?"

Hector stops talking and looks carefully at the occupants of a slow-moving Volkswagen Rabbit. He waits until it's gone past before continuing. "The confession was fine but we had to let him go. His girlfriend is a secretary at the Venezuelan Embassy, well liked over there. The Venezuelans asked us to release her, and she wouldn't go without him."

"*Hijo de puta.*"

"Yeah, fucking Venezuelans. They say it's cold and we say, Warm your dick in our asses."

"You let both of them go?" I ask.

Hector shakes his head. "I don't want to talk about it, it's too depressing."

A black girl yells up to us from the beach. She's been sifting garbage and beachcombing. She's about seventeen, very pretty in a gorgeous ripped yellow dress that someone who loved her once had given her.

"Blow job, five U.S.," she shouts at Hector.

"No," he says firmly.

"Five Canadian," the woman persists.

"We're Cubans, and we're police, you idiot," Hector replies.

"Police. That's why you're so fat," the woman mutters.

He could arrest her for that but Hector just shrugs. She has a point. These days most people in Havana have trouble finding food. Cops, tourist agents, and good whores are the exception. And as if inspired to burn off more kilos, Hector increases his speed. I'm limping a little now.

"What's the matter with you?" he asks.

"I tripped on the steps at my mother's place."

"When was this?"

"Couple of days ago. Ricky and I went to see her. Her building's a mess. She lives in one of those dumps near Ferrocarril."

Hector looks confused. "I thought she lived in Santiago," he says.

"No, Havana."

"There's something about Santiago de Cuba in your file."

"My father was from Santiago; my uncle still lives out there."

Hector grins. "Yes, that was it. Lovely city. I had a grandmother from there. Used to visit her in the seventies. Once we rode bicycles to Caimanera to look at the Americans. Did you ever do that?"

I shake my head. Even before it had gotten a bad reputation, I'd never had a desire to gape at the Yankees in Guantánamo. The Interior Ministry had mined the bay and surrounded the camp with hundreds of soldiers. A few people had tried to defect there but all had been caught. It was easier by far to try for the Keys. And even if I had gone to Caimanera I wouldn't admit it to Hector. The last thing I wanted to do was exhibit any kind of wistful longing for America.

He slows his pace. Easier now. My limp vanishes.

Hector is smiling to himself, probably thinking of his adventures with girls on that long, awful train from Santiago to Havana.

"You fell down some steps, Detective Mercado?"

"Yes, sir. Thieves have stolen all the streetlights on that—"

"When I was a child I fell down a well. Did you know that?"

"No, sir."

"An early sign of idiocy or an early sign of brilliance, what do you think?"

"Don't know, sir."

"The philosopher Thales fell in a well while contemplating the heavens. Heard of him, detective?"

"No."

"What did you study in college?" Hector asks.

"Dual major, sir."

"Dual major in what?"

"English and Russian."

"Hedging your bets, eh? I like that."

"Not really, sir, we didn't have much choice, we were told what to—"

"When was the last time you walked along here?" Hector interrupts.

"Yesterday. As a matter of fact, every morning. I—"

"Not me, must be a year since I *walked* here. I have a car, you know. A brand-new Volkswagen from Mexico," he says with pride.

"I didn't know that."

"No. You wouldn't." He sighs. "It's changed since the last time I was here. Worse. In Cuba things always change for the worse."

"Yes, sir," I reply and inwardly groan. From past experience I know that Hector is going to hit me with an expansion of this theory.

"Yes, things got worse for the indigenous Cubans when the Spanish came, then they got worse under the Yankees, then worse still under the little dictators, then worse under Sergeant Batista, then worse under Fidel. And you'll see, it'll continue to get worse under Raúl and the Venezuelans."

"And after Raúl?" I venture.

"Ah, you mean when the Miamistas come?" He looks at me with a glint in his eye. "We'll talk about that in a minute," he says mysteriously.

We walk along the seawall toward the curve of the Castillo. In the distance is the fort of San Carlos and the chimneys of the oil refineries on the bay.

The wind is blowing the smoke offshore, decanting it north to Florida, 150 sweet sea kilometers from here.

He lights a little cigar, offers me one. I decline. Two summers working in the plantations for the Young Pioneers cured me of any desire to smoke Cuban cigars. He hoists himself up and sits on the seawall.

"Sit next to me," he says.

I sit.

He smokes his stubby cigar and, feeling the need for more nicotine, reaches into the pocket of his beat-up leather jacket to remove a packet of Dominican cigarettes. He offers me one and this time I do accept. He lights it and I inhale. It's American. A Camel. He's hiding American cigarettes in a Dominican packet.

"Do you know the concept of *duende*, Mercado?"

"Something to do with flamenco?"

He sighs. "My father was at the lecture Lorca gave here in Habana on *duende*, in 1930. *Duende* is the dark creative energy, the opposite of the creative spirit of the muses. You must avoid that energy, that energy gets you in trouble, Mercado, killed, like Lorca himself a few years later."

I stare at him and say nothing. He's overhearing his own thoughts, trying to bring himself to the point.

He shakes his head. "Please at least tell me you're familiar with Lorca, Detective Mercado."

"Of course. Murdered by the fascists."

"Yes. Murdered by the fascists," he says slowly, making every word count.

Waves.

Gulls.

A chain grinding against a buoy.

"I've got property here," he says at last, pointing at the rows of derelict and bricked-up buildings on the Malecón.

"Really?" I say with surprise.

"Yes. Land money. Best kind. Seafront. Worth shit now. I got it for nothing. But in five years when the Yankees are back . . ."

"You think the Yankees will be here in five years, sir?" I ask.

"Give or take, and call me Hector, Mercado. Call me Hector."

"Yes, sir."

Beneath us more kids are combing the concrete-and-iron coastal defenses for flotsam or garbage, and farther down the shore in the cool light of day a desperate character is making a raft out of driftwood and polystyrene packing. I point him out.

"You want to fill in a lot of forms today? You didn't see him," Hector says.

"No, sir."

We sit for a minute and listen to the waves. A pale sun is rising over a paler sea. Traffic is starting to pick up on the road.

Hector clears his throat. "I'm not going to argue with you, Mercado. I know you. I know that you're stubborn and I know that you're clever and I know that your brother has already taken considerable risks, but I will say this, if you think you've pulled the wool over my eyes, you're mistaken. And if you can't fool me, then you're not going to fool anyone in the ministry either."

"What are you talking about?"

"How long have you worked for me?"

"Since college. Five years."

"*I* made you a detective. *I* promoted you. Me."

"I know that, sir, and I'm grateful, and I'll do everything I can to bring credit to the—"

He shakes his head slightly, narrows his eyes.

"Never had a daughter. Two boys," he says sadly.

"I know, sir."

"One works for the Ministry of Fruit Cultivation, the other one doesn't work."

I know that, too, but I don't reply.

"For a while there, Mercado, I thought we had a connection. Something special. The other day in the Vieja . . ." His voice trails off into a cough.

He doesn't continue when he clears his throat.

"Yes, sir?" I prompt him.

"Call me Hector. I prefer that."

"Yes, uh, Hector."

"I like the way you say that. Now, why don't I lay my cards on the table, and then you can do the same and you can try me with the truth. How does that sound?"

"Ok."

Hector smiles. He doesn't seem angry but he's bristling, and I can tell that I am irritating him. "Mercado, it's like this: your brother came back from America last week. He had to get permission from the DGI and the Foreign Ministry and then a license from the U.S. Department of State. The waiver he got was to attend some preposterous conference on Cuba in New York. The license did not permit him to travel outside New York City."

"I believe I told you that already, it's no secret. I—" I begin but he cuts me off savagely.

"Listen to me! I know, ok?"

"Know what, sir?"

"Your brother went to Colorado. Your father was killed in an unsolved hit-and-run accident in Colorado. He was living in Colorado under a Mexican passport. He was drunk, the car did not stop."

"My brother did indeed go out to Colorado but I think you've gotten things mixed up, sir. That was almost six months ago, that was a completely different trip. For that trip he was granted a special visa from the Foreign Ministry—"

"Two trips to the USA, both of them benign. End of story, right?" he mutters.

"Right."

"Wrong. I think Ricky went out there again last week, at your instigation, to do some digging into the accident. When he came back you two talked, he confirmed your suspicions, and that's why you want to go to America. It's nothing to do with the university. You've been planning this thing for months."

"You're mistaken," I say quickly in an attempt to conceal my panic. Old bastard had me cold. "My father is a traitor to the Revolution. He abandoned his family. I have had no contact with him since he left Cuba. I want to go to Mexico to attend UNAM. I am not going to the United States."

Hector flicks ash, nods. If it were me, I'd press the attack, but he doesn't, he merely sighs and throws his cigarette end off the seawall. It's been a while since Hector braced a currency dealer or a pimp; he's lost his touch.

Finally, after a minute of dead air, when I've collected myself, he does speak: "Police captains in the Policía Nacional de la Revolución have some influence, Mercado. We are allowed to use the Internet. We are allowed to look in certain files of the DGI and the DGSE. And most of us have to be of reasonable intelligence."

"I'm not doubting your intelligence, sir, I just don't know quite how you've got it all so wrong in this particular situation."

He rubs his chin, smiles. "Well, maybe I have. Come then, let's continue our little walk," he says casually. We sidle off the wall and as the sun begins to break over the castle he fishes in his pocket and produces a pair of ancient sunglasses.

He looks a little ridiculous in the sunglasses, heavy wool jacket, baggy blue trousers, scuffed brown shoes. He doesn't look a person of consequence, though perhaps that's part of his charm.

"How many whores would you say there are in Havana?" Hector asks.

"I don't know. Two, two and a half thousand."

"More, say three thousand. Conservatively they each make about a hundred dollars a night hard currency. That's about two million dollars a week. A hundred million a year. That's what's keeping this city afloat. Whore money."

"Yes, sir."

"Whore money and Venezuelan oil will keep us going until the future comes racing across the Florida Strait. Stick with me. Let's cross the street at this break in the traffic."

We dodge a camel bus and an overloaded Nissan truck and make it across in one piece. He leads me to a building at the corner of Maceo and Crespo—a decrepit four-story apartment complex that probably hasn't had any tenants since Hurricane Ivan.

"This is my pride and joy," he says. "*This* is the future."

Hard to credit it. Windows covered with plywood boards, holes in the brickwork, and you can smell the mold and rot from the sidewalk.

"Let's go inside," he says, producing a key and undoing a padlock on the rusting iron front door.

He fumbles for a switch and by some supernatural power lights come on to reveal a gutted, stinking shitbox filled with garbage, guano, pigeons, parrots, and rats.

"What is this?" I ask him.

"This is the building I've bought with all my savings. It's mine now and I can trace legal title back to before 1959, which will be important when the Miamistas come with their Yankee lawyers," Hector says.

"Why are you showing this to me?"

Hector grins. "This building is worth nothing now. Nothing. But in a few years, after Jefe and Little Jefe . . . A hotel. A boutique hotel right on the Malecón. A minute from the sea, a short walk to the Prado. This place will be worth millions of dollars."

I nod my head. "*If* the Revolution falters after Fidel and Raúl."

"It's a gamble, Mercado. Like everything in life. I'm not like the rest of these fucking Cubanos with their long faces and their gloomy lives. I see a future right here, in Havana. Not in La Yuma. Here," he says.

"Yes."

He lights another cigarette and leans against a crumbling wall. Pulverized plaster and tobacco smoke obscure his face.

A minute goes by.

Two.

"Uh, sir, I should probably be getting back. Those currency cases aren't going to solve themselves."

He sighs, disappointed. "Nietzsche said that knowledge kills action. Action requires the veils of illusion. That's the doctrine of Hamlet. When you go there and you meet them, what then, Mercado? What then?"

"Sir, I really appreciate the fact that you've trusted me with this—"

"I had hoped that here in *my* secret place you were going to tell me *your* secret. I naively thought that you trusted me sufficiently to give me your truth."

"I have given you the truth."

"Thing is, Mercado, you probably think you've got nothing to lose. But I have a lot to lose. I see a little glimmer of hope. I've got an investment. A dream."

"I won't tell anyone."

"Of course you won't, but you're still going to fuck me over. If you go to the United States and stay there, I'll lose my job, they'll take my property, they'll probably throw me in jail. My wife and kids will be destroyed. You want to see my wife blowing fat Swedes to feed our kids?"

He throws the cigarette. It bounces off my cheek, sparks flying.

"Is that what you fucking want?" he yells. His face is pink. He's really angry now.

"What are you talking about? The United States? I wanna go to Mexico, I have an interview at the—"

Hector reaches into the pocket of his roomy slacks and pulls out a Russian automatic. He flicks off the safety and, fast for a fat man, presses it against my throat.

"No more fucking lies, Mercado. I could kill you here in this derelict building. The ocean booming against the seawall, the traffic, no fucking witnesses, nobody would even find the body for months, if ever."

"Hector, I—"

"You want the DGI to destroy me? You want them to throw me in jail with all the people I've put away over the years? Is that what you want after all I've done for you? Made you a fucking detective, groomed you, made every other goddamn cop in the station treat you with respect. Answer me, Mercadito!"

The gun.

The dust.

His red eyes.

"I don't want to do anything to hurt you, boss," I say.

"Why do you think he was in Colorado posing as a fucking Mexican? Did you ever think about that? He didn't want to be found. He ran from the Cuba that raised him and he ran from the Florida Cubans who took him in. He ran and disappeared. He didn't want your help. Or anybody's help. He was a selfish motherfucker, Mercado. A drunk. A fuckup. He was the fucking town ratcatcher. Forget him."

He pushes the revolver hard against my windpipe, holds it there for a full ten seconds, but then, suddenly, he wilts. He lets the gun fall to his side, then takes a step back and sits on an old table.

The performance—if it was a performance—has exhausted him.

He looks in his pocket for his flask of rum but he's left it in the office.

"Just tell me the truth, Mercado. Ricky's a reporter. And despite the fireworks, a good one too. There was something he didn't like."

"I don't know wh—"

"The autopsy. He had the Mexican consulate conduct an autopsy."

"That's no secret either."

"No, but the results are or were. I found them, and if *I* can find them the DGI can find them too. They'll put two and two together like me."

"I don't see your point."

"The point is revenge. The pathologist discovered that your father was not killed in the initial accident. A lung was punctured and he fell down an embankment into the forest. He tried to climb back up to the road but he couldn't make it. Gradually, over a period of hours, I believe, in very cold temperatures, your father drowned in his own blood. That hurts, doesn't it?"

"Yes."

"Hurts bad. Both of you. You and Ricky. Ricky went and it's your turn now. You're going to go to Mexico City and you're going to find a coyote who can take you across the border into the United States. There you are going to make your way to Colorado and investigate your father's death and try to find the person who killed him."

I look at Hector. Off the street ten years, slow and old and fat and smart as a fucking whip.

"How did you piece it together?"

"Ricky."

"What about him?"

"Two trips to the United States in a year are bound to raise suspicions. Even though he's a Party member, Ricky was followed by the DGI. He did indeed cover a conference at the UN and a Friends of Cuba rally in New York City, but then the DGI lost him for four days. They think he was in Manhattan doing the tourist scene and probably fucking like crazy, but I suspect that during that time he borrowed some Cuban American friend's ID, flew to Denver, drove to Fairview, checked into a ski lodge or a hotel, and spent three days asking questions about his father's death. Then he came back to New York, crammed a week's worth of interviews into a single afternoon, and flew back to you with his results."

"This is your guess, not that of the Interior Ministry?"

"Yes."

"Am I under surveillance?"

"Neither of you is under surveillance. The DGI isn't interested in you. Not yet. But you've been clumsy, Mercado, you and your brother. And clumsy doesn't get ignored forever. Do you understand what I'm telling you?"

"I understand."

"So let it go. Just let it go."

"How can I?"

"Aren't you Cuban? Where did you grow up? Have you learned nothing? Don't you know the game is rigged from the start?"

"What are you going to do with these guesses of yours?" I ask.

He spits on the floor. "I'm no *chivato*, I'm not going to let them know about Ricky or the manner of your father's death or your plans, but I am going to stop them giving you that visa. If you go to America and get arrested or stopped at the border it's over for me. I'm not going to let you destroy me, Mercado."

"You can't do that."

"It's too late. It's done. I opposed your application. I sent them a letter yesterday telling them that you're too valuable an asset and that it would be a mistake to let you go to Mexico. They'll take the hint."

"What about what you said in the office?"

"Oh, that was just to give them an angle. They always want an angle. The boss who lies to his subordinates."

Now I'm angry. "You can't do this to me, Hector."

"I've been patient with you. Now, do me a favor, get the fuck out of my building, Mercado. Take the rest of the day off, and I never want to hear about this again."

"Fuck you and your fucking shitbox. I hope you choke in it, you old bastard!"

I storm out, cursing.

On the way up Morro a kid blows me the fucky-fucky. I flash my ID. Hassle him. Power: makes everyone a tyrant, and in a country where one in every twenty-five people is either a cop or an informant, that's a lot of tyranny to go around. Pat the kid. Fake ID, not interested, but sixty bucks Canadian is a good get. Pretty boy. A jockey. I take the cash, tell him to fuck off.

An old man sees the dough, hisses me from an alley.

"What?"

From under his coat he removes a packet of American Tampax.

"How much?" I ask without even thinking about it, for the Cuban generic is, of course, a complete disaster.

"Twenty U.S."

"I'll give you ten Canadian and I won't bust you," I say, hovering the ID.

"Ten it is," the old man grumbles.

Tampax and hard currency. Small comforts.

Walk to O'Reilly, climb the four flights to my apartment. Look at the coffeepot, the bottle of white rum. Ignore both. Slide back into bed. I don't sleep. I just lie there scoping the dump a detective in the PNR gets to call her own. Bed, dresser, color TV, half a shelf of poetry books, windows uncleaned since the last hurricane, hole in the floor, ant problem, Van Gogh prints tacked over the cracks in the plaster—*Night Café, Sunflowers*—washbasin leaking brown water because the bad plumber won't fix it, the good plumber only takes dollars.

Lie there.

Lie there all day.

Sun slanting over the Parque Central.

Fly buzzing against the window.

The phone down the hall.

Knock at the door.

The new maid at the Sevilla, a short plump girl from Cárdenas. Syphilitic nose, cross eyes. How did you get a permit to move to Havana? Who do you know?

"Phone call for you," she says.

Wipe her sweat off the mouthpiece.

"Your visa came," Ricky says breathlessly.

"What?"

"It came. Of course they sent it to Mom's. I'm here now. Hand-delivered. Good thing I was here."

"Jesus, it came?"

"It came. Seven days. Mexico City only."

"What's the date? Hector said he spiked it yesterday."

"He did? I thought he liked you? Well, I guess his influence isn't as strong as he thinks," Ricky says with a knowing lilt in his voice.

"*You* did something, didn't you? You talked to people. In the circle."

"I didn't. I really didn't."

"You're at Mom's? Aren't you the dutiful son? Wait there, I'll be right over."

Out of bed, wash off the makeup I put on for Hector, look at the woman in the glass. Pale, pretty, a little too thin, narrow eyebrows, uncomplicated green eyes, dark hair. Something about her, though, something a little intimidating. If she had glasses you might say she was severe, a librarian, perhaps, or a staff nurse, or a fucking cop.

Back down the stairs.

Out.

My mother's place is on Suárez next to the station. Filthy little building in a street of filthy little buildings. Black neighborhood. *Negros de pasas. Negros de pelo.* Most of the men are voodoo priests or initiates and all the women are Iyawó, brides of the orishas, the deities of the Lucumí religion.

A scary place after dark. Scary place anytime.

Barefoot children roaming the streets. "Give us some money, nice lady," they chant at the corner. Once I did give them money and they followed me all the way back to O'Reilly.

Mom's building. Broken front door, garbage and filth over the tiled stairs. Dog shit everywhere.

Usual soundtrack. Fights, the TV, American music, kids yelling, babies crying, Haitian music. Four flights. On four a woman my age says hello. I've seen her before, an Iyawó fortune-teller, *negro azul*, wearing bright West African clothes. Long black hair and even longer nails, cruel smile, creepy as hell.

"No husband yet," she says.

"No."

"I'll help you catch one."

"That's ok."

"Don't think you'll get one where you're going," she says.

"Oh. And where am I going?"

"You know," she says with an ugly laugh and with I-don't-give-a-shit slowness she closes her door.

Walk the landing. Mom's. Knock, knock.

Ricky opens it. Looks good. Blue cotton shirt and American chino pants and slip-on shoes.

"Hi, darling," he says, kisses me.

"Handsomer than ever," I tell him.

"I could say the same," he replies.

"But you won't."

"Of course I will, you look great."

"How is she?" I ask, my voice descending into a whisper.

"No worse than usual. I brought her some flowers. Cheered her up," he says.

"Again, you're such a good son," I tell him.

"Well, I want to be remembered in the will," he says with a grin.

I take his hand and step in. Mom has all the blinds drawn and the lights are off. No light anywhere except for the candles in front of the Santería shrine. Layers of dust, dust on the dust. Mom sitting at the table we bought her, looking at tarot cards. She doesn't even notice when I sidle next to her. She's wearing a tattered dress that exposes one of her breasts. Her face is haggard. She's lost weight since last week and the expression in her eyes is watery, remote, distant. "Hi, Mom," I say and kiss her.

"Hello, my baby girl," she replies, looking up for a moment and then going back to the cards.

I watch her for a while. I have no idea what she's doing and I don't want to know.

"She's lost weight," I tell Ricky.

"She trades her supply-book tokens for candles and spells from the priestesses."

The room's full of stuff like that. Lucumí gods and goddesses straight from West Africa. I recognize some, but most are utterly unfamiliar. And not just Lucumí—an eclectic mix from many pantheons: a brass Ganesh and his mother, Saraswati; a porcelain Virgin Mary; prayer flags from Tibet; a huge carved wooden Apollo.

Mom starts mumbling to herself over the tarot.

"She's gotten worse."

Ricky shakes his head. "No worse. She's doing ok."

"Doesn't look like it."

"You don't see her as much as I do," Ricky says with a smile to show that he's not criticizing.

"Those bitches really got their hooks into her with this shit. I'll tell them to leave her fucking ration book alone," I say angrily.

"I bring her food, she's ok," Ricky says.

"Quite the little saint," I say with a grin but also an edge.

Silence. Seconds turning into minutes. Claustrophobia. Get up. Walk around. I note again that Dad's ashes are gone from the mantel. I don't even want to think what she did with them.

More time. More suffocating seconds. God, I hate this place.

"I'm sorry, I can't stay here," I say.

Ricky nods. "At least tell Mom you're leaving the country."

She's dozing now. I kneel in front of her and take her hands and kiss them. She looks up, a little sparkle in those yellow eyes.

"My darling," she says.

"Mom, I'm going now. I'm going away for a while."

She nods and then, as if the veil has lifted for a moment, she says: "Be careful."

"I will."

Ricky walks me to the landing. "Don't forget your letter," he says, and hands me the forms from the Interior Ministry. Of course it requires a fee, but once paid, I'll have that rarest of rare things—permission to leave Cuba. An exit visa. A key to the prison door.

I hold it to the light and then I kiss it.

"How did I get this? You pulled some strings, didn't you?"

He shakes his head. "Even if I was fucking the minister's private secretary I wouldn't ask him for something like this. We'd all be headed for the plantations."

"Then how?" I ask.

He shrugs. "It's a mystery."

"Yeah, it is."

The Last Act.

The wee hours.

After all the tails have gone to bed.

Bang at my apartment door.

Who the fuck?

Open it.

"So you went above my head?" Hector says bitterly.

Rum breath. Bleary eyes.

"I swear I didn't."

"Ricky then?"

"I didn't ask him to."

"Own initiative, eh?"

"He says he didn't do anything."

He pushes past me, sits on my bed. "Can't stay, told Anna I was getting some air. Have a drink," he says and passes me the flask.

"No, thank you."

"Fuck Ricky and fuck you, Mercado. If you don't come back from the United States I'm finished. My family. Your family. All of us."

"I'll come back."

He shakes his head like a wet dog. "I could still tell them, you know. I could still tell the DGI or the ministry that you're going to La Yuma. I could tell them you've talked to me about defecting," Hector snarls.

"You wouldn't do that, Hector."

"No?" he says.

"No," I insist.

He balls his right fist angrily and thumps it on the bed. For a second I see him tossing the joint. Neighbors in the hall, phone calls, Hector pulling rank. But the fight's been ground out of him. He sighs. "No, I won't turn *chivato,* not now," he says.

He takes another drink, gets heavily to his feet.

"Can't stay," he says.

In the doorway he grabs my wrist, tugs me close. "Forget about it, Mercado."

I break free using first-week police aikido.

"Damn it," he says and stares at me, mentally wounded.

"Listen to me, Hector, I'm not dumb, I'm going to go to you-know-where, but I promise I will be back," I tell him. "Now, you should go home, Anna will be worried."

He looks at the floor and doesn't move.

"You're a poet, Mercado," he says.

"I don't know how that rumor got started."

"Ever read Pindar?"

"No."

"Homer's contemporary, except he really existed. He says, 'The gods give us for every good thing two evil ones. Men who are children take this badly but the manly ones bear it, turning the brightness outward.'"

"I don't see—"

"You can't fix everything. You have to let things go. Don't go to America. I'm begging you, Mercado, please don't go."

I don't reply.

I don't need to.

He nods, turns, and walks along the corridor. I hear him shuffle down the stairs, and from my window I check him for tails until O'Reilly becomes Misiones and he's finally swallowed up by the boozy Havana night.

CHAPTER 7

DESPIERTA AMERICA

*T*oo late, Hector. Too late now, my friend, to heed your words. I'm here and
    I've killed human beings and that chance to turn your brightness outward
is in the distant past.

I suppose I must have been awake, but it was only on the third or fourth
iteration that I became vaguely aware of the voice.

"María . . . María . . . *vamonos.*"

What?

"María, *vamonos.*"

María? Who is María?

"María, *vamonos.*"

Oh, yeah, I'm María.

"What time is it?" I asked.

"Six. I'm leaving for the day. How did you sleep?"

"Good. I slept good. The first full night's sleep . . ."

I didn't finish the sentence. The first full night's sleep I'd had in one hundred and eighty days. Six months since the day after my birthday in Laguna.
Six months since Ricky's phone call. Six months since I'd begun this plan.

"Look at me," Paco said.

I rubbed the blear out of my eyes. Paco was wearing jeans, work boots, a
heavy black sweater, a bright yellow hard hat. He seemed excited.

"Where are you going?" I asked.

"Construction site, downtown, do you like the hat? I look like a real

Yankee, don't I? A real American," he said, and then in a gravelly voice he added, "Do you feel lucky, punk? Do ya?"—an impersonation that completely escaped me.

"You look like a regular American," I agreed.

His grin grew even wider before a look of concern darkened his visage. "You better get up too, Esteban's already here to take the girls up the mountain. He's in a mood and he's dressed like a pimp."

"Screw him," I muttered and closed my eyes again. In Havana I didn't get up until I could smell the coffee brewing in the ice cream parlor on O'Reilly.

"Shit, María, they're calling me, I have to go," Paco said.

"Go then," I said, and then, remembering basic civility for someone who has slept literally under one's own roof, I added, "Have a good day, Paco, look after yourself."

"I'll see you tonight."

I nodded and drifted for a minute or two. I didn't hear him leave the room, I didn't hear the Toyota pickup full of Mexicans drive away, I *did* feel the poke of Esteban's snakeskin boot nudge my ankle.

I sat up with a jolt. "Who the fuck—" I began furiously and then remembered where I was.

"I'm running a business here, you got two minutes to make yourself look presentable," Esteban said.

"Sorry, I—" I began but Esteban cut me off.

"These are important people. You're a smart girl, you can see that our whole operation is on a knife edge. We gotta project a feeling of competence and calm. The feds didn't touch us. Everything's running smoothly. Get me? So no fuckups. This is your first day, I'd hop to it if I were you. I don't care how bad things get, I'll fucking can you and everybody else if I want to. Put this uniform on and meet me outside in the parking lot in two minutes," Esteban said.

He was wearing a charcoal gray suit. His hair was combed, his face washed, his beard trimmed. He had a large diamond ring on his little finger but apart from that he looked good. Few straight men can resist a compliment from a younger woman, so I gave him both barrels at point-blank. "I'm sorry for your troubles, Esteban, and I'm grateful for the opportunity. Can I just add I think you're bearing up very well under all this pressure? You look very together today."

Handsome like a bear, as we say in Cuba.

Esteban's mouth twitched and his cheeks took on a rosy complection. He grunted.

"Yes . . . well, uhm, I have to meet some of our clients this morning, reassure them that the Mountain State Employment Agency does not hire illegals and has not been affected by the INS raids."

"Well, you look great. I love the suit."

"Tailored. In Denver," he said, and then, remembering why he'd come, muttered, "Uhm, María, we all need to be downstairs in, say, five minutes?"

"Oh, no problem, I'll see you down there."

He stood there for a moment. Something was on his mind. He got to it. "I don't normally give people the choice, but, well, do you want to work what we call Malibu Mountain or would you prefer to be downtown, where it's a bit easier? You'll probably end up doing both, but the mountain's good because in about two weeks they're going to start giving out Christmas tips. Could be lucrative."

I had to work the mountain, there was no question about it.

"The mountain," I said.

"I have an arrangement with the other girls. Remember, I get half of all the tips, no exceptions, ok?"

"Ok," I said.

I'd be gone by Christmas. What the hell did I care?

Esteban seemed relieved. "Great. Thought I'd remind you. Didn't want to have to strong-arm you later."

"You think you could?" I asked with a smile, ironically flexing my skinny arms.

He grinned. "I like you, María. If this works out maybe you could even work for me in our office on Pearl Street."

"Ok."

"Good. I'll see you down there." He turned to leave and then paused in the doorway. "It won't be much, you know, don't get your hopes up," he said.

I had lost the drift. "What won't be much?"

"The Christmas tips. When we used to clean the Cruise estate, Margarita and Luisa got a thousand bucks each. But these fuckers we do now, they're all the lesser lights."

"That's ok," I said.

"Hurry up now," he said and finally left the room.

I put on the maid's uniform, a somber short-sleeved black affair with blue piping, but infinitely better than those I'd seen around the Hotel Nacional or the Sevilla. I smoothed the straggles from my hair, brushed my teeth, washed my face. I looked mousy but rested and fresh.

Angela, a slender young thing from Mexico City, had made Nescafé in the kitchen. I took a few sips of the acrid liquid before joining her and the other girls in the back of Esteban's Range Rover.

Esteban sped off, talking as fast as he drove. "Luisa, Anna, I'm going to drop you on Pearl Street. A lot of people are jittery, but I'm not. If the INS still has agents in town—which I doubt—remember that they're civil servants, so no one's gonna be up and about before ten o'clock. You understand what I'm saying?"

Both Anna and Luisa looked blank.

"Jesus. Am I the only one who does any thinking around here? You gotta be finished by ten o'clock."

Luisa looked at me and Angela with an expression I couldn't decipher but which Angela seemed to get. Angela nodded. Luisa leaned forward in the seat until her face was only a few centimeters from Esteban's. "Don Esteban, how are we supposed to do all the businesses on Pearl Street before ten o'clock? We are not miracle workers. You must be crazy," she said.

Luisa was an older woman from Guadalajara, and I could tell that she was allowed a little more leeway with Esteban than the others; but even so, Angela and Anna seemed surprised to hear her speak so freely.

Esteban stared at her for a moment, thought about one possible reply— almost certainly a profane one—but chose to select another. "Look, just do your best, Luisa. Make sure you cover the important clients: Hermès, Gucci, DKNY—you know, the big ones. Just get it done and get off the street before ten. We're in a jam and we all gotta pull together."

He dropped Luisa and Anna outside Brooks Brothers and drove off toward the so-called Malibu Mountain.

Before he'd gotten a block his phone rang.

"Yes? . . . Yes? . . . Yes!"

He hung up, reversed the Range Rover. Luisa was having a last cigarette while Anna was inside the store turning on the power. Esteban wound the window down and called Luisa over. He was excited. "They didn't get Josefina. She was at her boyfriend's house. Christ, when she didn't show up I thought they'd grabbed her. But she got away."

"Josefina? Ok," Luisa replied with considerably less excitement.

"So it shouldn't be any problem to get finished by ten, Josefina will be joining you," Esteban said.

"It'll still be difficult to do everything," Luisa said.

"Just get on with it!" Esteban muttered, and the window whirred back up.

"Good news," Esteban said, turning to the pair of us. "Great news. Who wants a Starbucks? My treat, eh?"

Angela rolled her eyes as if to say *he's only doing this to impress you.* But I wanted coffee after three days without.

"I do," I said.

Starbucks: my first experience of white America.

The smell of vanilla. Paul McCartney singing a love song. Scruffy men in five-dollar flip-flops working on five-thousand-dollar laptops.

White people *serving us.*

Esteban ordered for us, got coffee, croissants, and cakes, and put a dollar in the tip jar.

I sipped the *con leche* and it tasted almost like a *con leche.*

"How do you like your coffee?" he asked.

"It's ok, thank you," I said.

Angela had gotten a beverage that was covered in whipped cream and required a straw to consume. "Mine's absolutely delicious," she said.

"See, it's not like Rome, sometimes we're the masters," Esteban muttered apropos of nothing.

Esteban spotted a *Fairview Post* in the used newspaper rack. He grabbed it. The headline was "Tancredo Hails INS Raids." Esteban read the story and passed it across to me. "Can you read, María?" he asked.

"Letters and such?" I asked, doing my best peasant voice.

"Just read it, see what I'm up against," he said, ignoring the sarcasm.

Congressman Tom Tancredo (R-CO), hailed last night's INS raids in Denver, Boulder, Fairview, and Vail, which netted an estimated three dozen illegal immigrants. "It's only a small step but the message has gone out," Tancredo commented from Washington, "that Colorado is not a safe haven for illegal immigrants from Mexico."

Congressman Tancredo, who is running for President, will be on *Lou Dobbs Tonight* on CNN later today to talk about his new plan for dealing with the estimated 11 million illegal immigrants in the United States.

A spokesman for the Mexican consulate in Denver noted, "Twenty-six

Mexican citizens, all of whom have jobs and none of whom have a criminal record, have been detained by the Immigration and Naturalization Service. Their cases are under investigation."

With an estimated fifty thousand Mexican citizens living in Denver alone, an INS spokesman denied that these raids were only a cosmetic measure.

"Without us this whole country would grind to a halt," Esteban said.

I was about to pass the paper back when I noticed an ad: "For sale: Thorpe hunting rifle new 750 dollars. Smith and Wesson M&P 9mm good con with ammo 400 dollars OBO," with an address on Lime Kiln Road, Fairview. I carefully ripped out the ad, sipped the *con leche,* and said nothing.

Esteban nodded at the barista. "Romanian," he whispered under his breath. "Nothing to do with me. Whole different organization."

The girl was pale, blond, pretty, and, despite the hour, high.

"What's her story?" I wondered aloud.

"Come on, let's go outside. It's not too cold today," he said. Esteban sat us at a cast-iron table in the sun. It might not have been cold for Colorado in December but I was freezing. My teeth chattered and my hands shook as I sipped the coffee.

"Romanians and Russians," Esteban said. "I know you wanted to do nanny work, María, but I doubt that's going to happen. Up here they want European nannies. Most of them are from Eastern Europe. Sheriff Briggs brings them direct from Denver. He's the silent partner in the local company, Superior Child Minding Services—thinks it's a big secret, but I know all about it. Dumb fuck. Not as smart as he pretends to be."

"I see," I muttered, losing interest now.

"Pays a lot more than housecleaning. They're always desperate. Last thing the wives and girlfriends want to do when they come here is look after their own kids. The big guns have permanent help but the minor players are always looking. Shit, you can nail 'em for twenty bucks an hour and more. It's a hell of a racket."

He examined me for a moment. "No. Forget it. Won't even try, you don't even look Russian. And we're shorthanded as it is."

Of course I didn't tell him that I spoke a little Russian.

"Why do they want Russians?" I asked instead.

"They want Eastern Europeans because the wives like bossing white chicks around and the husbands think they can fuck 'em—which, of course, they can. You know, you're not bad looking, María, I can get you that kind of work if you want. Steady work. We cut in the Sheriff's Department, but you could be earning four or five hundred a week."

"I already told you I'm not a whore."

"Not a *whore*—a high-class call girl. Do it for a year or two, you've got enough saved for a little restaurant or something back in—where you say you were from?"

"Valladolíd in Yucatán."

"Well, I don't know if you want to live there, but you could move to the DF. Think about it. Anyway, finish up, enough chitchat, we're running late."

We finished our coffee drinks, got into the Range Rover.

Maybe now was the time to ask him about the dent on the front left.

"It's a really nice car," I said.

"My pride and joy."

"What happened to your—"

"Oh, fuck," Esteban interrupted and hit the brakes. Sheriff Briggs's shiny black Escalade pulled to a halt next to us. To my surprise I found that my hand was shaking. He wasn't on Ricky's list but that man made me nervous.

The Escalade flashed its lights.

"What does he want?" Esteban groaned, turned off the engine, and zipped the window.

Sheriff Briggs and Klein, his skinny, nasty-looking deputy, got out of the Escalade. Unlike yesterday Briggs was in full uniform. Black boots, dark green trousers, green shirt with a gold badge on it, dark green cowboy hat, black leather jacket, nightstick, flashlight, gun. The hat flipped me. Made me think, *Mierde, I'm in America.*

Briggs leaned into the driver's-side window of the Range Rover and took off his sunglasses. He stared at Angela and me in the middle seat before turning his attention to Esteban.

"Seem in an awful hurry," he said.

"I'm running late," Esteban replied.

"Hmmm," Sheriff Briggs said, then caught my gaze and smiled.

"Morning, ma'am," he said.

"Good morning, Sheriff," I said in English.

"How do you like our little community now that you've had some time to adjust?" Briggs asked.

"It's very beautiful," I said.

"That it is, that it is," he replied.

"Excuse me, Sheriff, but I really should get going. As you can imagine, today is not a good day to be understaffed," Esteban said.

Briggs nodded. "Oh yeah, almost forgot, how many did you lose?" he asked.

"Apparently seven got taken to the detention center in Denver. My lawyer thinks we can get one of them out tonight, Inez—she's engaged to an American—and there's another girl, Juanita, who Flora says is pregnant, so we might be able to get her out too. Won't release any of the men, of course. And that means we're still shorthanded at the site on Pearl."

Sheriff Briggs turned to his deputy. "Things are looking bad for our buddy Esteban here," he said.

"Looks like it, Sheriff," Klein replied.

"Not enough men to do the job," Sheriff Briggs went on, still talking to the deputy.

"But Sheriff, didn't you conquer the town of Subhan in Kuwait with just half a platoon?" Klein said, clearly having heard that particular story a couple of hundred times.

"I surely did, A.J., but it's well known that half a platoon of United States Marines can do just about anything in this world."

"Amen to that," Klein replied.

"Your Mexican, though. Takes a whole army of Mexicans to do the job of a few white men, ain't that right, Deputy?" Briggs said.

"I believe that you're speaking the truth," the deputy responded. "From the halls of Montezuma, as the song says."

"From the halls of Montezuma indeed," Sheriff Briggs agreed with a laugh.

Esteban was becoming impatient. "Sheriff Briggs, it is always a pleasure to see you, but today we are very late and some of my clients will need reassur—"

Sheriff Briggs cut him off. "Get out of the car, Esteban."

"What is this about?"

"Just get out of the car."

Angela started to undo her seat belt.

"No, no, you two little ladies can sit tight," Sheriff Briggs said.

Esteban got out of the car. The deputy turned him around and put Esteban's hands on the roof of the Range Rover.

"Nice monkey suit," Klein said, and both he and the sheriff laughed.

"Look, what is this about?" Esteban protested.

"Shut the fuck up!" Sheriff Briggs growled and cracked the end of his nightstick into the back of Esteban's legs.

The sickening crunch of metal on bone.

Esteban ate asphalt.

Sheriff Briggs hit him again, catching him twice more on a defensively raised arm.

"You can't do this to me, I'm a U.S. citizen," Esteban pleaded.

"Do what I damn well please in my town," Sheriff Briggs said, and he kicked Esteban in the legs. "Show him, A.J."

Klein reached into his pocket and threw a plastic bag that landed on Esteban's chest.

I sat up in the seat to get a better view.

"What is this?" Esteban groaned.

"That is five-hundred-dollar-an-ounce British Columbian hydro-fucking-ponic quality four-twenty."

Esteban tried to get up. Klein drew his gun and pointed it at him. I caught Esteban's eye through the car window. He stared at me. He didn't look scared and I gave him what I hoped was an encouraging nod.

"Is that what this is about?" Esteban asked.

"Yeah," Sheriff Briggs said. "That is what this is all about. Our deal was for cocaine from Mexico and you've been dealing ice and meth and pot, bringing it in from fucking Canada. Who do you think you are, *amigo*? Where do you think you are? Nothing escapes me, Esteban. Nothing. I know everything that goes on in this town. Everything you or anybody else tries to do, I fucking know it. Never forget that."

Esteban got to his feet and rubbed his forearm.

"Is that why you brought in the INS? To fuck me up?" Esteban asked.

The sheriff spat. "The feds don't tell us when they're coming. That's nothing to do with me."

Esteban nodded and closed his eyes for a second. Thinking. He opened them again and forced a smile.

"I'll come clean with you, Sheriff. You're right about this. It's an angle. I brought in the first small shipment as a trial. An experiment. I was going to tell you if it worked out."

"Apparently it has worked out," Sheriff Briggs said.

"Yeah. So far. Risky work, though. The real stuff is coming in tomorrow and then every month, once a month. I'm bringing in ice and pot. Good stuff. With your approval, of course. I was going to tell you all about it," Esteban said quickly.

"Sure you were," Briggs said.

Esteban appeared unfazed. "I can show you the paperwork. I'm being straight with you. I'm laying out thirty thousand capital for an expected hundred-thousand take. That's seventy net. I can give you twenty on this and every batch."

Sheriff Briggs nodded and hit his nightstick into his hand. "Thirty-five," Briggs said.

"Thirty-five? I'm taking all the risk," Esteban protested.

"Thirty-five and I want it by the end of the week."

"That's impossible! That's a month's supply, it'll take me weeks to deal it. I'm not unloading to some middleman, I'm selling it carefully to a very select group of people."

Sheriff Briggs looked at Deputy Klein. Klein grinned and hit Esteban hard in the gut with his nightstick.

Esteban staggered backward, caught himself on the hood of the Range Rover, bent over, and threw up part of a croissant and coffee.

"I guess you didn't hear me. Thirty-five by the end of the week," Briggs said softly.

Esteban grunted.

Sheriff Briggs nodded at his deputy. "See, I told you this was nothing to worry about. I was sure we'd be able to come to an arrangement, even if it is a bad time," he said.

Sheriff Briggs got back into his Escalade.

"What about the four-twenty?" the deputy asked.

"Oh, take the pot, I'm sure our old buddy Steve won't mind," Sheriff Briggs said, his dark eyes wide with pleasure.

The two cops got into the prowler, revved the engine for ten aggressive seconds, and drove off along Pearl.

No one had seen the incident, except possibly the Starbucks workers, and they knew better than to say anything about it.

"How often does this happen?" I whispered to Angela.

She put her finger to her lips. "You don't have to worry about any of this. We'll talk later," she whispered.

Esteban said nothing when he got back into the car. He dabbed his face with a silk handkerchief, got his breath back, and started the engine. He didn't look seriously hurt but I saw that he touched the wheel only with his left hand. In Cuba, where no vehicles had power steering or automatic gearboxes, he couldn't have driven at all, but here he managed.

He eased the Range Rover along Pearl and up the Old Boulder Road.

The Old Boulder Road. Ricky's black-and-whites. The phone call the day after my birthday.

"I'll leave you at the summit and you can work your way downhill," Esteban muttered.

We drove past huge houses that got bigger as we got closer to the top of the mountain. When we were almost at the peak Esteban pulled the Range Rover into a turnout marked VIEWPOINT on a small green sign. He turned to us and gave Angela a key chain with various house keys on it. Each was attached to a piece of card with a number on it.

"Angela, you'll be with María today, show her the ropes. Show her where the cleaning supplies are in each house and don't forget the alarm boxes." Esteban turned his gaze on me. "You know what an alarm system is?"

I shook my head.

"Each house has an alarm, which we disable when we enter and enable again when we leave. It's very simple. Understand?"

"Yes," I said. I'd never been in a house with a burglar alarm before but I got the concept. It would require a consistent electricity supply and a prompt police response, two things Havana lacked.

"Angela, make sure you show her which clients need the full treatment and which ones only get a surface clean. There's no point in wasting time on clients who won't appreciate what we've done," Esteban said.

"Of course," Angela muttered.

"Ok, both of you out of the car, I want to show María something."

Esteban was a big man, and in my experience big men take longer to recover from an injury. He was still breathing hard and rubbing his arm as he led us away from the car toward a gap in the trees.

He forced a smile. "Ok, María, here we are. This is where you'll be working in the mornings. You can see the whole mountain from here. Below us is the Watson residence. Big movie producer. He has his own staff but I've been in there. Dealt him coke. Delivered it personally. That house on top of the hill with all the lights and the fence—Tom Cruise."

"*The* Tom Cruise?" I asked.

"*The* Tom Cruise. Lives here about half the year when he's not filming. I think his sister lives there year-round."

"I get to clean Tom Cruise's house?"

"No, no. He has his own staff. As I was saying, we only get the lesser lights. Not the Watsons and the Cruises of this world. But you might see some famous people. It's important not to react in any way. They hate that. You've got to pretend that you're not there at all. That you're invisible. Never make eye contact with any of the clients and never talk to them unless spoken to first. Understand?"

"*Sí, Don Esteban.*"

"Good."

Esteban took another few seconds to get his breath back. "I suppose you're wondering about what happened this morning with the sheriff?"

"Yes," I said quietly. Angela said nothing.

"The thing is, I'm an American citizen," he muttered with a smoldering sense of outrage.

I nodded.

"An American citizen, and if that bastard tries to come into my house I'll shoot him with my rifle. Shoot him. And they can't do a thing. Cop or not. War hero or not. Without a warrant, the law's on my side."

Esteban sat down on a flat, red boulder. He dabbed his forehead.

"Do you want us to go?" Angela asked.

"No. No. Let María get her bearings. Look around you, María."

I observed the mountains and the forests. Layer after layer of them stretching west for fifty kilometers.

I tried to feel something.

After all, this was it. The place where my father died.

I tried to force an emotion: anger, regret, sadness—nothing came.

"What do you think, María?" Esteban asked.

"Pretty country," I said.

"All this was Mexico once. A hundred and fifty years ago. Mexico. Our home. Stolen by the Yankees and they don't even know it. They don't even know their history. We invited them to our land and then when we told them they couldn't have slaves they turned on us. Like a changeling in the house of your mother. Like an ungrateful dog."

His face was pink. He was sweating. For a moment I wondered if he was having a heart attack. Tears welled up in his eyes. "Mexico. All the way to the Pacific. That *cabrón*. That fucking son of a whore," he muttered.

He started to cry.

"Come on, let's go," Angela whispered.

We left him.

I said goodbye but he didn't seem to hear.

We walked past Watson's huge mansion and entered the first house on the route. Angela put the key in the lock and showed me how to disable the alarm system.

This house only needed a quick dust and vacuum.

As did the next.

I was expecting palatial residences but they weren't grotesque. About the same size as those of high-ranking Party officials in Vedado but not in such disrepair and most with epic views over the mountains.

The job seemed simple. The first three homes were empty and not a problem to clean. A dead mouse in a sink was the only bit of excitement. The next was occupied by an actress who was in her basement running on a treadmill the whole time we were there. We put away her clothes, ran her dishwasher, cleaned her living space, rearranged the diet shakes and cigarette cartons in her gigantic refrigerator.

The next house, however, was the one I'd been in the night before. The retro-future place with all the curves. Minimalist furniture, a low leather sofa, uncomfortable high-angled chairs, stainless steel light fittings, an ebony living room table. Huge windows facing the Old Boulder Road to the east and the Rockies to the west. It looked better in daylight. Angela showed me how to get in and how to disable the burglar alarm. The code was still the default 9999. Jack Tyrone was in the kitchen reading a newspaper. He had a box of Frosted Flakes in front of him and a french press filled with what I could tell from the hall was overroasted coffee. There was a new bowl of fruit on the breakfast bar. More kiwis to steal.

I scoped Jack in the daylight. Ricky's notes and his party anecdote flashed in my head. Suspect 2A, Youkilis's employer, 31, born Denver, Colorado, Hollywood actor, pretty good alibi for the night of the accident—he was sixteen hundred kilometers away in Los Angeles—but I wouldn't rule him out until I'd spoken to him.

"Do we say good morning?" I whispered to Angela.

She shook her head. We took off our coats, found the cleaning supplies, and began work. I dusted, she vacuumed.

"Maaling, lallies," Jack said with a full mouth, attempting to carry his newspaper, coffee, and cereal bowl into the living room without a major accident.

"Good morning, Señor Tyrone," Angela said.

He looked better than when I'd encountered him last night. In fact, more than better, very handsome indeed if you went for pale, blond, athletic, *American*. And to my surprise I found that I went for 'em in spades. "Those corn-fed western boys," Ricky once said, and I could see what he meant. Jack's complexion was pale, but even preshower he radiated health and strength. His body was chiseled and his jaw downy but not weak. His hair was tousled attractively and his blue eyes were the color of the marlin-filled sea off Santiago, rather than last night's muddy Havana Bay. The blue eyes now were smiling at us. "Might have a job, ladies, Paul knocked a bottle of wine on the Persian. They tried to clean it last night and I fucking Pledged it and Oxy-ed it this morning but it's still there."

We looked at the stain. Jack's efforts had produced a yellow chemical burn. The rug was ruined.

While Angela explained the catastrophe I took the vacuum upstairs. I had to spend twenty minutes picking clothes and food items off the floor before I could begin cleaning.

I hadn't been up here last night, but this was obviously where Tyrone's personality fully expressed itself. There were movie posters on the wall and film stills. Apparently he was something of a rising star, but I hadn't heard of him prior to Ricky's report. I had seen one or two of the films he'd been in but Jack's presence had not made an impression. From the stills I saw that he'd appeared in *Mr. and Mrs. Smith* with Brad Pitt and *Mission Impossible 3* with Tom Cruise, but obviously in such small roles that his name hadn't gotten on the posters.

In his bedroom he had headshots of himself, several awards, and a gigantic signed and framed picture of a man and his double in a tacky-looking space uniform.

I examined the awards.

LATO Best Newcomer 1999, Sundance Best New Talent 1998, ShoWest Up and Comer Award 2000.

There was nothing recent, and this made me wonder if his career was quite as hot as it had been.

In the upstairs bathroom there were mirrors everywhere and enough hair care product to have started a salon. Even Party wives in Havana didn't spend this much time on their coiffure.

I was sniffing something called Plum Island Soap Company skin cream with appreciation when he suddenly appeared behind me in the mirror.

He was grinning. "I know what you're thinking. You're thinking of that Carly Simon song, aren't you?"

"Excuse me," I said, quickly putting the lid back on the cream.

"Carly Simon . . . the Warren Beatty song. Ok, you're drawing a blank, before your time, I guess, don't worry about it. Uhm, what's your name?"

"María."

" 'María, I just met a girl called María,' " he sang in a thin baritone. It was a song I didn't know, but I smiled encouragingly.

"I haven't seen you before, when did you start?" he asked.

"I was here last night," I said.

"Oh, God, you were? Saw me at my worst. Sorry about that. Honestly, I'm not that big of an asshole."

"No, you were very polite to me," I said.

"I was? Huh. Well, of course I was. Mind if I just brush my teeth? Paul's coming in a minute."

He began brushing his teeth while I made the bed.

"What do you think of the old abode?" he asked, foaming at the mouth.

"Very nice."

"Yeah, I like it. Live here a lot of the year, ski season. L.A. the rest. That explains the headshots. Want to be clear about that. I'm not a nutcase. I mean, you never know. Veronica Lake in the coffee shop. Natalie Portman walking down the street."

I had no idea what he was talking about.

He noticed my bafflement, spat, and rubbed a towel on his face.

"The headshots. On the wall. I rent this house out when I'm filming. You don't know who'll be staying here. Casting agents, whatever. Hence the headshots. It's all contacts. That's all it is. Talent is about five percent of it."

"*Sí*. Contacts. You meeting me, for example. My cousin is Salma Hayek, she's looking for a costar," I said.

His eyes widened, but before I could further extend the fib I broke into a smile. When he saw that I was kidding, he laughed out loud. A pleasant, infectious laugh that filled the room.

"Oooh, good one. I'm going to have to watch out for you, I can tell. Where are you from?"

"Yucatán."

"The Yucatán, uh, that's down somewhere, uhm, in the Central American area, I think, right?"

"Geography is not your strong suit," I said.

"Wow, you're totally unimpressed by me. Refreshing. I had a maid in L.A. who sold my pubes on eBay."

I didn't know the words *pubes* or *eBay* but I could tell from the creases around his eyes that he was being funny, so I gave him a smile.

"She got a hundred bucks. Not a lot, and I put in two fake bids to get the price up." He leaned against the wall and shook his head. "It's a crazy business. Crazy. I could tell you stories. I won't, though, I know that guy you work for, uh, the one with the beard, keeps you on a pretty tight schedule."

"Esteban."

"Yeah, Esteban, Paul says he can get us just about anything we . . . well, never mind that. Have you time for one quick story?"

"*Sí, señor.*"

"Jack, please."

"*Sí, Señor Jack.*"

"Just Jack, but anyway, so I'm on *MI3* with Cruise. Two-page role. Probably doesn't remember me. Been here a year now and not one invite to the fucking house, excuse my French. Lost my train of . . . Oh, yeah, so the grips tell me on *MI3* that he has a special shredder in his trailer that vaporizes everything, burns everything to a crisp, you know, so no one can go through his garbage and sell it on the Net. What do you think of that? Paranoid, huh?" Jack said. His face fell. "Not much of a story, actually, was it?"

"It was a good story. Tom Cruise is very famous," I said in slightly more broken English than I was capable of. Better if he underestimated me a little.

Jack sighed and looked unhappy.

Below us the front doorbell rang. "That'll be the brains of the operation. I better go," he said. "It was nice meeting you."

"You too, *señor,*" I said.

I finished cleaning and when I went downstairs Paul was in the hall impatiently waiting for Jack. The man from last night. Paul Youkilis. Again Ricky's file: 39, born in Austin, Texas, Ivy League, Jack's manager and fixer, no known alibi for the night of the accident, hence suspect #1 or #2.

He was wearing a bright red shirt, yellow tinted glasses, black shorts, and flip-flops. He seemed dressed for a beach in Havana rather than a mountain town in Colorado. For some reason this sartorial choice filled me with annoyance.

"And who are you?" he asked, like Jack, failing to remember as far back as ten hours ago.

"María, I'm new. I work for Esteban."

"New. I don't like new," Paul said.

Jack appeared, also in shorts and carrying a racket of some kind.

"All set?" Jack said.

Paul sighed. "I hate fucking squash. When are we going to get to go skiing? Isn't this supposed to be Colorado? Where's the fucking snow?"

Jack laughed. "Skiing? Skiing, you say? Nobody under forty goes skiing anymore, you old man." He turned to me. "Ever been snowboarding, María? It's the bomb."

"No, *señor.*"

Jack punched Youkilis on the shoulder. "Anyway, it's your fuckup, dude. Cruise makes his own snow. Get us invited to his house and we can ski all fucking day."

"I'm trying man, I'm trying," Paul said.

"Try harder. David Beckham's coming for the weekend and he's like huge all over Europe and Asia. I was just telling María here what big buddies me and Mr. Cruise are. Don't show me up, brother."

Paul examined me again. "When did you start working for Esteban?"

"Yesterday," I said.

"Yesterday?" Paul muttered.

"Yeah, didn't you read today's paper, Paul? Looks like our old buddy Esteban is going to have a lot of new people on his staff," Jack said.

"What are you talking about?" Paul asked.

"*Fairview Post.* María here very cleverly escaped the net," Jack said, winking at me.

"I have no idea what you're blathering about," Paul muttered.

"As per fucking usual," Jack muttered. He waved, blew kisses at Angela and me, and led Paul outside.

When they were gone, Angela called me over. "María, can you keep a secret?" she asked.

"Let me guess, you're in love with Señor Jack," I replied.

"With Señor Tyrone? No. A thousand times no, he's skinny and has all those mirrors. Didn't you see that he has pictures of himself on his bedroom wall? He's crazy."

"Ok, what's the secret?"

"I wanted to tell you before, but I wanted to see if I could trust you."

And because I did such a good job vacuuming carpets you reckon you can? I thought but didn't say.

"What is it?" I whispered.

"When we get back to the motel tonight, we're clearing out of here for Los Angeles. Victor has bought a Volkswagen bus and we're driving to L.A. We've had enough of Esteban cheating us, paying us nothing, and now with the *federales* breathing down our necks, it's time to go. We can get good jobs in L.A. Better jobs. And we won't have to work for that fat thief."

Ahh, so that's what all the furtive looks were about.

"Who's going?" I asked.

"Myself, Anna, Luisa, Victor, Josefina. We can take you if you want to come," Angela said. "To L.A.?"

"*Sí*, we can just disappear. Victor has cousins out there. He can get us Social Security cards, driver's licenses, good jobs. And no Esteban."

"I'll think about it," I said.

"There's no need. You haven't even seen winter here yet. In January and February we have to walk up this hill in the snow and ice. L.A. doesn't have snow."

"I'll think about it," I reiterated.

"No, no, no, we need a decision now."

"Then it's a no."

She stared at me and shook her head. "Let me call Luisa and tell her you're coming. You won't be sorry." "No. Don't. Look, Angela, I don't want to move so soon. We only just got here and I have a lot of things to do," I said. The words were out before I could call them back.

"What things?" she asked.

I knew I had to change tack immediately.

"Nothing. Forget it. Look, the person you should ask is Francisco. He'll go with you, especially if you tell him that he'll make more money."

"You and Francisco are not together?"

"Of course not."

"Then I will ask him."

"Do that."

Angela's lips narrowed and she went back to the trash bags and I picked up the cleaning spray. Through the living room window I watched Jack and Paul reverse out of the driveway.

Things to do, I thought.

Things to do.

CHAPTER 8

THE GARAGE

When I was thirteen I won a poetry competition—the Dr. Ernesto Guevara Young Poets' Prize. The competition was open to all children under the age of sixteen, though really it was open only to the children of Party members. The prize was a trip to St. Petersburg to study composition at the Pushkin School. My poem wasn't very good, it was about the harbor lights on Havana Bay watching themselves on a still January night. I imagined all the events the harbor had seen over the last five hundred years and wrote about them. The metaphors were weak, the images childish, and the good bits were echoes from José Martí and García Lorca. It was a bad poem but my father knew how to play the game. He changed my title from "Night Harbor" to "Time Can Be Either Particle or Wave" and threw in a line about quantum physics. It was the early 1990s. Things were changing in Cuba. We were ending our ties with Russia, America had a new president, and for a brief while all things seemed possible. It wasn't quite our Prague Spring but it was something. The judges read my poem and lapped it up. I won the prize and at a big ceremony in the Teatro Karl Marx I got a medal from Vilma Espín—Mrs. Raúl Castro.

Of course they never flew me to St. Petersburg. The trip kept getting pushed back and pushed back and finally, after Dad defected, it was quietly forgotten about. I didn't write any more poems after that. But the point of this story isn't my aborted poetry career, or the evils of the Party, or my father's cunning—no, the point is the change of title. "Night Harbor" would never have won anything, but "Time Can Be Either Particle or Wave" sounded very hip back then. As Dad said, you've got to give people what they want, not what they need. You have to change yourself to fit the circumstances. When you're an undercover detective you have to own every room you're in.

Like a lot of actors I began with the clothes. I had bought an outfit in Mexico City, an expensive-looking dark gray suit: pencil-thin skirt, light, well-cut jacket, white blouse, black stockings, black high-heeled patent leather shoes, black fake Gucci clutch purse. I'd had to spot clean the jacket since it had been tossed from my bag and had lain on the desert floor while I killed two men.

I had the suit, I had the lie, I had a card.

My voice wasn't my voice. My face wasn't my face. Red lips, dark eyes, and that unpleasant local look—a thick layer of orange bronzer that made the skeletal Fairview women resemble victims of some nuclear disaster.

There wasn't much I could do with my hair but I had gelled it for more bulk and I sat with the poise of an American businesswoman, cross-legged, relaxed, coolly regarding the glossy magazines in the waiting room.

Marilyn, the blond, good-looking, fortysomething secretary, finally announced me: "Miss Martinez from Great Northern Insurance," she said.

I entered the office.

"Miss Martinez," the man said, not getting up from his desk.

"Mr. Jackson," I replied with a smile and passed him the card with the fictitious name and cell phone number.

"I'm a very busy man, what's this about?" he asked, taking the card Ricky had made for me, crumpling it, and throwing it in a wastebasket.

"The next piece of paper I'm going to give you will be a subpoena, I hope you take better care of that," I said, annoyed but inwardly thanking him for letting me enter the role without the necessity of small talk.

"You can't touch me, you're not a cop," he said with a little tremor.

"No?" I said with a look that told him I knew everything. Every little scam he'd pulled over the last five years. A bend of the law here, a few false accounts there. There wasn't a garage in the world that hadn't defrauded an insurance company at some point, and the Pearl Street Garage of Fairview, Colorado, was surely no different.

He grimaced. His mouth opened and closed like a dying snapper.

I sat back in the chair. Breathed. Watched.

The TV news tells us that Americans are all bloated capitalists but this was not the case in Colorado. The trophy wives on Pearl Street, the Hollywood types, the hardworking Mexicans in the Wetback Motel—lean. Mr. Jackson was no exception. Mid-fifties, but trim. Skinny arms, prominent Adam's apple, dyed black hair, and dead, beady, blue-black eyes. Like those of a stuffed animal. I had the feeling that Mr. Jackson was one of those people undergoing a starvation diet in the hope of living longer.

There was certainly something not quite together about him.

Sweat on the temple. Tremble in the lip.

It made me depressed. Did everyone have a dark secret? Did everyone lie? No wonder cops got worse as they got older. Ten years in you'd need a machete to cut through the layers of cynicism.

I couldn't bear to look at his face so I examined his clothes. A color-blind ensemble. Beige shirt, purple slacks, bright red tie with some kind of crest on it. After the clothes the room. Neat freak. A few landscapes on the wall. Empty desk. Phone. Pic of wife and four kids. A long sofa where he and Marilyn probably fucked.

Behind him, in the distance, I could see a ski lift carrying little empty chairs up a mountain. Empty because there wasn't much snow, I assumed. I watched them for a while.

The silence cracked him, as I knew it would.

People, and especially people in sales, hate quiet. It reminds them of the eternity of lost mercantile opportunities under the coffin lid.

He fished the card from the trash. "Inez Martinez, Great Northern Insurance," he read slowly. I nodded. "What can I do for you, Miss Martinez?"

"I'm investigating a fraudulent insurance claim," I began. "I think you know what I'm talking about."

His face whitened and he sat on his hands to stop them shaking. Christ, this character would last precisely thirty seconds in one of my basement interrogation rooms.

"I, I *don't* know what you're talking about," he said.

"Mr. Jackson, let me put your mind at rest, this has nothing whatsoever to do with your garage or the work you're doing."

An all-too-visible sigh of relief. *Come mierda, lela,* you should be on the stage, you'd be too big for the movies, but perfect for the theater. Everything's right there on your face.

"You're not investigating us? But why would you? We run a very tight ship here. That kind of thing is a stranger to our . . . I mean, we're not the . . . What I mean is, we always maintain the highest standards of . . ." He lost his train of thought.

"Mr. Jackson, my company's experience with your garage has always been first-rate, so let me just say again that this is nothing to do with you or the work you've done for us."

His smile broadened and I knew I had to hit him now while the relief endorphins were at full tilt. "It's nothing major, but my supervisor in the fraud department asked me to come up here and ask you for a favor since he knew I was going to be in Denver for a quite different matter," I said.

"Of course. What can I help you with?" he asked.

"Well, as you know, fraud is most common in cases of personal injury, but sometimes we do see it in fully comprehensive cases too. It's unusual but it does happen."

"Yeah, I guess it does."

Thin smile, more sweat.

"Generally it's not worth the risk unless you have double or even triple insured yourself. With different insurance companies, of course."

Mr. Jackson nodded enthusiastically. "God, yeah, I see what you're saying. Someone had an accident. We did the work and he claimed it off more than one insurance company, is that what you're talking about?"

"Exactly."

"So, like you said, this, uh, wouldn't be a reflection on the work we've done. We'd be, uh, we'd be—"

"Tangential."

"Yeah, yeah, tangential. Hit the nail on the head. Ok, what do you want me to do?"

"Since this is an ongoing investigation I am not permitted to reveal particulars of the case."

"No, of course not."

"What I need are your records for the last week of May."

"Of this year? May 2007?"

"Yes."

"No problem. Hold on."

He pressed an intercom on his desk. "Marilyn, can you bring me the accounts book for May, the red one. The red one," he said.

She brought the red book. The official book, not the real book with what things actually cost. I scanned the names.

The two names for the twenty-seventh and twenty-eighth were the same ones that Ricky had already found. I passed the book back.

Two minutes' work. Two thousand miles. Two dead men.

"Is that it?" he asked.

That was it. Marilyn saw me out.

Pearl Street was busy. Zombie *perras* in high-heeled boots, bearded men in sandals and ripped jeans. Pepper-spray perfume. Mustard-gas aftershave.

I started to lose character. Shoulders drooped. Face relaxed.

"Miss Martinez?"

I turned. Marilyn.

"Yes?"

"Mr. Jackson remembered something else that might be of use."

Back inside.

The office again. Stuffed animal eyes. Fuck sofa. Empty ski lift. His stomach making a rumbling noise.

"Yes?"

"Look, I don't know if this is important or not."

"Go on."

He coughed. "Well, like I say, I don't know if this is a big deal or not but two other people have been asking questions about our records for the end of May."

"Have they?"

"Yes."

"Do you mind if I—"

"One of them was a Latino reporter from Denver, a few weeks back, apparently he talked to one of our mechanics."

Ricky.

"Who was the other?"

"Sheriff Briggs."

* * *

The day departing behind mountains, saying goodbye with yellow hands and an orange-colored carapace.

Angela shook her head and dissolved in the lotus light. "It's not just that Esteban pays shit and he's unreliable. He drinks and he has a gun and he deals drugs."

Paco looked at me with stupid, tired eyes. "What are you going to do, María?" he asked.

I was dead tired too. I didn't want to make a thing of it.

"I'm staying," I said simply.

The Volkswagen microbus honked its horn. Luisa slid open the side door and waved to hurry us up. I acknowledged her wave and shook my head.

"I don't know," Paco said.

"We'd like you to come," Angela said, touching him on the arm.

"Jualo and all my crew are at the other motel on I-70, some of them are in Denver, are you gonna take those guys?" Paco asked.

Angela shook her head. "We've got room for two more. Come with us, Francisco. Come on, we want to have you, things will be better in L.A., please come," Angela insisted.

She hadn't begged me this much. She liked him. She was a sensible girl. She'd be good for him.

"Listen to her. You should go, Paco, you'll have more opportunities in Los Angeles," I said.

"But Esteban's done so much for us," he replied lamely.

"Fuck Esteban," Angela muttered.

The VW honked again.

"*Vamonos!*" someone shouted.

"Well?" Angela asked.

"How far is L.A.?" Paco wondered.

Angela shrugged. "L.A.? I think it's just over the mountains. A few hours. Not far. Not very far."

"Do you have a map?" Paco asked.

Angela was getting impatient. "I don't know. L.A. is huge. You can't miss it. You just keep going west."

Paco looked at me. It was hard, if not impossible, to read him but I had a stab: "Francisco, my friend, my brother, do not feel that you have an obligation to stay here because of me. I am able to look after myself," I said in formal Spanish.

He grinned. "María, that I know only too well. But we've been through a lot together and I don't want to go anywhere without you," he said, and his eyes flicked down to the motel parking lot to cover his embarrassment.

"You could make a lot more money in L.A.," I tried.

"So could you."

Angela spat. "You're both crazy," she muttered. "Come on, I need an answer."

"I'm not going," I said.

"Me either," Paco agreed.

Angela nodded. "Well, it's your funeral," she said in English.

I hugged her and kissed her on the cheek. Paco hugged her. She ran across the parking lot and Luisa helped her into the VW.

They waved as they drove out, honking the horn and flashing the lights like they were going to a fair, which I suppose they were, after this shitty town.

Lucky they left when they did. Twenty minutes after they made the highway Esteban's Range Rover pulled in.

Paco and I retreated to the kitchen to prepare dinner but one of Esteban's remaining goons must have told him what had happened, because soon after we heard him yelling and screaming and running from room to room to see who was missing. When he found us in the kitchen he wasn't relieved, he was pissed off. "They didn't want you? What's your fucking problem?" he demanded.

"Watch your language, there's a lady present," Paco said.

Esteban snorted, glared at us, and then left without saying anything more.

"Dinner?" Paco asked.

"I'll make something," I said, more than happy, again, to cook for someone else. For a man.

I opened the freezer and found strip steak. I fried it in garlic and olive oil.

We could still hear Esteban outside yelling and ranting like a child but we ignored him. In another pan I fried squash and plantains. Paco put on the rice.

He cut me two kiwifruits and an orange.

The juice ran over his fingers and for a moment I wanted him to feed me the fruit from his sticky hands. His hair had fallen over his face again and he smelled of pine and sun.

I took a beer from the fridge and pressed it against my forehead and asked him to set the table.

There were at least a score of other people in the motel at that moment and most of them worked for Esteban, but even so, for some reason, when he'd calmed down he came back to us.

He was carrying a bottle of tequila and three glasses.

"Excuse me," he said when he saw that we were eating.

"Pull up a chair," Paco said.

"Join us," I agreed.

I halved my steak and gave him rice and a tortilla.

He poured three measures of tequila.

"*Salud*," he muttered.

We knocked back the tequila and Esteban refilled our glasses.

"Eat something," I said.

He ate. "Not bad," he admitted.

"How are you doing after this morning?" I asked him.

Esteban grunted and told Paco an abbreviated and much more heroic account of this morning's episode with the sheriff.

"Sheriff seems to have a lot of power around here," I said.

"Don't worry about him. I have him in my pocket. He's a fool, he acts big but he has the brain of a cow."

"I heard some of the guys say he was in the war. He was in Iraq," Paco said.

"No, no, not this war, the first one. He was in the Marines. He was in Kuwait. Not this one," Esteban said with a dismissive sniff.

"He is a frightening man," I found myself saying.

And he did frighten me. Why was he at the garage? Why was he looking into the accident? What was *his* angle? Something Ricky missed?

"Worry not, little rabbit. He is nothing. If this were Mexico I would deal with him, but here . . ." Esteban muttered and waved his hand in the air with contempt.

"He seems to have a finger in a lot of pies," I asked, probing perhaps too hard. Esteban glanced at me, took another sip of tequila. His eyes narrowed a little and even Paco gave me a second look.

Too many questions.

I played meek, eating, looking down at my plate. I tuned out as the boys talked soccer. Esteban swallowed tequila, two shots for every one of ours.

Finally he stopped eating, banged the table with the flat of his hand, looked at me, time traveled back to the end of our conversation.

"No, don't worry about him. He thinks he's a player. He thinks he runs this town. If truth be told, it's me—I run it. He doesn't know half of what's going on. Not half of it. Motherfucker, he'll get his one day, you'll see. You'll see."

His eyes dark, violent.

I thought about his Range Rover.

Of course, as Ricky pointed out, if you were very stupid, or very bold, you could hit a man, kill him, and never bother to get the car repaired at all, just drive around without a care in the world, knowing that up here the life of a dead Mex wasn't worth a goddamn thing.

Esteban swallowed the last of his steak, smacked his lips. His cheeks were red, his face puffed.

I switched the conversation back to sports and Esteban tried to explain the difference between rugby and American football. Of all the subjects I wasn't interested in, this proved to be near the top.

Time dragged.

When he was finished with his meal Paco thanked me solicitously and gave Esteban such a black look that despite his mood he remembered his manners. "Oh, this was perfect, María, thank you so much for making it for us," he said. "There's nothing like good food to raise your spirits."

"It's just something I threw together," I replied, finding that I wasn't immune to the compliment.

"No, no, it was delicious," Esteban replied.

We had no sweetmeats but we had cigarettes and the rest of the tequila.

We moved together to the upstairs balcony of the motel.

Esteban stared at us and shook his head. "They didn't trust you. Too new. Fuckers. Ungrateful fuckers. I'll show them," he said, and he stomped off to his suite at the east end of the motel.

"He's drunk," I said to Paco.

"No, he can hold it better than that," he replied.

But either I was right or Esteban had serious mental problems, because a couple of minutes later he came out of his room with a hunting rifle. He shot it into the woods half a dozen times yelling *Chinga tu madre* and other obscenities, and when he tired of that he went into his room and turned on his Mexican polka music at full blast, singing along, shouting the lyrics over the desultory sound of electric accordions.

"This place is messed up. We should have gone to L.A. with the others," Paco said sadly.

"You should have gone, I need to be here," I replied.

Paco looked at me for a long time. He could sense that I was keeping something back. "Tell me," he said, at last.

"There's nothing to tell," I said weakly.

"Oh, I know this one," Paco said.

I listened to the tune but I didn't recognize it.

"I don't know it."

"Really? It's called 'Ghost Dance,' it's very popular. It's about the Day of the Dead," Paco said, giving me another skeptical look.

"Blood and death! Blood and death!" Esteban was shouting until he grew hoarse.

Eventually the tape stopped and someone helped Esteban into bed.

The clouds cleared. Mars rose between the branches of a blue spruce, and after Mars, Venus and then the big glassy seashore of stars, the Via Lactea.

"Hell with this, let's go to bed," I muttered.

Paco smiled.

"Separately," I clarified.

"Of course," he replied with an even bigger smile.

But neither of us moved.

We sat there, smoking, listening to the silence and gazing at the Milky Way.

It was quiet now and I felt strangely at ease here in the town where my father had found comfort and lived and loved. "It won't last," I said.

"It never does," Paco said.

It never does because waiting in the wings are blood and death.

"Blood and death," I whispered, and Paco grinned.

CHAPTER 9

THE MEN FROM SASKATCHEWAN

Esteban prodded me awake at four-thirty in the morning. "Can you drive a car?" he asked.

"Wha?"

Paco woke on the other bed. "I can drive," he said.

Esteban shook his head. "No, we need you at the construction site. We're against a deadline there. We get penalized a thousand dollars a day if we're not finished by Christmas. The Ortegas going to L.A. has really screwed us."

"Yeah, I can drive," I said.

"Good, come on, let's go."

"What time is it?"

"Come on."

"At least let me go to the bathroom."

"Hurry."

In five minutes we were outside in the Range Rover. Esteban's right arm was in a homemade sling.

"Where to?" I asked.

"Drive downtown, we'll swing by Starbucks, it opens at five."

"And then where to?"

"Wyoming."

"Wyoming?" I said with surprise. "Wyoming's the one with the Mormons and the—"

"No, no, that's Utah. It's just up the road, couple of hours. Come on, foot on the brake, turn the key, yeah, that's it."

I pulled out of the parking lot and made the turn for downtown. Across the street from the motel a big rented Toyota Tundra with New York plates was parked in a turning circle. I took no notice of the car but my cop brain saw a man apparently sleeping inside.

At the Starbucks we were the first customers and the coffee was poor, almost undrinkable. Esteban seemed to like it, though, and he bought a couple of pastries to go with it. I had him get me two yellow bananas and a small bright orange.

Wyoming turned out to be ninety minutes north of Fairview. There were no direct highways but good double-lane roads with little traffic. An easy drive. Signs everywhere warning us about the dangers of elk, deer, and bears but I didn't see any animals at all. A few big rigs, a lonely pickup or two.

The Range Rover was good, though it caught the wind on some of the exposed sections. I let the sheer take me over a little more than I should so we could talk about the car, but Esteban didn't even notice.

"The car drives pretty well," I said.

"Yeah."

"A little top-heavy."

"Yeah?"

"See you got a dent on the front."

"What?"

"You had an accident?"

"Oh, that, that was nothing."

"What happened?"

"Just fucking drive, María, it's not far now."

A little over the state line Esteban had me pull off the road onto a Park Service trail that led to a frozen lake surrounded by snow-covered forest.

We finally stopped in a small, empty parking lot.

"Ok, where are we?" I asked.

Esteban grinned. "You like it? This place is perfect. The Park Service closes it from Thanksgiving through April. No one comes here. They don't allow ice fishing because although the lake freezes, the ice isn't quite thick enough for the health-and-safety people. So it's perfect."

"We're here to fish?" I asked.

"No. Don't you listen? It's not safe enough. You can walk on the ice but it's not safe enough for the little huts those ice fishermen build. No, rest assured no one will be out here the whole winter."

"I don't understand. So what are we doing here?"

"It's a meet."

The light dawned. "Oh, I see. Who are we meeting?"

"The men from Saskatchewan."

I wanted to ask more but Esteban put a finger against his thick chapped lips. The conversation had terminated.

After a few minutes it got cold and he told me to turn the engine back on.

He blasted the heat and scanned the radio for a Spanish station but the mountains were blocking the ones from Denver and in Wyoming the music choices were between soulless white people singing songs about Jesus and soulless white people singing about their marital problems.

As 7:00 a.m. approached, Esteban killed the radio and turned off the car. He removed the key and put it in his pocket.

"What's happening?" I asked.

Esteban reached into the glove compartment and pulled on a ski mask.

"What the fuck are you doing?" I asked.

He opened the passenger door, went to the back of the Range Rover, and took out a sports bag and his hunting rifle. He came back around to the driver's side of the car, gave me the bag.

"Listen to me, María, it's very simple. You give them the bag, they'll give you a bag. There's no need to sample the merchandise and they have no need to count the money. We all trust each other. Just bag for bag. It's that simple."

"Why don't you do it?"

"I'll be in the forest, covering you with my rifle," he said. "Don't worry, I can still shoot with my arm like this, and despite my stupidity last night, believe me, I'm pretty good."

"Wait a fucking minute. I'm meeting your d—"

Esteban lowered the rifle and pointed it at my chest. "I suggest you take it easy. They'll be along presently. I'll be covering you from the trees."

He backed away into the forest.

Thoughts racing. What would he do if I got out and ran for it? Shoot me? No. But why not? For all his fine talk about Greater Mexico, what was I to him? Another wetback expendable, a *chiquita* at that.

As he disappeared under the branches of a big pine I shouted after him:

"No wonder everyone's fucking off to L.A. if this is how you treat your workers!"

He didn't reply and in another two seconds I couldn't see him anymore.

I sat there.

Ten minutes. Twenty minutes. Thirty.

The men came.

Not men at all—kids. Blond-haired Canadians in big coats. Bags under their eyes made them look as if they'd hit their early twenties but the driver's licenses probably told a different story.

Their blue Dodge Ram stopped next to the Range Rover.

I got out. They got out. They'd driven all night and had the smell of exhaustion and fear people got in the MININT building on Plaza de la Revolución.

I gave them the money and they gave me a large clear bag filled with white powder and an even bigger bag of marijuana.

"What's the white stuff?" I asked.

"Ice Nine from Japan, via Hawaii," one of them said.

They were excited. They were surprised to be dealing with a woman and they wanted to talk about the drive down, the money, everything. But I had an uncomfortable feeling pricking at the back of my neck. I was concerned for them. In his angry, humiliated mood, I wouldn't put it past Esteban to assassinate both of them and keep the cash and the drugs. Kill all three of us, take that phony bandage off his hand, drive back, laughing all the way.

". . . and Dale's shitting it, like totally shitting it, man, and I'm saying it's not the Mounties, it's a fucking fire marshal—" one of them was saying until I cut him off.

"Beat it."

"What?"

"If you know what's good for you. My boss is in the trees with a rifle. I don't trust him. Get out of here. Scram."

They scrammed.

Five minutes later Esteban returned. He slid back the bolt on his rifle and took the round out of the chamber. Live ammo. He'd been ready to shoot.

"You did well, María."

"Thanks."

Silence on the drive back. At the outskirts of Fairview, Esteban took the wheel and drove without any seeming discomfort. He dropped me at the bottom of the hill on Malibu Mountain.

"What now?" I asked him.

"What do you think? Your regular route."

"No bonus, no day off for my help, no tip?"

"I've got a tip for you—shut up and do your job."

"I don't have a uniform."

"Forget that. Just go—and you better step on it, you're an hour late. Oh, and tie the garbage bags properly at the top of the trash can, we've had complaints," he said, passing me a key ring with the alarm codes and house numbers taped to individual keys.

"Tie the garbage bags," I muttered.

"What did you say?"

"I said you really are a bastard, Esteban. Worse than that sheriff. You're screwing your own people," I said.

He made a fist. "You watch your mouth, María. You want to be back in Mexico? That's an easy one. That's one phone call. You've been given a great opportunity here, don't blow it."

I nodded, lowered my eyes.

"Look at me," he said.

Our eyes met. He yawned and his voice assumed a more conciliatory tone. "Look, you did well this morning. There's something about you. You got an air of responsibility. I like it. Tell you what, when I go to Denver with Rodrigo to unload the ice, you can borrow the car. Drive to work, drive to Safeway, do a couple of errands for me."

"Thank you."

"You're welcome."

I stood there.

"What are you waiting for? Quit your gaping and get up there, we don't want any more complaints."

"Ok."

He wound the window and started to drive off but the Range Rover suddenly squealed to a halt.

"No. María, wait a minute. Wait there," Esteban said.

I stood in the ditch while Esteban fiddled with something in the front seat. A stretch limo drove past, heading up the hill toward the Cruise estate. I tried to look inside but the glass was frosted black like Jefe's car.

"Come here, María," Esteban said.

"I'm here."

He handed me three small Ziploc bags filled with the Ice 9 from Japan.

"What the fuck is this?" I asked.

Esteban rubbed his hand over his beard. "This is nothing. This couldn't be more straightforward. Number 22, number 24, number 30 on the Old Boulder Road. That's Rick Hanson, Yuri Amatov, and Paul Youkilis. Got it?"

"What's in the bag?"

"It's meth from Asia. Look, don't worry, you'll get cut in. Couple of days when I'm liquid. That's why I have to go to Denver."

He stared at me for a second and I took the baggies and put them in my coat pocket.

"Where do you want me to put it?" I asked.

"Listen to me. This is important. After you've cleaned each residence and as you're leaving, place each bag in the downstairs medicine cabinet."

"What's that?"

"The little cupboard thing behind the mirror. They all have one. Don't refer to the ice and don't talk about it if you're asked, just leave the baggie and go."

"Hanson doesn't have a downstairs bathroom."

Esteban spat. "Use your fucking head then! The upstairs cabinet. If they have any problems they'll contact me," he said. "Now, no more of your bullshit and get to fucking work."

He drove off in a squeal of rear tires and burned tread. I watched the car go, wondering how fast he drove up and down this road and if he'd even know the difference between a deer and a man in the dark.

The air was frigid as I walked up the hill to the first of the houses.

I found the key and the alarm. The instructions were idiotproof. Bell or buzzer first and then key if they're not home or asleep. Thirty seconds to disable the alarm and arm it again as you're leaving.

I pressed the bell. "Who is it?" Mr. Hanson asked through an intercom.

"Maid service."

"You fuckers," Mr. Hanson said.

A buzzing sound and the door opened but I didn't go in. Not yet. I was emotional. Angry. Tired.

I took a moment to have a dialogue with myself. It's ok, Detective, it's all part of the process, don't worry about it. This day is important. You found the place. The place you've dreamed about. So forget the anger, forget the drugs, forget the Canadian boys, forget the money, remember the lake.

Remember the lake.

* * *

Hanson was drunk. He was sixty, trim, handsome, tall, an avid skier. Angela said that he played doctors or lawyers in commercials or occasionally the father of a female lead in television dramas, but not sitcoms as his personality wasn't large enough for that. He probably thought that being inebriated at nine in the morning was charming, but it wasn't. I emptied his trash cans, swept his hardwood floor, cleaned his toilet, ran the dishwasher, and wiped the surfaces. He was still in bed and flipping through the channels when I appeared with the vacuum cleaner.

There was a french press filled with cold yellow urine next to the bed when I came in. He pointed at it. I emptied it in the en suite bathroom.

"Giuh hanbac for a hajaa," he said repeatedly.

It was only when I was leaving that I realized he was saying, "I'll give you a hundred bucks for a hand job."

Meth and booze are a killer combination as consistent as cocaine and heroin, so defying Esteban, I put the Ice 9 behind two shampoo bottles on the top shelf of the bathroom cabinet—hopefully he'd need to be reasonably sober to find it.

I closed the front door and walked up the hill to the next residence, an easy one, that of an actor called Bobby Munson who was in L.A. and apparently not coming to Fairview at all this winter. There I did some light dusting and flushed the toilets.

The next house, a weekend retreat for a rich Denver family, was also empty. They had a Dyson vacuum cleaner and it was almost a joy to run that thing around. I dusted, emptied trash, made beds, ate fruit from their fridge. Oranges, grapes, and a kiwi that I lovingly cut, peeled, and diced into quarters. They seemed just the type to have a hidden camera that spied on the help, but fruit was my American obsession and what difference did petty larceny make when I was planning a kidnapping and worse.

Yuri Amatov was a production designer—whatever that is—a skinny, bald man about forty. When I rang the doorbell, he took my arm and led me inside.

"Where is it?" he asked.

"Excuse me, *señor*?"

"Where the fuck is it?" he screamed.

I reached into my messenger bag and brought out the cellophane-wrapped meth. He snatched it from me. "Now fuck off," he said.

"The cleaning, *señor*?"

"What part of 'fuck off' don't you understand?"

Another walk. The gradient increased as you went farther up the hill; seemingly the climate zone changed too. The wind was blowing from the north, the temperature had fallen considerably, and the sky was filled with ominous gray clouds.

"Looks like snow," I said to myself with no excitement whatsoever.

These thoughts left my mind at Youkilis's house.

Gravel drive. Carved wooden door. Bell. Paul Youkilis came to the door in a sweatshirt, sweatpants, flip-flops.

"You're late," he said, looming over me.

"I'm sorry, we—"

Youkilis raised a hand. "I don't want the details, just get this shit cleaned up. It's driving me crazy."

"*Sí, señor,*" I said.

He smiled and added, "Christ, I sound like such a fucking feudalist. Get this shit cleaned up, *please*. I can't work in these conditions."

"*Sí, señor.*"

The conditions were Chinese food cartons, newspapers, a couple of beer cans, and what looked like dog excrement in the kitchen.

Youkilis's house was smaller than Jack's. A few downstairs rooms painted in bright primary colors and adorned with Mediterranean pottery. The windows looked out on forest and there was no mountain view. I couldn't tell if this was all he could afford or whether he had just taken it to be next to Jack. Presumably he got 10 percent of Jack's salary, but how much did Jack make? How much did a second-string actor get in Hollywood? I should probably find out.

Youkilis went upstairs. I'd been cleaning for about fifteen minutes when I became aware that Jack was upstairs with him.

As I was changing the vacuum bag both men came down.

Evidently they had been in the middle of a heated discussion, but now neither was saying anything. Jack was wearing jeans and a blue shirt unbuttoned to the navel. His hair was product-free and he looked tired, frazzled.

Something was going on.

"Plato thought everything had a true self, an ideal form, from which all things deviated," Youkilis said.

"What's that got to do with anything?" Jack snapped.

"Everything has to be perfect. For a movie to happen, all the stars have to align, there are so many things that can fuck up: the money, the director, the cast. Every single little thing has to be perfect."

Jack's face was red. "So what are you saying? I'm trying to read between the goddamn lines here. Have I lost the movie again? Are you fucking kidding me?"

Paul smiled. "Relax, buddy, you haven't lost anything. Focus still wants to do it. This is just a hiccup. A rag in the gears, not a sabot."

"I don't know what the fuck you're talking about, man! Can you speak English for once!" Jack yelled.

"Look, relax, I'll talk to CAA and get the story. As I understand it, the movie's been delayed but not postponed and not canceled. I'll get the information. Now just fucking relax. The script is finished. We have a completed script. Can you imagine how many people are really screwed because of the writers' strike?"

"Just get me the story, will ya?"

"Ok, ok. I'll do my best. Probably doesn't help that we're in fucking Colorado, not L.A. You sit there, I'll go and get this cleared up."

Paul went upstairs to make a phone call. Jack sat heavily in a chair and put his head in his hands. I finally changed the vacuum bag and rewrapped a worn piece of silver duct tape around the tube. The suction was lousy but Youkilis never had to use it so what did he care.

Suddenly Jack looked up at me. "Hey, would you mind shutting that fucking thing off," he said.

"*Sí, señor.*"

"Oh, it's you. Sorry about that. I'm at the end of my . . . I'm just . . . I'm going to lose the fucking movie. My first real lead and it's all going to shit."

I nodded but I couldn't even fake sympathy. Try working sixty hours a week for four dollars an hour like Paco, try living on a dollar a day in Havana. But although I was unable to give him a simulacrum of concern, I hadn't meant to look contemptuous. Jack smiled. "Yeah, I know what you're thinking: Spoiled Hollywood motherfucker, doesn't know a goddamn thing about the real world. Yeah? Something like that."

I shook my head.

"Listen, I know about the real world. I worked hard to get where I am today. Fucking hard. Thousands of auditions. Not hundreds, fucking thousands. You know, I lost out on one of the leads on *Battlestar Galactica* by a whisker. Gave it to a goddamn Brit. Since when have there ever been Brits in outer space? TV, I know, but steady work, look at Katee Sackhoff, two shows now. Look at me, if *Gunmetal* fails *again* I'll have nothing. Empty slate until the summer. That's an eon in Hollywood, I might as well be in a fucking coma."

"Who are you talking to? Are you on the cell phone?" Paul yelled down the stairs.

"See? Hear his voice? He's shitting himself. It's not just about the money. It's a house of cards. This movie falls apart, what's Plan B? There is no Plan B. And then there's the strike. Fucking writers. And then our guild goes out. That's a year. And there's a whole new crop of young actors up for your part. I should be in the fucking Cruise war movie. I can do an accent."

"Get off the phone, Jack! Don't discuss this with anyone. We don't know what's happening yet."

Jack walked to the bottom of the stairs. "I'm not on the fucking phone, you dick! Ok?"

"Then who are you talking to?" Paul shouted.

"Nobody. Ok?"

Nobody. That summed it up. But somehow it wasn't so bad. Jack had a twinkle in his eye as he spoke, as if he knew he was giving a performance, hamming it up even for the maid.

"What did you say?" Paul shouted again.

"I'm not talking to anyone," Jack replied, and this time he actually winked at me.

"Good. We don't know anything. If I can't get CAA, I'll call Danny Tucker at Universal," Paul yelled back.

"Do that. I'm dropping a load here. And you're wrong, I'm glad we're not in L.A., pressure would be killing me. Oh, and by the fucking way, isn't that your job, to take the pressure off me?" Jack yelled.

"Fuck off to your house, I didn't tell you to come over. Shit, shut up, I just got through to his secretary," Paul shouted and closed a bedroom door.

Jack stood at the bottom of the stairs, teasing his hair.

I turned on the vacuum and again began cleaning the study, lifting the throw rugs and running the old machine underneath them. Jack watched me for a second, walked over, and pulled the plug out of the wall.

"My head is killing me. Can you possibly do that with a sweep or a brush or something, or can you come back tomorrow?"

"*Sí, señor,*" I said.

I put the vacuum in the downstairs closet and began walking to the front door.

Jack came after me, stopped me with a hand under my elbow. "No, no, wait, today is fine, but please, no noise. And I'm really sorry about all the swearing. Lot of pressure on us at the moment, you know. I lost this movie once before. If it falls apart now, I mean, I don't know."

"Ok," I said.

I rooted around under the stairs for a broom and found one that looked like a prop from a movie set. The bristles were one big useless wedge. Jack went into the kitchen to get a drink. I looked at my watch. It was eleven o'clock. I was making good time. After Paul's, Jack's house was the last on my route. Apparently, on a normal day, I'd go down the hill and start cleaning some of the homes in lower Fairview and finish up by cleaning the shops on Pearl Street. But we hadn't had a normal day yet and Esteban wanted us to stay away from Fairview while he found out if the INS was still lurking.

It meant that after Jack's I would have the afternoon free to see Mrs. Cooper—the second interview subject on Ricky's list.

I was nearly finished sweeping when Jack came back into the living room, sat on Paul's sofa, and flipped on the TV. He was sipping a pink foaming beverage and muttering to himself, "Bastards, all the luck. That bald fucker."

The identity of the bald fucker was not immediately obvious but when a saturnine man with receding hair appeared at the front door I wondered if I was about to see some real fireworks.

"Can you get the door . . . uh, María?" Jack said.

I went to the door, opened it, and the man pushed past. "I'm expected," he said. Jack looked up but did not seem particularly enthused.

"Hey, Jack, how ya doing? How's the vacation going?" the man said.

"Bob, Bob, Bob, I'm screwed, old buddy."

Bob sat in the chair opposite Jack. "You seem upset. What's the matter?"

"Uhh, Paul got this urgent call this morning from Bill Geiss at CAA.

Focus is pulling the movie from spring. Earliest we can roll now is fall—if it's going to roll at all. I don't know what the fuck is going on."

"What movie is this?"

"The only movie, *Gunmetal*. Man, I had all my eggs in that *Titanic*. Jesus. Turned down a coupla things. Supposed to be in L.A. for rehearsals in two weeks. And of course Greengrass is in Fiji or somewhere, can't be reached."

Bob nodded. "What does Paul say?"

"He doesn't think it's dead. He's trying to get information. Tell you, this fucking project has been jinxed from the start. The things I've been through. You've no idea. The retooling. The re-fucking-imagining. *Halo* and *Doom* killed the original video game concept. Now it's about a nineteenth-century Brit thrown into the future."

"Sounds promising."

"Yeah, it does. Originally it was a Jude Law vehicle, about a million fucking years ago."

"Is it the writers' strike? Those bastards are lucky we allow them in the building. In Selznick's day he'd have fired the lot of them."

"No. Nothing to do with the writers, it's something else, I don't know what's going on."

Bob smiled reassuringly. "Look, don't get yourself worked up. You don't know anything yet."

Jack shook his head. "I don't need to know. I'm jinxed, man. I could've had Colin Farrell's role in *Minority Report*. Missed that by a whisker. That was a star-making vehicle, Christ. Me and Cruise for real, not just 'Here's your coffee, sir,' in *MI3*. Would have buddied up. Jesus, I'd've let him convert me, I swear to God."

"You should watch that tape on YouTube, you have to be certifiable," Bob said with a chuckle.

"Yeah, insane all the way to the bank. In Hollywood they're third only to the gays and Jews. No offense, Bob."

Bob smiled. "None taken. I've heard worse. I worked with Peckinpah."

"Really. What was the project?"

Bob shook his head. "The reason I bought a house here was to get away from the bullshit and shop talk."

"Sorry, yeah, me too. Yeah, you're right. You're right. Let's talk about something else. When did you get in?"

"Last night."

"From L.A.?"

Bob turned to look at me. "Can she be trusted?"

Jack smiled. "María? Me and María go way back. Don't be fooled. She's not a maid, she's remaking that Ally Sheedy movie, this is her method. Ain't that right, María?"

"*Sí,* Señor Jack."

Bob grunted and continued. "Might have a deal cooking. I'll talk to Paul. We might be getting *The Hobbit* sorted out. Hush-hush. Anyway, no, I was in Scottsdale. Hundred degrees in December. I was at the club. Ever been there, the Happy Valley Country Club? Nice place. Anyway, I quit my round halfway through. Except for those struck by lightning or in the throws of cardiac arrest, it was an event without precedent."

Jack nodded but I could tell he wasn't really listening. "Too expensive to quit," Bob explained. "Golf was meant to be played on rainy Scottish moors with the ambient temperature at a brisk fifty degrees or so. A hundred in the shade is not my cup of tea. Ever been to St. Andrews?"

"I don't play golf, Bob," Jack said.

I went into the kitchen and didn't hear the rest of the conversation. I had finished all the cleaning I could do downstairs. I rummaged in my shoulder bag, took out the Japanese ice, and put it in the medicine cabinet. I closed the cabinet door and examined myself in the mirror. I looked tired, older. The lack of sleep, the stress. I frowned in the mirror and found that I was oddly put out. What's the matter, Mercado?

I searched my feelings and found that it wasn't the mission that was bothering me, it was Jack.

Jack?

For some reason I was irritated looking bad in front of him, I was annoyed at his indifference and his joke at my expense.

"Good God, Mercado, this is the last thing you need," I muttered to my reflection. Surely you don't have a crush on the movie star? The reflection shook her head. No. I hadn't seen any of his films, he was vain, he was five years older than me, and he had the maturity of Lieutenant Díaz back in Havana.

No. That wasn't it at all.

I ran my finger under the faucet and smoothed out my eyebrows. I pulled the lipstick from my pocket and put some on.

I went back into the living room, nodded to Jack.

"*Adios,* Señor Jack," I said with a cheerful voice.

"Bye," Jack said absently.

"María, is that María? María, are you leaving?" Paul yelled from upstairs.

"*Sí, señor,*" I said.

"Could you come upstairs for a sec?" Paul asked.

"I'll go with you," Jack said, springing from his chair.

We went up together.

Paul was still on the phone. He was grinning. He gave Jack the thumbs-up.

"Shit. What's the word?" Jack asked anxiously.

Paul put his hand over the receiver.

"I'm on hold, but the word is good. As far as I can see it's a minor fuckup, nothing more. They're pushing the picture back a couple of weeks. Studio space in Vancouver is at a premium and Focus doesn't want to overpay, so we're waiting for the next lull. Walter says it's going to be a four-week push back, not more, give everyone more time to rehearse and you to get working on those pecs."

"It's not off?" Jack said, his voice trembling.

"Fuck no. It's not off. Look, buddy, that's why I told you not to read the trades. Let me and Stevie handle everything. All you have to do is learn your lines, bulk up, and grow a mustache. Don't Google yourself and don't read the trades. You blow everything out of all proportion."

"So it's happening?"

"Yes."

"Fuck!" Jack said with boyish delight and punched his fist in the air. He was happy for about two seconds before doubt seized him again.

"You're a hundred percent sure? Tell me the truth," he asked.

"This movie is happening, man. You're on your way to the A-list, baby."

Jack stuck out his hand and Paul gave him a complicated handshake.

"Oh, man, that's just great, that's just great," Jack said.

Paul grinned. "Listen, Jack, I need to talk to María here for a minute, you go back downstairs," Paul said.

"Bob's down there," Jack said in a whisper.

"Oh shit, has he been talking about Pebble Beach?"

"St. Andrews. But he mentioned *The Hobbit.*"

"Holy shit. Get back down there and agree with everything he says and talk about how great Peter Jackson looks now that he's lost a few pounds."

"I will."

"And Jack, please don't panic and don't talk about the movie to anybody."

"Nobody," Jack said and zipped his mouth comically.

"I'm serious, Jack. Make like Clarence Thomas in oral argument."

"I don't get the reference but I'll be good," Jack said, punched Paul on the arm, and went downstairs. When he was gone, Paul leaned in close. "María, did Esteban tell you to, uh, leave the . . ."

"*Sí, señor,* it's in the usual place. Downstairs bathroom cabinet."

Paul grinned. "Great, and listen, speaking of Vancouver, I'm going to need some of that quality hemp Esteban gets."

"*Sí, señor.*"

"You know what I'm talking about?"

"*Sí,* it is fresh in today."

"Great," Paul said, and with a big show he reached into his sweats, produced his wallet, and gave me a twenty-dollar bill. I put it my pocket and as I turned he patted me on the ass.

I turned again, furious. "*Señor!*"

Paul grinned. He looked like a Yankee in a Cuban newspaper cartoon.

"Hey, don't *señor* me. Come on, you're not bad-looking, María, I won't take it for free. You wanna drop by this afternoon?" Paul asked.

"I don't understand."

"Sure you do. Esteban says we can get anything we want."

"Ah, no. You are mistaken. I am not one of those girls, *señor,*" I replied.

He frowned and then nodded slowly. "Ahh, I see what you're saying. Look, it doesn't have to be anything formal. Just come by, you don't even have to tell Esteban, this could be just between you and me. Ever tried that fucking Jap ice? Blow your mind."

"No, *señor.*"

I could tell that Paul wasn't used to getting no for an answer. All residue of his smile faded like the last ration of condensed milk in the coffee cup.

He leaned close, put his hand behind my neck, squeezed slightly. "I'll make it worth your while," he whispered in my ear.

"*Señor,* I have to—"

Paul tightened his grip. "More than worth your while."

The curve of the staircase. Jack's voice. Paul's breath. The hold music coming from the phone.

Lightness.

Nausea.

The lipstick I'd put on for Jack, not you.

His fingertips greasy like yucca plant, his breath closer.

And I didn't want to hit him, I just wanted to dissolve, to slide out of his grip, down through the carpet, down through the floor . . .

"Seriously, you and me and that Ice Nine, greatest fuck you'll ever have—"

"Hi, sorry about that, Paul. Paul, are you there?" the voice on the phone said.

Paul let me go. When I got outside I crumpled the twenty and threw it away.

"*Cabrón,*" I said, and barring some surprising development with Mrs. Cooper either Esteban or Mr. Paul fucking Youkilis was going to be giving me a lot more than twenty fucking dollars.

CHAPTER 10

THE LADY FROM SHANGHAI

A bus stop. Mountains to the west and east. A spear of cloud in a cobalt sky. The road a straight line running through woods on either side of a broad valley. The outskirts of Fairview to the south, nothing but forest to the north. Forest all the way to Canada.

The sound of a chain saw.

I have changed again. This time black jeans, a white blouse, and a blazer that Angela left behind. I have combed my hair and taken the slump from my body language.

Like Jack, I too will be performing.

From the direction of Fairview the bus comes.

It stops but the driver doesn't open the door. He points at his watch and mouths the word *early*.

Sí, amigo, and if I were one of those tall trophy wives on Pearl Street—

Not that they'd ever ride the bus.

A sound behind me. A Mexican laborer carrying sticks. He puts them down, walks a little into the forest, and relieves himself against a fir tree.

"Come on," I mouth to the driver but he shakes his head.

Oh, America, you're making it too easy for me.

Seconds go by. The cool sun. The idling bus. The sound of streaming piss.

When it's exactly five minutes past, the driver pushes a button and a compressor releases its hold on the door.

A hiss of air. The smell of AC, coffee, people.

The laborer catches my eye. An older man. Not his first time over the border. I suddenly see his whole trajectory: a crossing in Juárez, a night journey through west Texas; a lecture in vulgar street Spanish from Esteban or a punk overseer just in from East L.A.; and then work all day until the sun goes down. Sleep in the Wetback Motel or some dive in Denver, up and work again.

A look passes between us.

A look of recognition.

Life is hard.

No fucking kidding.

The man nods. I nod back.

"Gittin' in, miss?" the driver asks impatiently. I step onto the bus and leave five quarters. Exact change. I don't wait for the ticket. I walk to the last row and take a seat. Six or seven passengers. I see them but I don't see them. They don't see me, either. Who does ride the bus in this town? Kids, DUI repeat offenders, foreigners. The door closes, the clutch slips, we shudder forward.

Ten minutes pass. Houses appearing through gaps in the trees.

I look for numbers on mailboxes. I spot 229 almost immediately and hunt for a way to stop the vehicle. I see a cable that runs along the window. I pull it and a bell rings and the bus comes to a halt at the next stop, a full kilometer up the road.

I stand, walk to the front.

"Thank you," I say to the driver.

"Uh-huh," he replies.

I exit. The bus moves away.

Back to 229. A two-story with four or five bedrooms, set off the road. Wooden deck running all the way around it, rusting iron sculptures littering a small garden. The trees big and oppressively close.

The path. The porch. Neat piles of raked golden leaves. A knocker shaped like a border collie's head. I rap it. Clunk of boots. Door opens. Young man, twenty-five, jeans, black sweater, pale Asiatic features, a suspicious look. Huge. What do they put in the water out here?

"We never contribute to solicitors," he says.

"I'm from Great Northern Insurance, I'm here to talk to Mrs. Cooper, if I may," I state quickly.

The man frowns, hesitates, opens the door wider. "Is this about the accident?" he asks.

"Yes."

"You better come in."

The house is dark, cool, and smells of vinegar. Mahogany paneling, stone tiled floors, a few more of the ugly metal sculptures. I follow the man into a small cluttered living room. Hummel figurines, crystal animals, Indian tapestries, a beautiful worn rug hanging over the brickwork at the chimney, Chinese-style screen prints on the other walls. An oval ball in the middle of the mantel.

"My mother," the man whispers, obviously referring to a white-haired woman sitting in front of a very large TV. A quiz show is on, people jumping up and down.

"I'm Jimmy," he says.

"Inez Martinez," I say, offering him my hand.

He shakes it firmly and quickly lets go.

"Mom, there's a lady here to see you about the accident," the son says. He repeats the statement but the woman is rapt in the show. This happens two more times and finally Jimmy resorts to turning off the set with a remote control.

Mrs. Cooper looks in my direction. She's a seventy-year-old Chinese woman in a beautiful blue floral dress. Trim, neat, tiny. She has an ethereal quality about her that sometimes you find in the dying or in junkies.

"Mom, there's a lady here to see you," Jimmy says.

"I was watching that," Mrs. Cooper protests.

Jimmy shrugs and rolls his eyes at me.

Over to you, Mercado.

Gentle voice. Fake smile. "Mrs. Cooper, I'm Inez Martinez from Great Northern Insurance," I say, enunciating the words the way they taught us in English elocution class—our goal seemingly to sound like American actresses from the 1930s.

"Yes?" Mrs. Cooper says, looking at Jimmy as if she's being sold down the river or carted off to that nursing home her son is always going on about.

"I'm eighty-one and I've never had an accident," Mrs. Cooper says.

"Eighty-one? I thought you were in your early seventies," I tell her, truthfully. With Americans, I realized, it was very hard to tell.

Mrs. Cooper smiles.

"Would you like anything to drink, Miss Inez?" Jimmy asks.

I can't resist. "Do you have any orange juice?"

American orange juice is light-years from the ersatz stuff they pedal in Havana.

"We've got some fresh-squeezed," Jimmy says. "Is that ok?"

Fresh-squeezed orange? It's like breakfast with one of Ricky's high-powered friends.

"That would be perfect," I reply.

Jimmy smiles. "I got this new machine for squeezing juice."

"Very nice."

"A present. Little bonus we all got. I work for Pixar."

Obviously Jimmy is trying to impress me, but I don't know what Pixar is.

"Pixar, very impressive," I tell him.

"We're setting up a studio in Denver at the old Gates Plant. Us and Redford. You know, Sundance. I'm not one of the creative ones, but, you know, we all do our thing—"

"What is this all about?" Mrs. Cooper wonders, looking at me sharply.

"Madam, I represent your former insurance company—Great Northern Insurance, I'm a claims investigator. We're looking into an accident that you had on May twenty-sixth of this year," I say.

"I'll get that orange juice," Jimmy says and slips out.

"What accident?" Mrs. Cooper wonders.

"The accident that occurred on May twenty-sixth, when you were driving your Mercedes," I say with a mild panic—I couldn't have screwed up the names, could I?

Mrs. Cooper shakes her head. "I wouldn't call that an accident," she says.

"Is there anything wrong?" Jimmy asks, coming back with a glass of orange juice.

"Nothing wrong at all, this is just routine," I say with a reassuring smile.

"Mother admitted fault and they told us that it wouldn't be a problem," Jimmy continues.

"Oh no, it's nothing to worry about, I'm only here to get the details of the accident, this doesn't affect the claim in any way. In fact, confidentially, I can tell you that the check has already been cut. But for anything over ten thousand dollars we need to interview the claimant in person, it's just our policy."

Jimmy nods. It sounds plausible, and once you tell people that money is on the way that's generally all they can subsequently think about.

"Mrs. Cooper, if I could bring you back to the afternoon or evening of May twenty-sixth, 2007."

Mrs. Cooper still isn't sure, though, and looks at her son for a prompt.

"Go on, Mother, tell her about it," Jimmy says. "It's all right."

"Well, now that I think about it I do remember a little. There was still snow on the ground. It was a terrible winter, did they tell you that? We had a terrible winter up here, seven storms in seven weeks. One of the worst ones I can remember and I've been here for fifteen years," Mrs. Cooper says with a soft and not unpleasant Chinese accent. The Chinese apparatchiks I knew in Cuba all spoke in harsh, clipped, imperative tones.

"Can you understand her, Miss Inez? Mother's from Shanghai. Dad met her just after the war, he was an airman, the Flying Tigers. English isn't her first language."

"I can understand her perfectly," I say with another reassuring smile. I give him a little nod as if to say, *And aren't you great, Jimmy, looking after your widowed mother—the things you must have had to put up with all these years.* A lot to convey in a nod, but I do my best.

Jimmy returns the smile, completely warmed to me now. He walks to the mantel, picks up the oval ball, and begins tossing it from hand to hand.

"Go on, Mom, tell her," Jimmy says. "Spill the beans."

"I was coming back from the market in Vail," Mrs. Cooper continues.

"You drove all the way to Vail to do your shopping?" Jimmy interrupts, shocked.

"No, no, of course not, but they don't have a Chinese market in Fairview. Where else am I going to go, Denver?"

"You can get everything at the deli on Pearl Street. Mr. Wozeck—" Jimmy begins.

"Mr. Wozeck is a robber baron who charges an arm and a leg for—"

A brief conversation ensues in Mandarin before Jimmy turns to me and makes a slight solicitous bow. "Miss Inez, excuse us."

"Not at all."

"You don't know, Fairview has really changed in the last few years," Jimmy says.

Mrs. Cooper takes up the theme. "Oh yes, the prices in those stores on Pearl Street and Camberwick Street are preposterous. And they never have anything I want. Expensive delicatessens. Import stores. No, no. There is the 7-Eleven, but that's in Brown Town. I wouldn't go there. Old woman like me. No. You see the movie stars . . ."

I can see that I'm going to have to bring her back to business. "Now, Mrs. Cooper, this is important. At the time of the accident can you remember what road you were on?" I ask.

"What road I was on?"

Mrs. Cooper had not filed a police report and she hadn't told the garage where the accident had taken place. This, therefore, was the key question. From this answer all things would flow. "If you could try to recall where the accident happened, I'll be able to put it in our report and get the claim resolved as quickly as possible."

Mrs. Cooper thinks.

Time slows.

The angel holds his breath. He knows. He can see the half dozen lifelines beating in the air above her head.

"I think it was on Ashleigh Street," she says.

I write that down in the notebook. "Ashleigh Street?" I ask for confirmation and show her my spelling, which she corrects.

"Yes, that tree on the bend there, where the old liquor store used to be, just after the turn," Mrs. Cooper says and looks at her son. "It wasn't my fault, dear, there was ice on the road, I know it was May but you have no idea what it's been like up here."

Ashleigh Street. A tree at a bend in front of a former liquor store. Might be possible to check. Paint scrape, glass, a million things.

I nod and smile. "At any point during that day, Mrs. Cooper, did you happen to drive on the Old Boulder Road?"

"The what?"

"The Old Boulder Road," I repeat.

"The Old Boulder Road? Never heard of it," she says gruffly, not too gruffly but enough to raise my interest.

Hmmmm. Maybe Ricky's hunch was wrong. Could this be our girl? And what the hell would I do if she was? Probably nothing. Probably I'd get the two o'clock bus to Denver and the first night bus to El Paso. Slip over the border. The plane from Juárez to Mexico City and an earlier flight back to Havana.

No one would be the wiser.

Hector would breathe a huge sigh of relief. Ricky wouldn't care. Better for everyone.

"The Old Boulder Road is the road that goes from Main Street to what they call Malibu Mountain," Jimmy says.

Mrs. Cooper nods to herself. "I know what you are talking about. Yes, that *was* the Old Boulder Road before they built the Eisenhower Tunnel. That was a long time ago. It is a freak-show road nowadays. Those movie-star types. Their helicopters. They're all in that cult, they can control things with their minds. Jane Adams's son, Jeff, he's in with them. She cries every night. He never calls her, they do not allow him."

Bring her back. "Mrs. Cooper, did you have any occasion to be on the Old Boulder Road on the twenty-seventh or even the twenty-eighth of May?"

The old lady shrugs. "I don't think so. I don't know, but I don't think so. My thing wasn't there though."

"Your accident wasn't there?"

"No. I just said. That's completely out of my way. Haven't been there for a long time. Not this year."

"Can you take me through the accident in detail?"

"I don't know about detail, but I remember it ok. I was driving on Ashleigh and I had on NPR, it was *Colorado Matters*. I hate that show ever since Dan Drayer left, he was good. Anyway, I slipped on the road and hit the tree and then, when I was pulling out, I don't know, I was all shaken up, I turned the car and I hit the stop sign at the corner of Ashleigh and Rochdale Road. Knocked it clean over. That's why we had all those dents on the hood."

"You knocked over a stop sign?" her son interjects, looking at me nervously.

"I did. They have it planted right in the road with a couple of whatchamacall-'em orange lines painted in front of it. How are you supposed to see those?"

"Mother, did you report the fact that you knocked over the stop sign?"

"Well, not exactly. I didn't tell the other woman."

"What other woman?" Jimmy asks.

"From the insurance company," Mrs. Cooper says.

Two women from the insurance company? Jimmy gives me a suspicious look.

"What was the name of this other woman?" I ask.

Mrs. Cooper fishes around in a giant glass bowl on the phone table. It takes forever but finally she passes me the card. "Sally Wren. Great Northern Insurance Claims Adjuster," I read out loud and pass the card to the son. "Miss Wren is no longer with the company," I say with mild disdain, and lowering my voice, I add, "That explains the delay. I'll make sure I expedite this very quickly."

Jimmy looks at the card and frowns at Miss Wren's imaginary crimes. He turns to me. "Is Mom going to get in trouble for the stop sign?"

I shake my head. "It is not my job to give information to the police, in fact it would be illegal for me to do so. If you or your mother want to report it, that's fine, but it is nothing to do with me," I bluff, assuming this to be the case from all those Yuma lawyer movies. I don't really know, though, and of course in Cuba anyone who fails to report a crime can be sentenced to up to ten years in prison under the general category "Enemy of the Revolution."

Relief courses over Jimmy's face. "You're a good person, Miss Inez. Tancredo's wrong about M—about immigrants."

But I'm hardly paying attention. The accident did not take place on the Old Boulder Road. She hasn't been on the Old Boulder Road at all this year.

Satisfied, I get up and Jimmy shows me to the door. He thanks me.

"Thank you, Mr. Cooper," I tell him and then, remembering my American TV, I add, "Have a nice day."

"I will, thank you. And when will that check be coming?"

"Oh, very soon," I say.

"Excellent. Thank you. Goodbye."

"Goodbye." I walk to the path and before the door closes I look at Jimmy. "Uh, you weren't driving the car anytime around the twenty-seventh, were you?"

"Me? No. I was in San Francisco," he says flatly.

"Ok, thank you."

When I'm out of sight of the house I let the air out of my lungs.

"Closer," I tell myself.

Now what?

Walk back. Process it.

Only a couple of kilometers to Fairview and another half a klick to Wetback Mountain.

Yeah, walk back, let it bubble like rum in the kettle.

The road, the trees, the endless mountains.

Beautiful, really.

No wonder you hid here, Dad.

The afternoon gone mad with migrating geese, volery after volery. Thousands of them. Where are you going? Mexico? Farther south? I wish you could appreciate what I can see. The cobalt sky, the light bending over the mountains, the vapor trails.

That why you came here, Pop? A landscape that is in every way the opposite of Havana? Or was there another reason?

I make it to the outskirts of Fairview, take out my map, and find Ashleigh Street. I go along about a kilometer before I find a burned-out liquor store. Sure enough, the stop sign on Rochdale Road has recently been replaced. I walk back a few meters and examine the trees. One of them looks bruised, bent, like it may have been hit fairly recently by a vehicle. I look close and change my angle to get the sunlight. Tiny fragments of gray paint on the trunk. I dab my finger on my tongue and raise one of them from the tree. I hold it in the palm of my hand.

The garage report said she drove a cream Mercedes-Benz.

Six months later cream and white probably weather to just about the same shade of gray.

I sit down on a nearby tree trunk.

The sky changes color as the sun sinks behind the Front Range.

Get up. Start back.

The road begins a long, slow incline toward town, and I find myself thinking about what Esteban told me. Not too long ago this road and the Malecón in Havana were both Spain.

Spain. Hard to believe it. Of course, they have long since parted and they don't remember that they were kin. Here, unlike the Malecón, no one walks. Cars slow, people stare. Who is that person on foot? What can they be about? No good, I'll be—

"María! María, is that you?"

I look up. A Toyota pickup with half a dozen Mexicans crammed in the back.

"How do you know—"

"It's me," Paco says from under a disguise of grime.

He helps me into the truck.

Handshakes. Hellos.

The boys pass me a Corona. I drink it. They tell me they've come from a garbage dump on the far side of the mountain, where they threw out perfectly good refrigerators, radiators, air-conditioning units, and other obsolescences that they've taken from the building they're remodeling on Pearl Street. The boys are mostly from Mexico City or Chiapas. None of them is over twenty-five. Paco seems happy to be with them. Sitting there with the others, drinking beer, telling jokes. He's a different person among these guys, more himself, funnier, younger. I'm a weight. A drag. "We shouldn't be sharing a room anymore, Paco, you should be with your friends," I tell him.

"No, no, I like staying with you," he insists.

"I'm a cramp on your style," I say.

"Never."

He grins, finishes another Corona, shakes his head. Someone passes me a bottle of tequila but I decline and the bottle moves on.

"Did you have a good day?" Paco asks.

A good day? Yes. A productive day. Unless she's got an Oscar stashed away, Mrs. Cooper was not the person who hit my father and left him to die in a ditch. Only one name left on Ricky's garage list. The perfect suspect. Arrogant, rich, careless. He clearly takes meth, pot, alcohol. Gotta be him.

In fact, he's almost too perfect, and if I were in Havana and investigating this case for Hector I'd at least look at a DGI angle—the prime suspect being set up as cover for a Party man. But this isn't Cuba. This is a simpler country.

And Esteban and his deer? A deeper look to take care of that. Maybe also see about that Scientology golf cart. Just to be on the safe side.

We bump along the road. Paco, utterly wiped, lies against me. His eyes are dark and weary. He's definitely not used to manual labor, no matter what he said before.

"Lie on my lap, little Francisco," I tell him.

"I'm dirty," he says.

"Lie down, close your eyes," I tell him.

He smiles and lies down. Some of the other men give him an obscene roar but he tells them to fuck off. I stroke his hair and his smile widens.

"Keep a look out for the motel," he says. "When you see it, tell Hernando to bang on the roof. They won't stop. Angelo's crew are all going to Denver."

More bumps. More beer. "Plenty of food, plenty of beer, plenty of fun, that's America," he mutters. America. Yes. In Cuba it's different. In Cuba you think only with your belly. And at the end of the month when the ration book is running thin, your belly tells you what to do.

"What are you thinking about?" Paco asks dreamily.

"My belly," I tell him, and he laughs and laughs.

"You don't even have one," he says finally.

I do, Paco. I have a cop gut and it tells me that Mrs. Cooper is innocent and time is running out and the real killer's days to walk this Earth are few.

CHAPTER 11

PRAYER IS BETTER THAN SLEEP

Black orchid sky. Black moon. Black dreams. Back on bruised-mouth island. The beat in Vedado. Doctors. Informers. Tourists. Whores. Secret policemen. Secret asylums. Secret prisons. Calling me home. But not yet, I'll come, but not yet.

I dream the song of waking and lie under the sheet, awake.

I pull back the curtain, look through the window.

It's well before dawn. The night is full of dying stars and hidden mass.

A noise on the outside steps. A person.

Who is that over there?

My eyes adapt to the light.

It's Paco. Kneeling. Fingering his rosary.

Does he do this every morning?

Poor kid. Must be scared shitless to be here.

I watch him, fascinated.

He finishes, lifts his head. I let the curtain fall back, lie down again.

A key in the lock. The door creaks open. He comes in.

He looks in my direction, squints, tries to see if I'm awake. Deciding that I'm not, he tiptoes to his bed and takes off his shoes. He removes a white bag of powder from his pocket and puts it carefully in the drawer next to his bed. He lifts the duvet, slithers under it, and rolls onto his side.

He drapes an arm over his eyes and tries to sleep. After a couple of minutes the arm falls to his side. His face assumes a different, more feminine posture. His eyebrows are thick and his features fine, his hair wiry but containable. It's the eyes that give up his wildness, his begging years, his time running with gangs in Managua, or his time—probably exaggerated—as a camp follower of the Sandinistas, a wannabe boy soldier.

Sleeping, he has the face of someone deeper than the front he projects to the world. It's a shame, Paco, that you love America so. You shouldn't fall so hard on the first date.

Not me. In matters of love I take my time. Too choosy, everyone says. The Havana girl whose exception proves the rule.

But you, Francisco, everything's coming to you too easily and too fast. Didn't you listen to Esteban? There's another side to this land, there's a—

His eyes flip open and he catches me staring at him.

"I could feel your look," he says.

"Did I wake you?"

"No. I was awake."

"What time is it?" he asks, sitting up.

"Six . . . Wait a minute, are you just getting in?"

"Yeah."

"Where were you?"

"Denver," he says after a pause.

"Denver? What were you doing there?"

"Manuelito came by at midnight, you were asleep. He was looking for someone to go with him."

"Who's Manuel?"

"You don't know him?"

"No. What were you doing in Denver?" I ask, surprised.

"Clubbing, man," he says in English with a huge grin. He pulls back the sheets and sits on the edge of his bed.

"Clubbing," I repeat.

"You should go."

"I don't think it's my sort of scene," I tell him.

"What is your sort of scene?" he says with a bit of an edge to his voice.

"Not clubbing in Denver," I reply.

He reaches into his boxers and scratches his balls. "You know what your problem is, María?" he says.

"I'm sure you're going to tell me."

"I *am* going to tell you. Your problem is that you act like you're fifty, like you're past it. Christ, man, you're twenty-seven years old. You're in a new country, full of opportunities and people and things, and you're over there hunched with the fucking weight of the world on your shoulders, like you're some old nurse in a cancer ward or something."

"Tell me about the club," I say, refusing the hook.

He shakes his head. "Man, those prices. And those white *chiquitas*. Shit, American girls. College girls," he says to annoy me, which, bizarrely, it does.

"You're disgusting," I let slip.

"Is that what you think?" he says, standing up and walking across the room.

He's all points and edges, and the booze or that white powder has loosened him up.

"Is that what you fucking think?" he repeats.

Oh hell, what next? The punch to the face? The stoned attempt at rape?

"You're high," I tell him.

"I'm not high, didn't you hear what I was saying? I couldn't afford to drink at those prices. Blow my hard-earned cash on ten-dollar beers? No thanks," he says, folding his arms, glaring at me from a few feet away.

"I saw the bag."

"Spying on me? Not that it's any of your business, Esteban asked me to sell it for him and his buyer didn't show, ok?" he says, his voice rising to an indignant bark.

"You're scaring me, Paco. Go back to your own bed, please."

"I'll go wherever I damn well please," he says, but after a moment he sits on his bed.

"We shouldn't even be sharing a room now that all those guys went to L.A. I'll talk to Esteban about it," I say firmly.

"Esteban's in Denver with his lady until Monday morning," Paco says. "But he'll do what you want. You must be the fucking golden girl."

"What does that mean?"

Paco throws something at me. Two things. I pick them up. It's the key to the Range Rover and a cell phone.

"Franco's using the car today but Esteban says you can use it tomorrow to get supplies. Just give him a call."

"I see. That's good."

Paco shakes his head and continues to glare at me.

I've hurt him somehow. I don't need complications, I have to defuse this, now.

"Please, Paco."

" 'Please, Paco,' " he repeats mockingly.

"You *are* high," I say.

"So? You're not my mother. Been working hard. I earned two hundred dollars this week already. I'll make three hundred next week. Pretty soon I'll be foreman of one of the work gangs. And when it gets too cold in January and all these Mexes fuck off to L.A., they'll be begging me to stay."

He grins again, wolfishly. He's acting the big man but he can't hold it for long. Finally the lines crack and a wave of unhappiness spills across his face. He crosses the room, sits on my bed, takes my hand, and kisses it.

"María," he says.

"No, Paco," I say, pulling the hand away.

"No, I'll tell you what your problem is: you're a virgin, that's what's wrong with you. You're a virgin or a fucking lesbian."

"Get off my bed and get the fuck away from me."

"Fuck you," he says, and clicks his fingers in front of my face. He walks back to his side of the room with a satisfied look on his face, but again it doesn't last long. I'm in no mood for this game. I tell him so.

"Oh shit, I'm sorry, María, I'm not high. I tried a little, but I'm not high. I'm, I, I don't know. I'm tired."

He sits down heavily on his bed and closes his eyes. I know he's young and he's emotional, but there's something about his behavior that smacks of . . . what? I can't quite put my finger on it.

"You have every right to be tired. You've worked hard all week," I say conciliatingly.

"Not that kind of tired."

He rubs his hands through his hair, thinking about something. Suddenly he sits up straight, places his hands carefully in his lap, and looks at me. He takes a deep breath and begins: "Listen, María, I don't know who you are or what you're doing here, but I know you're not what you say you are. I know you're not from Mexico and that accent, that's not Yucatán. I had a cousin who played baseball, professionally, for four years in the Cuban league. His wife talks just like you. I don't know who you're running from or what you did, but I know you're not some fucking peasant girl from Valladolíd. You picked a pretty bad disguise. You don't talk like no Indian, you don't look like no Indian. You're a liar and not a good one, either."

He stares at me, trying to radiate trust through those dark green eyes.

For some reason it works.

We've been through the mill, Paco, you and me.

"I was never going to say I was from Yucatán," I begin. "I *was* going to say I was from Mexico City. I'd picked out a neighborhood and everything—Coyoacán—I walked the streets, memorized a few names, but I got spooked on the bus when you said you'd lived there for a while."

"So what are you?" he wonders.

"Cubana."

After a few beats he finds his voice. "That makes no sense. I mean, what game are you playing? Cubans are guaranteed a green card. You don't have to put up with this shit. You could be legal."

"I know."

"So what are you doing here?"

What *am* I doing here? Perhaps explaining it to him will explain it to me. And now it's me who crosses the room. Me who sits on his bed.

"I need to know that I can trust you, Paco."

"You can trust me. And look, María, before you explain, I was only kidding about those American girls. I don't care about them. I was trying to make you feel . . . I was . . . You see, over the last few days, I've become, I've . . ."

His voice fades.

Even in the half-light I can see that his face is crimson with embarrassment.

"Don't say any more," I tell him. "Please."

"No, I want to. I know it's a weird situation. All this. Maybe because we're sharing the same room or because of what happened in New Mexico. I should have protected you there. I felt bad. Terrible. And now this, me and you, you know, I didn't want this to happen, it wasn't part of my big master plan for America, it's just that, well, you know. You understand what I'm saying?"

"Yes."

"And what do you think?"

I shake my head.

He looks at the floor. "Yeah. That's what I thought."

"Besides, I'm older than you," I tell him.

"I'm older than you think," he mutters.

I put my arm around him and kiss him on the cheek. "Paco, I'm sorry. There are lots of reasons. You're too young for me. I'm not— You're not my type."

He looks at me. "You are gay," he says, hurt, angry.

"No."

He smacks his hand into his fist. "It's the fucking Americans, isn't it? All those gringo cocksuckers. They're all fags. They fake it for the movies, but it's a well-known fact that they're all sucking each other's dicks."

He's humiliated. He put it all out there on the line and I've shot him down.

"No, it's not them."

He mutters something I don't get and stands and looks at me, like an actor in a play who has forgotten his lines.

He shakes his head, walks to the window, and peers through the blinds.

Silence creeps into the room and lingers there like a louche relation.

"Cuba," he says at last.

"Yes."

"I can keep a secret," he says.

My lips part, my diaphragm contracts, I breathe in. Oh shit, I'm going to tell him. "I can't tell you," I reply, and then in a deluge of words I unburden myself of the whole thing . . .

Francisco, it turns out, has many shades.

I wouldn't have taken him for a good listener, but he is.

And the questions he does ask are short and to the point.

"How long was your brother in Fairview?"

"Three days."

"Is that long enough?"

"It's all the time we had. But Ricky's good."

"What did your father do here?"

"He worked for High Country Extermination—as a pest controller."

"What's that?"

"A ratcatcher."

"What if Ricky got it wrong?"

"I went to the garage. I looked at their books. I think he got it right."

"What if the person who hit your father didn't use the Fairview garage? What if they had their car towed to Denver?"

"Ricky managed to check the Fairview Towing Company records for all of May."

"Very resourceful, but what if they used a Denver towing company and a Denver garage to do the repairs?"

"In that case, they're going to get away with it. There's no way I can check every garage and every towing company in Denver for May and June."

"If you turn this over to the U.S. police—" he begins but then changes tack. "You already know, don't you?"

"I don't know. I've eliminated one suspect, but there are many things up in the air."

"Who's your prime suspect? Tell me. You know I'm not a yapper, I won't tell anyone," he says eagerly.

"No."

A pause. Yellow light filtering in through the window. Someone yelling in drunken Spanish at the far end of the parking lot.

"What are you going to do once you've found him?"

I shake my head. "I don't know."

His eyes narrow to a Mongolian squint. "You came here to kill him, didn't you? He hit your father and left the scene of the accident. He left him to die by the side of the road."

"It was worse than that. He knocked him off the Old Boulder Road into a gully. He tried to climb back up to the road but he couldn't make it. His lung was punctured. He drowned in his own blood."

Paco's face loses its color. "The Old Boulder Road?"

"Yeah."

"So this hypothetical driver of yours was one of those fucking movie people?"

I don't want him to jump to any conclusions. I don't want him going up there himself. *You were the man in New Mexico, María, but now I'll show you what I can do.* He's the type.

"No. Not necessarily. I don't know for sure."

"It's one of those guys whose homes you've been cleaning. Someone up on Malibu Mountain. It's Cruise, isn't it? Fucking Tom Cruise killed your old man and the Scientologists covered it up."

I roll my eyes. "Francisco, calm down, it's not Tom Cruise."

He nods, clucks his tongue. "So, when are you leaving town?" he asks casually, but we both know it's the key question.

I don't answer.

"Did you hear me?"

"I heard you."

"You don't have to tell me anything," he says.

He opens the window to let in fresh air. He keeps his back turned. He doesn't want me to see his face.

"I have to be back in Mexico by Monday night."

"Monday!" He turns. "What's today? Saturday? Monday! Christ, when were you planning on telling me?"

"I *was* going to tell you," I lie.

"You played me for a sap."

"No, I didn't. I don't have all the pieces yet, I have a lot to do, when I had it all I would have told you."

"Jesus, María. I should have stayed in Denver. No, I should be going to fucking L.A. with everyone else. I only wanted to be here because I thought you'd be here."

"I'm sorry I screwed you up."

"Yeah, you did screw me up. You fucking did."

"Paco—"

"*Chupame la turca,*" he says sadly, goes to the door, opens it, and tries to slam it behind him but even that fucks up and it catches on the back of his heel, tripping him.

"How far are you going to get in your socks?" I yell after him.

I wait for him for a minute. Two.

Bathroom. Mirror. Sink. Splash water. Reflect. My fault. A conversation I should not have had. There's a time for the truth and there's a time for silence. Any good interrogator knows that. Paco's too young to understand. Too immature to be any kind of a confidant for me.

Faucet off.

He opens the door, comes in, crying.

He falls on his bed like a kid.

I sit beside him, stroke his back.

"What will I do after you go home?"

"You'll be fine. You've got a job, friends, you'll be fine."

"I should have stopped those guys in the desert."

"No. You should have done exactly what you did. You kept a cool head and I'm proud of you."

"You've a boyfriend in Havana?"

"No."

"Maybe I'll come see you when I've got some money saved."

"Sure."

Sure.

"I saw you praying."

"Yes."

"What's that like?"

He shakes his head. He doesn't understand the question. He yawns. Time flowing forward in single breaths. Entropy maximizing.

"I'm tired," he says and yawns again.

He starts breathing like a cat.

Up on Obispo, at the Casa de los Arabes, lies Havana's mosque. You can get in only if you're a foreigner or a diplomat or a cop. I went once with Hector to question a man from the Iranian Embassy about activities proscribed by the Koran and also by Cuban law. We were there at dawn, when, Hector explained, an additional line is sung by the muezzin: *Come to the mosque, for prayer is better than sleep.*

I've always liked that. Prayer is better than sleep.

But what if you don't know how to do either?

I want to pray, I want to sleep, both, either, I want to feel something, or nothing. Paco starts to snore, unmoved by such concerns.

"I wish I was more like you," I whisper in his ear, kiss him, and put my blanket on him.

But anyway, it's a lie. I wouldn't want his certainty, the clarity of a believer.

Not yet.

I'll lean into the confusion. The gray area. The dark. Embrace it. Sleep can wait and prayer can wait and into the comfort of the profane world I'll go.

CHAPTER 12

MR. JONES

I need a gun. In Havana I was lit by neon. A rep. The kind that floats up. Only my immediate superiors and the goons in the DGSE or the DGI could fuck with me. But in America the border taught me that life is cheap. The life of an illegal worth less than a dog. And Paco's right. It's Saturday. I've got one day left. The investigative part of this operation is almost over.

Not Mrs. Cooper.

If I can eliminate Esteban's Range Rover and the silly golf cart, it will all boil down to the garage.

There were only two cars in for repairs in the Pearl Street Garage that whole week. Mrs. Cooper's Mercedes and Jack Tyrone's Bentley.

But Jack was in L.A. the night of the accident.

Youkilis was here. Youkilis driving Jack's car? Got to be. It fits with the man, it works with the evidence. Twenty meters from Jack's house, fifteen from Youkilis's front gate. Jack's car and Youkilis drunk or high or both. Coke and ice. Ice and coke. Foreign and domestic. Gives you two trips, two lives.

Youkilis. Take him. Break him. Make him talk. Make him admit it.

And then . . .

Is there any real alternative? The Cuban Interests Section of the Mexican Embassy?

Sure. The ministry claims that Luis Carriles put a bomb on a plane that killed seventy-three people. To this day the Yankees have refused to extradite him to Cuba.

It has to be in-house. I'm ok with it. It feels right.

For all of recorded history and for the million years before that humans have taken vengeance into their own hands. A simple code. Kill one of ours, we'll kill one of yours. The simplest code there is. Only in the last century or two have people given this job to outsiders. To police, lawyers, courts. And no one really buys into that 100 percent. Certainly not in Cuba, where the old ways walk the streets of Cerro and Vedado. This is what Ricky doesn't understand. He's never walked those streets. Cops and the rule of law are a blip in deep time.

No, we don't completely believe in them and some part of us remembers that revenge isn't just a right—it's a sacred obligation.

And why else did I come here? Why?

Overthinking. Need to be doing, not thinking.

Supplies. Duct tape, cuffs, map, markers, sledgehammer. And most of all—a gun.

In another ensemble from Angela's cupboard I walk out of the motel. Brown cotton skirt, beige blouse, black sweater, black jacket. Backpack. No lipstick, no makeup. Wool hat low over my eyes. No attempt to look my best. This is the business end of my journey here. An ugly business.

I turn left for Fairview and again note that Toyota with the New York plates. No man sleeping inside this time because it's later.

One sighting was bad but two have me worried. Someone's keeping an eye on the motel. An INS agent? A fed following up a lead from New Mexico?

It's *something*. Think about it.

Down the hill to town. I walk past Starbucks and Dolce and Gabbana and a Ferrari dealership. Dean and Deluca. Whole Foods. Past a paradise of fruit and bread.

I turn on Arapahoe Street and enter the Safeway.

Aisle 2: Hardware. Knife, tape, rope.

Aisle 3: Winter clothes. Ski mask, gloves.

Aisle 6: Electrical. Flashlight, batteries.

Aisle 8: Grocery. Coffee, butter, bacon—so the purchases don't look quite so menacing.

Pay.

Load up my backpack.

How many dollars left from my carefully husbanded bribe money, payoff money, and wages?

Six twenties and a five. Is that enough for a firearm? I walk down Manitou Road to what passes for the bad part of town.

A 7-Eleven, a couple of liquor stores, boarded-up shops—notices on the boards that all this has been rezoned for urban renewal.

Next to a sex shop is Fairview's only pawnbroker.

In the window: a bicycle, a baby stroller, a fur coat, guns.

I go inside.

Skinny kid in a blue T-shirt reading an SAT prep book. Looks up at me briefly and back down at his book.

A whole row of handguns in a glass cabinet in front of him, the cheapest a .38 police special for $180. I'm fifty-five bucks short. But it doesn't matter anyway—a sign on the wall says HANDGUNS FOR SALE TO US CITIZENS ONLY and another informs me that BACKGROUND CHECKS WILL BE ENFORCED AT ALL TIMES.

This kid doesn't seem the type who is authorized to haggle or bend the rules.

Damn it. I turn, go to the door. Kid looks up again.

"Help you with anything?" he asks.

"No, thank you."

He goes back to his college book, and as I nod goodbye I notice something that actually might be very useful. Behind him on a rack are half a dozen sets of police handcuffs and above that, cans of pepper spray. I've used pepper spray before in the PNR but it's a controlled substance in Havana and private citizens are not permitted to purchase it. Pimps like it, though—gun possession is an automatic year in jail, whereas having a can of pepper spray can be bribed out of court. Once I traded two cans of CS gas for twenty bucks and a week's tickets from the ration book. Eggs, sugar, flour. Ricky and I made a birthday cake for Mom.

"How much for the pepper spray?" I ask.

"Twenty dollars."

"Do I need a permit to buy it?"

"No."

"And how much for the steel handcuffs?" I ask.

The boy looks at the price label.

"Fifteen."

Out into the street two minutes later. A snow flurry. I pull on my wool hat. I still need a gun.

Plan B.

I fish out the ad from the *Fairview Post*: "For sale: Thorpe hunting Rifle new 750 dollars. Smith and Wesson M&P 9mm good con with ammo 400 dollars OBO."

The address is 44 Lime Kiln Road, about two kilometers north out of town. I don't have the cash but my plan is not to buy the weapon.

Risky, but I don't see any other choice. Esteban has a rifle in his apartment but Esteban's in Denver, the apartment's locked, and no one else in the Mex Motel owns a gun.

Noon.

Go there now before you lose your nerve.

I walk to the crossroads at the liquor store. Lime Kiln is a narrow two-lane curving northwest into the mountains. No sidewalk but there is a trail next to the tree line.

Walk it.

Twenty minutes along the wood.

Cars and SUVs racing past on the downhill lane at close to a hundred kilometers per hour.

The dull clothes better than camouflage, just another Mex going about her silent business, just another invisible with no plans or dreams or thoughts in her head. No one slows to avoid showering me with stones, no one notices me at all.

After half an hour the gradient increases and the trees thin out and there are half a dozen houses next to one another. I read numbers on mailboxes.

Number 44 is a little yellow trailer home set off from the others.

A whole lot of people around. Kids playing, people raking leaves, a lady with a blanket over her legs reading a book.

All these witnesses. This is fucked. Should have scouted this yesterday. This is a night op.

It's two kilometers back to town. I'm not going back.

Before they notice me I dart into the woods to check out the approach from the rear.

Some of the houses have tall antibear fences but number 44 does not. Just a grassy yard and a well-worn path leading into the woods.

Tires, a workbench, a lathe, half a Dodge pickup parked in the yard.

If I was a pro I'd scout and make notes and wait but I have no time for that, and besides, something tells me to go for it, now. That something is desperation.

I walk out from under the tree cover and approach the rear of the trailer home. I reach into the backpack, remove the ski mask, and pull it over my head. I put the knife into the lock on the screen door. Pull. The plastic gives with a loud snap.

Two houses over, a dog barks. The barking becomes a low growl and then stops.

Heart hammering. *This is crazy. Get out now.* I turn the handle on the back door and enter a tiny, dirty kitchen. Pots and pans on a gas stove, a box of pancake mix on a table next to a carton of milk. A smallish black dog is sleeping in a wool-lined box near a washing machine. The dog blinks and looks up at me. He registers my presence and rests his head back down on his paws.

This is stupid, Mercado. Get out of here.

I tighten the grip on my knife and push the door to the next room.

A living/dining room and a man, watching TV in a reclining chair. His back is to me but I can see a white hand holding a can of beer. I can't tell if he's big, small, young, old. The other hand must have the TV remote because every fifteen or twenty seconds the channel flips.

The room is painted a dull yellow and, apart from a few newspaper fragments on the floor, is quite tidy. There are cupboards along the wall, and through the front window I can see the children throwing an American football to one another.

The longer I stand here the harder it's going to be.

I pad gently across the floor with as much silence and economy of movement as my nerves will permit.

I look at the knife.

How am I going to do this?

Quickly.

One op. No second chances.

I stand behind him, look down at the top of his head. Bald, with a gray fringe around the edge.

I grip the knife, take a deep breath, and in one fast slice of air it's at his throat.

"Don't move," I tell him.

"The fuck," he says but doesn't move.

"This is a hunting knife and it's on your jugular vein. Don't move or I'll cut the vein and you'll be dead in under a minute. Do you understand?"

"Yeah, I understand," he says with surprising equanimity—as if one of the hassles of everyday life was the occasional knife-wielding maniac jumping up from your sofa while you're watching TV.

"Put down the beer," I tell him.

"What do you want from me?" he asks.

"Put down the beer."

He sets the beer can on a side table next to the chair.

"What do you want from me?" he asks again.

Keeping the knife against his vein, I reach out with the handcuffs and place them on his thigh.

"Very slowly handcuff your wrists together," I tell him.

"I ain't gonna do it. You're going to kill me," he says.

"No one is going to die. Soon I'll be leaving and you'll go back to your TV show. I promise if you do what I say you will not be hurt."

"Hmm, I don't know," he says.

"Do I sound like a killer?"

"I wouldn't know."

"Just do it!"

He slides his wrists into the cuffs. "Never had a pair of these on before," he mutters.

When his hands are fully clipped I step out from behind the chair. The ski mask startles him and I take that stunned second to check the cuffs. Tight. Good.

He's not what I'm expecting. About sixty-five, maybe seventy, wearing a plaid shirt and dark blue jeans. His face says that he's lived a lot of life. Blue-collar outdoor stuff. His eyes are green and sharp and kindly. It would be very hard to have to kill this man.

"Why don't you sit down?" he says.

"I will."

I turn off the TV and sit in the rocking chair opposite him. Rocking chair. A heartbeat ago I was in Santiago de Cuba watching little Ricky sitting down triumphantly in Uncle Arturo's rocking chair, winning the game, Mom laughing, Dad winking, Lizzy bursting into floods of tears. A blink and the years are gone like playing cards. And Cuba's gone and I'm in the dream world, America, opposite an elderly man in an unnamed hamlet outside a mountain town in Colorado and Dad's dead and Ricky's gay and Mom's got pre-Alzheimer's and I haven't spoken to Lizzy or Esme or Uncle Arturo for a decade.

"Well," the man says. "What can I do ye for?"

"Pardon?"

"What can I do ye for?"

"I have come about your advertisement in the newspaper."

"What ad?"

"For the guns."

"I can detect by your accent that you ain't from around these parts."

"No."

His eyes twinkle. "Well, I have to tell you, ma'am, that in general this here thing with the knife and the handcuffs is not how you're supposed to respond to a small ad in the newspaper."

"I need the handgun," I tell him.

He nods, scratches his nose. "Why is that? If you don't mind me asking," he says.

"I need it for protection and I don't have enough money to buy one downtown."

He clears his throat. "Ok. Just let me get this straight. You think someone's trying to harm you and you want to get a gun to protect yourself, but you don't have much money, so you thought you'd break into my house and steal one of my weapons?"

"Yes."

He thinks for a second and nods. "Well, ma'am, if you're willing to take a risk like that then I reckon you're in a heap of trouble, all right."

I nod in agreement.

"I got two daughters myself. Both in California."

"Hmmm."

"Two daughters, four grandchildren. All girls. Not a boy among them. Don't get me wrong. I ain't complaining. Thank the Lord they is all healthy."

"Mister, uh . . ."

"Oh, you can call me Jonesy, everyone pretty much calls me Jonesy. And I won't take it as a sign of disrespect if you don't want to tell me your name considering the circumstances.

"Thank you, sir," I say.

A pause and then a look of cunning. "Well now, missy, how much money you got?" he asks.

"About ninety dollars."

"Ninety bucks? My oh my. You're right about that. That ain't a whole lot of nothing these days. Well, I know you've kind of got me over a barrel here, but I'd be very reluctant to part with that brand-new Smith & Wesson nine-millimeter for less than a hundred dollars, no matter how I come to it, but I've got some older models you might wanna use for personal protection. Good guns. Stop any ex-boyfriend, ex-husband, that kind of thing. Stop a bull elephant if you was close enough. Lessen you is set on the M and P."

"I don't care what the gun is as long as it works."

He smiles. "Yup, that's what I reckoned. Well, if you'll open that red cupboard over there. The key is on top of the TV."

I find the key and open the cupboard. Half a dozen hunting rifles and a drawer full of revolvers and semiautomatic pistols. Many more guns than he needs for personal protection. Obviously a dealer or a collector of some kind.

I look back to check that he's still sitting. He hasn't stirred.

"Ok. You want an M and P? Good choice, by the way. The new one is over on the left-hand side but I got one with a little bit of scoring on the handle, very similar gun, 1997, shoots real good, just under the—"

"I see it," I say, pulling it out. Looks perfect, not heavy. The grip a little big for me, but not too unwieldy.

"You like it?" he asks.

"Yes."

"Excellent, ninety bucks even for her and no questions asked. She's a beaut, shot her myself behind the old homestead here. Fires pretty steady up to fifty feet."

"I'll take it." To prove my honesty I remove four twenties and other bills from my pocket and hand them to him. He grins, showing a couple of missing teeth, the first American I've seen with that very Cuban look.

"Tell you what, let's call it seventy. Can't say fairer than that. That's a good gun. Serial number filed—not by me, I don't do that kind of thing. Not my line. Serial number's gone but it wouldn't be fair dealing if I didn't tell you that in the Salt Lake City police department there's a ballistics report saying that there handgun was used in an armed robbery. Smart cop might be able to trace it back. You shoot that ex-boyfriend of your'n and they'll have you for armed robbery too. And of course, if you ever brought up my name I'd deny everything."

"I understand."

"Good, good. Well, we're almost done here, I reckon."

"We are done, thank you."

"Don't go running off now just yet. You and me got off to a rocky start, but ain't that the way sometimes? We're fast friends now."

"I've got what I came for."

"Wait a minute, you're going to need something from me and I'm gonna need something from you."

Suspicion makes me frown under the ski mask.

"What do I need from you?"

"Don't you want some shells?"

For a second I don't understand what he's talking about. Why would I want shells?

"Ammo," he clarifies.

"Yes, of course."

"Fair trade, I'll give you enough for a clip. Gratis. But you gotta remove these here handcuffs. There's no way I can tell any of the neighbors around here to cut 'em off. Laugh themselves silly. And as for calling Sheriff Briggs, forget it."

"What are you saying?" I ask him.

"Bottom drawer of the cupboard. Standard nine-millimeter rounds. I want you to load your clip and when you're done, throw me that handcuff key. I'll uncuff myself, you'll take your gun. You go out the way you came in and we'll say no more about it."

"Sounds reasonable, as long as the ammo isn't dud."

"It's good stuff. A-grade. Dry as a hornet's nest."

I find the ammo box and load eight rounds into the clip. The spring has a little more give than I would like but it's not bad for an older weapon.

I throw him the handcuff key. He fumbles with it but eventually uncuffs himself. I take the cuffs and key and put them in my pocket.

"What now?" I wonder.

"There is no *what now*," he says. "What now is you going and me staying and us never meeting again."

He sits in his chair and picks up the beer can. He hits the remote and the TV comes to life.

I walk into the kitchen and slip out the back door and down the yard.

I'm half expecting a shotgun blast tearing up the air around me, but nothing happens.

I dart into the woods and take off the ski mask.

No one follows me on the road back to town and everything's real smooth until Sheriff Briggs in his black Escalade pulls in beside me.

Bad judge of character—I didn't figure the old man for someone who would call the cops.

Briggs leans out the window. "Aren't you one of Esteban's . . . Wait a minute, I know you. I got you myself, day before yesterday. What the hell are you doing down here?"

No, Mr. Jones isn't a *chivato*, this is just the Mercado luck.

Briggs handbrakes the car and takes off his aviator sunglasses.

Looks at me. I look at him.

A spark.

That man and I know each other. In other lives or other universes our paths have crossed. We're right to be wary.

Let me see you, Sheriff. Let me really see you.

Skin the tone of a throat-cut murder victim. Eyes the blue ice of an alien moon.

"Asked you a question."

No muscle in his face moves when he speaks, his voice slipping between his thin lips like one of Mother's voodoo spirits.

"I must have gotten lost, sir," I say in Spanish.

"Lost? Christ on a bike, your people managed to fucking walk here from Siberia and you can't find your way around a town with half a dozen streets?"

"I took a wrong turn," I suggest.

After this remark, which seems to highlight a prima facie case of falsehood, he hesitates for a moment and then pulls out a packet of cigarettes.

Something's up, something's not quite right.

"Lost, eh?" he repeats.

"*Sí, señor.*"

"Gonna tell you one more time, cut out the Mex."

"Yes, sir."

He opens the car door and gets out. "Gonna search you, sister. If you got any large sums of money on you, you and Esteban are in for the fucking high jump. I don't care if the INS is fucking with the program, I'm not that desperate. I run this town, not him, get me?"

"Yes, sir, but I have no money, sir."

Just a ski mask, a gun, a fucking sledgehammer.

"I'll be the judge of that. Take off the pack."

I let it drop. Gently.

Towering over me, he pats me down, his big horrendous paws touching my sides and ass. He looks inside my shoes and pulls my sweater forward to look down my bra.

"What's in the backpack?"

Lies. Lies that won't get believed.

Here it comes—

The big paws pummeling me. Smashing down and down. Blood pouring from my nose and mouth. From my eyes. Drowning in blood. Screaming nerve endings. Pain. Mercy shot to the head. Shallow grave in the woods. A missing Mex. The world doesn't hesitate on its ellipse.

"Fucking deaf? What's in the backpack?"

"Cleaning supplies."

"Open it up."

The radio crackles inside the SUV.

"Sheriff?"

Briggs reaches through the window and grabs the mike. "This is Briggs."

"Sheriff, we got a twenty-two on the Interstate. Messy one."

"Shit. Deaths?"

"I don't know, Sheriff, at least three vehicles. One of them's on fire, so I reckon Channel Nine will send up the chopper."

"I'll be right over," Briggs says and gets back in the Escalade.

"Mex town is at the top of the hill and turn left," he says.

"Thank you, *señor*."

"And don't let me catch you in this neighborhood again. Decent folks along here."

"No, sir."

He starts the engine, drives off.

When the SUV disappears over the brow of the next hill my body wilts.

Relief. Exhaustion.

I sit down on the grass verge. December in Colorado, but the sun is shining and it's warm—not Havana warm, not hot enough to melt that lake in Wyoming; but a dry, wearisome mountain heat.

Get up. Hoof it.

After a klick I find a sign on a forest trail that says ROAD CLOSED— SUBSIDENCE DANGER. That might come in handy. I roll up the sign, put it in my backpack. As I'm zipping another car slows and a voice says, "Me to the rescue. Need a ride?"

CHAPTER 13

THE PRINCES OF MALIBU

The white Bentley, Jack leaning his head out the passenger's-side window.

"Yes, please," I replied, and once again I was annoyed that I wasn't wearing lipstick or looking my best.

"Get in. Ever been in a Bentley before?"

"No."

"Get in, get in. I'll put the top down. You can't put the top down without a beautiful girl next to you, it's obligatory, says it right there in the owner's manual."

I sat in the passenger's seat. He pressed a button and the roof slid back. The Bentley accelerated away from the curb with a feline roar.

"I'm probably the oldest 'girl' you've had in this car."

"How old are you?"

I gave him what I hoped was an ironic look.

"Yeah, I know, not the sort of question you're supposed to ask. Tip— don't ask actors, either."

"I know how old you are," I told him.

"You looked me up in Wikipedia?"

"I don't know what that is. At that party you had I heard you say that you tell producers you're twenty-nine, but your older résumés say you're thirty and really you're thirty-one."

"Goddammit, *in vino veritas*, eh? Shit."

"I don't think it was vino."

"No it wasn't. A-rated, two-fifty-a-spliff Vancouver hemp—that's what it was. We got it in for Pitt, except he didn't stay. His loss—supremo shit. Course I don't need to tell you, you're from Mexico."

I gave him another look that he missed. "If that acting career doesn't work out, I'm sure they'll hire you in the diplomatic corps, Señor Jack."

He burst out laughing. "Yeah, I guess that was a bit crass."

I smiled to show I wasn't in the least offended and for some reason this made him grin like an idiot. He touched me on the leg. The Bentley had barely been going thirty but as the undulating road flattened out he gunned it up to seventy. It accelerated so smoothly it was as if we were in a studio and the landscape was a back projection.

"Beaut, isn't she? Valet parkers fucking kill themselves for the keys. Like it?"

Like it? Nothing in Cuba moved like this. The fifties Yankee cars with Russian engines and jerry-rigged suspensions, the cheap Chinese imports, the Mexican Beetles. I thought all cars rattled and roared until I rode in the back of Sheriff Briggs's Escalade.

"It's ok," I told him.

"Yeah, it'll do," he agreed.

It was a break to actually be in this car with him. I couldn't let it go by.

Men loved to talk about their cars. "Is it from this year?" I asked prepping the ground so I could slip in an important question.

"Oh yeah, 2007, I'll keep it for a couple of years and then I'm thinking of getting a DB9. Course it won't be a DB9 in a few years, but it'll still be an Aston Martin. The valets will love that, too."

"I noticed a little repair on the hood."

"Oh God, yeah. My dad told me once, never lend a friend money and never let anyone drive your car. Never."

"What happened?"

"Few months back, I was in L.A., something wrong's with Paul's Beemer. Borrowed the Bentley to drive downtown. Couldn't handle it. The Bentley needs care and attention. You treat it like a lady. Jesus, he's a fucking idiot. I love him, of course, but he's still an idiot."

"He was in an accident?"

"Oh yeah, but he was fine. Dent and a ding. No big deal."

"He crashed your car?"

"No, no, well, yes, but it wasn't a biggie. The garage fucked up the repair, if you want to know. You shouldn't even be able to see it. Nearest dealership is in Texas and I'm not driving it to Texas. So anyway, what about you? What are you doing out here?"

"I wanted to see some of the country."

"Should have been here a few weeks ago, the leaves were at their peak."

When we hit the outskirts of Fairview, Jack turned to me. His face had assumed a rigid intensity. He was either about to lie to me or he was going to try some of his acting.

"Listen, uh, M . . ."

"María."

"I remembered! Come on. María, of course, listen, I've been invited to this dinner party and they said bring a date and I called Paul and he couldn't come up with anybody this late and I know this is kind of short notice, but, hell, do you wanna come?"

"Paul won't be there?"

"No."

"I'll come."

"What's the matter, you don't like Paul?"

"No."

"Lot of women don't like him. He's a good guy, you know, comes across as a bit of an ass. But basically a good chap, a really good egg."

"Yes."

"Can you tell that that was an English accent?"

"I don't know, I've never drunk tea or met an Englishman in my life."

"Lucky old you. L.A. is plagued by them. They're all very insecure. I know a couple of writers. They're the worst. Chain-smoking Marlboro reds, ridiculous."

"You know English writers? Have you read the poet Philip Larkin?" I asked him.

"The what? The who?"

"It doesn't matter."

"Anyway, where were we? Oh yes. So you'll come?"

"To a party, yes," and wordlessly I added *It's been a trying day.*

"You'll come? You'll be my date?" he asked insecurely.

"I said yes."

"Ok, well, don't freak, but I'm kind of on my way over there right now."

I wasn't following him. "Why would I *freak*?"

"It's a party. Don't you need, like, three hours to get ready?"

"No, but I'll bet you do."

He laughed. "Low blow, yet strangely accurate. We're all fags now, although I'm not as vain as some, believe me, I could tell you stories," he says, fluffing his gelled hair in the rearview.

"But I do want some time. Look at me."

"You look great."

"Pull in there."

Gas station. He spent a small fortune filling the Bentley while I washed my face and attempted to make my hair slightly interesting with the hot-air hand dryer.

I pinched some color into my cheeks and applied red lipstick.

I looked ok and if anyone said I didn't I had a sledgehammer and a Smith & Wesson to change their mind.

"Whose house is it?" I asked when we're back in the car.

"Oh, no one you would know, unless you read the trades, which you probably don't. Not someone conventionally famous, but very A-list, a producer, big enchilada in a behind-the-scenes kind of way."

"What's his name?"

"Alan Watson. Look him up on IMDB, more movies this year than Judd fucking Apatow. Producing or coproducing credit on half a dozen flicks. Playa with a capital P. Total wacko, of course. All the big ones are. The house is only two doors away from the Cruise estate at the top of the mountain. And with Cruise shooting pickups for that Nazi movie, this week Watson is the big bear on Malibu Mountain."

The house was indeed only two doors from the Cruise estate at the top of the mountain, but those doors were at least half a kilometer apart. The homes up here were all huge *poronga* affairs, faux Swiss chalets or supersized mountain ski lodges with ample grounds, guesthouses, outdoor Jacuzzis, pools, stables. Esteban said that Cruise and a few others had their own private ski runs to the valley and even chairlifts that ran back up to the house.

Watson's house did not have a private ski run that I could see but it did have three floors and was the size of a small Havana apartment building. The style was Spanish hacienda with ultramodern features: radio antennae, quadruple garage, satellite dishes, swimming pool, solar panels, and a wind turbine that probably massacred local birds by the score. Even without Esteban's and Jack's prep it would have been obvious to me that Watson was in the upper echelons of the power elite.

Judging from the cars outside, the party appeared to be a small but upscale affair. Two Mercs, a Rolls-Royce, a Ferrari, and Jack's Bentley.

We rang the bell and I admired the paintwork on the cars. In Havana all vehicles except for the very newest are finished in glossy outdoor house paint, but these were in subtle attractive shades: racing green, midnight blue, morning gray. As you got wealthier, I speculated, your tastes rebelled against the primary colors of the common herd.

Jack had yet to learn that lesson with his white Bentley.

We rang the bell again and someone said, "It's open!"

We walked through a bare marble foyer into an equally spartan dining room that looked west upon a sunset and eight or nine layers of mountains. We were the last to arrive, and a fortysomething redheaded woman in a beautiful emerald couture dress hastily introduced us to the four other guests. Jack knew only one of them personally—a shaven-headed man wearing a black polo-neck sweater, black sweat pants, and diamond earrings.

"Mr. Cunningham, this is my friend María," he said.

Cunningham took my hand and kissed it.

"Delighted to meet you, miss," Cunningham said with such a warm smile and wonderful manners that I knew he was homosexual. Actually, it turned out that all the men were gay except for Watson, who, as Jack had predicted, proved to be a bit of a wacko.

I was seated next to the redheaded woman, who called herself Miss Raven, and a young man in a plaid shirt, jeans, and glasses who said he was "Mickey, just Mickey," in a throwback New York accent straight from the Yuma movies of the fifties.

Miss Raven opened two bottles of sparkling wine and the chat flowed between the men. They talked fast and I found myself dipping in and out of their conversation.

"Jack, I loved you in that thing you were in. Your acting is an homage to a bygone age."

"What about those writers?"

"What about them? Jack Warner said they were 'scum with Underwoods.'"

"No shop talk. Did any of you see that Richard Serra show? It was appalling. What a confidence man that character is—all those pseudoscientific names for his pieces. That's how you spot a bad artist—the pseudoscientific name. 'Trajectory Number Five.' 'Tangent on Circle.' Of course, the *New Yorker* review and Charlie Rose were positively supine."

"I hardly read *The New Yorker,* not since they got a pop music critic called Sasha Frere-Jones. Frere-Jones indeed. I imagine some twenty-three-year-old Barnard girl whose parents are influential condo board members in the East Seventies. I occasionally glance at the odd movie review. Such poor grammar. Lane's sentences have more clauses than a fucking Kris Kringle convention."

"I saw him once in Vail."

"Vail? Good God, I wouldn't be seen dead in Vail."

"Clooney loves it."

"He's a bullshit artist like all the others. I mean, do you really believe Clooney when he tells us that Budweiser is the King of Beers?"

Miss Raven didn't speak but smiled at me from time to time, as if to apologize for my exclusion from the shop talk and gossip. I appreciated her concern but I wasn't getting annoyed. The wine was delightful and the view excellent and from the kitchen came the smell of good things. I could see that Jack was frustrated, though, itching to jump in, but he lacked pluck. Why they'd invited him was a mystery—perhaps he was a last-minute replacement for someone else.

When we were halfway through the second bottle of sparkling wine, Watson appeared with hors d'oeuvres on a silver tray. He was wearing a leather bondage suit, a leather mask, handcuffs, and leg irons. When he served us he kneeled on the floor next to Miss Raven until she clicked her fingers and he removed the empty tray.

I had been in Havana's many brothels dozens of times and had seen a lot worse. Jack, too, appeared unruffled, always acting, this time giving us the fixed smile of someone dancing with a little girl at a wedding.

More bottles. More food.

And gradually he and I were brought into the talk. I was passed off as an old friend who worked in the hotel business. I went along with the lie and let Jack build the cathedral—I was looking at land here in Fairview for the Mandalay Bay group. Vail was over and Aspen hopelessly passé—Fairview, with its easy access to Denver and a back road to Boulder, was the place to invest. I was pushed on the veracity of these claims and my unwillingness to confirm any of the details impressed everyone with my discretion. Miss Raven seemed pleased that I was there. Watson's antics had long since ceased to amuse her and when the conversation became drearily shoppy she talked to me about the weather and clothes.

Jack found his niche and as he relaxed he allowed himself to speak more freely. He drank and began to enjoy himself. I suppose this was the kind of slightly risqué high-powered party he'd been expecting to find in L.A. and hadn't ever gotten invited to. It wasn't exactly the dinner feast of the Satyricon but it wasn't bad. Oysters and shrimp were followed by duck, all three flown in from some picturesque spot in Alaska that very morning, and the excellent wine was from Watson's own vineyard in Sonoma.

Time and food and conversation flowed, and when Watson went into the kitchen to load the dishwasher, Miss Raven produced a 150-year-old vintage Madeira and preembargo Monte Cristo cubanos.

With a bottle under his belt Jack was waxing on his favorite topic: the up-and-down career of Jack Tyrone. "Yeah, the Independent Spirit nomination was a real boost, I'm getting leads now. I'm doing this movie called *Gunmetal*, medium budget, I play a British Victoria Cross winner in the Crimean War. You wouldn't believe the script changes. It's based on the video game but it's gone in a totally different direction. We're throwing this Brit guy into the future, steam punk, all that."

"You're playing a Brit?" Mickey asked skeptically.

"But of course, my dear sir," Jack said in his faux English diphthongs.

"Don't like the title. Don't see the connection," another of the other producers said. He was a svelte, tanned man in a tailored polo shirt and an expensive toupee.

"But that's the whole thing, you see," Jack said. "All the Victoria Cross medals are made from gunmetal from cannons that the Brits captured in the Crimea. So the title sneakily refers to the medals but it's also about the first-person shooter."

The dishwasher loaded and the kitchen cleaned, Watson came back and kneeled next to Miss Raven. She drummed her fingernails on his leather-encased head while Jack went on and on. Some of the men were looking bored and I wished Jack would give it a rest, but unfortunately he wasn't capable of that. Cunningham finally interrupted the flow.

"Who's this with?"

"Focus, for Universal."

"I'll speak to them. *Gunmetal* won't fly. Sounds too John Woo. Doesn't work for a historical."

Jack wanted to defend his picture, which hadn't even begun rolling yet, but he had the sense not to offend the producer. "Do you have any suggestions?"

Cunningham puffed cigar smoke and considered it. "Keep it short, go with *Crimea*."

"Well, it's not really up to me," Jack said.

The producer with the toupee looked at him, strangely, as if regarding a particularly rare specimen in a butterfly net: My God, who is this person that eats with us yet doesn't have the power to change the title of a movie?

I sipped some of the Madeira. It was sweet, rich, very good.

Miss Raven stared at me, hoping that I had something to say.

Titles, I thought to myself, what do I know about titles?

Time Can Be Either Particle or Wave.

"I like *Gunmetal*," Watson said, surprisingly, from behind his mask. "But it *is* too John Woo. *Gunmetal Sky*, *Gunmetal Gray*—those work better and they're short. Titles should be two or three syllables at most."

Watson's words hung in the air like a failed bon mot. It was easy to ignore him as long as he wasn't saying anything, but now that he'd broken the spell we couldn't help but see this bondage-encased man kneeling on the floor next to us.

Watson knew he'd screwed up and with a haughty look from Miss Raven he scurried off to the kitchen.

The party ended in anticlimax. Miss Raven asked us if we would mind forgoing coffee as she had urgent business to attend to in the dungeon. The men said it was no problem. She thanked everyone for coming, asked them to see themselves out, and with a bored sigh followed Watson into the kitchen.

Jack and the others walked outside and Jack gave Cunningham his phone number. It was cold now. Jack took off his jacket and placed it around my shoulders.

We said good night and got in the Bentley.

Jack wasn't happy. Something had upset him. "What's the matter?" I asked. "You're upset about the movie-title thing?"

"No, titles are like gossamer. Change all the time. Did you hear what Mickey said earlier? He said that my acting was an homage to the icons of yesteryear."

"Isn't that a compliment?"

"Like fuck it is. He was saying I was a lousy actor. Fucking queer, what does he know?"

"Mickey likes you. Miss Raven told me so."

Jack's mood did a one-eighty. A grin like a Party kid meeting Jefe at Pioneer Camp. "Really? Really? She said that?"

"Yes," I assured him.

"Oh, shit, really? Maybe I got the wrong end of the stick there. Yeah, he's a good guy. And you know, it's not true about my acting. I've gotten good notices. Paul says I just missed out on a SAG award, and A. O. Scott said that in *We'll Always Have Parricide* I was 'the sole bearer of a lifebelt in this shipwreck of a movie.' Clever, right? Did you ever see that one? *We'll Always Have Parricide*? It was a black comedy, you know? Bandwagon stuff, Luke Wilson vehicle, I was third banana."

"I didn't see it."

"Well, you didn't miss much. I've got the DVD at home if you want to take a look."

"Sure."

We accelerated out of the driveway and the gates opened for us as if by magic. Jack paused to see if there was anything happening at the Cruise estate but the lights were off and the Cruises abed.

"Can I give you a ride to Wetback—to the, uhm, I mean, the motel?"

"Don't worry, I know what everybody calls it."

"It's just a joke. It's not mean."

"I'm not offended."

A look of obvious conspiracy flashed in his eyes followed by that boyish salesman smile. "Or, or, would you, uh, like to come back to my place for coffee?"

"Your place. Coffee," I said quickly.

The ride to Jack's took fifteen minutes. It was a five-minute drive but Jack had had that bottle.

The irony did not impress me at the time because I was tipsy too, but I saw it eventually.

This car. This road. An intoxicated driver. Me. Dad. Enabler. Avenger.

We arrived at the house. I stumbled as I got out. Jack caught me before I fell.

I had never had such heady stuff in my life.

Tipsy, but not drunk.

I knew what I was doing. I knew what was going to happen. There were a million opportunities to back out. No one put a gun to my head.

A gun to my head. Yeah, that's right, more irony.

"Shall we go inside?"

"Please."

"Let me get your bag."

"Leave it."

"Christ, that's heavy, whatcha got in there?"

A telephone call to the motel would have put a stop to it. *Paco, come.* But I made no calls. Didn't want to. Jack was the antithesis of all those cadaver boys in Havana.

Jack was alive, funny, insecure, overconfident.

Jack was all those Yuma movies and TV shows.

Jack was America.

We went in and he took off his jacket and surreptitiously wrote something on a pad next to the phone table.

"Martini?" he asked. "Even when I'm sort of on the wagon I allow myself one at the end of the day."

"Yes," I said.

"Tip from Paul. A stiff drink and one—but only one—Ambien and all the cares of the world disappear . . . How do you like yours? Your martini?"

"Whatever way you're having it."

When he went into the kitchen I looked at the note he'd made on the scribble pad. It said: "1) Chk Richard Serra MOMA/Met? 2) New Yorker— tell Paul subscribe."

Very sinister.

"You want me to find that Luke Wilson DVD?" Jack shouted.

"If you want to."

Jack came back with the martinis and began showing me the various objets d'art and interesting pieces of furniture he had in his living room. He had somehow forgotten that I had been in this house twice already and dusted all this shit.

I listened. He told jokes. I laughed.

Upstairs he showed me his awards, his film books, his signed scripts, and that hideous framed poster of the twins in spaceship uniforms.

"What do you think?" he said, pointing at the poster.

"Who are they?"

Jack's jaw dropped and hung there.

"It's Kirk! From *Star Trek*. The two captains. Look, down there, signed by Shatner himself."

I had heard of *Star Trek* but that particular Yuma series had never made it to Cuba.

"I thought the captain was bald," I said.

"Jesus Christ, that's Picard! Forget him, this is the main dude. Bill's the man. Did you ever see *Fight Club*? Remember what Pitt said when they asked him who he'd want to fight in the whole world?"

"I did not see *Fight Club*."

"Shit, man. No *Star Trek*, no *Fight Club* . . . I mean, you had electricity, right, where you're from, right?"

"Electricity? No, we only just got fire a few years ago, but that was useful because it helped scare away all the dinosaurs that kept marauding the village."

Jack laughed and kissed me on the cheek. "Oh, María, you crack me up. You're funny. No, no, let me tell you, I'm proud of this. It's from 'The Enemy Within,' episode five, you know, the two Kirks? I wanted 'Mirror Mirror,' but then I figured that if I ever got an opportunity to meet Nimoy, I'd get him to sign a 'Mirror Mirror' poster, the two Spocks. Good idea, huh?"

"Very."

"I'd thought about getting a goatee myself like the evil Spock for *Gunmetal*, but everybody's nixed it. The Brits back then wore mustaches, not goatees. Besides, after all the 'Mirror Mirror' parodies you'd feel like an idiot."

"Yes."

"Probably should move the poster to my place in L.A. More traffic through there, tell the story, impress them with my *Trek* lore. Youkilis says I should move full-time to L.A., but I'm a Colorado boy and Fairview is white hot for celebs right now and it's still got that small-town feel."

"It does."

"Yeah, you really get to know people and the big rooster himself is up the hill. Shit, if we could get Spielberg to move out here we'd really have something . . ."

I stopped listening after a while. I liked Jack better when he wasn't saying anything. He was several years older than me but he seemed younger, younger than Paco, even. I finished my drink.

"Get you a refill?" he asked.

The martini. Words. Another martini. More words.

"I'll have to introduce you to my friends and I'll have to meet yours . . . You should see my place in L.A. Seriously, why not?"

Jack's shirt. His breath on my neck. A joke. A question.

Yes, Jack, I do. I want to feel your body on top of me, I want you to give yourself to me utterly, completely, all of you, Jack, even if only for a night.

Another refill and I caught him looking at his own reflection in the window. He grinned sheepishly. It's ok, Jack, this is you at your peak, lead rolls in the pictures, money, women, fame. This is you on top, before the injections and the rejections. You shouldn't be ashamed to look. You're fabulous.

"New haircut, not sure I like it," he said and pulled a strand or two.

Oh, don't speak, Jack, just come over.

Why is it always the woman who has to show the man? I thought, drained the third martini and got up from the couch. I stepped out of my skirt and panties, I let the blouse fall to the floor, I unhooked my hair.

"Two hundred dollars in a new place on Pearl and they didn't even trim my sideburns," he said, still looking at the haircut, but then he saw me and his common sense kicked in. His mouth closed. He put down his glass.

"Fuck," he said.

"My sentiments exactly," I replied.

CHAPTER 14

KAREN

Blindfolded dawn. Sound, then light. A timer clicks, a motor whirrs, and the curtains pull back by themselves. Snow at morning's door. A pinkish-white dusting on the balcony rail.

The sun inching over the Front Range but as yet invisible behind a smother of low gray clouds. Above the clouds, a red sky turning American blue.

Hairs on the back of my neck standing up.

Something's wrong. A shiver.

"Jack?"

But Jack's asleep. Dreaming of Oscars and Spirit Awards.

I sit up and look around the bedroom.

Maybe Youkilis has come in early.

Maybe I've overplayed my hand.

No, the alarm box in the bedroom is still blinking. It hasn't been disabled. No one's come in.

Is there someone outside? A deranged fan? I have read about such things in French magazines.

I slip out from between the covers, find a pair of Jack's sweatpants and one of his T-shirts. I pull on the sweatpants, tie the band tight, and tuck in the T. The T-shirt says "Total Loser" on it. Why would someone buy that? It must be an American joke. How long would I have to be in this country to stop feeling like an alien? Did Dad ever get over it? I think of Mork in that Yuma show from the seventies—that was Colorado too.

I walk to the glass doors and scan the balcony and the gravel drive that leads to the road. Chairs. Bird footprints. *Snow.* Once I would have run outside. Not now. I'll never see it again after tomorrow. Not until Jefe and Little Jefe finally go to be with Marx.

Hector's voice: *Well, Mercado, what else do you see with that keen cop eye of yours?*

A water tower rising like a Wells tripod from the trees. A breeze ruffling the upper branches. A plane on the approach to Vail.

No psychotic stalkers or fans.

Spotlights at the big Cruise estate at the top of the mountain are making a kind of false dawn. Spotlights and a flashing red landing beacon. The helicopter bringing Mr. Cruise will be here soon.

I walk to the window nearest the bathroom and check the garden and Jack's car. The gate is closed and the car is still in its spot.

There's nothing out there, I say to myself.

I sit on the ottoman and pull the hair back from my face. On a desk I find some other one-night stand's scrunchie and make a short ponytail.

What now?

I could do breakfast, but Jack's TiVo says it's only 6:15. Too early to get up quite yet.

I don't want to go for a walk. I don't want to sit here.

Hell with this.

I lift the duvet, slide back underneath the cover, and sidle my way next to him.

"Jack," I whisper but he's out.

His breathing hushed, slow. One of my hairs falls on his face. His nose twitches.

What am I doing here with this lovely boy? The psalmist has words for you. But not me. I'm content to say nothing, to lose myself in the silence, to ripen in your good looks.

Oh, Jack, you'll never get taken seriously as an actor with that face. You ought to be in Attica judging beauty contests between Hera and Aphrodite. You ought to be out in the earthblack woods, butterflies alighting at your passing, does sniffing the air.

You're so un-Cuban. So finely sculpted—masculine, poised, confident. Like the statue of David I will never be allowed to travel to see. You can. You can do whatever you like. You're one of those imperialist Yankees we read about in high school. One of those white men who run the globe. Sure, I'll meet your friends, Jack, and you can meet mine. Tell Paco he'll never be a big cheese like you. Tell Esteban that this isn't Mexico anymore. This is your land, Jack. You beat them all to it. You were here before Columbus slipped anchor for China. You were here first. Flying your *Enola Gay*. Singing "Jailhouse Rock." Bunny-hopping on the moon. Let me be here with you, Jack, let me stroke those washboard abs, that botticino marble skin, let me ride that long American cock and lick the sweat from your back.

I slide my hand between his thighs but the Ambien and martinis keep him down.

I'm leaving, Jack. I'm going soon. You'll come see me? Defy the U.S. Treasury. Rendezvous in the Hotel Nacional. A good career move. Maybe they'll put your picture up next to Robert Redford's.

He grins in his sleep and I close my eyes. Feel his warmth. Lie there.

The winter sun burning through clouds. Ice melt. Water tap-tap-tapping on the window. My boy smiling in his dream.

I touch his cheek and his eyelashes flicker.

Wake up and we'll skip this scene. I could be legal by noon. Drive me to the FBI office in Denver. This year alone five thousand Cubans have come over the border from Mexico, all of them now on the path to citizenship. Citizen Mercado and her boyfriend, Jack.

You like the sound of that?

And I'll forgive Paul or Esteban or Mrs. Cooper.

María is the sovereign lady of forgiveness.

Forgive. Yes. I don't even think I'd care if it was you, Jack. Not Youkilis, Youkilis covering for you somehow.

It wouldn't matter, would it, Jack?

Uhh, he says in agreement.

I put my arm under him. My breasts press against his back.

Yes. Let's slip away.

You'll understand, Dad, won't you? After all, what did you ever care about any of us? What were you thinking about on that slope? Did you see my face? Ricky's? Not Mom's. Probably you were drunk or high. Crying out for Karen or the girls you had on the side. Drunk and happy like you were the day you abandoned us in Santiago. Did you see me as you lay dying? You were not on my mind. I wasn't even in Havana. Wild goose chase for a wife killer. Train to Laguna de la Leche. Reading one of Hector's extensive collection of banned books. Thucydides. Given to me as a birthday present. Yeah, that's right . . . the day after my birthday. Well, Pop, did you even bother to look down on me on your way to eternity? You would have liked Pajero, near Laguna—a perfect shithole. Moonshine shacks, tin houses, open sewers. Our killer—of course—long gone. Girl on a bicycle brought me a message from town. *Señora,* a phone call from Havana. Phone call? *Sí, señora.* Back together on the bike. Two of us. East among the sunflowers. East into the dying sunflowers, the words of Pericles by the lake, while you were being unmade.

Ring-ring on a rickety black café phone from the thirties.

Ricky's voice as distant as the moon.

How did you find me?

Listen, darling sit down, are you sitting? I'm sorry, Dad's dead, some kind of accident in Colorado.

What? Where?

Colorado.

My first thought: Good riddance. Not one letter. Not one dollar.

But then the memories flooding back.

Crying and Ricky's voice: I can get permission to go.

How?

Strings. Blow jobs.

Me laughing through tears.

Hang up the black Bakelite receiver.

The café owner, a police narc: Bad news?

Yeah. My father. Dead.

On a road in the mountains of Colorado.

That road, out there. Out the window.

Oh, Papa, there's nothing I can do for you. This is the Castle of No Escape. And I like it here. Yuma, land of the Yankees. I like it. I asked for the key to my own dungeon, a thousand miles from the dandelions on the salt trail and the bean-fed boys and the red dirt fields and the teardrop skies.

That road. *That road.* There through the glass.

A creak on the deck outside.

Someone there. This time I'm certain.

I'm alert, fully awake, flooded with adrenaline. I sit up quickly, look for shadows on the balcony. Nothing, but I know I'm not imagining things—that was no squirrel or stray dog. That was boot on wood.

I throw back the duvet, jog to the fireplace, and grab a cast-iron poker with a vicious-looking hook at the end.

I undo the lock on the french doors and walk onto the deck, checking blind spots and the roof.

Fresh powder under my feet.

"*Hola?*" I ask.

No one answers. But the birds are quiet.

The gate's closed, no strange cars, nothing out of the ord—

Wait a minute. Bootmarks in the gravel. Bootprints coming to the house.

"Hello," Sheriff Briggs says behind me.

I bite down a yell and turn.

He's wearing an overcoat but I can tell he's got the full uniform on underneath. He's come as a cop.

"You scared me. I didn't see you there," I tell him.

He flashes the pearly grin, rubs the bottom of his chin.

"Yeah."

He looks at my breasts through Jack's T-shirt. Fishes into his pocket and pulls out a cigar. Other pocket, Zippo. I shouldn't be waiting out here. It looks guilty. I should go back inside.

"Excuse me, *señor,* but I—"

He shakes his head. "No, you don't."

"But Señor Tyrone is—"

"I'm not after Jack. I'm looking for you."

Meek. Eyes down. "For me?"

"Yeah, for you."

"What do you mean, *señor*?" I say in Spanish.

He grins, blows a smoke ring. "No, no, don't do that to me. I know your English is just fine. Now be like a good little puppy and take a seat over there."

He points at a wooden deck chair. I brush off the thin layer of snow and sit. Water seeps up from the wood, through Jack's sweatpants and against my skin.

"You weren't in the motel," Briggs says, leaning forward and taking the poker out of my hand.

"No."

"Weren't in the motel so I asked around and figured you were here."

"Have I broken a law?" I ask.

"Well, if you were whoring here and not cutting Esteban or myself in, I'd say that you were breaking a law, but I don't think you're whoring, are you?"

I shake my head.

"No, María, I don't think you're whoring, because I don't think you need the money."

"I do not understand, *señor*."

"It's just a hunch, but something tells me you don't need the money that badly," he says with another grin.

The cold is making me tremble. No. It isn't the cold. I force myself to stop it.

"If I haven't done anything wrong, I'd like to go back inside," I tell him.

"You're not going anywhere until you answer me a few questions."

"Ok."

"'Ok' . . . Yeah, that's the fucking spirit. Ok. How long have you been here? Three days. You should know the score by now. Question number one. Whose fucking town is this?"

"Your town, *señor*."

"My town. Absolutely goddamn right. My fucking town. I'm the sheriff. I'm the representative of the republic. I'm the fucking Lord High Executioner. That's right. We got Tom Cruise but it's my fucking town."

His voice has risen. His face is red.

Something's happened. He's found something out.

Did Paco blab about New Mexico? Have the *federales* followed our trail here? What has leaked? Calm. Keep calm. It's ok. Remember the Havana rule: say nothing—twice.

He unbuttons his coat, places his boot on the arm of my chair, and continues. "You think something could happen here and I wouldn't know? You're very much mistaken, *señorita*. From Malibu Mesa to Wetback Mountain and all the way to fucking Vail, I know what's going on. It's my job to know. Get me?"

"Yes, *señor*."

"The last time I existed in a state of ignorance was Gulf War One. We thought we were the invasion but we were only the diversion. No one's played me like that since. No one and certainly not some Mex cunt who's too fucking proud to whore for us. Why are you so fucking proud? You think you're going to get Jackie here to marry you? You think he's going to knock you up?

Is that your fucking plan? Or is blackmail more your game? Play both angles at the same fucking time?"

The other shining leather boot lands on my chair with a clump. He crosses his legs and those eyes bore into me.

Take it easy, I tell myself. He doesn't know anything for sure. He's still fishing. He's got something but he doesn't see everything. Yet.

"No answer?" he says.

"I don't know what you mean, *señor.*"

"What did you hear? What rumors are they spreading in that Mex motel of yours?"

Spittle flying from his lips. Real anger in his words. And now I'm afraid. Afraid of those big hands more than the gun. Beat me to death with two blows.

Again an image of a naked body, yellow and blue, bloated, a skull for a face, maggots for eyes. That's me there in that soft brown earth, under those big trees, unloved, unfound forever.

He pauses to get his breath back, squints at me. "Well?" he says.

I'm supposed to answer.

"But I don't know what you're talking about," I say truthfully.

"You don't know what I'm talking about? I think you fucking do. I think someone has been shooting their mouth off and you've seen the chance for a few dollars more. A chance for the big score. Is that right? I mean, why concern yourself with blow-job money when you can shoot for millions?"

Anything I say will only provoke him.

He waits me out.

"Perhaps you could tell me what I have done wrong?"

He nods, smashes his fist into his hand, gets up, and walks behind me. I stare straight ahead. If I don't look back the monster won't be there. Right, Dad?

A car driving past on the road. A helicopter landing at the Cruise house.

Surely he can't kill me out here with all these potential witnesses.

His breath against my cheek.

"You were at the Pearl Street Garage in town. Asking questions about an incident last May."

The grave. The trees.

I'm fucked. Should have bribed Jackson.

Hector's first rule of police work: secure your snitches. But where would I have gotten enough money on a salary of thirty dollars a month? Burned most of my savings on the coyote. And besides, Jackson told me about you, why wouldn't he tell you about me?

And now. Fucked.

Don't say anything. Don't deny it, just say nothing.

Briggs takes a long breath, breathes out. Cream, coffee, tobacco. "So why does Little Miss Nobody want to know about a dead Mex? What are you, María? A blackmailer? An opportunist? An undercover journo? What's in it for you, Señorita X?"

His gloved hands pinch a fold of skin at the back of my neck. He twists it. Pain. Terrible pain as he lifts me off the seat.

"I could fucking paralyze you with this if I wanted to," he says or seems to say—I can barely hear him through the fire in my nerve endings.

I try to hit his arms. My legs kick out.

"Stop it!"

"Speak, you little bitch, speak and tell me everything. Why did you go to the garage? Did Esteban put you up to this? What does he want to know?"

He squeezes so hard that I'm seeing stars, passing out . . .

One second, two, blackness.

He lets go the pinch. My head slumps forward.

He's facing me.

"Why were you at the garage?" he whispers.

Play for time. Big breaths. Got to get out of here. Hit him with something.

"Why were you at the garage?"

"*Señor,* I think you're mis—"

He grabs a handful of hair, drags me out of the chair, and throws me to the deck.

"Who put you up to this? Who? Is Esteban too fucking chicken to do his own legwork? How much did he pay you? What's his angle? What's his fucking angle? Answer me, you little bitch."

I try to scramble away from him but he grabs my ankle and pulls me back across the deck. He kneels down on my legs and draws his gun.

"We're going to get some fucking answers or you are gonna fucking disappear."

He slides the hammer back on his .38 and points it between my legs.

"Maybe I'll just blow your cunt off. Won't be able to whore then, will ya? Won't be able to fuck movie stars on the side. What's Esteban's cut on that little racket? Eh? Still not talking?"

He pushes down on me with all his weight, crushing my thighs. He points the gun at my head.

"Nah, forget that, I don't want to wound ya. One in the temple, a group of three beside it to triple check. That's the ticket. Vanish you off the face of the Earth. Message to that Mex bastard: Mind your business, Esteban."

"*Señor*, I don't know what you're t-talking about," I stammer.

"You don't know what I'm talking about?" he says, leaning forward to slap me across the face. My lip catches a ring on his hand and starts to bleed.

"Think I'm stupid? Is that what you think? Think because you fucking speak English you can beat me in a battle of fucking wits? I've been through the fucking war, *señorita*. I've been farther than you'll ever fucking go. Farther than Esteban, farther than all of ya."

"*Señor*, I—"

"No. No. Forget it. Don't talk. I'll get it from him. You're history, little girl. Nobody knows you from Adam. You're life ain't worth shit. One less dumb whore for us to worry about. Close your eyes, sugar."

He climbs off me and stands back so the blood splatter won't get on his coat. He points the gun, squeezes the trigger.

I start to scream from somewhere deep. From New Mexico. From Havana. And deeper still. Louder than the helicopter at my uncle's house in Santiago, louder than the prisoners in the Cominado del Este.

Scream and scream.

"Jack! Help me! Help me! Jack!"

"There's no help coming, little sister, this is my t—"

A blur. A smash.

Jack barreling into him. Knocking him down. The gun going off and simultaneously flying out of Briggs's hand. No bluff. He would have killed me. Jack punching Briggs twice on the head. Briggs thumping Jack on the back of the neck. Jack crumpling. Briggs getting to his feet, kicking Jack in the stomach. Briggs looking for the pistol, looking on the deck, under the chairs, behind him, and finally at my right hand.

"Ok, now, steady on. Hold on a minute. Let me explain something, let me explain just a little."

I put my finger to my lips. "Ssshhhh."

He shushes, puts his hands up.

Jack dry heaves and manages to get into a sitting position.

"What's going on, María?" Jack says, choking out the words.

What to say? "I don't know, Jack. I think Sheriff Briggs has gotten me mixed up with one of the other girls. Since coming here I have broken no laws and I have kept to my own business. I only want to work hard and stay out of trouble."

Briggs looking at the gun. Eyes wide. Still can't believe it. Are you scared? Are you having a premonition?

"What in the name of all that's fucking holy is going on, Sheriff?" Jack asks, furiously. Boxer shorts, T-shirt, no shoes. His face white with anger. Jack gets to his feet and I offer him my hand. Show solidarity. Jack takes the hand.

Briggs's brain up to Mach 5. Thinking escape routes, consequences. The movie star. The movie star's lawyers. The wetback with the gun. He clears his throat.

"I think I've made a terrible mistake here, Mr. Tyrone. I got a tip that someone from the Mex motel was asking questions about the, uh, car trouble, that, uh, Mr. Youkilis, that we dealt with in May. I thought it might be a blackmail attempt or an attempt to get a scurrilous story into the tabloids. I showed pictures and María here was ID'ed."

Jack looks at me, doubt flashing between his eyes. In one sentence the fucker's changed the game back again.

"But I was with Jack," I say, though of course Briggs didn't say when it was.

"She was with you?" he asks Jack.

Jack nods. "Sheriff, María was with me. She wasn't asking anybody questions. She wasn't doing anything. She was with me," Jack insists.

Briggs frowns.

And now is the moment to turn that pond of doubt into an ocean, to show him that I'm completely innocent, that he or someone else has gotten this thing entirely wrong, that the tip was garbled, the ID screwed. Something.

I smile meekly, take two steps across the deck, and offer him his gun.

The barrel glistening. Bullets in the chamber. The death end pointed toward my heart.

He looks at the weapon, looks at me, nods.

He takes the revolver and puts it back in its holster.

"I'm sorry to have caused all this trouble, *señor*," I say in my best Mex, my best *invisible*.

Sheriff Briggs grimaces and it shows me that I've convinced him. For now. Somebody fucked up. He'll find out who.

Briggs shakes his head. "It's me that should apologize, ma'am, you're a, uhm, a guest in our country and I thought I was acting in the best interests of the town and I see that I've gotten incorrect information. I've made an error and I'm sorry."

Jack grins. "Well, I'm glad that's sorted out," he says cheerfully. "Glad and a little disappointed. That's the most heroic thing I've ever done and all for some stupid mistake. That's not going to make a good story."

"If you do not mind, Señor Jack, I will go and put some coffee on," I say.

"Wonderful. By all means, excellent idea. Thank you very much, María," Jack replies.

I look at Sheriff Briggs. "Would you like some coffee, sir?" I ask him.

His face is red with embarrassment. I repeat the offer of coffee and he shakes his head. This little encounter has given me breathing room. It'll take him a few hours to pin down the real story—maybe all day. That's all I need. One more day.

"No, ma'am, no, thank you," he says stiffly.

I go inside the house and once I'm out of view I run to the kitchen, press the button on the coffeemaker, and wind open the window so that I can hear their conversation.

The two men are standing close, intimately so, like brothers or lovers or confederates.

"Is Youkilis in some kind of trouble?" Jack asks.

"I don't think so."

"What's going on?"

"I'm not sure. Maybe nothing. Probably nothing. You know that girl Marilyn from Ohio that works for Jackson?"

"Yeah. Sure. Not bad-looking."

"She used to work for me at the sheriff's station. Got rid of her. She thought it was Bond and fucking Moneypenny. We're still close, though. Good head on her shoulders."

"What about her?"

"Calls me up last night and lets me know that someone's been asking questions about the accident. The day the Mex got killed."

"Shit. Is it something we should be concerned about?"

Briggs shakes his head. "I don't know. Something might have gotten garbled down there. I'll check it out. I'll ask Esteban. No, to hell with *ask,* I'll brace the fucker. I'll find out what's going on. You don't have to worry about a thing."

"Should I tell Paul?"

"No, I don't think so. I'll look into this, really look into it. Let you know Monday."

"Ok."

Briggs shakes his head, ruefully gestures at the overturned chair. "And, and I'm sorry about all this, Jack."

Jack, not Mr. Tyrone.

"It's a bit much for a Sunday morning. You scared the shit out of María."

"I'm sorry about that. Maybe made a mistake about her. Anyway, I'll let you know what's going on by tomorrow."

Jack murmurs something that I can't hear.

I press my face right against the bug screen but I still can't catch it.

Jack and the sheriff shake hands. Briggs picks up the poker and hands it to Jack.

Jack laughs.

The sheriff laughs.

Very cordial. Very anglo. Is this how they do things here? In Cuba you don't let a man rough up your woman. You put him in the fucking hospital. You kill him.

This . . . this seems too easy.

Briggs points back at the house. I shrink from the window. He puts his hands on his hips, spits.

"Thing is, Jackie boy, even if she's clean, I mean, really, the maid?"

"She's great."

"You don't see me running around with easy pickings and I've got plenty of opportunity. You gotta get your act together," the sheriff says.

"Hey, I wanna—"

"Wait a minute, hear me out. I mean, what do you want? What do you really want out of life?"

"I want a career. A good career," Jack says.

"You want to do good work, you want to be remembered. Right?"

"Yes. That and friends and a family."

"You don't think I want that? You don't think I want to get married again, have kids? I'm not getting any younger. But I'm trying to build something up here. A town. A community. Something that will last. Even if the Scientologists don't come, I'll have made something that'll be here a hundred, a thousand years from now. This was barely a village before we got started; in a few years we'll be in full competition with Aspen and Vail. You gotta get with the program, Jack, you have to take life more seriously. Your friend María, Esteban, people like that, they're not thinking about the future—I doubt they're thinking at all—don't let them drag you down to their level. Set your goals high, Jack, make some sacrifices. It's not about instant gratification, it's about the long term, it's about posterity."

Jack nods solemnly. Briggs puts his big paw on Jack's shoulder.

Gives me a spine shiver from neck to ass.

Briggs walks down the gravel path. Jack waves and then says, "Hey, Sheriff, you were in the Marines, right?"

"Yeah."

"You think we could talk some time? I'm playing a British Army officer in this movie I'm doing. Maybe we could have coffee and you could give me a few hints."

"Sure. Let's do that. I'll call you Monday."

Jack waves again and comes back into the house.

When he appears in the kitchen the coffee's ready. I pour him a cup.

"Thanks," he says.

I wait a beat, then two, then almost half a minute before finally he remembers to say it: "God, María, I'm really sorry about Briggs."

"I was so scared," I tell him, giving him a big slice of the truth.

"It's ok, it's ok, it's ok," he says.

I sit on his lap and have coffee and a stale bagel. Not once does he offer an explanation but several times he looks at his watch.

I shower, scald myself with the water. Wither away that expensive olive oil soap.

I change into my *invisible* clothes from yesterday. No lipstick, no makeup. Wool hat over my forehead.

Jack's on the phone when I come out of the bedroom. He hangs up with an enormous smile on his face. "Fucking hell! Sunday lunch at the man's! Can you believe it? Can you believe it? Beckham's gonna be there. Not to mention Kelly and Katie. Fuck, he didn't say Travolta but if Kelly's gonna be there, who knows, right? Me and Mister C. Jesus! Jesus! Gotta tell Paul and Danny."

208 · ADRIAN MCKINTY

"That's great," I say without inflection.

"Wow, he remembered me, all right. Did I tell you we were in *Mission Impossible 3* together?"

"Yes."

"I was little more than a glorified extra, but he must have remembered me. See, that's how things go. It's all contacts. And Paul's right. Do some indies, the big pics follow. I'm not even thirty—officially—and I'm moving into the territory. Lead in *Gunmetal* and then maybe a second lead in a Cruise flick. Maybe the quirky best friend. Second banana in a Cruise movie. Fuck! That'll pay the pension. Ever see *A Few Good Men*? The guy can act. Oh, and don't think I'm discounting Travolta, hell no. *Pulp Fiction, Saturday Night Fever,* man, two of the all-time classics."

His eyes glaze over and he stares through me. His face falls.

"Oh, honey, look, I'm sorry, forgot to say, invite's only for one. Wait a minute, look, tell you what, do you want me to call up and ask if he'd mind or . . ." His voice trails off.

I try not to smile. Would he really do it if I asked him?

"No, no, thank you, Jack. I have a million things to do."

Relief. Maybe Katie or Kelly has a sister.

I kiss him on the cheek and he calls Youkilis. I don't think he even notices me when I slip out.

Five minutes later I'm walking back down the hill to the crossing.

In town I stop at Starbucks and order an espresso. It comes in a giant cup. Even when I add sugar it's about as far from a Cuban coffee as *A Few Good Men* is from a real depiction of the naval base at Guantánamo Bay. The espresso costs a dollar seventy-five, which is more than the average daily wage in Havana. I can't bring myself to finish it.

I shoulder the backpack and continue on. Past the trophy-wife stores, the ski shops, the delis, up the other hill to Wetback Mountain.

A police cruiser waiting outside the motel.

Might be a deputy, might be unrelated to me and the garage, but I can't take the chance. The last thing I want is another encounter with that psychopath. I step off the road and disappear into the woods. I walk through the pine cones and fallen branches and sit on a log.

There's a river running through the trees. The quiet glade reminds me of Río Jaimanitas, just outside Havana.

Time to think. Think about suspects, think about the clock.

Suspects. Their talk has more or less cleared Esteban. They thought he was involved in a blackmail plot about the accident. Ergo it can't be him. I never thought it was. Ricky's hunch—who kills a man and leaves his car unrepaired for six months? Still, I'd like one last interview to ask him about his deer.

Not E. Not Mrs. C., not in a million years. It's Y.

Jack has given him to me. Jack and his good buddy the sheriff. Y. Y. Y.

The clock. Sunday morning. My flight from Mexico City to Havana is early Tuesday. So by this time tomorrow I need to be on the bus to El Paso. Cross over, to Juárez. Flight from Juárez to Mexico City. Jesus, it's tight. I certainly don't have all the information. In Havana I'd call this half a case. I'd need another full week's work before I'd even think about going to Hector with the file. But that's there and this is here. Here Briggs is on my neck and my options have collapsed into one simple thought: *If I'm going to do this then it has to be tonight.*

* * *

Fairview disappeared. The road narrowed from four lanes to two and the houses on either side quickly became swallowed up by forest. Beech Street was not meant for pedestrians. There was no sidewalk, and when cars approached they pulled all the way over to the left lane, annoyed at the presence of someone on foot.

In another five minutes so thick were the trees that it was hard to believe there were any houses at all. Mailboxes and driveways the only clues. The smell of douglas fir, aspen. The crunch underfoot of golden, red, and black pinecones.

I counted down the addresses on the mailboxes. 94, 92, 90.

A cold, prickly feeling on my scalp as I got closer, and I had to pause for a moment when the mailbox said 88.

"This is it," I said aloud.

When Ricky came to Fairview, he'd gone to the garage, he'd walked the Old Boulder Road, he'd visited the motel, he'd taken photographs of Jack's car and Esteban's Range Rover, but this little job he'd left for me.

I hesitated at the gate and then went in. Cement driveway. Underfoot more pinecones, beech leaves, a flattened Starbucks cup. The path bent to the left and there, suddenly, was the house. Single-story Colorado ranch style. Modest in proportion to other homes in Fairview but boldly painted yellow and elaborately festooned with flowerpots and hanging baskets, some of the blooms gamely hanging on even though it was December.

It was shady here and frost coated a neat square of garden and several of the close-trimmed rosebushes that surrounded the house like a primitive siege defense.

I stepped over an ornamental gnome with a fishing pole, half a dozen free newspapers, and squirrel shit. I knocked on the door.

She took a minute to open it.

She was pretty. She looked about thirty but I knew she was older than that. She had black hair cut short in bangs, cornflower-blue eyes, arched, surprised-looking dark eyebrows, high cheekbones, full lips with a crease in the lower. If it wasn't early on Sunday and if the past few months hadn't been such an obvious trial to her, she'd be a knockout. Dad's type? Certainly. And I had a feeling that a year from now she wouldn't be alone.

"Hello?" she said, groggily. Her breath: coffee, cigarettes, last night's red wine.

"My name is Sue Hernandez, I'm from the Mexican consulate in Denver," I said and offered her my hand. After a second's hesitation she shook it.

"What can I do for you, Señorita Hernandez?" she asked.

"We're looking into the death of Alberto Suarez. I've come here to ask you a few questions, if that's ok."

She stood there in the doorway, pulled her nightgown tighter about her. It only accentuated her big breasts.

"On a Sunday?"

"I'm very sorry for the inconvenience."

"Fuck it. What's all this about?" she asked.

"Señora Suarez, your husband was a Mexican citizen, and the embassy routinely investigates all suspicious deaths of Mexican citizens in the United States."

"Not this again."

"This will be the last time, I assure you. May I come in?"

She shook her head. "The place is a mess."

"I don't mind that," I said, realizing that I was actually more desperate to get in the house than I was to meet her. I wanted to see relics: family photographs, art, souvenirs. The interior of number 88 would be a ghost house filled with memories.

"No. I've been through this before. With the cops and someone who phoned me from your embassy, already. And now you're here. Clearly, the left hand doesn't know what the right hand's doing."

I smiled. "It's just a few questions. Please, may I come in?"

"No, you can't. Look, I don't have all day. What are your questions?"

"They're about the accident."

"Yeah, you said that. Just ask the questions."

"You husband worked as a pest controller."

"Yeah, he was overqualified for that. He was a smart guy. Killing rats, trapping raccoons, it was gross."

"Yes. But what was your husband doing on the Old Boulder Road? According to our records his last job was at the Hermès store on Pearl Street. He didn't have—"

"He was drinking."

"I'm sorry?"

"I didn't like him to drink, so he used to go up there. There's a viewpoint two-thirds of the way up, a cliff where you can see the whole Front Range. A couple of kids committed suicide there. He used to go there, drink, look at the mountains, walk it off before he saw me."

"So he *was* drunk the night of the accident?" I asked. The local paper had said he was drunk but there hadn't been obvious signs of alcohol and the consulate hadn't felt the need to conduct a tox report.

Karen shook her head. "I doubt it. We had a big blowup last year, I threatened to leave him, I've never seen him blind drunk since then. He was smart about it."

"I see, so he may have been drinking when the car hit, but he wasn't intoxicated."

"Something like that."

Hmm. Ricky said that it was just a coincidence that it had happened on my birthday. But maybe not. All those years without letters, without sending us a dime, maybe guilt had finally got to him. Had he had too many? Was he staggering all over the road? Maybe the consulate in Denver had hushed up the toxicology for fear of contributing to a stereotype. Maybe a million things.

Karen sniffed. "I hope he was drunk. I hope he was totally hammered."

"Why?"

"Lady who found him, walking her dog. I know her. She talked to me. She told me the truth, the people around here are pretty blunt."

"What did she tell you?"

"Told me his face was frozen. It was May but it's been cold up here. Face frozen, fingers broken, blood and dirt all over him, he'd been trying to climb up that slope all night. It took him four or five hours to die. Drowning in his own blood the whole time, drowning, freezing, ribs broken, the pain must have been awful, and just a few feet from rescue up on the embankment. The goddamn torment. I wouldn't put my worst enemy through that. So yeah, I hope he was drunk."

My head felt light. I swayed back on my heels.

"I, uh, I only have a couple more questions. Are you sure we wouldn't be more comfortable inside?"

Karen gave me a skeptical glance. Feelers out. Nervous.

Damn it.

"All this is irrelevant anyway," she said.

"How so?"

"I told you guys, Albert, or I should say Juan, wasn't Mexican," she said.

"I don't understand," I said, affecting surprise.

"He was Cuban. A defector. He came over in the early nineties."

"But our information was that—"

"He bought that passport in Kansas City. It cost two thousand dollars. A passport and a Social Security number and a green card."

"But—"

"So you see, Señorita Hernandez, you've wasted your time. This isn't a job for your people at all. I told you guys already, ok? Who do you think called his family in Cuba? Me. They flew his son out. *From Cuba*. Christ, how dumb are you people? So thanks for the interest but really, I've got nothing to tell you."

The brush-off.

"Well, that certainly contradicts the information I've been given. I'll need to confirm this against our records. Do you have any photographs or—"

"For Christ's sake. Wait here."

She took a step backward and went into a side room. Now I could see tantalizing glimpses of a smallish living room. Hardwood floor, white sofa, white chairs. More flowers and paintings, perhaps done by Karen herself. Dad was never much in the drawing line and I couldn't imagine that he had changed so greatly that he taken to painting fairies in forest glades and white horses galloping across impossibly sandy beaches. Karen's "mess" appeared to be a few piles of laundry on the living room floor.

She came back with a fifteen-year-old Cuban driver's license and handed it over.

"You can have this if you want. No good to me."

I looked at the black-and-white photograph of Dad in his Russian wool suit and that little mustache he thought made him a dead ringer for Clark Gable. Ricky and I used to tease him about it, but in fact he really did resemble the late Yuma movie star. Quickly I put the license in my purse for fear she'd snatch it back.

"This doesn't much look like the man in the autopsy photographs. Do you have a more recent photograph?"

"Oh, Jesus. Never ends. Hold on. I'll get you one."

An inner voice warned me that this wasn't necessary, I didn't *need* a photograph, I just wanted to open the floodgates, to wallow in the emotion. *Careful, Mercado, once the sluices open, they're pretty hard to close.* She came back with something she'd just taken out of a frame.

"Here," she said. "I put them all away. It was too painful to have him around looking at me, but I couldn't throw any of them out."

The photograph was of her standing next to a bearded man, a little heavier, but with sharp brown eyes and mostly black hair. He had a sarcastic, self-mocking expression on his face. I hadn't seen him for fourteen years but it was definitely him. He looked like one of those public intellectuals on Channel 1, talking about trade with China or the Glorious Revolution's prospects in the twenty-first century.

"Satisfied?" Karen asked, taking the photo back.

"Perhaps I could ask you a few more questions for the record?" I wondered.

"You can have one more minute. This is all still pretty hard on me. And *Jeopardy!*'s on early on Sundays and I never miss it. It's a routine. Routines help you get through the day, don't you find?"

"Yes. I don't mind if you watch while we talk. Perhaps if I could come in for just a—"

"I'd prefer not."

"So there seems to be at least some confusion, regarding Señor—"

"There's no confusion. He bought that passport because he wanted to pose as a Mexican permanent resident called Suarez, so he could work in the United States."

I smiled. "Ah, but this is where I am confused, Señora Suarez. Cuban defectors are automatically granted green cards, Social Security numbers, and so on, are they not? Why would your husband even need to pose as a Mexican?"

Something came into Karen's face. A darkening. A suspicion.

"Where did you say you were from, Miss Hernandez?"

"I'm from the consulate in Denver."

"Can I see some ID?"

Mierde.

On to me.

The old man must have prepped her. If someone comes asking about me, ever, check their credentials at once.

My mind raced while I fumbled in my purse. Who was he hiding from? He was a defector hero among the Miamistas. Cuban intelligence never went after defectors. There were literally millions of them in the United States: baseball players, boxers, politicians, doctors, engineers. And Dad was a lowly ferry attendant. What was his game?

"Well, this is a little embarrassing, Señora Suarez, but I think I must have left my papers in my other bag back in Denver. I could come back the day after tomorrow and show them to you if that will help?"

A slight nod of the head. A narrowing of the eyes. She didn't like that one bit. A furtive sideways glance into the bedroom. That's where she kept the guard dog or the phone or the gun.

"I'll come back when I have my ID?" I asked.

"Yes, I think I'd prefer that," she replied in a frightened monotone.

"Shall we say Tuesday at ten in the morning?"

"Fine."

"Tuesday, excellent. Well, in that case I'll be on my way. I apologize if I have inconvenienced you in any way and hopefully we can get this resolved next week."

"Yes," she said, her voice barely above a whisper.

I smiled, turned, and walked down the driveway. Bye, Stepmom.

I didn't look back but I knew she was in her bedroom, calling someone, looking for the emergency cash, packing a suitcase . . . Dad had told her about this day and the day had come.

I couldn't begin to understand it.

Was his death not an accident? Was he something more than met the eye? Had Ricky gotten it completely wrong?

When the house was out of sight behind the trees, I crossed the road, vanished into the forest, and waited.

It took only an hour for her to load a beat-up eighties-style Volvo with suitcases and cardboard boxes. She turned right on Beech Street. I cursed at not having Esteban's car to tail her, but it didn't really matter. Right was south toward I-70, the big cross-country highway that could take her all the way to Los Angeles in the west or New Jersey in the east. I memorized the license plate, wrote it down for future use, walked back up the driveway, broke in through a side window. The white furniture was the only thing that wasn't tossed, although the sofa had been pushed way up against the wall, maybe to give her room to pack.

And pack she had.

Drawers opened, clothes scattered, pictures ripped from the walls, a bed stripped. Method to the madness. *They had rehearsed this.*

No photographs, no diaries, no books.

No books. I thought at the very least I'd see some of his books, maybe flip through the titles while Karen made me a cup of coffee.

I rummaged in the trash but even that gave no clues, just a few nondescript bills. Everything incriminating gone. Tonight it would be burned and dropped in a trash can at some random truck stop.

I put a plastic bag over my arm and shoved it down the U bend of the toilet, but that was clean too.

I did the whole house. A quick brace and then a longer backward trace. Nothing.

I sat on the sofa.

Memories. Guilt. Tears. Ricky said not to fall for that trip, and he was right.

Be like an alchemist. Transmogrify guilt to anger. Easy after Karen had brought his death so vividly to my mind.

I stood, addressed the void: "I don't know what you thought you were doing here, Dad, I don't know what you filled her head with, but you did a number on her, all right, just like you did on us. And . . . and I want you to know something: I'm angry at you, I'm angry that you left us, that you didn't write, that you missed my *quince* and you sent nothing. I haven't done a poem since you left, and Mom's half crazy, and we're all stuck in Cuba. You fucked us, old man, fucked us good."

I left through the front door and had gone a kilometer along Beech before I turned and walked back.

Something was nagging at me. Something about the sofa.

In through the window.

No reason for her to move it.

I shoved it and found the place where she'd tried to rip up the floorboards.

She'd spent some time on it but she didn't have a claw hammer and she was in a terrible rush.

I did have a hammer.

I smashed out the nails and ripped up the floor. One board, two boards. Dirt. A plastic bag. Inside the bag another bag, inside the second bag a gun.

Dad's? I looked at it. It was strange. It was certainly a clue. If I had the time I'd check it out.

I sat back on the sofa. Sat there for a long time. Light marched across the floor.

The patterns changed.

A gnawing sound. A mouse investigating the mayhem. It looked at me with surprise.

Run, mouselet, I spare thee.

Yes. Run, run, run from the Cubans and enemies real and imaginary.

I fished in my pocket, found where I had written Karen's license number, ripped it up, and flushed the pieces down the toilet.

You'll be safe, Karen.

Safer, at least, than your husband's killer.

No. That poor bastard. I wouldn't want to be him a few hours from now, on a sad, cold, December night in Nowhere, Wyoming.

CHAPTER 15

THE BOOK OF CHANGES

he arithmetical process of elimination. Our two primary suspects and Esteban were three of the solutions to the case, but they weren't *all* of the solutions, and I knew I wouldn't be comfortable until I had dealt with every possibility, no matter how remote. At this last stage of the game I knew I was going to have to see about Ricky's golf cart. I probably should have investigated this one first, but I'd been putting it at the back of my mind. It would be a ridiculous way for a man to die. Run over by a purple golf cart whose speed topped out at ten kph, but all ways to die were equally absurd and somehow in all this craziness it wouldn't have been inappropriate.

The Scientology Drop-In Center was next to Donna Karan.

I decided to drop in.

Metallic walls, massive air-conditioning pods, dark, uncomfortable-looking chairs around an ebony coffee table. Scientology magazines, newsletters, booklets, and of course various texts by L. Ron Hubbard. The reception desk was a long curve of black marble. I'd never seen black marble before and I was impressed.

I stood there and ran my fingers along the grain.

The receptionist looked up.

Pretty, with a Stepford hairdo and dress, she had a glazed Hero of the Revolution expression about her.

"Yes?"

"I was wondering if I could see Toby. I'm an insurance inves—"

"Oh yes. Toby's available right now if you want to go in. It will have to be brief, he's auditing at two. IV Room number two, first on the left."

IV Room #2.

Toby was sitting behind a desk, surfing the Web on a tiny silver Toshiba laptop. He was skinny with a raggedy gold sweater, blond hair, and a sallow, distant expression. His eyes were black, tired, and startled when I came in unannounced. He quickly pulled down the cover on the Toshiba.

"Can I help you?" he asked.

"Yes, I read that you crashed a golf cart at—"

Toby stood and offered me his hand. It was moist, limp, the nails dirty and bitten to the quick. He rubbed his face, sat back down, and reached into a drawer under his desk. He brought out a long white booklet and a pencil and passed them across to me. He didn't appear to have taken in what I had begun to say. "I suppose they told you that this is going to have to be quick. I've got an audit at two," he muttered.

"So they said."

He stood again, his left eye twitched alarmingly for a moment, and then, abruptly, he left the office.

"Wait a minute," I said. I went to the door and tried to follow him but it was locked from the outside.

"Excuse me! Excuse me!" I called out.

The door opened and the receptionist came back in. She was holding a glass of water.

"Oh, please take a seat, Miss . . ."

"Martinez."

"Please take a seat, Miss Martinez. Just fill out that questionnaire and Toby will be back in to see you in a moment. And do drink the water, it's very dry in here."

She gave me a winning American smile and I found myself sitting.

The door closed.

I drank the water, opened the questionnaire.

I faked the career history and personal data pages, info dumping a fictional CV I was quite proud of. Inez Martinez 3.0 was a young Latina from Denver, who had become an insurance agent after attending Harvard University. Hmm, was that credible? Harvard, well, it was too late now. I'd made her magna cum laude and a member of the basketball team.

I started answering the other questions. It was amusing. A distraction.

They grew increasingly weirder as the pages turned. I cannot remember them exactly but they were along these lines:

Q. 43: "If extraterrestrials were proven to exist would you A) Be worried? B) Be pleased? C) Be angry? D) Have no opinion?" I wrote D.

Q. 77: "When you see a clam do you feel A) Hungry? B) Happy? C) Strangely sad? D) None of the above?" I wrote D.

Q. 101: "Would you rather have an A) Average income? B) High income but less than your neighbors? C) Low income but more than your neighbors? D) None of the above?" I wrote D.

I had just finished question 200 and closed the booklet when Toby came back in.

"That was good timing," I said.

He took the booklet. "No, I was watching you through the monitor.

Toby began drawing a line through my answers, forming a kind of chart.

"Well, this will give us *some* idea," he said. "If I wasn't pressed for time, we could do the proper thousand-question test; that's the real deal."

"Uhm, look, Toby, I'm an insurance invest—"

"Ah, you're from Denver! Denver, Denver, Denver!" Toby exclaimed, his eyes wide, his fist pounding the table.

"What about it?"

"Denver holds a special place in our pantheon. Is that the right word? No matter. It was in Denver that *Battlefield Earth* takes place, surely Denver's claim to fame as a city."

He leaned across to me and his eyes now took on a furtive expression. "Do you want me to spill?

Do you think you can handle it?"

"Spill."

"There are some of us who don't think it's a novel at all."

"No?"

"No. Not a novel, but a . . ." he lowered his voice. "Prediction."

"Ah, I see."

"That's just between us."

"Of course."

"That's why some of us think Mr. Cruise has moved to Colorado. And when Xenu returns . . . No, forget that, I've said too much, but let's just say that the rumors about Mr. Cruise's bunker aren't just rumors."

I leaned back in the chair while Toby finished his chart. When he was done he passed it across the table and began explaining it. It looked like the stock market index after a turbulent week, but according to Toby the fluctuations weren't the problem, the problem was that the high points and the low points were in the wrong places. My life was a mess, I was rudderless, confused, clearly unhappy; however, there was an answer. He further explained that the Church of Scientology could help me iron out these personality defects, with the assistance of the thousand-question audit, and motivated people like Toby.

After this little speech he began biting his nails and, when he thought I wasn't looking, exploring his ear canal with the eraser on the top of the pencil.

When he began nibbling at the eraser I decided that as amusing as this all was, I'd had just about enough of it.

I was a serious person, here on serious business.

I gave him my card and heavy hit him with words like "dead Mexican" and "hit and run" and "intoxication" and "manslaughter" and "leaving the scene" of an accident.

He was already fragile, on edge. He began to simper and confessed that he had been drunk the night of the golf cart incident, but he'd only been trying to drive from the Scientology Center on Pearl Street to his apartment on Arapahoe, that there was no way he could get up the mountain, and in any case everyone had been given strict instructions to stay away from Mr. Cruise's estate and not to invade his personal space. The sheriff's department hadn't cared.

Still, he groaned, he knew it was wrong to get drunk, it was weak, and if *they* found out that he'd been drinking he could get into big trouble. He wanted to talk about it but I'd had enough.

I assured him that his secret was safe with me, exited IV#2, and, forsaking forever my chance of being accommodated in Tom Cruise's bunker when the aliens returned, walked back out into Fairview.

Within a minute I had dismissed Toby from my mind and had steered my trajectory back onto its proper course.

Got to eat. Call Esteban and eat.

The long road back.

The motel.

Upstairs, look for Paco.

A note: "Overtime! See you tonight!"

Stomach rumbling. Needed some food.

I had money left.

Paco said there was a good burrito place downtown on Logan Street. Good because it was too greasy for the white people and it was cheap.

Out again.

Sun, but a chill in the air, and a hundred meters from the motel Mr. New York Plates still there in a turning circle by the forest. Sipping a coffee, reading a *Denver Post*. Latino, bald, forty, chubby. Shifty-looking character, possibly an INS agent, possibly not.

I crossed the street.

"Good morning," I said to him.

He pretended not to hear.

I tapped the glass.

Window down, paper down. "Yes?" he said in accentless American.

"Do you know the way to San Jose?" I asked.

He grimaced. "I'm a stranger here myself," he said.

"A stranger in paradise, well, that's ok. Have a nice day."

The window whirred back up.

Now that he's been made, I'll never see him again, I thought with what turned out to be poor powers of prescience.

I walked down the hill.

I was wearing my third change of clothes of the day. Blue jeans, black shoes, a red blouse, and a raincoat Angela had left for some reason. Didn't she watch the movies? All those Yuma flicks with Bogart, it's always raining in L.A.

Main Street. Gray clouds. Few people about.

A family with kids. A gaggle of high-maintenance girlfriends buying apres-ski gear. Half a dozen individuals sitting outside Starbucks and Peet's Coffee and Tea, some of them still defiantly in flip-flops and shorts.

They didn't notice me.

I didn't register them.

I did see Mr. New York Plates again, following me on foot.

An INS agent almost certainly—the FBI investigating a murder in the New Mexico desert would surely do a better job.

I found the intersection for the burrito place, turned the corner on Logan, and ducked down an alley.

Garbage cans, Dumpsters, squirrels.

I waited for Mr. New York Plates.

He passed by in a hurry.

I waited until he had turned at the next block and then I ran back up the hill to the Wetback Motel.

His Toyota was still there in the turning circle.

On my second day in the force Lieutenant Díaz showed me a trick with a coat hanger that can open practically every car on the planet. I've used it many times. But I didn't have a coat hanger, and why not give the INS a little of their own back?

I picked up a log and smashed the passenger's-side window, opened the door, looked inside the car.

A sleeping bag, McDonald's wrappers, soda cans, a water bottle filled with urine. Nothing interesting until I found a digital camera in the glove compartment. I took it, slipped it in my coat pocket, and went back down the hill again.

Our paths did not cross as I had hoped they would.

I found the burrito place, ordered a beef fajita, and scanned through Mr. New York Plates's photographic work on the digital's tiny screen.

Pics of the motel, of trees, several of squirrels, of himself, and finally the jackpot: several shots of me, Esteban, Paco, and a few of the others.

Yeah—INS. Didn't bother me but I'd have to warn Paco. He should have gone to L.A. If they deported him now he'd be back to square one again. Poor kid.

I ate the burrito and drank a warm Corona.

"You're not good at this," Mr. New York Plates said in Spanish.

I looked up.

"Not good at what?" I asked, attempting sangfroid.

He didn't look angry, just tired. He put his hand out. I gave him the camera and he put it in his pocket.

"I like the ones of the squirrels best."

"What else did you take?" he asked.

"Well, I was spoiled for choice: the bottle of urine or the McDonald's wrappers?"

"Good day," he said and turned to go.

"Wait. Who are you?" I asked.

"Me? I'm someone who doesn't like to get dicked around by stupid fucking bitches!"

"I can't imagine you get much opportunity if that's an example of your small talk."

He sighed. "You think you're smart? We'll see how smart you really are," he said and walked out of the restaurant.

I didn't think of a snappy comeback until he'd been gone five minutes. "I'm only smart in comparison to some."

It was happy hour, so I ordered a Negra Modelo and considered him for a while, but I didn't have enough information to work up many hypotheses. And besides, I had other tasks.

I found the phone Esteban had left for me.

"Hello."

"Who is this?" Esteban asked.

"María."

"What's up? You wanna borrow the car?"

I did want to borrow the car. I needed the car tonight, but that's not why I was calling.

"No."

"Good. Fucking walk to town. Fed up with people using my property for their personal convenience. You all have it easy. Twenty years ago you'd all have had to work for a living. Don't know what I was thinking. Don't even try it. I'll have them check and see if it's in use with the GPS. Same to everyone else—no one uses the car until I get back on Monday. Give them an inch they take a mile."

"I haven't used it at all."

"Somebody's been driving it. I've logged it. Abusing their privileges. Oh yeah, and what's this I hear about you asking questions about some accident? Briggs left a crazy message on my voice mail."

"That's what I wanted to talk to you about."

"What?"

"A private investigator's been asking everyone questions about an incident that happened here in May. He's been hired by the Mexican consulate in Denver. Apparently someone killed a Mexican on the Old Boulder Road and he noticed that your car was involved in an accident around then. He thinks you might be implicated somehow."

I took the phone from my ear while Esteban threw out a complex series of curses involving the man's mother and all sorts of unlikely forms of intercourse.

When he was finished I pressed home the point. "What should I tell him? He wants to have your car towed to a lab for a forensic examination."

"My God, I leave town for one day and Briggs is going crazy and they're towing my car? What the hell is happening out there?"

"Look, Don Esteban, it's ok. I can handle this. He seems to be a little taken with me, but what should I tell him?"

"This is so fucked. I hit a deer. And that was a week before that accident. I was with Manuelito and Danny Ortega. We swiped an old doe. Jesus. And besides, everyone knows what happened to that dead Mex."

"Oh—"

"Oh yeah, that's no secret, one of our friends up the hill killed that poor bastard. Those fuckers. Briggs covered it up for them, I'll bet my life on that."

"One of the Hollywood people?"

"They can do anything they want in this town. That's why we gotta squeeze a big tip outta them. Has anyone mentioned tips to you yet? Christmas isn't far off."

I ignored the sidetrack. "So I should I tell the investigator it was one of the Hollywood people?"

"No, no, don't tell him anything. This isn't our concern. Say nothing."

"Ok."

"But I know. Oh yeah, they think they can keep me out of the loop? That's bullshit. Yeah, and just between you and me I'm pretty sure I know who did it."

"Who?"

"Well, I can't say over the phone. It's not exactly confidential formation. You remember him. He smashed up that big white Bentley. You know who I'm talking about? From the party? I think he's one of the houses you clean. No big secret."

Silence.

Youkilis.

And everybody knows.

And no one cares.

"Are you still there, María?"

"Yes."

"You sweet-talk him, María, don't let anyone touch my car. I'll fucking kill them."

"Ok."

"Ok. Good. Hold the fort. I'll be back. See you Monday."

● ● ●

It wasn't late. The room clock said nine but Paco was already asleep, exhausted from a day's overtime.

I needed sleep too.

Quietly I stored my supplies in the backpack and wrote a quick note for Paco. It didn't convey much of anything. "Paco, you've been more than a friend, but this next step belongs to me alone. If all goes well I will see you tomorrow before I take the bus to Mexico. If all does not go well, I want to thank you for everything. Love, María."

I read it, reread it, thought of crumpling it, left it.

I laid out my clothes, the backpack, the keys to Esteban's car.

I climbed under the sheet. Closed my eyes.

My head hurt. The wires were all fucked.

Next door a man stumbled in, drunk. He pushed his bed across the floor with an ugly screeching noise. He started to sing. Paco didn't stir. Poor kid. I examined his face. The bruise on his cheek from New Mexico had turned yellow. He looked young, vulnerable. We were all vulnerable. We were all on the box here. Above the trapdoor.

Time went past without sleep choosing to descend.

I looked at my watch. Ten minutes to eleven.

Fuck this. Call Ricky. Talk to him.

The lobby. Deserted. Early for America but late Mex time. Everyone up since four digging ditches or removing brush or cleaning rooms or minding kids or making food.

I took out the calling card and rang him direct. Please be in, just this once, *hermano.*

"*Ciao,*" he said.

"Isn't that goodbye?" I asked him.

"Honey, it's you!"

"It's me."

"How are you?"

"Good . . . Listen, Ricky, I thought I would let you know, I'm going to try for it tonight."

A pause. "Is it our boy?" he asked cautiously.

"Yes. You were spot on, Ricky. I've wasted enough time."

"What are you going to do?"

"I don't want to say over the phone."

"Of course. Sorry."

A longer pause. My phone card minutes being eaten up.

"I talked to Mom yesterday. She sent you a message," he said at last.

"From Mother? There's a message from Mom?"

"Yeah."

"What is it?"

"Well, you know how she is," Ricky said sheepishly, preparing me for something about Yoruba gods or a warning about rapists or a request to pick up some oranges for Dad so he could sell them at the Pan American Games.

Ricky cleared his throat. "She says to tell you that she cast the fifty-second hexagram. You're to study the fifty-second hexagram. I think it's a reference to the I Ching."

"Yeah. I know. Did Chinese my first year, remember?"

"Yeah."

More silence, more talk without words.

"What happened to her, Ricky? Do you think it was Dad leaving or the time in jail?"

"Nah. It's just one of those things."

A voice in Ricky's apartment asked him something. "Hold on," Ricky hissed with his hand over the receiver.

Let him go. He can't help. "I have to run. I love you, Ricky."

"I love you too, big sis. Remember, you don't have to do anything, you can just come home."

"I know."

"Be careful."

"I will."

"Bye."

"*Ciao.*"

I hung up, looked at the phone. Ricky *hadn't* helped. I didn't feel validated. I felt worse. I felt bad and cheap, as if this whole thing was some monstrous vanity project. Jack and I weren't that far apart. I should have seen it in the desert. Should have seen it before now.

The script fluttered in the wind: Mercado walks back to her room. Close-up on her face. She looks tired. She turns the door handle. The door creaks. She goes inside. The room is filled with moonlight . . .

Too slow. Skip to the end. Is that me walking on Malecón or am I on some slab in the Jefferson County Coroner's Office?

The last page had been ripped out.

I sat on the bed. Good old Paco, still out for the count. A million TV ads for sleep aids in this country. You want a good night's sleep? Work like a fucking Mexican.

I slipped between the sheets, set the alarm for two hours hence. Pulled the covers over my eyes and tried to get some z's. After all, two hours was better than nothing and there was going to be an even longer day ahead.

CHAPTER 16

GUNMETAL

The highway goes silent. The forest holds its breath. The mountain sleeps. The image of the fifty-second hexagram is also a mountain—the youngest son of heaven and earth. The male principle is at the top, the female principle beneath. It is a hexagram denoting stillness. But in the Book of Changes rest is only equilibrium between forces. Movement is always on the verge of breaking out. Why that one, Mother? But then again, why any of it? Why the cards, the yarrow stalks, the Santería church? Why would someone who has no future care about the future?

My eyes flutter. Open.

The floor. The wall. The two beds.

I haven't slept.

Paco's still out. I can tell when he's deep down because it's almost as if he's dead. When he does meet the horseman they're going to have to hold a mirror over his mouth.

As if reading my thoughts, he smiles. One of those little grins that means so many things. He's got back doors, does Paco.

I walk to the window. Snow coming down like cherry blossoms. Floating. Not the way I imagined it to be. In the old reel-to-reel Soviet flicks that we used to get on Saturday nights it always seemed harder, more painful, somehow. Not soft like this. Why would all those French soldiers fleeing Moscow complain about this? It's beautiful.

My watch says 12:30. It's already Monday. Shit. I have to go.

I grab my clothes, open the front door, ease out the heavy backpack.

Better to get dressed on the outside walkway than risk having to deal with him. If I tell him he can't come, he'll see it as an assault on his manhood.

Snowflakes as big as mandarin oranges. I put out my hand and catch a few. Lick them off.

Dress: black jeans, black long-sleeved T-shirt, thick black sweater, black ski mask, light jacket, black gloves, black sneakers. I check the backpack: rope, knife, sledgehammer, duct tape, road map, two guns.

Snow over everything.

It's ok.

I zip the main pocket, heave it on my shoulders, go downstairs.

Ice crystals on the bottom steps. The smell of pine and laurel.

I walk to the Range Rover, throat dry, eyes filled with tears, knees shaking.

Not cut out for this. They saw that in Cuba, or they would have promoted me before now or invited me to join the DGI. They knew I wasn't made for the rough stuff. Few women go high in the Party brass, but some do and are rewarded with those elusive travel visas to Vietnam or North Korea or China.

They don't hand those out to lightweights. *Like me.*

I take out the car key, press the button, the car unlocks. Always seems like a miracle.

I shiver. Get in, put the key in the ignition, start the engine, turn on the heat.

"Now what?"

Get on with it, that's what. But I sit there, warming my hands over the vents. Reluctant to move. The gun's been bothering me. I wonder if Mr. Jones is still awake.

The gun.

Esteban's cell phone.

On the second ring Mr. Jones picks up. "Hello?"

"Mr. Jones, I'm sorry to bother you at this hour, you probably remember me, I was the lady who broke into your house."

"Yeah, what can I do ye for? In the market for another weapon? I'm up, I'll be up for a couple of hours."

The Range Rover purrs into life. Very quiet. I like that. Almost as quiet as Jack's Bentley. I put the ski mask on, drive out onto Lime Kiln Road.

Mr. Jones's lights are the only ones still burning.

A little tremor of doubt. Maybe he has hard feelings.

Park. Walk the drive. Ring the bell.

No answer.

This isn't about the gun. Who gives a fuck about the gun? What the hell am I doing *here*? It's what the PNR psychologist would call "displacement activity."

It's bullshit, is what it is.

The truth is I don't want to see Youkilis. I don't want to torture the truth out of him even if he does deserve it.

I ring the bell again. While I'm waiting I take the ski mask off.

Finally Mr. Jones opens the door. He's wearing a coat, dark blue jeans, and work boots. He's covered with mud.

"So that's what you look like. Figured you was older. Come in, come in."

I sit down in the living room. Funky smell. TV blaring. He turns it off.

"Drink?" he asks.

"Sure."

He comes back with a mug a quarter filled with clear liquid. I drink it. It doesn't burn like Havana moonshine.

"It's good," I say.

He smiles. "Excuse the dirt, I was out checking my traps," he says.

I nod. "I'd like to show you something," I say.

I produce the gun. He takes it, holds it up to the light.

"A thousand dollars," he says. "It's a fair price. I can get three times that, but you can't."

"I just want to know about it. It looks unusual."

He nods. "You've a good eye. It *is* unusual. Real collector's item. It's a Russian Stechkin APS pistol, Cuban-made, 1993 to 1999—you can tell that because it's manufactured from gunmetal, not stainless steel—good stock, sights set for twenty-five meters, at one point it was fitted with a silencer, it—"

"Gunmetal" catches my attention.

"Excuse me, what? Gunmetal? I've heard that before. What is that?"

"Gunmetal is a type of bronze, an alloy of copper, tin, and zinc. Where I'm from—Macon County, Alabama—they still call it red brass."

"It's a metal? That's what they make guns out of?"

He laughs. "Not anymore. Everybody uses steel. That's how I spotted this little beauty right away. I don't know if you know much about Cuba, but after the USSR collapsed they couldn't get steel. Went back to gunmetal for their Stechkin knockoffs."

I nod but I'm confused. My PNR pistol was a standard Chinese revolver. I'd never seen one of these before.

"So where did this gun come from, I mean, who has these?" I ask.

"I reckon they made about two thousand of 'em. I can check my book. As far as I know—and what I don't know ain't worth shit—they was for KGB, the Cuban KGB, whatever they is."

"The DGSE, internal security, or the DGI, Raúl Castro's secret police."

"Yeah, something like that. Where'd you get it?"

The room spinning, the walls closing in.

I get up. "I have to go. You can keep the gun. I don't want it."

He shakes his head. "This belongs to you," he says.

Ok. I throw it in the backpack, forget about it.

A thank-you. A goodbye. Even a good luck.

I get out, breathe the cold air.

What does it mean?

Dad had a spook's gun. Did they send someone to kill him? Had he survived the attack and taken the gun? Was he a spook himself?

No, they were after him. That's why he was calling himself Suarez and living as a Mexican. Had he stolen the gun in Havana? Bought it? Killed someone? How long had he been planning his defection? What exactly happened that weekend we went to Santiago?

Too many questions. Information overload.

Fuck it. Just drive.

I get in the car. Hit the lights. Back to town. Malibu Mountain. The Old Boulder Road.

Cruise. Watson. Tambor. Tyrone. Lights off.

Youkilis. Lights on.

Park the car. Cut the beams. Wait . . . Wait . . . Wait.

Snow stops. Moon comes out.

A car drives past. Damn it. Can't sit here all night.

"I'll kill half an hour at the motel and then come back," I say to myself.

Down the hill.

I pull into the motel parking lot and there, standing in front of me with his arms folded, is Paco.

T-shirt, boxer shorts, coat, cigarette, no shoes. Furious. A button winds down the driver's-side window. "Francisco, you'll catch your death, go back inside," I say like a big sister.

He walks to the Range Rover. "I'm not cold. Where are you going?"

"That's my business."

He shakes his head. "No. It isn't. It's our business. We're in this together."

"Nicaraguan idiot. You're out of your depth."

"I think it's you that's out of your depth," he says.

He reaches into the car and tries to grab the keys.

"Fuck off!" I tell him and push his hand away.

"Get out of the car!" he hisses.

"Who do you think you are?"

"I'm someone who doesn't want to see you get killed. Get out of the car."

"Why the hell should I?"

Paco thinks for a moment. "For one thing, you don't know that Esteban's changed his plans. He's going to be back tomorrow morning by seven and he seems the type that'll notice if his fucking car is missing. He'll call the cops. How long were you planning on taking it?"

Two-hour drive to the lake. One-hour interrogation. Two hours back. Not enough time. On my return the police would be looking for a stolen car.

"*Mierde*," I mutter.

Paco nods. "Let me get dressed. I'll drive you to the house."

"What good will that do?"

"You can steal Youkilis's car," Paco says with a wolfish grin.

He's figured out everything.

I underestimated him. What else have I got wrong?

"Won't someone report that his car has been stolen?" I ask.

"Who? Youkilis will be in the trunk, going wherever it is you're taking him, and you can leave a note on the kitchen table that says, 'Gone for drive, back at noon' or something . . . Right?"

"Right."

"Good, now wait there," he says and runs upstairs to pull on his jeans and a sweater.

I shift to the passenger side.

Make a decision.

Whatever else he says, he's not coming with me.

"You're not coming with me," I tell him when he returns.

"Why not?"

"This is personal. This is nothing to do with you. And . . . and I want to do it by myself."

He doesn't answer. "Did you hear what I said?" I ask him.

He turns to look at me. He nods, slowly. "I heard and I know why you said it," he replies hesitantly.

"But what?" I ask.

"But I'm just not sure you can handle it. Kidnapping a man from his house, interrogating him. It's not you."

"I'm a cop. I'm in the Cuban PNR. A detective. I've done my fair share of shaking people down, bracing defendants. All the heavy play, all the games. I know what I'm doing."

"A cop? You?"

"Me."

He coughs to hide his skepticism. "Well, ok, but when I was a kid in Nicaragua—"

"Jesus, if I never hear that line again . . ."

"This is pertinent."

"I don't want to hear it."

"Your loss. I am a fucking font of knowledge," he says with a laugh.

"Come on, I don't have time for this."

Paco fakes a hurt look, nods, reverses the Range Rover out of the spot, and heads it up the mountain.

"How did you figure it was Youkilis?" he asks.

"I could ask you the same question."

"The way you looked at him. It was the way you looked at those men in New Mexico."

"I had him from the get-go. My brother, Ricky, ran the garages and found that only two cars had been brought in that weekend. An old lady called Mrs. Cooper whose story checks out and Jack Tyrone's Bentley."

"Tyrone."

"Yeah, except that Jack was in L.A."

"So you think Youkilis was driving Tyrone's car?"

"That's what I'm going to find out."

Paco looks at me doubtfully, knitting the eyebrows of his kid's face. "You've covered all the angles?"

"All the ones I need to cover."

"Why was your father hiding under a Mexican passport?"

"I don't know. He was paranoid. I guess he thought the DGI was going to kill him, which is just crazy—a million Cubans have defected and the DGI is going to go after him?"

But then those doubts again. The gun. Karen's escape plan.

I hesitate and continue almost to myself, "Shit, Paco, maybe he wasn't so paranoid, maybe they did come after him."

"What do you mean by that?"

We stop at a traffic light. Paco repeats his question. The light goes green, snapping me out of it.

"Oh, I was just rambling, I don't mean anything. The important thing is I've got what I need to go on."

Paco nods again. "Well," he says finally, "if you're happy with what you've got then I'm happy."

"It doesn't matter two fucks whether *you're* happy or not, Francisco," I say with irritation. Stupid kid. I should never have told him anything, should never have brought him in.

We hit Pearl Street.

Everything's closed, but the big plate-glass windows are still illuminated. I read off the names for the last time. Versace. Donna Karan. Armani. Ralph Lauren. Hermès. Harry Winston. De Beers. Starbucks. Peet's Coffee and Tea. Another Starbucks. The mystery bookstore. The hand-woven yoga mat shop. The Tibetan shop. The organic food store. Power Yoga. Mystic Yoga. Dance Yoga. Namaste Yoga. The BMW dealership, the Mercedes dealership.

Not a cop anywhere. None necessary. No crime. Briggs runs a tight ship.

We drive through the last stoplight and finally get on the road to Malibu Mountain.

Paco slows at Jack Tyrone's house and stops outside the ranch-style house next door. The lights are off. Youkilis is asleep.

"You're sure about this?" Paco asks, his voice descending half an octave, an attempt to sound more mature. A punk kid, yes, and yet there's something about him that isn't young. "You know about the alarm systems and guard dogs and that kind of thing?" he says in a flat voice that has no hint of condescension about it, but still, it's annoying. He's second-guessing me. Hinting again that this is a man's job.

"I've been in the house three times. I've scouted the alarms. I know where they are. I've got the fucking code. I know what I'm doing," I say firmly.

"You think you know," he says in an undertone.

"Thank you for driving me, but I want you to go now, Paco. I've prepped as best as I can. If it fucks up it's my fault and I don't want you or anyone else involved."

"I don't mind," he says.

"Yeah, but I do."

I unclick the seatbelt and grab the backpack. I put my hand on his leg. "Paco, when I get out of the car, I want you to drive back to the motel and go to bed. I don't want you driving up and down this road haunting me. I want you out of the picture. I need this, Paco, I need you to promise me that you'll do that."

He shakes his head in the dark. "If that's what you want . . ."

"It *is* what I want. This belongs to me."

He hesitates. "Will you at least tell me your plan?" he asks reasonably.

"No. I don't want you following me."

Paco sighs, rubs his chin. "You don't want any help from me at all?"

"It's not like that. You would be a terrific help. But this is about me. Me and Ricky and Mom. That's why I'm here. To get some of the answers, to get some part of the truth."

"I don't think I'll be able to go back to sleep."

"Try."

"Tell me when you're going to be back."

"I, I don't know. I suppose I'll be back before noon."

"And if you're not?"

"It means I'm in jail or dead."

"Mother of God," he mutters.

"If they do arrest me or kill me, they might come to the motel asking questions."

"Don't worry about me, María. Worry about yourself."

"I do. I don't want you dragged down in the wreckage of my sinking ship."

"Jesus, look at you. You're shaking," he says, taking my hand.

"I'm all right."

"Do you need a better coat?"

"No, this thing is really thick, there's a layer of fleece and a layer of something else."

"Let me come with you. You don't know what you're doing. I was with the *guapo* army in the jungle when I was eleven."

"This isn't like that. This requires finesse."

He bites his lip and we sit there holding hands like children.

"I'm going to go," I say, my voice barely above a croak.

He leans across the seat and kisses me. "You'll need these," he says, and gives me his Mexican cigarettes.

"Hey, and for sugar, this."

An orange.

I get out of the Range Rover, shoulder my heavy backpack, and close the door. He turns on the engine and drives back down the mountain.

I wait until the Range Rover's lights are gone before I pull on the ski mask.

I look at my hands. He was right. They are shaking.

And now I feel utterly alone.

Scared.

Maybe I could do it tomorrow.

No. Tomorrow I have to leave for Mexico and I have to be in Havana the day after that, otherwise Hector and Ricky and Mom will all get taken.

"Ok," I whisper to myself.

I walk to the rusting metal box next to Youkilis's gate.

I key in the code.

The gate swings open.

I step inside and stand there.

After half a minute the gate closes behind me.

I might as well go on. It's like launching a raft into the Gulf Stream: once the current takes you there's no going back.

Snow is still falling. Lighter now. Little diamonds on my jacket and padded black sweater.

I scope the place. No lights. No sound.

I walk over the gravel drive to the path.

Clouds drifting across the half-moon. The night holding her breath.

I fumble in my pocket and touch the key.

I look over the wall at Jack's house. The house is dead but he might still be awake watching the tube in the master bedroom.

I wonder how his party went at the Cruises.

How will you take it if I have to kill your buddy?

I walk down the zinc-colored footpath, making footprints in the snow.

If it all goes to shit those footprints will be useful to the cops.

I reach the front door and take the maid's key out of my pocket.

Breathe. In. Out. In. Out.

I put the key in the lock, turn it, and push. The door opens.

I now have thirty seconds to put the correct code into the alarm box. I walk in, flip open the box, and key in 9999—the default. The red light flashes green.

Big breath.

I close the front door.

I take the backpack from my shoulders, unzip it, and remove the flashlight and the gun. Reshoulder it, walk upstairs. Nineteen steps on the curve. Second door on the left. This is the time for surprises. A houseguest. A new dog. A whore from Denver. An old girlfriend who's driven up from Vail. Jack, feeling lonely, staying over.

I wait for something. Anything. The tension is bending my back like a coconut palm.

Nothing. Yet. Stand there at the top of the stairs.

The carpet I've cleaned and cleaned. An ancient Greek drinking vessel. A poster from the motorcycle show at the Guggenheim.

Autographed pictures. Friends of Jack, friends of Peter. Famous friends only. Clooney, Affleck, Pitt, and the neighbors, Cruise and Tambor.

The master bedroom.

The handle.

Bladder feels full. A noise. Look behind me—nothing.

Ski mask restricting my field of vision, making me claustrophobic, jumpy.

Pressure on the handle.

The door opens.

I go in.

The TV's on, bathing the room in a zigzaggy blue light. Gun up. Flashlight off. Fumbling, I drop the flashlight and it crashes to the floor with a thud. Down on one knee, raise the gun. Wait . . . Nothing.

Stand again. Check the corners. Go in.

Youkilis lying there on top of the bed, naked, asleep. The TV playing images on his belly.

I walk to the bed. Look at him. Deep gone. Drug sleep. Scan the room. No one else.

Back to the TV. Perfect if he'd been watching child pornography or a snuff movie or something bourgeois and decadent, but it's not, it's just the Discovery Channel. A show about blue whales.

I turn it off.

He doesn't stir. He's sleeping, spread-eagled with a grin on his face. A ten-milligram tab of Ambien and a glass of hundred-year-old cognac must be the recipe for bliss. What if he'd taken the whole packet of sleeping pills? That would let me off the hook. Wouldn't it, Dad? Wouldn't it, Ricky?

I roll up my sleeve and look at my watch. 1:30.

Where did the time go?

I stand there with the gun pointed at him.

He's not even snoring. And he's happy.

On the nightstand next to him there's an open drawer. I look in. A Ziploc bag filled with drugs and currency. I take it, sit on the bed.

"I really don't want to do this," I whisper to myself. Then don't. Go. Walk back down the hill, get a good night's sleep and the bus to El Paso. Go. Ricky won't mind. Mom doesn't care. Karen's moved on. It'll be better for everyone. Go, little birdie.

I stand but before I'm even on my feet the chemical messengers have done their work and my synapses have flashed back through one of the good times. Before the affairs, before the blowups, before Santiago. Dad laughing as Ricky and I steer the ferry on the first run of the day, the sun rising over the bay, seagulls on the deck, water sluicing through the gunwales.

Another time: Aunt Lilia's wedding, Dad in a blue suit, Mom in a black dress, me holding his hand in a sepia photograph and dancing with him to a Yuma tune.

And one more: Ricky, Dad, and me watching Cuba win everything at the Pan American Games, me complaining of thirst and Dad from nowhere producing mangoes he had hidden for hours.

You took all of this, Youkilis. You ended it and now it belongs to you.

You own it and I want it back.

I walk around the bed.

I look at him and force myself to poke him in the ribs with the gun barrel.

"Ugh," he says and doesn't move.

I poke him again.

Another "Ugh." But he still doesn't wake.

Damn it. Now what?

Use it, Mercado.

Yeah. Use it. I roll him over. I put his hands on his back above his ass. He starts to snore. He's way deep. Fathoms. Kilometers. I put the flashlight on the bed, take off my backpack, and remove the duct tape.

Five minutes later it's done.

His wrists are duct-taped together and the Ambien-cognac combo has kept him out.

The next step?

The car.

I go back downstairs and through the kitchen to the garage. I need the keys he keeps on a hook by the door.

I turn on the flashlight and there they are, but even if they hadn't been there it would have been ok. Every Cuban knows how to hotwire.

I pop the trunk and throw out a crate of seltzer, a pair of ski boots, and a lawn chair.

Nice and roomy.

Back upstairs.

Sleeping beauty sleeps still.

I rip off another line of duct tape and slather it over his mouth.

That's what wakes him. He groans. Jolts upright. I flip the lights. Ski mask, gun, the twenty-first-century equivalent of the devil in the forest.

Screams behind the tape.

He scrambles away from me, falls off the bed, and bangs his head on the nightstand. I let him lie there for a minute to gather his wits. Then I point the gun at his heart. It's in this moment I decide that I'm not going to speak. Not a word until he's at the lake.

He looks at the gun and nods his head. He struggles to his feet.

I point at the door and sidle around the bed so that he's ahead of me.

He turns and stares at me. He's wondering if this is a nightmare.

Yeah, it is.

I point at the door and give him a little push and he walks ahead of me, slowly, onto the landing.

I flip the lights.

All that stuff.

The celeb pics. Caricatures. Expensive art I hadn't noticed before. Small postwar Picasso lithographs. Jack's preferences are for the big and splashy but Youkilis, if I recall, attended Princeton. Taste. Class. Discretion.

He comes to the stairs, hesitates, looks back at me, afraid.

What's he thinking? That I'm going to push him?

I point down. He shakes his head. He's trembling all over. His penis has practically disappeared.

I point again, this time with the gun.

Gingerly he makes way down the inside part of the curve, rubbing against the railing with his left arm. His back twitches at the bottom and he takes another look at me.

I don't like it.

He's up to something, I better keep an—

Suddenly he trips and falls against the phone stand. The phone and a notebook and a cell phone clatter to the ground on top of him.

Accident? Was he trying to call 911? Quickly I pick up the phone and put it back in the cradle.

He's groaning. He's cut himself across the chest. I have no sympathy. I kick him in the ribs and direct him to get up. His eyes are calmer, less wide.

I'm uneasy.

He did something there. I don't know what. But he did something.

I look at the phone and the wall—everything seems ok.

Better get the hell out of here. I point at the kitchen.

We walk in and I open the door to the garage.

I point at the garage door and while he goes ahead I swing the backpack around in front of me, unzip it, and take out the pepper spray.

He stops at the open trunk of his BMW, turns, and looks at me. He shakes his head. He's not getting in the trunk. Trunk equals death. If he stays in the house he has a chance, but if he gets in the car he's going to die.

I've been expecting this. I pepper spray him in the face.

He screams, his knees buckle. I run at him and ram him onto the lip of the trunk. He's six-five and built, so if he falls to the ground it's going to be a hell of a job to get him in there. I drop the gun and pepper spray and shove his pelvis with both hands. Even blinded and in agony he fights me, kicks, but it's too late, I have him in. I punch him in the nose and, stunned and winded, he tumbles backward into the trunk.

I lift the backpack, take out the tape.

He's sobbing, bleeding, but he'll live.

I grab his ankles, pin them under my arm, and wrap them in the duct tape. The punch and the pepper spray have winded him and he's as docile as a lamb. But that won't last forever. This has to be *tight*.

Roll after roll.

He starts to fight and buck.

Another loop over his mouth.

I close the trunk.

Muffled screams.

I don't feel good about this.

I stand there for what seems like forever, then go back into the house and turn off all the lights.

Back to the garage.

He's quiet.

Maybe he had a heart attack.

It would still be murder.

I click the button that opens the garage door and open the passenger's-side door of the BMW. I throw my gear in the backseat, get in, close the door, turn the key, start her up, and drive out.

Lights on.

Seatbelt on to stop the alarm.

The BMW drives like a tank, and I would know, since I did part of my military service on a T-72.

The driveway. Full beam. Heart pounding.

I look behind to see if the garage door is going to close by itself.

It doesn't.

I have to do something. I fumble around until I see a small box clipped onto the sunshade. A button says OPEN/CLOSE. I press CLOSE.

It closes.

I drive toward the gates.

Somehow they know I'm coming and open automatically.

I turn left down the mountain road.

I take off the ski mask and focus on driving.

I forgot to leave that note about being back in the afternoon. It's ok. Forget it. The help won't notice anything's amiss. I'm the help.

The icy road. The trees. He starts to make noise back there.

I click the radio. Flip, flip, flip until I get a Denver classical station playing Shostakovich.

I take out the map book, hit the interior light.

Where are we?

Ah yes.

The Old Boulder Road to the first junction.

I turn the light off and drive.

Trees. Houses. The junction.

The road splits. The 34 goes east into Rocky Mountain National Park, the 125 goes all the way up to Wyoming.

I want the 125.

I recheck the map. Straight shot to the state line.

Nothing behind me. Banging from the trunk. Ahead on the 125 the lights of cars, trucks.

The snow petering off but still a nuisance. Windshield wipers. Radio louder.

I turn left onto the 125 and accelerate the BMW up to sixty.

When I get on the road, I gun it to eighty and then ninety.

Minutes go by. Ten, twenty, forty-five.

Shostakovich gives way to Purcell gives way to Mozart.

I slow down to go through the small town of Walden, which at this hour is completely dead. I accelerate again, and not long after Walden we're in Wyoming. A sign says WELCOME TO THE COWBOY STATE. Below that someone's scrawled "Cheney Cuntry."

An inner voice as persistent as a teenage pimp says this is a big mistake. This is the gamble of your life. And for what? For what? You still don't even know for sure.

Shut up. Only about twenty minutes now.

But actually the BMW gets me there in fifteen.

We're going so fast and so effortlessly that I almost miss the turnoff for the lake.

Brakes, a skid.

I drive down the dirt road.

Pitch-black.

Here too early.

Can't go on the ice in the dark.

Have to wait.

The moon is in the eighth house.

But I want the sun.

I kill the engine.

I pull out the pack of Mexican cigarettes and lift the orange from the floor.

CHAPTER 17

FIFTY GRAND

Images from Al Andalus. The dogwood minarets. The ice-lake *sajadah*. The raven muezzins. A lake in Wyoming. America.

I try to think of a Cuban metaphor but I can't. There's nowhere in Cuba like this.

Clean. Cold. Quiet. Safe.

But even America is only an idea for those who don't live here. Here you see that it's a place like other places.

My hand under his arm.

Keeping him up.

My fingers turning blue.

He listens to the story.

I came from Cuba to investigate the death of my father. The poor dead Mex. The town ratcatcher. An anonymous wetback with false papers and a fake ID. A nobody. Barely a mention in the paper.

I posed as a maid in your home. I gathered material. I got evidence. I eavesdropped. It wasn't Mrs. Cooper. It wasn't Esteban. It wasn't Toby. It was you. I know it was you. Jack told me. Everyone told me. You hit my father and you left him to die by the side of the road.

Well . . . Now you know.

What have you got to say?

Nothing.

He can't speak. He can barely breathe.

The backwater of breath encircling our mouths and merging with the smoke from the cigarettes.

Tell me. Be quick and I will be merciful. For Paco is right, I have no stomach for this. For any of it. Come on. Speak. Let's get this over with.

Say it. Now. Save yourself. "Tell me."

Death is mist on the surface of the ice. It collapses his resistance.

"But, but, this is crazy, I didn't even do it. I wasn't driving."

"You would say that, wouldn't you? Now, for the last time tell me the truth."

"That is the truth. I wasn't driving."

"If it wasn't you, then who?"

"Jack," he says with single-syllable finality.

"Of course, bite the hand the feeds, blame the boss. Unfortunately, the boss has an airtight alibi."

"No alibi. It was h-him," he insists.

"A lie. Jack was in California. In L.A."

"No, he wasn't. Believe me. He definitely was not."

Jack *was* in L.A. Ricky did the research. Jack was in L.A at a rehab clinic. It was Jack's car but Jack was in L.A. Jack confirmed it to me himself. This pathetic attempt is doing nothing but making me angry. Your life is in the balance, Youkilis, you need my goodwill, not my wrath.

"Tell me the truth!"

"That is the truth."

"Jack already told me you were driving the car."

"That's the lie. That's the lie we made up," he says.

His eyes close.

Open.

They're red. Weary. Something about those eyes. This doesn't look like the ploy of a desperate man. This—this has the smell of verisimilitude.

"Jack was in California," I attempt again.

"Jack was in F-Fairview."

"No."

Teeth chattering. Lips blue. Pupils dilated.

"He'd auditioned for this movie. D-down to him and s-s-someone else. David Press at CAA told him he'd m-m-missed out. They went another d-direction. This was a lead in a major m-m-movie. Jack lost it. Went drinking. Flew to Vail. Came here looking for m-me. I w-was in Denver. He went to a bar, some guys b-bought him drinks, not many. He felt ok to drive up the m-mountain. He m-must have hit him on the way home."

"No," I mutter. But it's only a word. I know truth when I hear it.

Fact is, I've known it all along.

Youkilis was easy to hate. Jack was easy to like.

A one-minute cross-examination and he gives me the whole sorry tale: Youkilis gets back from Denver, finds Jack, sees the car, sees blood on the car. Waits for a cop. No cop comes. Maybe a deer, he thinks. Or a dog. Or, at worst, a hit-and-run with no witnesses. He doesn't panic. His instinct kicks in. He drives Jack to Vail and charters a plane. It lands in L.A in the middle of the night. A limo takes him to the Promises Rehab Center in Malibu. Youkilis leaks a story that Jack's been in there for two days and is doing well.

I've put the wrong guy in the grave.

Maybe I made you detective too soon, Hector said.

Yeah. Maybe you did.

Mind racing. Wait a minute. He's still guilty of the cover-up. Accessory after the fact.

"You put him in the rehab and that was it?"

"That was it."

"But you bought off the cops."

"No. That was later. Somehow Sheriff B-Briggs f-figured it out. He shook us d-down for fifty grand."

"Fifty thousand dollars?"

"Fifty grand. It was n-nothing. We were relieved it was so l-little. He d-didn't even take it for him-himself."

"What do you mean?"

"He p-paid it into the p-police b-benevolent fund."

Fifty thousand for a dead Mex. Fifty thousand for my father's whole life. An insult. Horrible. But . . . but no reason to kill him.

At least not reason enough.

At least not for me.

"Oh no," I say to myself. "No, no, no."

"What are you g-going t-to d-do?" he asks.

"Fuck!" I yell out loud and put down the gun.

Going to have to lift you out, you bastard. Going to have to try and save you. How? Under the armpits, drag him. "Put your arms out," I tell him.

But in the last minute hypothermia has started to set in. His eyes are fixed. The cigarette is burning him and he doesn't even notice.

"*Mierde!* I'm going to fucking save you."

I rip the cig from his mouth.

I kneel behind him, shove my hands under his wet, frozen shoulders, and try to heave him out backward.

I can't get purchase.

I pull again.

Distracted, I don't notice, behind me on the hill, Jack Tyrone, Deputy Crawford, Deputy Klein, and Sheriff Briggs get out of the black police Cadillac Escalade. I don't hear Sheriff Briggs talk about the panic button on Youkilis's house phone or the homing GPS in his BMW. I don't notice them examining Youkilis's car or see them as they follow the footsteps that lead down to the lake. I don't see any of them look up, startled, when they hear me yell.

And what do they see?

POV shift to the main man, Briggs. Furious. Jubilant. A rifle in his hands. Like John Wayne at the end of all those Yuma flicks. Here with the Seventh to save the day.

"Let's go, boys," and they run through the trees to the water's edge.

Briggs sees me trying to pull Youkilis out of the hole, but it can't be obvious that I've changed my mind, that I'm trying to save him. Probably he thinks I'm administering the coup de grâce.

Maybe he doesn't care what I'm trying to do.

He unslings a high-velocity .270 elk-hunting rifle with a manual sight. The sight is set for a hundred meters and I'm a little closer than that.

Aim a tad high, he thinks.

He's never shot a woman before. But he doesn't feel that that's an issue. He's calm, focused, professional. *Don't even think of her as a woman. God-damn wetback bitch. And besides, this is your job. This ain't nothing. This is taking out soldiers on the Basra road. This is bagging boar in the Rio Grande brush country. This is a duck shoot on the Kansas line.*

He fixes my skull in the T of the manual crosshair.

He sniffs the breeze, adjusts for it, and moves the T to the back of my head.

"Yes," he says, and just like that, the whole of the sensual world goes—

CHAPTER 18

CITY OF HEROES

The bullet struck me on the head. *Ice gone. New Mexico gone. Colorado gone. All of it . . . gone.*

And that was good. That was as it should be.

I shouldn't be here. I need to be elsewhere. Across America, across the sea. Back to the island of the crooked mouth. Over the forests and plantations. Over the jungle. Across the years.

Smell is the most basic part of memory. What is that smell? The aroma of cigars and mangrove and somewhere bacon soldering itself onto an unwatched pan.

A lazy day in autumn. A school holiday.

We'd taken the train to Santiago de Cuba. That long, long train. No matter how much you pack, all the food runs out and the water runs out and it breaks down and you think it's never going to get there. You could walk faster than that train for much of the journey.

Ricky and I do, slipping out of the last carriage and running behind and jumping on again.

My uncle's Arturo's house. A large, white two-story sugarbeet overseer's place from the twenties. An American UFC man built it and my uncle took it after the Revolution. I say Santiago but it's not really in the city at all. An unnamed village on the edge of the mangrove forest and the sea. Four streets. A road. Swamp.

Country cousins. And every other kid a friend.

Hot.

Very hot . . .

Some of the kids were playing hide-and-seek at the far end of the road, where the neighborhood was almost swallowed up by abandoned plantations. Halfhearted attempts were being made to look for people and there were halfhearted attempts to hide.

Ricky and I were lying in the yard, watching everything from under the shade of the big warped palm tree. Palm trees curve up at thirty degrees but this one had a gentle slope that bent back on itself, as if it had been designed for climbing. Even toddlers could get halfway up it—there had been accidents.

It was 1993, right in the heart of the "special economic period." Communism had collapsed in Russia, and Cuba had no friends. This was before the Venezuelans or the Chinese or the roaring comeback of the sex trade. Blackouts were common in Havana and there was no traffic anywhere.

A nice day.

Some of the older people had brought chairs to catch a few rays of the sun before it vanished behind the stone wall of the graveyard. Mostly women, knitting, repairing clothes, talking. Mrs. Ramírez and her sister in the street in front of us saying things about the decline of morals among kids today. Mrs. Ramírez reckoned that a decent haircut would improve the behavior of most of the unruly boys in Santiago, whereas her sister favored a good kick in the ass.

When they began talking about what was wrong with girls today I stopped listening.

"Come on, little guy, come on."

I looked up sleepily. Ricky was trying to coax one of the swamp iguanas to come into the garden with a ropey string of sausage. But all the iguana wanted was to be left alone.

"Where did you get those 'izos?" I asked Ricky.

"Kitchen."

"Aunt Isabella will kill you."

"She'll never know," Ricky said.

"Iguanas only eat insects," I said.

"Not so, Dad says they eat mice. Meat," Ricky said.

"Kids, are you outside?" Dad's voice.

"Get rid of those sausages, Dad will go crazy. You know what he's like about wasting food," I hissed.

"They're not from the ration. Aunt Isabella has half a dozen strings like this in the pantry."

"Get rid of them."

"What do you want me to do?" Ricky asked.

"I hear you. Wait there, kids. Don't go anywhere," Dad yelled from an up-stairs window.

I grabbed the string of sausages and hurled them up into the palm tree branches. They caught first time.

"Dad, we're over here," I yelled back.

Dad came out of the house. He was wearing a loosely buttoned white shirt, tan army trousers, and a pair of checked slip-on shoes. He had shaved and combed his unruly hair.

"Hi," we said.

Dad nodded, walked past us, and looked down the street. He said *buenos días* to Mrs. Ramírez, even calling her *señora* instead of comrade. She smiled when he spoke to her. Everyone did. Dad was well liked and he got on with all strata of society. Mrs. Ramírez asked him about his job and he said some-thing about how he loved it, how he always wanted to sail the seven seas. Mrs. Ramírez laughed, because the only stretch of sea Dad's vessel ever went to was from one side of Havana Bay to the other.

When the pleasantries were over with the neighbors he sat on the white, dusty ground next to Ricky and me.

His eyes were dark like his hair, his nose long and angular. In fact, he was all angles. Skinny even. He was about forty, but he looked younger and was still very handsome. Childbirth, especially Ricky's breech, had ruined Mom's looks. She had a worn, worried expression all the time that was no doubt exacerbated by the monthly food crunch and by the throwaway affairs Dad had with women he met on the ferry.

"Why aren't you playing with your cousins?" Dad asked me.

"I don't know," I said.

"Did you have a fight?"

Sometimes María and Juanita put on airs because they lived in a big house and we only lived in a scuzzy Havana *solar*. But that didn't happen often be-cause we could always call them country bumpkins, or if we were really feel-ing mean we could point out that they were *leche con una gota de café*, because their grandmother (like many people in Santiago) was from Haiti.

But today there hadn't been a fight. We didn't want to play baseball or hide-and-seek with them because we were just too hot and too tired after the Havana train.

"No, no fight, we're good," I said.

He smiled and looked at me for a long time and when I caught him, he turned away. He pretended to be fascinated by a creeper Ricky had twisted into a rope but after a moment he just couldn't help himself.

"My little girl," he said.

"Yeah," I replied, rolling my eyes.

"And my little man," he said and ruffled Ricky's hair.

"Hey," Ricky said, pushing Dad's hand away.

Dad grinned again and stared at us so hard it hurt.

"What?" I asked.

"Nothing," he said and shook his head.

"Stop that," I muttered.

"Stop what?"

"Looking at me like that."

"Well, kids, how are you liking your vacation so far?" he asked, changing the subject.

"I'm bored, there's nothing to do here, when can we go back to Havana?" I asked.

"They don't even have TV here," Ricky said.

Dad grimaced. For a second, that old Mercado rage took, but he didn't let it possess him; instead his face filled with and then lost its fiery color. Equanimity returned.

He reached into his pocket. I thought for a moment he was going for a present or money but instead he produced a hip flask. He took a swig and put the flask back in his pocket. Dad seldom drank even beer, and it was disturbing to see him swilling rum like some *frito flojo* on San Rafael.

"Yes," he said apropos of nothing and then he lay on his back, put his hands behind his head, and gazed up into the palm tree. How he missed the sausages I have no idea. He muttered something to himself—the words of a song, I think—and then after a minute he turned to me.

"We better go inside. Isabella's getting your cousins, we're having an early dinner," he said.

"I'm not even hungry yet," Ricky said.

Dad ignored Ricky and lifted him onto his shoulders, something he hadn't done since Ricky was about five. I took his hand.

We walked into the house.

Dinner. The UFC man's dining room. A hardwood floor elevated so that you could see through the Spanish windows to the old coffee fields beyond. China plates, silver serving spoons, and even a chandelier that had been in the house since the twenties.

We had changed into our best clothes, Ricky in a stiff shirt and me in a black Sunday dress.

It was still hot. The house had an electric fan but it wasn't working.

Around the table: Aunt Isabella, Mom, Dad, Ricky, me, Uncle Arturo, María, Juanita, Danny, Julio, and the new arrival, little Bella. I was jealous of María and Juanita that they had a baby in the house and I wondered when Dad and Mom were going to make a sister for me.

Servants were forbidden in Cuba, but Uncle Arturo had two: a black woman from the village called Luisa Pedrona who made the food and a girl from Las Tunas who brought it to the table. Aunt Isabella was famous for her inability to cook, but the fiction around the table was that she had made everything.

"These plantains are amazing," Mother said.

"Did you try the *ajiaco*?" Aunt Isabella asked.

Mom said that she had and that it was delicious too. She turned to Dad but he merely grunted and I could see that he'd hardly touched anything.

I wolfed it all. Luisa was good at Cuban specialties and this was a Cuban meal that included such exotic things as fish, beef, and fresh fruit.

The men talked baseball and the woman talked children and the children said nothing at all.

We were onto the *coco quemado* when the phone rang. Juanita got it and announced that it was for Dad.

The phone was in Uncle Arturo's "study," a small adjoining room that had a patio and leather chairs. It was where Uncle Arturo kept several hundred of the UFC man's English books locked in a glass case, and it was where he had his own stash of Marlboro cigarettes and pornographic magazines in a rolltop American desk.

Dad bowed to Aunt Isabella, excused himself, and went into the study. The adults resumed their talk, which was something about President Clinton and the Miamistas. I was nearest the study door and couldn't help but listen in on Dad's end of the conversation.

"Yes? Yes? What is it? . . . Impossible. I'm in Santiago. You know what that train is like. How can I . . . No, no, no, of course not . . . They can go to hell . . . Yes. I'll get the overnight. I hope this is not indicative of the state of the rest of the . . . Ok . . . Goodbye. Wait, wait, please tell José to remember the diesel."

The conversation stopped.

Uncle Arturo was fortune-telling: "I predict that President Clinton and the pope will come together to Cuba for a visit. Mark my words. Remember this date."

I remember. October 1, 1993.

The phone. The cradle. Father running his hand through his hair. He came back to the dinner table. His coconut pie was cold. He looked at Mom. He grinned at me and, reassured, I went back to my dessert.

"What was the call?" Uncle Arturo asked.

"Aldo got sick, my stand-in. They want me for the morning."

Arturo was appalled. "You can't go back. You only just got here. The kids haven't had any time to play with their cousins. We haven't even been to the beach."

Dad shook his head. "No, no, everyone will stay. I'll get the ten o'clock train back tonight."

"Can't they get anyone else? Why is it always you?" Mom asked.

"I'm the only one they trust," he said, then walked over and kissed her on the forehead. Mom frowned, wondering, I suppose, if it was really Aldo or some hussy from the Vieja that Dad had been planning to see the whole time.

Sundown.

Games of canasta and poker and my favorite, twenty-one.

Uncle Arturo told a stupid joke: "What do you call a French sandal maker? Answer: Philippe Flop."

Dad told a subversive joke: "What are the three successes of the Revolution? Answer: Health care, education, and sport. What are the three failures of the Revolution? Answer: Breakfast, lunch, and dinner."

Supper of nutella on toast.

The bed. Ricky on one side, me on the other.

The fields alive with insects and huge colonies of Jamaican fruit bats blotting out the moon.

Dad in for the goodnight story and the kiss.

Rum breath. Tears in his eyes. No story. Nothing. Not even goodbye.

Next day.

The beach. The tide out and the sand wet, freezing. Kelp on the dunes, see-through jellyfish. My hands blue. A cut on my right thumb hurting in the wind.

There was nothing to do. The others had gone on ahead and I was too late to catch them. I walked along making trails with my feet and wrote my name in the sand with a piece of driftwood. I picked up a length of seaweed and popped some of the float pods on the strands. They went snap and briny water came out of them, trundling down my fingers onto Aunt Isabella's white shawl.

Farther along the shore I noticed a dead gull. Its wings were covered in what looked like a thick gray film but was really dozens of little crabs.

Drizzle, clouds.

Flocks of birds heading for South America. Other lands. Other countries. No one I knew had ever been to another country, but Ricky and Dad had once seen Haiti from the headland at Punta de Quemado.

More beach.

A dead shark with its black eyes pecked out. Its belly had swollen. I found a stick and cut it open to see if there were other fish inside. I poked, guts spilled. The perfume of death. Intestines. Stones. No fish.

I walked on. It started to rain. Now I was wet and alone. I cursed my stubbornness. Uncle Arturo had gotten everyone up at nine, for baseball and a day at the beach, but I woke in a huff about Dad, furious that he had gone back to his stupid job, ferrying stupid people across the stupid bay in his stupid boat. I refused to go. Mom begged me and was embarrassed but Aunt Isabella pretended I was sick and brought me moors and christians and soup and a shawl and a book of poems by José Martí.

After they all had left, guilt finally got me out of bed. I rummaged for clothes, found a green dress and the shawl—no shoes, no underwear—and went after them, but I couldn't find them. And now I was a little lost.

Rain. Sand. Black clouds. A dog came bounding over. Black labrador, sandy paws, floppy ears. "Good boy," I said, grabbing him by the collar. His tag said he was called Suerte—Lucky.

I patted him. "Are you lost too? Are you? Where did you come from? Do you want to be my friend?"

I didn't see many dogs in Havana—you had to get a special permit to own a dog and often they caused resentment. Dogs ate meat, and for many people that was rubbing it in.

"Lucky, I like that. Lucky you met me."

A boy walked over the dune. Black, a little older than me, wearing shorts, a yellow T-shirt, no shoes either.

"Your dress is soaked, I can see through to your papaya," the boy said.

"You shouldn't be looking," I replied, my cheeks burning.

"I, I was only joking."

"I don't find that joke very funny."

"That's my dog," he said.

"You can have him," I said, pushing the dog away from me.

"Hey!" someone called up from the dirt road beyond the dune.

"Who's that?" I asked.

"I don't know," the boy said. "But I know you."

"Oh yeah? Who am I?"

"You're staying with your cousins in the Hacienda Mercado."

"That's right."

"Your uncle is a very bad man," the boy said, taking his dog and keeping it close to him.

"Why?"

"He beat me for talking to Juanita."

Uncle Arturo was an important official in the regional government. He had every expectation of his daughters marrying well and moving to Havana. It didn't surprise me that he'd beaten this poor black kid from the village for talking with the lovely Juanita.

"What's your name?" I asked.

"Patrice."

"What kind of a name is that?"

"Haitian, I mean French."

Ricky ran down from the road. He was breathless. "We should go, there's some kind of trouble. Uncle Arturo got a tipoff that the police are coming. He sent me to look for you."

Patrice, Lucky, Ricky, and I ran back together.

It was almost dusk when we made it to the village. The rain had eased and there was a helicopter. My mouth went dry. In Cuba only the army flew helicopters. What kind of trouble meant the army? We walked closer until we saw police vans and cops blocking the roads in and out of the village.

"Get down," I said and pulled Ricky to the ground. Lucky ran back to his house and Patrice followed him. "Hey!" I called after him, but some instinct told Patrice to get away from us.

To one side of the settlement were three big fields that had been zoned for a new coffee plantation, which for one reason or another had never materialized. The fields had been left to grow wild and palms and mangrove trees and tall grasses had sprung up. Excellent cover. We ducked off the road and into the undergrowth, crawling toward the hacienda. Scores of police and troops and plainclothes DGI and DGSE men. The helicopter, a huge Russian thing, was shining a spotlight down onto the village.

We got on our bellies now and slithered all the way around to Uncle Arturo's yard.

A confusion of soldiers, cops, civilians. The street had been blocked off by army jeeps manned by troops toting enormous machine guns. The police had their guns drawn and there were still more soldiers in green fatigues with black armbands kneeling and pointing rifles at the hacienda. The villagers were congregating behind the jeeps—almost everyone in the little hamlet had come out to enjoy the spectacle. The helicopter came lower and its spotlight began scanning the house, the yard, and the fields beyond.

"We're going to be seen here," I whispered to Ricky.

"What do we do?"

"The palm tree," I said. "In the break between the beams. Stay with me."

We scrambled into the yard and climbed the palm tree at the back of the house. From up here we could see everything better. All told there were about fifty soldiers and as many police fiercely surrounding Uncle Arturo's house as if it contained lost survivors from the Bay of Pigs.

A lead policeman in a civilian suit was trying to speak into a megaphone but he couldn't get the thing to work.

The big helicopter was landing. It was probably running low on gas.

The noise was incredible. We watched it until it went behind the trees, thundering, shaking coconuts out of the branches. Other cops had set up a generator and when they turned it on arc lights flooded the scene.

I hadn't stopped shivering since the beach and six meters up a palm tree was no place for a fainting fit.

"What do you think Uncle Arturo did?" Ricky asked.

"Maybe this is about the American cigarettes and those magazines."

The policeman with the megaphone finally got it to work. He stood on a tree stump and started telling the other police officers to get the civilians away.

"Why is he doing that?" I wondered.

"In case there's a shootout, of course."

"How do you know he has a gun?" I asked.

"I've seen it. Juanita said— Hey look, it's the sausages," Ricky said, pointing to the line of 'izos three branches up. "That was a pretty good throw for a girl; pity girls can't play baseball."

"They can and they do."

"In America," Ricky said dismissively.

In the typically Cuban way, a man pushing a food cart appeared from nowhere. He was selling flan and beer but the police made him go away after confiscating all his merchandise for themselves.

Finally, when the policeman with the megaphone was satisfied that the crowd was sufficiently safe, he turned his attention back to the hacienda. He was a short guy with shiny black hair and boots.

"Arturo Mercado, come out with your hands up," the cop said.

The crowd went silent and then much to our surprise Uncle Arturo answered: "What is this? I've done nothing wrong!"

"Send out your family," the policeman said.

"I have a right to know what this is about. Under the Cuban Penal Code all persons have a right to know what they are being charged with," Arturo shouted.

"You are not being charged with anything, Mercado, not yet. We want to question you. Be a man, at least send out your family."

"How do I know they'll be safe?" Uncle Arturo said.

"Of course they will be safe. There are hundreds of witnesses."

"Give me your word."

The cop blanched for a moment but then recovered his poise. "My name is Captain Armando Beltre. I give you my word that if you release your family to my care, they will be unharmed."

Five minutes later the cousins, Mom, Luisa, and Aunt Isabella came out. Everyone was carrying suitcases and bags as if they might be going away for some time. I was impressed. Uncle Arturo had clearly had some time to prepare. They walked past Captain Beltre and were grabbed by the leading edge of the police. The children were separated from the women, who were all bundled together into a police *julia*.

"Did you see that they took Mom to the police van?" Ricky asked.

"I did. Don't worry. Mom didn't do anything."

At around midnight there was a shot from inside the house and everyone screamed. One of the policemen shot back and then another and another. The order came to cease fire. The policeman with the megaphone shouted into the house to see if Uncle Arturo was all right, but there was no answer. Not long after the shooting another older policeman turned up. He looked to be pretty high up and he seemed displeased with everything that had been going on. Immediately after talking to Captain Beltre, he ordered the street cleared. The cops and the army started moving everyone back into their houses or way down the village into the fields. The older policeman took the megaphone and said that if Uncle Arturo didn't come out he would order the army to storm the place and Arturo would be responsible for the consequences.

Uncle Arturo came out.

He was wearing a white shirt and there was blood on the shoulder. He was holding his hands in the air. He walked to the front of the house and lay down in the yard. Policemen ran and cuffed him.

"This is fantastic," I said to Ricky.

"Yup," he replied breathlessly.

Both of us were shaking with excitement.

Uncle Arturo was bleeding into his shirt and his eyes were red and his hair was everywhere. I'd never seen him without even a tie before. Two policemen in riot gear hauled him to his feet. Uncle Arturo didn't resist. He looked exhausted. Like us. Like everybody. I was staring at the blood on his shirt and wondering if he'd been shot or not. I'd never seen anyone shot before either.

The soldiers pushed Uncle Arturo toward one of the army trucks, but suddenly he stopped and looked up into the tree where the pair of us were hiding.

Ricky grabbed my arm and I grabbed him right back.

Uncle Arturo grinned. "I see you," he said. "I see what you did with those sausages."

One of the policemen looked up into the branches but he didn't notice anything. He shrugged his shoulders and shoved Uncle Arturo from behind.

"Come on," the policeman said, and he led Uncle Arturo under the canvas flap of one of the trucks. After a couple of minutes, they transferred him to a police car and turned the siren on. Shortly after that the car drove off toward Santiago. Ricky was shaking and holding on to me tightly. We were both frightened and exhilarated at the same time.

"What do we do now?" Ricky asked.

"Now we climb down the tree," I said.

We climbed down. I tapped the nearest cop on the back. He turned.

"We surrender," I said.

Later, years later, I found out that Uncle Arturo had spent the night destroying papers that implicated him in dozens of bribery and blackmail schemes. He needn't have bothered. The police weren't interested in him at all. In fact, within six months he was back in the hacienda with his government salary and position restored.

No, the police had come because my father and some others had hijacked one of the Havana Bay ferries to Florida. Previous attempts had failed because the ferry had run out of fuel, but my father and his cronies had trundled in dozens of drums of diesel. They'd taken the fast ferry, a gift from the Japanese government, because it could do twenty knots. They'd gone on the very first run of the day, straight out of the harbor and north for Key West. It took the sleeping authorities an hour to realize what was happening and the hijackers confused them by saying that they had left the harbor only because the steerage was jammed. Then they reported a fire, and by the time the government realized it was a hijack they were halfway to the Keys.

Uncle Arturo was suspected of complicity but he knew nothing about it. None of us did.

The cops reunited us with our cousins, and María told me the details at our grandmother's house. "Your father is a dirty traitor. He has joined the Yankees in Miami."

They took Mom to Havana and kept her in a DGI dungeon for a week and then let her out.

She had bruises on her back and thighs.

She never talked about what they did to her. She just got on with things.

The power cuts, the end-of-the-month scramble for food, mending our school uniforms, the TV repairman who would take payment only in dollars . . .

Eventually she got a job as a maid in the Hotel Nacional—one of the best jobs in Havana because of the tips—and saved enough so that Ricky and I could go to college.

Uncle Arturo denounced Papa in the newspapers and, of course, after that we never went to Santiago again. And nothing came from America. No letters. No money. We heard that he had remarried. He moved from Miami to New York.

And then he disappeared.

Drifted from our lives.

Dissolved, like he was never there.

Vanished like a dandelion on the curve of air.

And that's all that needs to be said.

He isn't here.

He isn't anywhere.

He's not a character in this story.

He's a template. A tabula rasa. For me to write my narrative, for me to invent myself.

And now, dying, I understand why I came.

It isn't for him.

It isn't for justice.

It's in spite of him.

It's for truth.

I am the girl on the beach looking inside a shark for other fish.

I am the sleepwalker awakened. Awakened on the edge of the precipice.

I needed the bullet. I needed the bullet to show me that I want an end to the lies.

You betrayed us, Papa. You didn't tell us. And I came here to show you that truth is important. The truth wipes everything away. All the forgotten birthdays. All the tears. All the hurt. You enjoyed that other world. The infidelities. The Cuban game. But it wasn't a game to Mom. Or us. Is that what you liked most of all? The deceit? The deceit more than the conquest.

And now I see deeper still. It's truth, but also pride. To show you that despite your lack of concern for your family we turned out well, Ricky and me.

Look at the pair of us, doing everything we can to discover who killed you.

Look at us, sticking our toes in the waters of revenge.

Risking everything for you. Dying for you.

I'll never find out why you left. You had a wife who loved you, two kids, a good job. You were never a political person. You didn't care about politics. Why did you jump? Where did you get that gun? I don't know. All of that information died with you on the mountaintop. But it doesn't even matter.

Do you hear what I'm saying, Papa?

I didn't come for you! I'm here for me! I'm here for us!

Cold.

Freezing.

Not the cold of Santiago.

Winter cold.

The cold of frozen water.

Ice.

My mind aswim. Shouting. Gurgling.

Blood in my mouth. Cold grabbing my shoulders like the secret police.

I sink into consciousness.

They're talking.

Their song swells.

I find that I understand them.

I reshape the world. Gone is the palm tree. The 'izos. Here is the wind, the wet.

Voices.

"Fucking one shot. Blew her the fuck away."

"We got ninety-nine problems but the bitch ain't one."

"Paul, you ok?"

"I don't think he's still alive."

"Get him out."

"He's breathing."

"Get him out and put *her* in the fucking hole."

"Shouldn't we call the, the federal authorities?"

"We're all in too deep for that."

"I want no part of this."

"A part of it you have got, a big fucking part. Now shut up. Take his arm. We might be able to save him."

"Call a helicopter. We've got to get him to a hospital."

"No hospitals. We'll get him back to the car."

"We have to take him to a hospital, for Christ's sake, man."

"Listen to me. I've got adrenaline and a CPR kit in the prowler, we'll do this ourselves. We're fucked if we go to a hospital."

"Jesus! Wait a minute. Wait a fucking minute. I think she's still fucking breathing."

"Is she now? Have you got her gun? Good. Ok, lemme see, lemme— Fuck me, would you look at that, you're right, all surface, only grazed her."

"Told you, you should have used the three-oh-oh."

"Yeah, I guess."

"Well, we'll soon put a stop to her fun and games."

I open my eyes. Deputy Klein. He's holding a 9mm, a meter from my face. There's a halo of water vapor around his head. He looks like the Angel of Death.

Is that one in your tarot cards, Mother? Did you see that one in your voodoo ceremonies?

Breathing hard.

Grinning.

Excited.

Spittle frozen on the lapels of his coat.

His eyes iron planets. His mouth a gutted fish.

"I don't know what you wanted, you crazy fucking bitch, but I hope you find it at the bottom of the lake. Say your fucking prayers."

He lifts the gun, rests his finger on the trigger, takes careful aim, squeezes . . .

CHAPTER 19

OUR LADY OF MERCY

I am copied in your eye, mother of the golden breeze, lady full of grace, lady of the moon. Between ice and the gilt morning. I am copied in the patterns of your stars.

You don't get two chances. One they'll give you. But not two. Not at point-blank range. Not so close that you feel the powder burn. Prayers, you say? Well, again it's that old dilemma. In Cuba the state religion is unbelief. The high-church religion is Catholicism. The street faith is Santería. Who would I pray to? Who would I pray for?

And yet.

A breath escapes. And every breath a petition.

The muscles in his face as taut as a halyard on a sail.

Smile not, friend.

Lillies grow from your mouth. Think not of drinking blood from my skull. Your corpse is food for trout.

Don't you see her? She is the image in your eye too.

His face relaxes, transfigured by the mystery.

Death has made him special, given him a secret that I do not possess.

A full second after the bullet strikes I hear the crack.

I roll to the side.

He falls where I have been.

A puff of ice. Another crack.

Preoccupied with Youkilis, Sheriff Briggs belatedly turns to see his deputy lying next to me, the back of his head caved in like a melon that's fallen off a truck.

Briggs looks at me, sizes up the situation immediately.

"She's got a fucking accomplice. Everybody hit the deck."

"What?"

"Hit the fucking deck, assholes!" he yells but only he and Jack fall fast enough to escape the gunman.

A sound like *sssssipppp* and Deputy Crawford gets one in the leg. Gravity does the rest and he's down too.

Briggs pulls out a .45 and shoots randomly at the tree line.

I count them off. *BOOM, BOOM, BOOM*. One, two, three.

"What's happening!" Jack screams.

"You see anything?" Crawford yells.

"I don't see a goddamn thing," Briggs replies and turns to his deputy. "How you doing, buddy?"

Crawford grunts. "I'm ok. Fat shot. No arteries or veins."

"Thank God. Get your gun and look for the muzzle flash," Briggs says.

"Shouldn't we kill her?" Crawford wonders.

Briggs slides his body around to look at me. "Yes, we fucking should."

Another puff of ice, another crack.

Briggs arcs the .45 in my direction. *Mierde.* I grab the body of Deputy Klein and drag him—*it*—in front of me, blood pouring from the hole in the skull, coating the ice beneath us in a red film. It pools under me, sticky, warm. The .45 slugs punch into Klein. *BOOM. BOOM. BOOM.* At this range they could easily burn right through Klein and into me, but I get lucky, they snag on bone and muscle and internal organs.

And then somehow Youkilis gets to his feet. Naked, hallucinating.

"*Aaaaggghhh,*" he screams. Guttural, horrifying. He looks confused, hurt. The noise he made scared even himself. His hands are burning him, his lungs agony.

"Get down, you fucking idiot," Briggs says.

"Get down, Paul, get down," Jack says.

But Youkilis isn't getting down. He wants to escape the water, the ice, the hurt.

He can't. There's no way ou—

Cunning flits across his eyes when he spots me. *Her.* All this pain is something to do with her. *"Neaaaahhh,"* he says and comes for me, hands out like Mitchum in that Yuma flick with the kids and the money.

He growls, staggers, trips on Jack's leg.

"Grab him!" Briggs yells at Jack.

But Jack keeps his head down.

That's my boy.

Youkilis steps around his boss and lurches closer. He's going to kill me if he can. He's going to bring me into his world.

"Get down, you fool," Crawford says and makes a grab for him. "Jack, tell your fucking buddy to get down."

But a nearby rifle shot sends Crawford diving for the ice.

I hug Klein like a lover and his body protects me from the bullets and his blood protects me from the cold, seeping into my shirt, coating my skin, slithering into my underwear and down my leg, warming, purifying—as intimate as mother's milk.

"Faaaking bittch!" Youkilis says, staggering to within a few meters of me.

"Go away," I hiss at him.

He laughs and is gearing up for the final zombie shuffle when a rifle shot buries itself in his back.

He drops to one knee.

"Faarg!" he screams, and he looks at me with savage, cold fury.

Somehow he gets back to his feet. Fucking unstoppable. Naked, inhuman, a thing from beyond the grave. I'm afraid of him. And then Briggs resumes firing at me. *BOOM. BOOM.* A bullet rips through Klein's neck and almost gets me, missing my head by centimeters and zipping across the ice. Briggs changes the clip.

More rifle puffs. Youkilis swatting at the bullets like the monster in *Frankenstein* trying to catch musical notes. Finally the anonymous marksman makes the kill shot. A hit behind Youkilis's ear—the expanding lead rifle round ripping through his eyes and forehead. He staggers on for one more beat and falls on top of Klein.

You did it, you got here.

"Fucker!" Briggs yells, and he shoots the reloaded .45. *BOOM. BOOM.* But now there are two corpses to give me cover.

"We gotta get out of here!" Crawford says.

"The fuck! How? Fucking pinned," Briggs replies.

"Been watching. It's one guy, he's in the trees by the car," Crawford says.

"Or it's two guys, taking their time," I suggest.

"Shut up, bitch, you'll get yours," Briggs says.

"If you surrender I'll make sure they don't kill you," I yell.

"Shut the fuck up, you fucking cunt," Briggs says. "Crawford, can you get an angle on the bitch?"

Crawford tries a shot that plows into Youkilis with a sickening squelch.

"I don't think so," Crawford says.

"Maybe we should give ourselves up," Jack contributes.

"Cut us down like dogs," Briggs says.

Briggs fires several more at the tree line and his clip runs out again. It holds eight. The bad news seems to be that he's brought several spares.

A different noise. Thunder. No.

A ripping, tearing, a—

Beneath all of us the ice starting to crack.

"Jesus Christ!" Jack yells, his hands still over his head.

"We're fucked!" Crawford says.

"We're not fucked. Keep it together!" Briggs orders.

Another puff of ice. My unknown confederate adding to the mix.

"Fuck it, let's go!" Crawford says.

Holes appear and water starts gushing up through the ice in frothy freezing bursts. One of the sharpshooter's bullets skims past my feet. Shit. Was that a mistake? Is he really an ally after all? Is he trying to kill all of us? Esteban, is that you?

Water bubbling underneath me. This is what you get for playing Nemesis.

I scramble away from the blood and the surging water on hands and knees toward a firmer piece of ice a few meters from the bodies.

This looks better. But how would I know? Cuba doesn't even get frost.

I kneel on the raw plain of ice, completely exposed.

When I was child I used to play a game. If I closed my eyes I could make myself disappear. As long as I couldn't see me no one else could. Keep 'em closed and you'll be ok.

The bodies. The blood. The shooting—the rifleman from the parking lot, Briggs and Crawford firing back into the trees.

Don't look in my direction.

Don't look.

I'm invisible.

I'm not here.

A grinding, gurgling sound. I open my eyes just as Youkilis slips beneath the surface. Klein follows him into a fissure, his body turning and his cat black eyes staring at me before disappearing into the slime of the lake bottom.

Ice cracks all around me and I get to my feet for balance.

My sweater is dyed red, like a target, like Che storming the barricades, but he had a gun and I'm a sacrificial la—

Wait a minute.

The backpack.

A 9mm and a clip.

My father's gun.

"Jesus, there she is! Got a shot?" Briggs yells.

"Yeah, I got one, fucking ice breaking, hold on, yeah, try this on for size, ya fucking bitch!" Crawford replies.

BOOM.

Down. Hard. Nose cracking off the surface.

"Missed her!"

"I'll try!"

Triage. Everything seems— *BOOM, BOOM, BOOM, BOOM.* Briggs, a gun in each hand. The right firing at the parking lot, the left shooting at me.

I lie flat on the ice, a tough shot for both men, as long as my friend keeps them pinned and I don't stand up again.

They're going to have to get lucky—but they need to be lucky only once and I need to be lucky all the time.

Use your brain, Mercado. Do something smart. Work 'em. Jack is the weak link. Work him while you make your way toward the backpack, six meters to the left, on the edge of a hole in the ice.

"I'm a federal agent! We've got you surrounded. Drop your guns and surrender and we'll all get out of this in one piece," I yell.

"You're no fucking cop!" Briggs says.

"I'm an agent. Sheriff, this is crazy. You covered up a vehicular homicide. That's not a huge crime in the big scheme of things. You'll lose your job and get probation. You won't do a day," I yell, switching from the formal English we learned in school to the Yuma English of the movies and TV.

"If you're the feds, where's the SWAT team, where's the fucking helicopters?" Briggs yells. He's no dummy.

"They're on the way, believe me. Now cease firing and let's all get out of this alive," I shout.

Briggs takes aim at me and pulls the trigger. The bullet whizzes over my head. Close, but he's gotta stand to get the kill shot.

Work the others. "Crawford, you're a veteran, you won't do a night in prison. Jack, if you plea-bargain you're looking at thirty days. We don't need to lose our lives for this. I'm the one that's fucked anyway."

"What do you mean you're fucked?" Crawford asks.

Another puff of ice, another rifle crack.

"I'm fucked because I didn't have the authority to bring Youkilis up here," I say. "I screwed this whole operation up."

I slide slowly toward the backpack; its shoulder strap is in the water, the ice cracking around it. Please don't fall, please don't sink.

"You hear what she says, Briggs?" Crawford yells.

"You've done nothing wrong, Crawford, not a thing. If you kill me, a federal agent, it's the death penalty," I tell him.

"If you're a fed, tell your buddy to stop shooting," Briggs demands.

"My radio's at the bottom of the lake. Just cease fire and drop your weapons," I yell at him.

"What do you think, Sheriff?" Crawford asks.

"She's fucking lying!" Briggs says.

Five meters from the backpack. Freezing water. Ice burns all over my fingertips.

"Let me show you my ID. We'll see who's fucking lying," I shout. "Cease fire! That's an order."

"Yeah, you'll all be fucking ok, but I'll go to jail for manslaughter. My career will be finished," Jack says.

"You'll be fine. Vehicular manslaughter ain't jail time, look at your buddy Matthew Broderick. I say we stop this madness right now," Crawford says.

But the sheriff isn't falling for any of this bullshit. He looks at me, smiles, and shakes his head. "She's no fed. She's got one friend. Two of them. Take 'em out one at a time. That's the way we do it."

"How?" Crawford wonders.

"Get a bead on the trees. Look for the muzzle flash and unload a fucking clip, pin him down. I'll take her. And when she's dead we'll get across to the other side, away from our lone gunman and before all this fucking ice cracks."

"Don't listen to him, Crawford! It's a death sentence!" I yell.

"She's fucking lying," Briggs says.

Two meters from the backpack. It's sitting on top of a seven-centimeter fissure somehow defying gravity. Don't fall. *Don't fall.* I keep it from plunging to the lake bottom by sheer force of will.

"What do you want me to do, Sheriff?" Crawford asks.

"Don't listen to him, Crawford. You've done nothing wrong at this point. I'm the only one in real trouble here! Jack, if they kill me, you'll be accessory to a murder, you'll get life in prison for that."

"We've got to do what she says," Jack yells desperately.

The crack widens, the backpack starts to tilt. I spread my weight and try to touch it.

"Like fuck we do! She's a lying cunt," Briggs says.

"We can't just kill her. We'll get—"

Closer . . . closer . . . closer.

"We'll get nothing. She's some dumb Mex on a fucking trip. Never find her. Crawford, you ready?"

I touch the backpack, grab it, start to unzip it.

"I'm ready," Crawford says.

"Pin the rifleman, I'll take her," Briggs says.

Rifle shot. Muzzle flash.

Crawford gets up on one knee, bites through the pain of his wound, stands, and starts firing at the trees. But Briggs doesn't keep his side of the bargain. He's too chicken. He's still trying to shoot me lying down. *BOOM, BOOM, BOOM.* All misses. Get up and kill me, asshole. Where's your *huevos*? Thought you were a fucking war hero.

"Did you get her?" Crawford asks.

"Angle's wrong," Briggs replies. "Don't worry, I'll fucking kill the bitch. Keep plugging at that shooter."

"Rifleman's reloading," Crawford says. "We got ten clicks."

And now Briggs does stand up. All six foot five of him and still somehow wearing his fucking cowboy hat. He flinches, bracing himself for a bullet in the brain.

I rummage through the stuff in the backpack: pepper spray, ski mask, rope, duct tape, finally the loaded 9mm Stechkin APS pistol that hadn't been cleaned or fired in years.

Briggs walks toward me, striding over the ice fissures, holding his .45 in both hands. Six meters away. Impossible to miss. He beads me, lifts the gun. "No more chances now, whore," he says. His eyes narrow, focused, concentrating, his grin wide.

"None necessary," I reply, sliding up my father's pistol and shooting him in the neck.

Briggs falls to his knees, drops his weapon.

Hands at his throat, blood seeping between his fingers.

Ssssffff! The rifleman in the trees has evidently reloaded. Crawford hits the deck.

"Did you get her?" Crawford says.

The ice cracks beneath me as I walk to Briggs's .45 and kick it into the water.

"Damn it, man, did you get her?" Crawford says, firing the last of his clip at the marksman in the woods.

The sun breaks over the tree line. New-born photons bisecting the lake into a world of shadow and a world of light. Water seeps into my shoes, I lose my balance, put my arms out, regain it, step over a widening fracture, and come up behind Crawford.

He turns.

"Cocksucker," he says and slams home a fresh clip but can't get off a round before I put one in his groin, one in his thorax above his body armor, and one in his mouth.

I wave at the man in the parking lot.

He stands up, waves back.

It's too skinny to be Esteban. It has to be Paco.

I wave my hands over my head. "Stop! Stop! That's enough! They're dead."

Silence and then a distant voice. "Are you ok?"

"*Sí.*"

"I'm coming."

I walk to Jack and kneel beside him.

He's terrified. He smells bad. He's defecated himself.

I smile in a kindly way.

"W-who are you?" he asks, his voice quivering.

"I'm María."

"Why have you done this?"

Well, it ain't because you're a lousy tipper.

A groan behind me. Briggs, living yet. That type needs a stake through the heart at a midnight crossroad.

"Wait here," I say to Jack. "Don't go anywhere."

Dodging cracks and fissures, I walk back to Briggs. The ice is cracking all around him. Blood and water, water and blood.

I kneel beside him.

Our eyes meet.

Are you close now? Do you have any answers?

I don't. Hector says the meaning of life is to be found in the quest for the meaning of life. But that's Hector.

Briggs looks at me. A croak. "Help me," he says.

I look at the wound. I suppose if we rushed him to a hospital there'd be an outside chance.

I shake my head.

"Why?" he asks.

Why indeed?

I can't tell you about the tarot or the Book of Changes or that I am sent by our lady of the moon. But I must tell you something. I must tell you because, before the minute hand on your watch makes another revolution, I will be the instrument of your transfiguration.

For you, I suppose, it was the fifty thousand.

"The fifty grand. The price of a dead Mex."

He thinks about it, doesn't get it.

"That my father's life could be bought so cheap," I explain.

He nods.

His breath has taken on the sweetness of death. His face is white, his eyes crimson. There are splinters of ice in his hair.

"Is there a deity with whom you confer?" I ask.

"No, no, wait . . ." he gurgles.

"Make thy peace."

He grabs my arm with a bloody hand.

I release his grip, step back, raise my father's gun. This is not retribution. I have no authority for that. Nevertheless, I deliver you from this world of tears.

"No, wait, we can make a—"

Lead crosses the space between us, rips his skin, passes through muscle and bone, punches a hole in his skull the size of a baby's fist, and exits through his spinal cord.

He looks at all the blood and lies backward on the ice, dead.

Jack's hands are above his head.

He's crying. "Don't shoot me. Please. I'm so sorry. Oh God, I'm so sorry. Whatever I did, I'm so sorry." Tears, an anguished look. More tears. "Oh God, please don't, please."

"This is your best performance," I say.

"It's not a performance, I'm so sorry."

"For what?"

"For whatever it is that you're so angry about," he says. Lips quivering. A cackle at the back of his throat. Snot, spittle.

The scent of death all around me, in me, makes me want to throw up. On the edge of the ice lake I see Paco in a black coat and carrying Esteban's rifle. He waves. I wave back.

He yells something but I can't hear what it is.

"I can't hear you!"

"I said, I saved your Cuban ass."

Gingerly he begins walking across the ice. He's almost comically slow. I imagine they don't have many frozen lakes in Nicaragua.

"Oh God, oh God, oh God, you're going to kill me, I'm going to die," Jack says.

He bends over and throws up what's left of the hors d'oeuvres from Tom Cruise's house.

"I'm not going to kill you."

"You're going to kill me. You're going to murder me like you killed those others. I'm going to be dead. This is the last thing I'm ever going to see. I don't even know where we are, I don't even know where we are!"

"Wyoming."

I sit down next to him on the ice. I turn his face so that he's looking at me.

"Listen to me, Jack, that's my friend Paco coming over to us. That kid has a jones for killing. He says he fought with the Sandinistas in Nicaragua when he was only a boy, and he was so good with the rifle that I think I believe him."

"Wait a minute, I'm not going to—"

"Shut up. This is important. Paco's going to come over here and he's going to say: 'No witnesses. This one too. I don't care if he's a big star. All of them in the lake. We gotta protect ourselves.'"

"What are you doing?" Paco yells. I look up. He's not advancing at record speed. The ice is spooking him but we've got about five minutes here, tops.

Shit. This is not the way I thought it was going to be. Rushed. Bloody. Incompetent. This isn't the kangaroo court of my imagination. Me remembering the good times and telling my dad's killer what I've lost because of him, because of his drunken carelessness.

"It was you, Jack, you were driving the car, you were drunk. You knocked my father off the Old Boulder Road. You killed him."

"I don't know what you're talking about," he says.

"Don't lie to me."

"I'm not lying. Please don't kill me," Jack says, tears running off his eyelashes in his greatest-ever audition tape.

"I'm not going to kill you, Jack. I'm sick of this. I'm sick of all this."

He's looking at me with a desperate hope in his eyes. Can she really mean that? His cheeks vermillion. A green stain on his neck. His jeans soaked with piss.

"I want only one thing from you," I tell him.

"What?"

"I want the truth, Jack. I want you to tell me what happened that night. The night you hit the Mex and Youkilis covered for you and said that you were in Malibu and had been there for days."

"I wasn't there, I don't know—"

"Look, look over there at Paco. He's coming. Now, I'm not going to kill you, but he's going to want to and it's going to be up to me to persuade him otherwise. You understand? You dig?"

"I understand."

"Youkilis told me everything. Let me hear it in your words. And fast."

"W-who are you?"

"I'm the daughter of the dead Mex. The anonymous fucking wetback that you killed and that your manager decided was worth fifty thousand dollars. Fifty thousand bucks. How much do you get for a picture?"

"It depends, sometimes I work for scale on a—"

"How much?"

He starts to shake.

"I got two million dollars for the last movie I made. I was third lead."

"Two million dollars."

"I didn't see all of that, of course. Agent's cut, manager's cut, taxes. So really, when it all boils down—"

"And my father's life was worth a measly fifty grand."

In Havana fifty thousand could buy you out of a murder rap. You could become a general officer in the army for ten thousand. But here that was an insult.

"How many days did you work on that movie?" I ask.

He shakes his head. "I don't know, I—"

"Out with it."

"Five-week shoot, I think."

"So my father's life was worth roughly one day's work for you."

"Well, you see, that's what I was saying before—"

I click the hammer back on the 9mm to shut him up.

Let the silence hold you. I want you to sit with those details for a moment. A man's life for a few hours' work on a movie set.

Paco waves. "This thing is a fucking death trap," he yells in Spanish.

"Yeah."

"It's cracking. Do you see it's cracking?" he says.

"I see."

Back to Jack. "Ok now. Tell me what happened that night."

He closes his eyes, shakes his head. Sweat pouring from him.

"Speak."

"I can't," he says.

"Why not?"

"I think if I tell you, you'll kill me. You say you won't kill me but I think you will."

"Open your eyes. Look at me. Look at me!"

He opens his eyes, finds mine. I rid them of the red mist, the crazy, dark stuff from Santiago de Cuba, from New Mexico, from everywhere. I make them reveal what I am feeling right now. The calmness. The exhaustion.

"Can you see what I'm thinking? You gotta fucking trust me, I'm not going to kill you. Not now, not ever."

"Ok," he says. He fakes a grin, falters, blinks.

"Now speak, quick, before Paco comes."

"It hadn't been a good year. I was up for a Spirit Award, I didn't get it. I'd never been nominated for anything major in my whole life, I never won anything in my life. But I got odds on that I would win that night. And they gave it to that bastard Jeremy Piven, who's won everything. And then after that I lost a couple of big roles and then I was up for this movie *Gunmetal* and they said I had it in the bag and then those fuckers at Universal gave it to someone else."

"The accident."

"I lost the movie. But I didn't go apeshit, not like in my twenties. Cool head. Paul was here. I flew to Vail on a charter. I went into town. Just for one drink. But they know me here and a couple of guys bought me drinks. I didn't buy anything. I didn't buy a drink the whole day. Nothing."

"How many drinks?"

"I don't know. Couple of beers. I wasn't *drunk* drunk. I used to go to AA. I used to have a problem. This wasn't a bender. This was just a few beers. And I don't know, maybe it was the altitude or whatever, I'd been in L.A. all week."

"What happened?"

"I'm driving home and I think I'm doing ok and I get to the hill and then there's this dude alongside the car and *clunk*, you know, and I think I might have hit him but I'm not sure and I look in the rearview mirror and there's nobody there, so I don't know what to think. I stop and look back and there's nobody there. I'm tired, and with the altitude and the beers and everything, I think I might have just hallucinated him or something."

"Is everything ok?" Paco yells from barely twenty meters away.

"Interrogating," I tell him.

I look at Jack. "Go on, fast," I whisper.

"Ok, so I get home and just fucking go to bed. Next day, I don't remember anything, just the car. So I dump the car at the garage and later that day they find the Me—the, uhm, your father, I mean, and I tell Paul and he just takes over. Private charter to L.A. Gets me into Promises and leaks it that I've been there for three days, in other words I never left L.A. Would never hold up if anybody really looked, but I'm not a big enough star for anybody to really look. Just another B-lister going into rehab. Nobody cared."

Unattractive self-pity in those azure eyes, but not yet guilt, contrition, understanding.

"And then what happened?"

"Well, then nothing. I stayed at Promises for a couple of weeks and went back to Fairview to read scripts. Someone dropped out of *Gunmetal* and they offered it to me again and I took it. It was all good until that son of a bitch came snooping around."

"What son of a bitch?"

"Briggs. Fucking Briggs. But again Paul took care of it. We paid him off. Fifty thousand to some cop charity, a couple of photo ops. Paul promised to use his boys as fucking extras in the next movie. Christ, it was all so pathetic. So fucking small change."

I grimaced.

I'd like to think that that might have been the first of many payments. Briggs was smarter than that.

"How did you find us up here tonight?" I ask.

"Paul hit the panic button and Briggs traced the GPS in his car. Woke me up, got his deputies. He could have APB'd it, but he knew it was something to do with this. We had to keep it quiet."

I nod, smile. "Ok. Good. You've been very good, Jack. Now, listen carefully. Paco is going to want to kill you. He thinks you'll go to the police about this, but we have to convince him you won't go to the police."

"I won't go to the police."

Tears, trembling, hands together in prayer.

"I know you won't go to the police, because if you do, I'll make sure the press finds out that you killed my father and you and your manager conspired with the local police to cover it up. That's manslaughter and conspiracy. You might not get a lot of time in jail, but you will go to jail and your career will be finished."

"I'm not going to go to the police. I'm not," he says desperately.

"My friend Paco is old-school. He's from the jungle. They take an eye for an eye literally down there. We can't let him know that you were the one driving the car. Understand? So don't say anything, I'll do the talking. Ok?"

"Ok."

He looks at me with gratitude and fear. "Why are you doing this? You have every right to kill me. I killed your father."

"Killing you won't bring me one gram of comfort, I see that now. It'll only make things worse. Much worse."

Relief. More fucking tears. Probably real.

Paco almost beside us. My voice descends to whisper: "I'm going to stop him from killing you, but I want you to do something for me."

"Anything. I owe you."

"I want you to stop drinking. I want you to stop the bullshit. I want you to live an exemplary life. I want you to become engaged with the world. I want you to give a sizable portion of your income to charity. I want you to go to Africa. To India. I want you to improve the lot of Mexicans who work in your town. The invisibles. You can still act, that's what you do, you can still make movies, but I want you to be a force for good."

He nods. Really bawling now. "Of course. I will. I'm lucky. I'm lucky that you were the one, that it was you. I, I'll never be able to bring back your dad, I can't do that, but, but, I'll do what you say."

"I don't need to threaten you. You know what will happen if I discover you're caught with cocaine or DUI—"

"It will never happen. I promise."

"Good. Ok. Now, here's how we handle Paco—we're going to pin this on Youkilis. We're going to tell him that he was driving you from the bar and *he* hit my father and covered it up. Paco's sharp. He can spot a lie so I'm going to have to hide the truth. I'm going to tell him that Youkilis wouldn't confess to it, but I'm sure it was him."

"What do you want me to say?"

"I want you to say nothing. Nothing at all until I tell you to talk. Understand?"

"Yes."

"Ok, shut up, here he is."

Paco. Grinning, rifle slung. Knight in fucking shining. My hero. I hug him and burst into tears.

"You saved me," I whisper in his ear.

"Damn right."

"I told you to stay out of it."

"Man, I haven't seen this much action since I was eleven."

"Christ, you saved me." I kiss him on the mouth. Hungry for him. This *kid*.

"What about this one?" he says, pointing the rifle at Jack.

"Nothing to do with it."

His eyes narrow. "Who killed your father, María?"

"Youkilis. I think."

"You don't know for sure?"

"It was Youkilis."

"You're not lying to me, are you?"

Jesus, Paco, I was lying to you from the very beginning. My name's not even María . . . But, nevertheless, I want you to believe me. I want this to end.

"It's over, Paco. Youkilis is dead and Briggs is dead. It's finished."

"You've come all this way to find the person who killed your father and you're going to leave it like this?"

"I'm tired and I have to get back. If I don't a lot of people I care about will be in trouble."

Paco takes a step away from me and sights the rifle at Jack. Jack puts up his hands, cowers, whimpers. Oh, Jack, please, act the man for once in your life.

"It was him, wasn't it? Youkilis covered it up to protect him. He was in Fairview that night. He was drunk."

I shake my head and look hard at Jack: "Tell him. Tell him what you told me."

"I was after this part and then I was at a bar and Paul, well, Paul," Jack begins hesitantly.

"Just tell him about the drinking and the drive home," I interrupt.

"I'd had a few beers. I was too hammered to get back up the mountain. I called Paul and he came and picked me up. He didn't even know I was in town. He thought I was in L.A. He'd had a few too, but not many. He wasn't drunk. We were going up the mountain and I'm in the backseat and Paul's turning around to talk to me, you know, and we hear this sort of clumping noise. Paul looks forward and doesn't see anything. We stop the car but we don't see anything. So we drive on. Day after that we read about the dead guy by the side of the road. We put two and two together. Course, by then we'd left the car at the shop. That's how Briggs tracked us down."

I'm staring at Paco.

Don't hit him, please, he'll crack like the first *huevo* of the day. Let him be.

Paco looks at me. "This is good enough for you?"

"We're done here. Finished."

"But this one, he will go to the police," Paco says.

"We've talked that over. He covered up a crime. He's an accessory to vehicular manslaughter. He'll get jail and it'll destroy his career."

Paco closes his eyes. Thinks. I take his hand, squeeze it. "No more death," I whisper.

Two in New Mexico, two here. Four men I've killed. Four too many.

"You're bleeding," he says.

"Yeah. I got shot."

"You got lucky."

"Yeah."

"Let's go," Paco says.

Two bodies under the ice.

A third and fourth faceup, staring at us.

"What about them?"

"Sink them."

"They'll come up," I say.

"Their vests will drag them down."

"Three cops go missing. Bound to be an inquiry."

He points at Briggs. "Does this one have a phone?"

"I don't know."

Paco hands me the rifle, searches Briggs. He removes a silver cell phone and a wallet. He skims the wallet. About a thousand dollars in scratch, which he puts in his pocket. He takes out his own cell and smiles.

"Find Briggs's number," he says. "It'll be on his menu."

I flip Briggs's cell, find the number, and tell Paco.

Paco dials it. Briggs's phone rings and Paco waits for the voice mail. He grins at me and affects a chingla Mexican accent. "Briggs, man, where are you? We got the fucking stuff but we don't see you. We went through a lot to get here. If you don't show, or you try to pull something, man, you gonna be sorry."

He hangs up. Grins.

"They won't buy that," I tell him.

"It'll give them something to think about. We'll sink the bodies, put Briggs's phone in his car, leave the car where someone will find it. Ok, let's go. Can you guys help?"

Paco stares at Jack and me. We're both exhausted.

"Hell with ya, I'll do it," he mutters in Spanish.

He walks to Briggs, slides him into the nearest ice fissure. Briggs rolls over, floats for a second, and then sinks in a froth of bubbles. Paco does the same to Crawford, who joins his buddies at the bottom of the lake.

Carefully Paco picks up all the shells and puts them in his pocket. He points at Jack. "Ok, we go back. You first, and you better not run and you better not fall in the fucking water."

Jack begins walking to the shore. Paco puts his arm around me.

"I think we'd better kill him," Paco whispers.

"No," I insist.

"Are you sure it wasn't him?"

"It wasn't him. Just an unlucky guy. A passenger. Wrong place, wrong time."

Paco nods. "What's that you've got?" he asks, looking at my father's gun.

"You can have it," I tell him. I'm done with guns.

We get to the shore. Paco starts telling Jack about the cars. We'll drive one each. Jack will take Paul's BMW. I'll take Esteban's Range Rover, which of course Paco drove here since Esteban isn't expected back until tonight—a white lie of his that nearly got me killed. Paco will drive Briggs's Escalade. We'll dump the Escalade at a truck stop on I-25 and Paco will drive Jack back in the Beemer.

The plan seems sound.

I change my sweater, smoke a cigarette, take a last look at the lake.

Cracks already freezing over.

It reminds me of a poem by Basho: *An old pond / a jumping frog / ripples.*

This was not the way I wanted it to be. I don't really know what I wanted it to be, but it wasn't this.

Blood, gore, corpses under the water.

Hector's niece is a nurse who works in a hospice for terminally ill babies. Babies who won't live out a year. She feeds them, and cleans them, and loves them, and every night she whispers over them, "Grow, little baby, grow."

That's what a hero does.

Not this.

I shiver.

Paco puts his hand on my back. "Ok," he says. "Let's go."

CHAPTER 20

MARIA

Denver. The Greyhound Station. The bus to El Paso. His unruly hair brushed, his face shaved. He's wearing a black leather jacket, jeans, cowboy boots. The clear green of his eyes twinkles.

Our lips part.

He looks at me.

Not my best. Pale, bruised, and a beanie hat on to cover the bandage above my right ear.

"Do you really have to go back?" he asks.

"I do," I tell him. "If I don't, my boss, my mom, and my brother will all get in big trouble."

He grins. "So the Cubans think you've been in Mexico this whole time?"

I nod.

"Quite the little secret agent," he says.

The bus driver starts the engine.

"It's a long drive to El Paso. You got something to read?"

I shake my head. "I'll think."

"Four hours from now you'll be sorry."

"Maybe."

He looks at me. I look at the ground.

"Well," he says. "You better . . ."

"Yeah."

I kiss him again. This time chastely on the cheek. I pick up my bag.

"Is there anything I can do for you, Paco?"

"Plenty," he says and grinds his hips.

"Not that," I say, laughing. "I'm serious."

He considers it.

"You saved me," I explain. "I owe you."

"My mother has cancer," he says.

I peer into his face. He has never talked about his family. In fact, I know nothing about him at all. Brothers? Sisters? Orphan? He's a cipher, a nowhere man.

"Your mother has cancer?"

"Yes. It's breast cancer. The doctors rate her chances as fifty-fifty. I'd like to increase the odds, if possible."

"Bring her to Cuba, we have some of the finest doctors in Latin America. They will treat her. I'm sure it's better than Nicaragua. Bring her. And besides, I, I'd like to see you again."

He shakes his head. "I'd like that too, but I can't bring her to Cuba. She's not well enough to travel and I have to earn money in the U.S."

"What do you want me to do?"

He clears his throat. "If you have the time I would like you to light a candle for me at the shrine of Our Lady of Guadalupe."

"Our Lady of Guadalupe? I've heard of it but I'm not sure what it is exactly," I reply.

"It's in the north of Mexico City. I know you're in a rush to get back, you have a plane to catch, but if you get the time."

"I never pegged you for the religious type," I say with a little smile, and as soon as the words are out I remember that time I caught him praying.

Paco grins. "In many ways, María, you're not very observant at all."

"What does that mean?"

The smile widens. "It doesn't mean anything."

I punch him on his arm. "Ever since you saved my life, there's a sly confidence that's come over you that I don't like at all."

"Oh, you like it."

The bus driver revs the engine. All the other passengers are on. I kiss him one more time. Lips. Tongue. Lips.

"The shrine of Our Lady," I say seriously to let him know that I will do it if it means that much to him.

He clasps his hands together in fake prayer.

"God is generous to virgins," he says and begins muttering in pretend Latin.

"I'm not a—"

"Sssh, you're spoiling it."

"Are you getting on or not?" the driver asks me in Spanish.

"*Sí. Momento.*"

"Hurry," the driver says.

"Say goodbye to Esteban for me."

"I will."

"And watch out for the INS."

"I'm one step ahead."

I get in. Doors close. I find a seat at the back.

Paco waves as the bus pulls out onto Broadway.

The last thing I see him do is hail a cab.

The Denver to El Paso bus is all Mexican, and before we're even out of the city, I've been offered cake, seen baby photographs, watched part of a tele-novela, and entertained one semiserious offer of marriage.

Eventually I pretend to fall asleep. South through New Mexico.

Gone are the mountains, the great spine of North America. Gone is the snow. My last look at snow until after the Castro brothers leave us. But it's ok, I'll remember it, cold and white on the lakeshore and red from our foot-prints dipped in the blood of dead men.

* * *

The #4 subway train to Martín Carrera. The #6 to Villa Basilica. Thread through the religious souvenir stands. The knockoff merchants. The lame. The halt. Pickpockets.

Traffic, street noise, the kind of density of people and vehicles you never see in Havana. Motorcycles, scooters, ice cream vendors, big cars, small cars, trucks.

The stalls are there to cure you of piety. Jesus pictures with eyes that move. Gaudy life-size statues of María. A photographer who will take a picture of your kid and produce a print of him sitting on Christ's lap in a shady dell. The tip of the iceberg as you get closer to the Basilica of Our Lady. Crosses of every type, María pics, holy water, holy blood, holy dust. Hundreds of icon mer-chants and thousands of people buying stuff. Worry beads, rosaries, postcards.

Everywhere the sick, the old, the young, parties of school children, pilgrim tourists from all over Latin America, Europe, the United States.

The hill of Cerro Tepeyac.

Here, five centuries ago, the Aztec nobleman Cuauhtaoctzin saw the Holy Virgin. The bishop demands proof. An image of *la virgen morena* appears on the nobleman's coat. A church is built and then a bigger one and finally an entire complex. In 2002 Pope John Paul makes Cuauhtaoctzin a saint. The context for a doubter, for a daughter of the Revolution, for a Cuban: when Cuauhtaoctzin sees the Virgin, Aztec civilization has just been destroyed by Cortés—the Aztecs and their gods are on the run and Cerro Tepeyac is the most important shrine to the brown-skinned female harvest goddess Tonantzin. So you could say worship of the goddess continues in another form.

Dad never believed in any of that stuff, nor Ricky, and Mom believes too much. Her ghosts and goblins are another inoculation against a moment of revelation.

The plaza of the basilica.

An old church, earthquake-damaged, being held up by scaffolding. Side churches and temples. The new church, which looks for all the world like an unfinished terminal at José Martí Airport. But this is where the pilgrims are going—this is where María haunts the building. I'm now wearing a black beret to cover the bandage above my ear. I take it off when I go inside.

Midnight mass, but only a few empty seats in the swooping basilica.

I am unaccustomed to religious services and the thing is still in Latin despite Vatican II. Men and women beside me, kneeling, standing up, reciting the rosary. I copy them. Stand when they stand. Kneel when they kneel.

Where is the María?

What is it that they have come to see?

A girl comes by with a collection plate. I throw in a few pesos and am given a picture of the dark-skinned Virgin. I realize that it is the double of a big picture behind the altar. The focus of the church. The mother of Jesus, the goddess protector of all Mexicans, of all women.

For many Cubans, of course, the dark Virgin is Ochún, the sensuous Santería goddess of love and protection.

When the ceremony is over, I light a candle and place it as close to the image as I am permitted.

I bow my face.

"Accept this candle on behalf of another," I whisper.

The Virgin sees. Understands.

A moving walkway means that no one is allowed to remain directly under the image. It seems like a joke, but it isn't. The devout are in tears. Mothers are showing the Virgin barren wombs, deformed babies, terminal cancers.

Crying, candle smoke, prayers.

Too much.

I back away and run outside.

Take a breath.

My head hurts. It's a reminder. A centimeter to the left and that .270 round would have smashed my skull. A centimeter to the right and it would have been a clean miss and Briggs would have gone for a chest shot before I'd even heard the crack of the first.

A policeman asks me if I am ok.

"Fine. Too many people," I tell him.

"You should have seen it last week, the holy day of Guadalupe is December twelfth." He waves at the plaza. "There were two million out here."

The subway.

Basilica to Martín Carrera to Consulado to the airport.

My plane is at four.

The airport. The special Cuban line. The ticket.

A delay. Newsstand. A headline in the December 18 *Miami Herald:* "Wire Service Report: Fidel Hints at Retirement."

The plane. Cubana flight 131. Take off over the glittering city. Circle to gain altitude, and already the lights are lost beneath the nighttime haze; only the beacons on Popocatépetl and Iztaccíhuatl peeking through the dark.

East across the forests of Yucatán.

I take out the image of the Virgin María. For a while we shared a name, you and I.

I rest my eyes, even sleep a little.

I feel the plane descend and a stewardess asks me to return my seat to the upright position.

I open the window shade.

When Columbus saw Cuba for the first time the landmass was so large that he knew he had made it to one of the islands of Japan. He landed near Gibara and brought the astonished Taino Indians gifts and respectful greetings for the Japanese emperor. When the shogun refused to show up, Columbus gave the

Indians instead the cross and slavery and smallpox and death. Cortés took the cross from Cuba to Mexico. The old gods fell and the father god took their place. Wise Cuba threw off the shackles of all the religions, found truth in Hegel, Marx, Engels, and Fidel Castro. The very first thing we learned in school was that religion was the opium of the masses.

And yet.

I am copied in your eye, lady of Guadalupe, lady of the moon.

Accept this candle for another, blessed mother, generous to virgins . . .

Havana.

The bay surrounded by mist.

A pink sea.

The plane descends.

I put María in my pocket.

Dark when we took off and not quite morning when we land at José Martí.

Yawns, a smattering of applause.

The Jetway is broken and takes a long time to dock to the plane. I thank the pilot and the stewardess and walk down the ramp back into *la patría*.

As soon as I enter the terminal building and before I even make it to the metal detectors I spot Sergeant Menendez, the DGI spy in Hector's office.

He nods to two men in blue suits.

"Chivato cabrón," I say under my breath.

They arrest me.

"What's the charge?" I ask them as they lead me outside into the dark, warm, drizzly Havana rain.

"Treason."

Treason. Yes. The great catchall. And one of the many, many offenses in Cuba that carries the death penalty.

"Come on. Get in."

I get in the car, a Russian police Lada.

The engine turns over.

The lights come on.

The engine dies.

"Everyone out," the driver says.

The rain again.

A gun in my face.

"Help us push."

"No."

"Do it or I'll shoot you."

"You won't shoot."

The smell of earth. Fruit rotting in the fields. The sea.

"Forget it then."

The men push, the car moves, the clutch slips, the engine catches, the men jump in, and, having no alternative, forward into the day we ride together.

CHAPTER 21

FINCA VIGÍA

Cheap handcuffs. Cheap cologne. On either side of me cheap suits. The empty highway from the airport. Morning mist. Women with bundles on their heads, Africa style. *Negros de pasas*, *blanquitos,* all the same. In Cuba everybody walks. Kids carrying broken bicycles, old men pulling donkey carts, hitchhikers putting their hands down when they see it's a cop car.

Where are we going?

Not the ministry. Not the meat-hook basements in the MININT building, ten floors below Che's beard.

"Where are we going?"

"Shut up."

The southern suburbs. Shanties, tin towns. Unmetaled roads, hurricane-fucked streets.

I don't recognize this neighborhood at all. Is this where the DGI has its torture house?

A hill. A Spanish colonial village turned into slums. Pigs rooting in the street. Old men sleeping in gutters.

The beginning of sunrise.

Climbing.

This area a little more familiar.

"Is this San Francisco de Paula?"

"We told you to shut up."

Four of us. A driver and these two DGI goons.

San Francisco de Paula. I haven't been here for years.

A turn off a dirt road, the Lada slewing in mud. A big gated nineteenth-century hacienda on a hilltop.

G5 and DGSE guards at the gate, snoozing under bougainvillea.

The Lada honks its limp-dicked horn, and as if to compensate our bull-necked driver shouts obscenities through the window.

A soldier in green fatigues opens the gate.

A long driveway lined with jacarandas and mango trees. Parrots, tocororos, and yellow-necked finches roosting in the branches. And above them frigate birds with scimitar wings hanging eerily in the air.

The house is a one-story Spanish colonial. Outside the embassy area all these homes are falling to pieces, but this one has a new roof and a fresh lick of cream-colored paint. Parked outside is a black 1950s Chrysler New Yorker.

"What is this place?"

"*Mira, chica,* how many times do we have to tell you to shut up?"

The Lada stops. The driver helps me out. A young man in a blue uniform I don't recognize approaches the car and puts a finger to his lips.

"What is all this?"

"Quiet. He's still sleeping," the young man says.

"Who?"

"Would you like some coffee?"

"What? Yes."

I start to walk toward the house. The shutters are open and you can see through from one side to the other, and all the way to Havana.

"No, over here," the young man says and leads me to a shack at the back of the house. Seven or eight tables. A half dozen MININT men drinking coffee.

"Alex, spare another cup, this one's just got in from Mexico."

Alex, an old guy with white hair, *muy negro,* produces a coffee cup and leads me to a table away from the MININT men.

He smiles at me, looks at them, and mutters "Vermin" under his breath.

He returns with a pot of coffee and a bowl of sugar.

"We've got nothing to eat, I'm sorry," he says.

"That's ok. Where are we?"

He looks at me in amazement for a moment. "Finca Vigía," he says and walks off.

The name rings a bell, but I can't quite place it. I pour coffee in the espresso cup and add a cube of white sugar. Before it's fully dissolved I take a sip. Cuba does two things well, cigars and coffee. Local beans, local sugar, local water. And strong. The hit is instantaneous and even in this state of incipient panic I can't help but smile.

My head feels clear for the first time in days. I lean back in the white plastic chair and breathe out.

Ok, Mercado, why don't you try to figure out what's going on?

We're in some kind of garden. A beautiful one. Hibiscus, oleander, Indian laburnum, blossoming hydrangea. The scent heady and overpowering. Under the trees there are half a dozen species of orchid and a small scudding sea of Cuba's national flower, the brilliant white mariposa. There are a score of security guards but that's it, which means this is not Jefe's house. The Beard's gotten even more crazy as he's gotten older and doesn't go anywhere without half a battalion of soldiers surrounding him. One of the other ministers, perhaps, or an ambassador from the—

Inside the house a clock dings the hour six times.

I hear someone stir.

My legs start trembling. I'm wearing tight black American jeans and low-heeled black pumps, not exactly designed for making a break for it through the garden and over the wall.

I pour myself another cup of coffee.

The young man in the blue uniform returns. He has very long eyelashes and a nice smile.

"He wishes to see you. Please come," he says.

Who?

He leads me around the front, past a pool, and in through a set of double doors.

The house is a museum. Old-fashioned furniture, a range in the kitchen. No modern appliances. When I see the hunting trophies all over the walls I remember what Finca Vigía is. We're in Casa Hemingway. Preserved the way Hemingway left it in 1960. I haven't been here before but I've read about it. The large open-plan hacienda, the immaculate pool, the expansive garden, the shutters open to the dawn and the early morning mist and distant sea. But for the trained assassins waiting outside, a truly charming spot.

Along the walls ibex and antelope heads and more dead animals on the floor. White-painted bookcases overflowing with volumes. Desks covered with magazines: *The Field, The Spectator,* a *New Yorker* from November 1958. Bullfight posters. Paintings by Miró and Paul Klee. An armoire with a cheetah skin draped languidly across it. A Picasso of a bull's head. And the pièce de résistance, there, sitting on the edge of a twin bed, as freaky and unreal as the Picasso, in his pajamas and a black silk dressing gown, Raúl Castro.

What's left of his hair has been dyed. Tanned leathery skin hangs loose on his face and under his neck. There are bags around his yellow eyes, but unlike Fidel he has his own teeth and even this early he looks a lot younger than his brother.

When he sees me he puts a finger to his lips and points at the bed. A girl with him, sleeping still. It's not a scandal. For although Vilma Espín only recently passed away, Raúl had been separated from the mother of his children for two decades.

He points to the kitchen. The house is all on one floor with rooms bleeding into one another. Only the kitchen has a big thick door that closes.

"This way," Raúl whispers.

Two DGI men slip outside as we enter.

Raúl gently closes the door, leans on a pine table, and opens the shutters. "What time is it?" he asks.

"Six-fifteen," a voice from outside mutters.

Raúl yawns and looks through the window. "Coffee," he says.

He sits down at the table and motions for me to sit too.

"This can't take long, we'll have to have the house open for tourists by ten."

"I don't know what *this* is."

Raúl smiles and rubs his jaw. In every other Cuban that gesture is a discreet reference to the Beard, but for him it's just an assessment of his stubble.

A coffeepot is passed through the shutters, along with two cups and a bowl of sugar. Raúl pours himself an espresso and adds no sugar. That explains the teeth.

"This, *this*, Comrade Mercado, is an interrogation."

Fear. Great pulsing sine waves of the stuff. Worse than the ice lake. Worse than the hangman himself. All those DGI and ministry men outside but Raúl is going to do this himself.

"Would you like a cup?" he asks.

I shake my head.

He takes a sip. "Not bad. Are you sure you don't want one?"

"No."

"Do you know who I am?" he asks.

"Of course."

"I am the deus ex machina of your little adventure, Mercado. I am the person who will finally get things done right."

"I don't under—"

"Who killed your father, Comrade Mercado?"

I try not to appear taken aback. "I don't know, I have no idea. It was a hit-and-run in La Yuma."

Raúl shoots me a puzzled frown. He obviously isn't up on his subversive slang.

"La Yuma. The United States, in a place called Fairview, Colorado," I clarify.

"Who killed him?" Raúl asks again.

"I don't know."

Raúl sighs and looks out at the garden. The smell of hibiscus drifts through the window.

"You came in through the front of the house?"

"Yes."

"Did you know that Ava Gardner swam naked in that pool?"

"No."

"Do you know who Ava Gardner was?"

I shrug my shoulders. "I think I've heard the name."

"Young people. What do you think of me sleeping in Hemingway's home? In his very bed?" Raúl asks.

"I don't think anything."

"You don't consider it profane?"

"No. It's just a house."

Raúl grins. "Yes, I suppose so. It is just a house like any other. My brother never sleeps in the same house two nights running. He is afraid that the CIA is still trying to kill him. For a while it was the KGB too. But now only the CIA."

His brother. Jefe the unkillable, the immortal. I mask my nervousness and fix an expression of polite interest.

"Do you know why I sleep here, in this house?" Raúl asks.

"No."

"We are the past, the present, and the future of the Revolution. We must be safe. In Iraq U.S. pilots were not allowed to hit cultural, historical, or religious buildings. Perhaps I am paranoid, but I feel safe here and I like it."

"It's a nice place," I agree.

Raúl sighs. "I met Comrade Hemingway twice. Once at a fishing competition in Havana and once at Floridita. Have you been in Floridita, Comrade Mercado?"

"Only to arrest someone. It's too expensive to drink there."

"You should treat yourself sometime."

"Sure."

"Yes, I like it here. Surrounded by books and artifacts. Genuine history."

"It's, uh, special. I suppose I should have visited before now."

"You should have. When were you born, Comrade Mercado?"

"May twenty-sixth, 1980."

"When did your father, the traitor, defect to the United States?"

"1993."

"When you were thirteen. Hmm. Thirteen. Before your *quince*."

I grimace. Two years before my *quince*. My fifteenth birthday—the most important day in any Cuban girl's life. "I was his only daughter but he never saw it. My uncle Arturo said Dad would send money for the party. But he didn't. He didn't even send money," I blurt out.

Raúl nods. As a father of daughters and granddaughters he knows just how important the *quince* is.

"Have coffee, Officer Mercado."

"I had some, already. A whole pot."

"In Mexico City?"

"No, here."

"Real coffee."

"Yes."

"Good, good. Now I think you'll admit that despite your father's defection we have been very generous to your family," Raúl says.

"Generous?" Ricky, my mother, and I got the same rations as everyone else. We all lived in the same crumbling apartments. Mom's place didn't even have hot water.

Raúl nods. "Generous. Despite your father being a traitor, we let your brother, Ricardo, travel there to dispose of his remains."

Gooseflesh on my back. Leave Ricky out of this.

"Ricky's a Party member, a former president of the National Students Union, an executive member of the National Union of Journalists," I say quickly.

"Yes, yes," Raúl agrees dismissively.

"Ricky has been out of the country many times. He's traveled to Russia, to America, to Mexico. He has always returned. He's proved himself many times to—"

Raúl puts his hand up like a white-gloved transit cop. "Enough," he says. "What have you done with Ricky? Have you arrested him? Where is he?"

Raúl seems amused that I have the effrontery to question him.

"I have no idea where your brother is. More than likely in the bed of some newspaper editor or a Chinese diplomat or one of our generals."

Mierde. He even knows about Ricky's *counterrevolutionary tendencies.* Of course he does. They know everything. One person in every twenty-five is a *chivato* like Sergeant Menendez.

He waits a beat. "And your mother, did she know of your mission to America?"

Hesitantly: "I don't know what you're talking about. I didn't go to America. I went to Mexico City. I'm applying to the university to study criminology."

Raúl snaps his fingers. One of the DGI goons leans his head in through the window. "The file," Raúl says.

The DGI man goes away and comes back quickly with a small green folder. Raúl snatches it out of his hand. "You flew to Mexico City last Tuesday. The day you arrived you had a tour of the university and were interviewed by a Professor Martín Carranza in the Department of Criminology. On Tuesday evening you checked repeatedly for tails and obviously you found our man. You took the subway to Coyoacán. You went to the house of Leon Trotsky." Raúl puts the file down and smiles at me. "You have a sense of humor, Officer Mercado, I like that . . . Let me see . . . Ah yes, you entered the house but did not leave. Somehow you exited without us noticing. I have been to that house, Comrade Mercado. It's a walled fortress, not easy to slip out of there."

"No."

"You escaped our tail and found a coyote to take you across the border. You went to the United States to investigate your father's death."

"No."

"Who killed your father?"

"I don't know what you are talking about."

"You went to America to investigate the death of your father," Raúl insists.

"No, that's not true. I've never been to America."

"Your boss, Captain Hector Ramirez, recommended that we deny you an exit permit. He said you wanted to go to Mexico but he suspected you might be a risk for defection."

Hector sold me out.

"Well?"

"Captain Ramirez thought as much, yes."

Raúl Castro sips his coffee and examines me like an M.E. performing a difficult autopsy. After a while he smiles, not unkindly.

"We overruled him," he says. "We. The DGI."

"What?"

"The Foreign Ministry denied your application to travel to Mexico, but we overruled them."

My head spinning. "The state security police got me the exit permit?"

"Yes."

"Even though you knew I was going to go to America?"

"Ah, so you admit you went to America?"

Damn it. The only way in Cuba was to deny, deny, deny. For years if necessary.

"I didn't go to America," I say again, quieter now.

A dog starts barking in the garden.

"Someone take him for a walk!" Raúl yells.

"Your dog?" I ask desperately, trying to change the subject. Raúl nods. "What type?"

"A mutt. All other breeds are bourgeois," he says smugly.

"As bourgeois as that big black Chrysler outside."

Raúl grins. "You saw my car. There's a story behind that vehicle that, alas, must be saved for another time. Now, I'll ask again, what is the name of the person who killed your father?"

"I don't know."

Raúl taps the table, rubs his chin. He decides to try a different tack.

"How do you think we've survived for nearly fifty years on this island, *mano a mano* with the most powerful country on Earth? We are a poor country, with few resources. How did the Revolution survive with so much stacked against it?"

"I don't know."

"Because, Comrade Mercado, we are smart. Everyone underestimates us. Again and again. You did well in Mexico City, you suspected that we would put a tail on you and you were right. What you did not appreciate was my personal involvement in this case. You did not appreciate that the DGI would anticipate your caution."

"What do you mean?" I wondered.

"We wanted you to see the tail. We wanted you to see him. And we allowed you to think that you'd got rid of him, but you missed the real tail, Comrade Mercado. You're good, but you're just a police officer and we are the Guardians of the Revolution. We are the DGI."

A second tail.

No. He's bluffing. He's trying to trick me.

"I, I don't believe you," I tell him.

"We followed you to Terminal Norte, where you took a bus to Gomez Palacio. You found a coyote and you went across the desert that night. You had an unexpected and unpleasant episode at a place called Bloody Fork—don't you love those English names?—and our operative says you did very well at that encounter. In fact, after that episode he recommended that we continue the family tradition and recruit you."

Family tradition. Our operative. Pick a question.

"Your operative?" I ask.

Raúl yawns, the big jowly fold of skin under his neck swaying from side to side.

"Our operative in the coyote van."

Our operative in the coyote van.

My Guardian Angel.

Oh my God.

Paco.

An agent for Cuban intelligence.

The phony trips to Denver, his skill with the rifle; the man in the rental car, Mr. New York Plates—his contact. Now it all makes perfect—

"I see by your face that you understand," Raúl says.

Best course now is the truth. Fast. To save my life. To save Ricky, Mom. Truth.

"Yes. I went to America."

He nods. "Take off your hat," he says. "I want to see."

I take off the beret. He looks at the bandage above my ear.

"A graze. Don't think you're special, Mercado. I once saw a man who was shot between the eyes. The bullet exited through his lower jaw and two weeks later he was back fighting with us in the mountains," he says.

"He was lucky."

"Yes and no. Later we had to hang him for rape . . . Now, who killed your father, Officer Mercado?"

"A man called Youkilis, a—"

"My patience has its limits," he interrupts. "I'll ask that question once more and this time, if you do not tell me the truth, I'll consider it a crime against the state. A conspiracy that involves your whole family. Do you understand?"

"Yes, Comrade Castro."

"Who killed your father, Officer Mercado?"

"It was, it was . . . It was an actor, a Hollywood actor called Jack Tyrone. He lived in Fairview, Colorado. He was driving home drunk, he hit Dad and knocked him into a ravine, and then he drove off. In America they call that a hit-and-run."

"I heard the death was unpleasant. If it's not too painful I'd like to know the full details. How did your father die?"

"Dad's pelvis and legs were broken. His rib cage was shattered. He tried crawling back up to the road but couldn't make it. Blood filled his lungs. He drowned in his own blood. Slowly. It took him hours to die and when they found him his face was frozen."

A flicker as he tries to conceal a reaction. He nearly succeeds, but not quite. He waits for a beat or two to feign casualness.

"A Hollywood actor called Jack Tyrone."

"He's young. Thirty. Up and coming. You won't have heard of him."

"No, I am familiar with him. Not, of course, through his films."

Through Paco's report.

Sunlight finally breaks through the mist, sending yellow beams through the house. Parrots start screeching on the rooftop. Soon all the other birds will begin too.

"You discovered that Jack Tyrone killed your father but you did not kill him?" Raúl asks.

"No. I didn't kill him."

I wait for the other shoe to drop. It drops.

"Why?"

"I killed the man who covered it up. I drowned him in a lake in Wyoming. I killed the police officer who helped him cover it up. I let Tyrone go. He was drunk. He didn't even remember the accident. And afterward he did what they told him to do. He followed his lines, he played his part. He's an actor. He's not a . . . He's not evil." Raúl's face is twitching with anger as I continue my explanation. "I told him I'd be watching him. I told him that if he didn't lead an extraordinary life, an exemplary life, that I'd be back. I'd be back to kill him then."

Raúl cocks his head, as if mercy is known to him only as a theoretical concept, not one that he's seen in practice. "You killed the men who covered it up but you let Tyrone go?"

"Yes."

He doesn't like the answer. His face reddens. He smacks his hand down hard on the kitchen table. The coffee cups jump. A goon looks in through the window.

"It wasn't your call to make!" Raúl shouts.

"I don't—"

"Don't speak! It wasn't your call, Mercado. I sent you there. *I* sent you. I sent you to do a job for me! Juan Mercado belonged to us, not the Yankees! We . . . I made the decision to spare his life and someone else overruled me!"

In the black books, in the samizdats, they quote the Jesuit schoolmasters who taught the Castro boys. Fidel was wild, aggressive, a bad loser, a prodigy. Raúl was the levelheaded one, unemotional, slow to anger. I always believed that but the books were wrong. Raúl's face is scarlet. He's shaking. Spittle on his lips. His hands have become fists. He's capable of anything. If he said the word one of those DGI men would take me outside to the jasmine trees and put a bullet in my head.

He stands and stares at me for so long that I begin to think he's had a stroke. But then his yellow eyes glaze and he calms down.

"It wasn't your call to make," he mutters again.

Finally he sits, takes a sip of coffee, breathes.

"Why did you go to America, if not to kill the man who killed your father?" he asks in a quiet tone.

It's not an unreasonable question. It's the same question I've been asking myself. "For the same reason I joined the PNR. The truth. Do you remember the truth?"

"Don't get smart with me, Officer Mercado. I could have you and your captain and your brother and your mother thrown into a dungeon for fifty years. Your whole *solar*. Everyone you know."

I look at my feet. Save yourself. Save yourself. You did it on the ice. Do it now. "I beg your pardon, Comrade Castro. I spoke hastily."

He grunts. "Apology accepted, Comrade Mercado."

A long silence.

The guards muttering. Someone warming up the car. Parrots and macaws screeching as they walk along the tree branches.

The question has been hanging here the whole time, but I can't ask it. Not yet. Why are *you* so interested in my father, Comrade Raúl?

"Do you like Hemingway?" Raúl asks in a stern pedagogic voice.

"I haven't read much. The Cuba novels in school. *The Island of Streams, The Old Man in the Sea*."

"*Islands in the Stream, The Old Man and the Sea*," Raúl corrects.

"Of course."

"For the chief it was always *For Whom the Bell Tolls*. Hemingway wrote that book in the Ambos Mundos in Habana Vieja and he bought this very house with the first royalty payment. The book is about the necessity of killing one's enemies. Killing without favor or malice or mercy. But you have killed, Comrade Mercado. Four men."

The watery eyes boring into me.

"Four in a little over a week. How does that make you feel?"

"Sick."

"I myself have never killed anyone."

I can't help but raise my eyebrows. He sees, grins. "But I have signed the warrants on many. I signed the warrant on your father at his trial in absentia."

"I know." And that's the opening I want. Now is the time. "If I may ask, Comrade Raúl, why—"

"Your father worked for me. Juan Mercado was a DGI officer. G6."

"He was a ticket taker on the bay ferry."

Raúl smiles. "Wasn't he, though? I'll bet he met everyone in Havana at one point or another. He was with us right from the start. From boyhood. The early days."

"Not once did he talk to us about the Revolution," I say, my voice trembling, my composure going.

"No. He wouldn't."

"It's not true." Desperation. For all his faults, Dad was no rat.

Raúl regards me, lifts his cup, waits. There's no point in saying anything. We both know he's not lying.

"Why?" I manage.

"We needed men in the exile community in Miami. A mass defection has always been the best way of inserting agents. Your father was well known, well liked. We knew he would go far. We arranged the whole thing. Your father was one of half a dozen agents on that boat. Of course we knew that as soon as they landed in America, they would all be given U.S. citizenship with only the briefest of background checks. And Juan's record was clean. Ah, yes. I ran that operation personally. It was the last one I did before I retired. I was proud of it."

"What did he do for you in America?"

"Oh, he got a job. He joined the right groups. He gave money to the right causes. He knew the right people. He was as popular in Miami as he was in Havana. We were grooming him. He could have gone far."

"Could have gone?"

Raul blinks rapidly, sighs. "He met a woman, a younger woman."

"Karen."

"Karen, yes. She was at the University of Miami, studying for her teaching license, but she was from North Dakota. When she finished her degree she went back to North Dakota. He followed her. They got married. North Dakota is of no use to us. There are no Cubans in North Dakota. We had six good agents on that ferry. One died of AIDS. Two came back to Cuba. One ended up in an American prison for dealing cocaine. And one found Jesus Christ. Your father was the last one from that insertion. I did not want him to leave Miami. We ordered him not to leave Miami, but he went."

"You must have more than one agent in America?"

Raúl laughs. "Dozens. But for me this was personal. This was my operation. This was my man. I told him to return to Miami or we would kill him. It was clumsy. We could have accommodated her . . . enough money will soothe most people . . . I made a mistake, I spooked him."

Raúl looks out the window and holds up the empty coffeepot. Almost instantly, another one is brought, along with sweet cakes and dry black bread. Raúl offers me a cake but I decline.

"You should eat. After this interview who knows when your next meal will be, Officer Mercado," Raúl says.

Sound advice. I eat the cake. And besides, I'm on the hook. I want to see where the story goes. "What happened next?"

"He disappeared. We lost him. Our hit teams could not find him, and after a while I called them off. My family is from Sevilla, and there they have a saying, 'You hunt the wolf for a year and a day and then you must let him go.' We put out the word that all was forgiven, but your father didn't trust us. For five years he stayed hidden until he turned up dead in Colorado with a Mexican passport."

I look at Raúl to gauge his reaction. "You were glad?"

"Glad? No. Not at all. But I was curious. A ratcatcher in Colorado? Perhaps that was the only job he could get. Perhaps he had lost none of *his* sense of humor. In a manner of speaking, that had been his job when he worked for me," he says, his eyes narrowing at the half joke, the skin fold under his chin jiggling.

He coughs, clears his throat. "In any case, when your brother asked to travel to Colorado to bury your father, we let him go without making any difficulty. Your brother is a good reporter. When he brought back many documents and gave them to you, we knew you were going to go too. We knew you were going to find the man who killed him and that you were going to exact a child's revenge."

"I don't think—" I begin, but Raúl puts his finger to his lips.

In Hemingway's bedroom the girl is stirring.

Raúl appears startled. "Quickly, get up. If she sees you here there will be a holy row. These officers will take you back to your apartment."

Warily, I get to my feet. "I'm free to go?"

"As a bird."

I look at the tame parrots walking on the balcony rail. "You clip their wings."

Raúl smiles. "Only the songbirds, Comrade Mercado. You're not a songbird, are you?"

"No."

A voice from the bedroom. "Raúl!"

"Coming. Just taking care of something!" Raúl shouts and leads me outside.

He leans on the black Chrysler and taps me on the shoulder.

"Big changes are coming, Mercado. Sooner than you would think."

I raise an eyebrow. He points at Casa Hemingway. "All of this will be a luxury. They won't allow me to sleep anywhere that isn't reinforced against the Yankee bunker-buster bombs, despite my talk of cultural protections."

I'm not following him.

He frowns. "You see, that's why we have to take care of all of the unfinished business now. In a few months I will have bigger fish to fry."

"Yes," I say, still confused.

My obtuseness is starting to irritate him. He sighs and changes the subject. "What should we do with you now, Comrade Mercado?" he whispers.

"I don't know."

"Do you want to join the DGI?"

"No."

"What do you want?"

"I want to go back to my old job."

"Then go."

Raúl signals the guards to bring the Lada.

"Comrade Castro, can I, may I ask *you* a question? Two questions?"

Raúl looks inside the house. "Quickly. Quickly. Estelle is very un-Cuban in her attitude to infidelity."

"What do I tell Hector? I mean Captain Ramirez."

"Tell him the truth. You spent a week in Mexico City. You saw the pyramids, you prayed at the shrine of the Virgin. Your second question?"

"Will I see Paco again?"

Raúl looks puzzled, but then he understands. "Paco. Paco? Oh, Francisco. Yes. I picked that name for him. There is an old joke that Hemingway was fond of. Do you wish to hear it? I will tell you: A father in Madrid puts an advertisement in *El Liberal:* 'Paco, meet me at Hotel Montana, noon today, all is forgiven—Father.' The Civil Guard has to come to disperse the crowd of eight hundred Pacos who respond to the ad."

"His name is not Francisco?"

"No."

I should be angry but I'm not. I lied to him. He lied to me.

"And I doubt that you will see him again. He lives in Miami."

Raúl offers me a hand.

I shake it.

"Good luck, Officer Mercado. I hope to never see your name in any future report that crosses my desk."

"You won't."

"Now, go."

The goons show me to the car.

They drive me into town and drop me on the Malecón.

I walk to O'Reilly.

Outside the *solar* there's a dead dog on the porch, a border collie. Flies around her eyes. Belonged to the family on the top floor.

Up the stairs.

A note on my apartment door from the landlord. My room has been broken into while I was away. They changed the locks.

I go down to the basement and bang on the landlord's door. He appears with a baseball bat. I give him an IOU for a five-dollar bill.

Up the four flights. New key in the new lock.

Yeah, broken into, and not by the DGI—they don't let you know they've been. This place has been ransacked. Thugs. The TV gone, my twenty-kilo bag of rice gone, my clothes gone. Poetry books gone.

I sit on the edge of the bed and cry.

Hector was right.

What was it he told me that Pindar said? *The gods give us for every good thing two evil ones. Men who are children take this badly but the manly ones bear it, turning the brightness outward.*

Yes. Something like that.

I sit there and cry myself out.

The sound of rats. The sea. Clanking camel buses. American radio.

I need a drink. The man down the hall makes moonshine in his bath. I knock on his door and buy a liter bottle for another IOU. I pour a cup. It burns. I go downstairs.

"Use your phone?" I ask the landlord.

I call Ricky. Oh, Ricky, I was so stupid. To think that I could outwit *them*. To think that I could do anything right.

"You're alive," he says.

"Yes."

"I was so worried."

"Don't be."

"Did you find what you were looking for?"

"I think so."

A pause.

"I believe I'm being followed," he says in a whisper, as if that will fool the DGI bug.

"No, that's all over. You won't see them again," I assure him.

Another pause while he takes this in.

"You're alive, big sister."

"Yes. I'm alive. And that's something."

CHAPTER 22

A HAIR IN THE GATE

I wasn't there. Airtight alibi. I was working a case in the Vieja—a dead German tourist, a dead prostitute, a missing pimp. I wasn't there. It was nothing to do with me. I read about it the next day. It made the Mexican papers.

Jack Tyrone had just left his Hollywood Hills home. It was very early. He was going to an audition. A good role. They wanted him to play the part of Felix in a James Bond movie. Not the biggest lick, but worldwide exposure. He was drunk. At six-thirty in the morning. Jack Tyrone had well-documented problems with alcohol. His car went off the road right outside his house. He wasn't wearing a seatbelt. The windshield shredded his pretty face, the fall down the canyon broke his back. The car landed on top of him and caught fire.

Even for the DGI it was good.

They'd probably gotten into his house in the middle of the night. Drugged him, tortured him, injected alcohol through a vein in his foot, rolled him down the canyon.

They broke the car windshield from the inside and smeared his blood on the steering wheel. How they got the car on top of him isn't much of a mystery. They brought a truck with a winch. They were careful. They didn't want it to crush him, just pin him sufficiently so they could burn him alive.

That's how they do things.

Dad was their man. He was retired, but he belonged to them. No one else had the right to terminate his existence. Officially the L.A. coroner's office said that death would have been instantaneous, but the coroner and I knew better. Minute for minute, life for life. The DGI looks after its own.

I should have seen it coming but I don't speak their language. Hector would have taken Raúl's hints but I didn't get them. I'll never get them. That's not me.

I read Jack's photo obit in *People en Espanol*. Banned but readily available. Photographs of him at Cannes, in Darfur, at a Vegas party with Pitt and Clooney. His eyes staring at the camera, his body well positioned between bigger stars.

I looked at the pictures, I read the words.

Hollywood didn't pause in its journey around the sun. It rolled along fine without him.

Dad didn't get an obit anywhere.

Or did he?

A plaque somewhere in the Foreign Ministry, or on an anonymous wall in that big, windowless, Che-covered Lubyanka in the Plaza de la Revolución?

Maybe. I don't know.

A week after the hit a DGI colonel came to see me. He was carrying a cardboard box and something wrapped in tissue paper. He put the box on my table and made me sign papers in triplicate saying that I'd received it.

The thing in tissue paper was my father's pistol.

I put it in a drawer.

I let the box sit there until dark.

I flipped the switch and the lights came on.

I opened the lid.

Letters. More than a hundred, from Dad to me. Some of them contained money. Five hundred-dollar bills for a dress for my *quince*. Stories, poems, drawings, kisses for me and little Ricky. The last letters were from 2006. Dad was in Colorado. It was cold, he said. He had to be vague, because he knew the letters would be read by the DGI before being passed on to me, but he described the forest and the mountains, snow. He talked about books he'd read, and Karen, his girl. He knew that Internet use was strictly controlled but he had heard that the Ambos Mundos had a live webcam. He wondered if I could possibly go there at a certain time and wave into the camera. He would wait by his laptop. He would wait, night after night.

Of course—tears.

Tears all night and into the morning and the next day.

Oh, Papi.

It's going to come. The end of days. Even for you, Jefe, Little Jefe, even for you.

I read the letters, showed them to Ricky and Mom.

I took a sick day. Then I went back to work. The autopsy. The German Embassy. Reports. I began a letter to Francisco, and on the Prado I ran into Felipe, the waiter/baby killer I had arrested the night Ricky returned with his notes. He grinned at me, unable to quite place where we had met before . . .

Sleep.

Wake.

So go the days.

The Malecón at dusk. The castle before me, the faded grandeur of crumbling hotels, boy jockeys along the seawall, fire belching from the oil refinery in the bay.

The lights on the water are fishing boats and perhaps, beyond the horizon, American yachts in the Dry Tortugas.

I walk on the Malecón and I see the future.

Cell phones, personal computers. The end of ration cards, the end of ID papers, the end of summary arrest. And what happens to the policeman then?

I walk on the Malecón and I see the past. I know you now, Papa. I know your real name. That secret part you concealed from us. You went and you didn't take us with you. You lied. That was your job, but still, you lied.

I missed you.

I missed you my whole life.

I walk on the Malecón and I see the present. No one sleeps. Everyone sleeps. The police, the beachcombers, the pretty boys and their teenage pimps.

Oh, Havana.

City of hungry doctors.

City of beautiful whores.

City of dead dreams.

I'm tired of you.

I want to be the sea.

I want to spirit myself away. Under the moon, across the starlit waves, with my arms spread out, with fresh-cut flowers in my hair.

Where will I go?

Santiago. Nueva York. Miami.

The forbidden places. The other world.

North, with the egrets and the spoonbills and the blue-plumed tocororo.

Across the cays.

Into the stream.

Dark waves.

Sea spray.

Skimming the blue.

And no one sees. Not the police. Not the navy. Not the brides of the orishas skilled in Santería.

North.

As the sailfish jump.

As the marlins dive.

North.

Always north.

Until the stars cease their wanderings.

Until the sun opens her tired eyes.

And I'll fly alone.

And I'll forgive the past.

And I'll turn the brightness outward.